PRAISE FOR MARY ELLEN TAYLOR

"Mary Ellen Taylor writes comfort reads packed with depth . . . If you're looking for a fantastic vacation read, this is the book for you!"

—Steph and Chris's Book Review, on *Spring House*

"A complex tale . . . grounded in fascinating history and emotional turmoil that is intense yet subtle. An intelligent, heartwarming exploration of the powers of forgiveness, compassion, and new beginnings."

—*Kirkus Reviews*, on *The View from Prince Street*

"Absorbing characters, a hint of mystery, and touching self-discovery elevate this novel above many others in the genre."

—RT Book Reviews, on *Sweet Expectations*

"Taylor serves up a great mix of vivid setting, history, drama, and everyday life."

—*Herald Sun*, on *The Union Street Bakery*

"A charming and very engaging story about the nature of family and the meaning of love."

—*Seattle Post-Intelligencer*, on *Sweet Expectations*

THE WORDS WE WHISPER

"Taylor expertly employs the parallel timelines to highlight the impact of the past on the present, exploring the complexities of familial relationships while peeling back the layers of her flawed, realistic characters. Readers are sure to be swept away."

—*Publishers Weekly*

"A luscious interweaving of a spy thriller and a family saga."

—*Historical Novels Review*

HONEYSUCKLE SEASON

"This memorable story is sure to tug at readers' heartstrings."

—*Publishers Weekly*

WINTER COTTAGE

"Offering a look into bygone days of the gentrified from the early 1900s up until the present time, this multifaceted tale of mystery and romance is sure to please."

—*New York Journal of Books*

"There is mystery and intrigue as the author weaves a tale that pulls you in . . . this is a story of strong women, who persevere . . . it's a love story, the truest, deepest kind . . . and it's the story of a woman who years later was able to right a wrong and give a home to the people who really needed it. It's layered brilliantly, and hints are revealed subtly, allowing the reader to form conclusions and fall in love."

—Smexy Books

THE
BRIGHTER
THE
LIGHT

THE BRIGHTER THE LIGHT

MARY ELLEN TAYLOR

Text copyright © 2022 by Mary Burton
All rights reserved.

Published by Montlake, Seattle

www.apub.com

Amazon, the Amazon logo, and Montlake are trademarks of Amazon.com, Inc., or its affiliates.

ISBN-13: 9781542032599
ISBN-10: 1542032598

Cover design by Shasti O'Leary Soudant

Printed in the United States of America

THE
BRIGHTER
THE
LIGHT

PROLOGUE

RUTH

Nags Head, North Carolina
Sunday, January 2, 2022, 8:00 a.m.

Off these shores, the Atlantic Ocean is greedy. She swallows ships, goods, men, and hungrily guards her treasures and mysteries. Days, months, centuries can pass without a whisper of truth, and then smooth waters crackle, briny depths churn, and somewhere deep below the surface, a grip slackens, and a secret is revealed.

Now, standing on the shore before dawn's untethered sky, Ruth could feel the looming change in her eighty-four-year-old bones. She huddled deeper into her coat, warming her arthritic fingers as sunlight burst above pale clouds ferried along the horizon by cold, salty winds.

"No one saw the storm coming but us, Mama," Ruth said to herself. "I felt it like you once could." None of the news stations had forecast that depressions off the African coast would head west, mingle with the warm waters of the Caribbean, and snap free as a Cat 4 storm. No one had expected evacuations so late in the hurricane season. And no one had predicted the damage.

Ruth had wanted to ride out the storm, but the sheriff had ordered her out. She'd argued but, in the end, let him drive her over the Wright Memorial Bridge to the mainland, where she'd spent a long night in the Currituck County High School gym with hundreds of others. Worries over the damage swirled in the crowd as winds howled and lights flickered.

Funny thing was, Ruth hadn't been worried. Annoyed, sure, but not anxious. She'd known before she'd left her cottage that her hotel, the Seaside Resort, wasn't going to survive. Like her, it had run its course. Their time had passed.

Her family had owned and managed the Seaside Resort for over one hundred years. Her daddy liked to brag that he'd won it in a card game, but the place hadn't been much until Mama had seen fit to marry him and take charge of him and the resort's day-to-day operations. On this day in 1938, she was born in Bungalow 28, which once boasted the best ocean view in the entire place. As the story goes, her mama found Ruth wrapped in a pink blanket, with no sign of the woman who'd given birth to her.

Edna took her wailing discovery home to her husband, Jake, and the two decided after seventeen years of marriage that a baby would be just the thing for them. They folded the little girl into their lives and, together with the hotel, weathered all of Mother Nature's punches.

A wave crashed against the shore, pushing water right up to the tips of Ruth's worn athletic shoes.

She turned from the ocean and walked up the dune, past the sea oats that brushed her fingertips. Looking at the Seaside Resort's remains still pained her. One-hundred-and-fifty-mile-an-hour gusts had torn up the trees and shrubs and dumped them in the pool, rippled the asphalt parking lot, and ripped off the roofs of most of the bungalows and main building. Gallons of rain had poured inside the structures.

On the other side of the dune, she moved toward what had been the main building. The carpet in the lobby, which she'd just installed two years ago, was soaked with rain. The seashell wallpaper was peeling off the walls in large strips, and sunlight streamed in through the cracked roof. The Seaside Resort might have had more lives than a cat, but she'd used up her last.

"I've taken the offer on the property, Mama." The practicality of selling didn't soothe her guilt or anger. "Pained me good to sign the papers yesterday. But there was no way clear this time."

A breeze blew cold from the ocean, and she closed her eyes as she searched for signs her mother was listening. Of course, she didn't hear anything. Like Ruth, Mama never was a woman of many words. No bear hugs or sloppy kisses. But steady as she goes and always there. And Mama could guard secrets as close as old Neptune himself.

"I'm not crazy enough to think they'll save the hotel. Only a fool would try. Too expensive." She'd saved what she could from the damaged buildings and stowed it in her cottage, packing each room nearly to the ceiling. Tossing away what she'd paid good money for seemed sinful. "What remains of the resort will be razed. But maybe that's for the best. Time for something new."

The money from the sale of five acres of prime beachfront property would clear out Ruth's debts and leave her with enough to get her to the grave. There'd be no extra money for her granddaughter, Ivy, but Ruth's cottage, built a century ago with timbers from a demolished church, would bring a tidy sum.

"Blessed by God," her daddy used to say about the cottage. Considering it was two hundred yards from the Seaside Resort and hadn't lost a shingle, she reckoned that was true.

Whatever the reason for the cottage's endurance, Ruth saw it as a blessing. Ivy had a chance for a fresh start, whether she chose to live here or sell. No better gift Ruth could give.

Ruth turned her back on the ruins and faced the ocean. The brisk salt air burned her lungs and fisted around her heart as she moved across the sand. Wind brushed her face.

When she raised her gaze, she saw her parents standing on the beach holding hands with her daughter. She was tired and ready to join them. She'd be leaving Ivy alone, but that girl was the strongest of the lot. If anyone could heal the sins of the past, it was Ivy.

CHAPTER ONE
IVY

Four hundred and twenty-four. It was the number of miles between New York City and the Outer Banks of North Carolina. Seven and a half hours. That was the projected drive time. But it didn't account for the accident on the New Jersey Turnpike, the gridlock around the DC Beltway, or the new road construction miles before Norfolk. The calculation also didn't factor in a McDonald's stop in Delaware (hamburger and large Diet Coke) or the potty break in Fredericksburg, Virginia.

Eleven days. The time it had been since Ivy Neale had left home to attend her grandmother's funeral. It was the post–New Year's lull at the restaurant, so no one had minded when she'd taken off two days. There was a hurried flight to Charlotte and then back up to Norfolk, followed by a one-hundred-mile drive in a rental to the Outer Banks and then the thirty-minute funeral service. She'd seen friends and family, but the hugs had been quick and the conversations superficial. No time for the ex-boyfriend, the ex-friend who'd slept with him two months after she'd left for New York twelve years ago, their truly precious child, the hundreds of people who had loved Ruth, or a tour of Ruth's house.

She'd flown back to New York, the sea air still clinging to her sweatshirt, and inquired about an extended leave from her job.

Five seconds. How long it had taken her boss to reject her request for leave. One second for this last straw to break the camel's back and for her to quit. Three days to cut a deal with her landlord, sell her furniture, and pack up what remained. She had agreed to pay him the remaining two months on her lease once she sold the cottage or was making money again. He'd accepted, knowing money later was better than none at all.

It wasn't that she didn't love her job or the city. God knew they'd endured a lot together. But it was time to return home and clean out Ruth's house. She owed this to Ruth.

One thousand five hundred dollars. That was how much the 2005 van had cost her from the used-car dealer. It was green and had worn tan seats and a radio that worked as long as you didn't hit a pothole, which was a neat trick on nearly eight hundred miles of I-95.

Thirty-one dollars and three cents. It was the cost of gas and a large packet of M&M'S from the gas station before she crossed the Wright Memorial Bridge and left the mainland behind for the Outer Banks, the two-hundred-mile-long chain of barrier islands stretching along the North Carolina coast. They'd been inhabited for a thousand years by native tribes drawn by the fertile waters and since 1587 had been settled by Europeans.

Ivy's grandmother, Ruth, had lived and died by numbers. She'd always been counting the days until opening season, the days until the season closed, the dollars and man-hours required to keep her hotel in the black, and the miles per hour of the winds when a hurricane loomed close to the shores. The last hurricane that hit in December was the "widow-maker," as Ruth had said on the phone. It ripped and soaked Ruth's hotel beyond the point of salvaging. Ivy had vowed to return home as soon as the Christmas rush was over.

The wind whipped across the long bridge, forcing her to tighten her grip on the steering wheel to keep the tires aligned. Thick gray clouds unspooled over the bright full moon.

Across the bridge, Ivy stopped at the Wendy's and ordered up two bacon cheeseburgers, fries, and a diet soda. There'd be no food at Ruth's cottage, so the extra burger could double as breakfast until she figured out what stores were open in the off-season.

Ivy glanced in the van's rearview mirror, which tossed back a reflection of smudged mascara and a riot of black curls. As she stared at her likeness, Ruth's voice echoed: *Your shift starts at seven. We've got three parties this weekend, so no time for friends. We made it through another season.*

She grabbed a handful of french fries and gobbled several as she pushed through the drive.

It was another eight miles down the main road until the left turn by the mattress store at Milepost 8 took her down a side street to the beach road. A half mile south, she expected to see the Seaside Resort, but the barren, leveled land threw her off, and without the landmark, she drove past Ruth's cottage.

She was a half mile gone when she realized her mistake and did a U-turn. After she'd retraced north, she slowed and pulled onto the naked lot. In the last two weeks, the demo team had erased all traces of the bright-aqua main building, the twenty-four bungalows, and the neon SEASIDE RESORT sign.

Ruth had said she was going to sell the valuable beachfront property a day after the storm.

"It would take a lifetime to pay off the debt, and I'm too old. I'm letting her go," she'd said.

"To who?" She'd been in New York a dozen years, but the guilt over leaving always resurfaced when she talked to her grandmother.

"There's a developer."

"The land's worth a fortune."

"I know. And it's enough to pay off my loans and give me something to live on."

"If it's not enough . . ."

"It is," she said quickly. "Besides, I've been moaning for years that I'd like more time. Now I have it."

"I can be down there tomorrow."

"No rush, Ivy. I know how busy it gets in the restaurant at the holidays. Come when you can. Being here won't change much."

"I'll be there soon."

Ivy had grown up in that hotel. Stood behind the front desk when she could barely see over the counter. She'd swum in the long rectangular pool after hours more times than even she could count, eaten all her meals in the kitchen, and skateboarded on the parking lot in the off-season.

The kitchen was where she'd learned to cook. By age twelve, she was wearing an apron, standing on a step stool, and cutting, chopping, and sautéing meals for the guests. Never mind that her grandmother might have been breaking all the child labor laws. God only knew what OSHA would have said. But in truth, Ivy liked the work as much as Ruth did. She liked cooking, creating, and hearing feedback from the guests. By age sixteen, she was in the kitchen before and after school and seven days a week during the summer.

And now it was all gone. Ivy and her grandmother were out of tomorrows.

Regrouping, Ivy pulled out onto the road and then took a quick right onto the concrete driveway bounded by tall shrubs, bent and twisted by the constant ocean winds. She parked and stared up at the dark house perched on eight-foot posts. The staggered cedar shakes were grayer than she remembered, and the battered blue hurricane shutters were closed. The stairs appeared to be in good shape and the wraparound porch intact. How fickle weather could be.

Her headlights swept the underside of the house toward the small utility shed. The breakers would need to be flipped and the water turned on. An hour before the heater warmed the cottage and the old water tank made hot water.

She dug into her bag of french fries, ate several more, and savored each bite of the salty, fatty potatoes. She could have calculated the calories but decided in times like these, they didn't count.

How many times had Ruth talked about the magic of food? It lifted moods, healed broken souls, and made any task less daunting. She polished off the fries and slurped diet soda before she crumpled up the wrapper and shoved it in the bag next to the uneaten burger. "Ready or not."

After fishing a flashlight from the glove compartment, she clicked it on, got out of the van, and dashed to the utility room. The cold wind cut through her thick down coat, a veteran of twelve New York winters. She fumbled with the keys, her fingers awkward in the cold. The lock, rusted by the salt air, finally gave way, and she stepped into the small room and swiped her light across the walls and fuse box. Praying the salt air had not corroded the box and that the water pipes hadn't frozen, she opened the door and searched for the master switch, which to her surprise had been turned on.

She wasn't sure who'd turned on the juice, but she was grateful there was hot water waiting in the tank, intact pipes, and maybe a warm house. Closing the box, she turned her attention to the master water valve and realized someone had also turned on the water. "Whoever you are, bless you."

She closed up the shed and grabbed her one overnight bag, burger, and soda. Tucking her head against the wind, she climbed the steps to the front porch spanning the house's entire exterior. The rusty front door lock had been freshly oiled and gave way easily. After opening the door, she stepped into the warm, dark house and switched on a light.

Greeting her were wall-to-wall items from the Seaside Resort, including stacks of red leather banquet chairs, boxes of hotel linens, folded tables, cutlery, and signs. SEASIDE RESORT POOL. RECEPTION. NO PARKING. Ruth had rescued and crammed all the Seaside Resort storm survivors into her house.

"Shit."

Sixty-two days until spring; sixteen days until her thirtieth birthday, when she would inherit the cottage outright and could sell it.

She made her way to a couch by a dark stone fireplace climbing to the vaulted ceiling. Sitting, she dropped her overnight bag to the ground and dug her second burger out of the bag. Screw breakfast. She needed comfort now. She sat for several minutes focusing on the burger's flavor and sipping her too-sweet soda as she stared at the towers of clutter.

As the last of the soda gurgled up the straw, she rose and wove down a narrow path through the maze of items toward the back screened-in sleeping porch. The door's well-oiled hinges opened easily. Briny, cold air rushed toward her as she stared out over the crashing waves illuminated by the full moon dangling in the sky.

When she was a child, Ivy and her best friend, Dani, had slept on this porch more nights than she could remember. Dani and Ivy would giggle until midnight, when Ruth would finally shout from her first-floor bedroom for them to sleep. There was something freeing and exciting about sleeping out here with the ocean breeze cutting through the humid air dripping with moisture, the squawk of the gulls, and the gusts carrying the laughter of hotel guests still lingering by the hotel's pool.

When Ivy had first moved to New York, she had a terrible time sleeping. The honks and shouts of street noise were a poor substitute for the crashing waves that had lulled her to sleep ever since she was a small child. And lying on a cot in the YWCA, listening to two residents fighting, she'd wondered how she could have been such a shitty friend to Dani and a bad girlfriend to her ex, Matthew.

The three had run together since middle school. She'd started dating Matthew junior year of high school, and their dreams for the future had quickly tangled together. He didn't want college, like Ivy and Dani, and he believed the three of them should open their own business. She agreed, because she had no better idea. Dani was thrilled, admitting that she'd been accepted to art school, but the housing-market crash had made finances really tight for her dad. A year of making money would solve all her problems for the much-needed school tuition.

When Matthew announced he'd found a work-to-own arrangement for a small restaurant, Ivy freaked. Dani would leave in a year for school, and then she'd be here with Matthew in a *life* she wasn't ready for. And still it took a few weeks and four beers at a graduation party for her to screw up the courage to tell him she was backing out of the deal and moving to New York.

"What, you're just going to New York?" Matthew's wide grin faded, but he still seemed to be expecting a punch line.

"I'm leaving tomorrow." Her heart lodged in her throat, making it hard to draw in a full breath. She'd hoped spitting out the words would be a relief, but she felt sick with guilt.

"We're scheduled to sign papers in two days on the café!"

"I know."

"Is this payback because I forgot to pick you up for this party?"

"It's not payback. I'm leaving."

"Do you know how stupid this sounds?" Anger cut through his beer-glazed eyes. "You've only been to New York once, on the high school field trip last year."

The vastness of New York City had overwhelmed her on that trip. But she'd been so excited by the newness and energy, which had both followed her home. "Maybe it does, but I've got to try."

"Do you have a job?"

"No." But she had a list of places where she wanted to work and a seven-night reservation at the YWCA. If she got too mired in the details of this move, she would acknowledge how pie in the sky it was.

His laugh held no humor. "You really aren't kidding?"

"No." The more she spoke, the stronger her intentions grew.

"This is bullshit," he said. "We were supposed to open our own place."

"It was your place," she said.

"I thought *we* were a team." He gestured between them, sloshing his beer on her white dress.

"Sorry." They could go around and around, but she was not going to change her mind. She was not. And when Dani came up to them with three beers balanced between her long fingers, she must have immediately seen their tight expressions.

"What's going on?" Dani asked.

"Ivy is ditching us," Matthew said. "She's not signing the papers, and she's moving to New York."

Ivy drew in a breath, wishing she were drunker. "I'm not ditching you. I've decided to move to New York."

"No, you haven't," Dani said.

"I have." Telling Dani was harder for some reason. "I've talked to Ruth, and she understands."

"When did you talk to Ruth?" Matthew demanded.

"A few weeks ago." Her grandmother had needed time to find a new fry cook and overall kitchen manager. Ruth had taken her announcement with a shrug, hugged her, and whispered, "It's what we all got to do at some point."

"Weeks?" Matthew shouted. "Don't you think I deserved the same goddamned consideration? My deal depends on having you both working the business. Ivy, you were trained by one of the best cooks on the Outer Banks, and that means something to my backers."

Dani took a step back as if she'd been slapped. "You never said a word to me. We were going to enjoy this next year, working together."

"And next year, when you had your money for school, you were leaving," Ivy said. "Matthew would have his business up and running, and I'd still be in a kitchen working less than a mile from the place where I grew up."

"I didn't just pull my plans out of thin air," Dani shouted. "You knew I was leaving. You promised us both that the three of us would stick together for at least another year."

"I'm sorry. I can't keep that promise." Tears welled in Ivy's eyes. "It's now or never for me."

Dani set the red plastic drink cups down hard, splashing more beer. "I forbid you to leave. Not until we've hashed this out."

"No," Ivy said.

"Her word is worth shit," Matthew said.

"Apparently," Dani said, crossing her arms.

Ivy left for New York the next morning, operating on no sleep and sporting a wicked hangover.

Her resolve lasted all the way up I-95 and into the city parking deck, where she suffered sticker shock at the fees. She found her room at the YWCA, and over the next six days, she visited restaurants on her list plus a half dozen more. No one had heard about the Seaside Resort, and no one had a job.

On day six, chewed up by defeat, guilt, and loneliness, she pulled out her suitcase from under her bed and started packing until she caught herself. She had inherited her mother's recklessness but also Ruth's iron stubbornness, and the last thing she was going to do was return home with her tail tucked between her legs. She wasn't opposed to going home one day, but it would be with sails plumped with success. So she again hit the pavement the next day.

Her tenacity did pay off. She found a job in an Italian restaurant called Vincenzo's, two blocks off Broadway, as a fry cook and dishwasher.

The staff were all related to the owner, and she was the first nonfamily member Mama Leoni had hired in twenty years. Mama said she liked Ivy's look, the calluses on her hands, the faint scars on her arms from the Seaside Resort's kitchen fryer, and her *yes, ma'am*s delivered with eye contact. Mama Leoni explained that the restaurant had grown in popularity following a review on a blog site, and the chef, her husband Mario, and their son, Gino, needed help. Beyond grateful, she agreed to report to work that night.

While Ivy stirred the large pots of Italian gravy and cut, sautéed, and seared, Mario and Gino shouted at each other, relitigating arguments they'd likely been having for decades. Each fight ended with Mario escaping to the alley for a smoke. Not so different from Ivy and Ruth and the Seaside Resort kitchen.

When Mario became sick with cancer three years later, he cut back on his hours, Gino became head chef, and she rose to sous chef.

Mama Leoni told Ivy she was family. "You have Italian running in your veins."

And Ivy wanted to believe her. Family didn't always stick together, but it was supposed to in theory. And when the tough times came for Vincenzo's, and they did, Ivy worked double time to help keep the restaurant open.

And when the time had come for Ivy to take a leave of absence to return to North Carolina after Ruth's death, well, apologies and tears aside, Mama Leoni had needed only seconds to refuse. They'd abandoned her.

Karma. It had finally swung around and knocked Ivy on her ass.

CHAPTER TWO

IVY

Tuesday, January 18, 2022, 7:00 a.m.

Ivy was up as the sun was rising, a habit ingrained after years of rising early so she could scour the farmers' markets for the best produce. She'd been at the restaurant a year when Mario had invited her to the early-morning markets and begun introducing her to the vendors. The outings reminded her of the North Carolina farmers' markets, where she'd bought fresh fish, whole chickens, sweet potatoes, corn, and collard greens. In New York, she hunted for varieties of tomatoes, cuts of prosciuttos and veal, and spices she'd never seen. She grappled with and then marveled at the sensory overload as Mario explained why he made his choices, which vendors were honest or affordable, and how much product was enough for the evening dinner service. Wasted food was lost revenue, and like the Seaside Resort, Vincenzo's operated on razor-thin margins. She never felt closer to Ruth and home than she did during the morning market trips.

By her last year at Vincenzo's, she was going to the market alone. Mario's cancer had gone into remission, but his knees were bothering him, and his diabetes, which he refused to acknowledge, left him light headed at times. Gino had three babies at home now, and he was finished with early mornings. The extra sleep, Gino said, would do him good.

And so she'd risen early and been at the market by sunrise, moving among the venders, tasting the fresh vegetables and fruits, smelling meats, squeezing melons. It had always remained a feast for the senses and a boost to her creativity.

She slid on her jacket and shoes. The sun peered up from under the horizon as she moved outside toward the dunes and watched the waves crash hard against the beach, pebbled with a line of seashells. As tempted as she was to walk along the beach and inspect the ocean's latest offerings, the primary objective was to get coffee and then a few groceries. Tomorrow morning, with a coffee warming her hands, she might linger and enjoy the sunrise.

Back in the cottage, she dug a gallon-size zip-top bag filled with toiletries out of her suitcase. She went into the first-floor bathroom, still containing Ruth's toothbrush and a half-squeezed tube of toothpaste. She gently touched the brush.

Lifting her gaze to the mirror, she groaned and dug her own supplies out of the bag. She brushed her teeth, combed her dark hair that looked so much like Ruth's, tied it back in a ponytail, and applied a little lipstick to brighten her face.

She grabbed her purse and hurried outside through the cold to the van. Unless the world had turned upside down, Dotty's Pancake House was still two miles north and open during the off-season. The five-minute drive rewarded her with Dotty's flashing red **OPEN** under the giant pancake-shaped sign.

The few cars in the lot were trucks and service vans, indicating that the local tradesmen tasked with the endless list of off-season fixes and repairs were grabbing breakfast. Inside, she inhaled cinnamon and bacon scents that immediately sent a hit of dopamine through her brain. Many of Ruth's guests often remarked that the smell of the Seaside Resort's apple pie always righted the wrongs of the world.

Ivy stood behind a tall guy in line. He had broad shoulders, dark hair curling out from a black knit hat, and a thick tan work jacket. The jeans were clean, but the cuffs were as frayed as the boots were scuffed. He smelled of soap, hints of sawdust, and cold, salty air. At the register when he ordered, his voice triggered waves of memories. He was Dalton Manchester, her old ex–best friend Dani's older brother.

They had gone to high school together, but he'd been a senior when she was a freshman. Smart, athletic, nice, he wasn't dashing or overtly sexy, but his gray eyes always focused when he spoke to you. No drive-by comments or half listening. When you had his attention, you had it. Anyone on campus with a heartbeat was aware of Dalton.

Not ready for a trip down memory lane rutted with her own failings, she ducked her head and held back as he paid for his order. At the register, she selected the number four, which included eggs, bacon, pancakes, and a bottomless coffee cup. She handed the cashier a ten.

"That's four dollars and five cents change." The cashier was a few years younger and had dark hair pulled back into a ponytail. Her bronzed face set off blue eyes already feathered by crow's-feet.

"Great price," Ivy said.

"You're the first to say so," she said. "We raised prices January first by a dollar, and I haven't heard the end of it since."

Ivy shoved the change in her jeans pocket. "I've been living in New York for a few years."

"Well, that explains it. The only time I went to New York was for my junior high school trip. I remember paying eight dollars for a plain bagel and a small coffee."

"Was the bagel good?"

She grinned. "Not bad, but I'd put Dotty's pancakes up against it anytime."

"I'm counting on it." New York's fast pace still ingrained deep into her bones, she skipped the chitchat, filled a white stoneware mug with coffee, and found a table in the corner.

She took several sips of coffee, savored the flavor and kick, and then reached for her phone. Automatically, she opened her email, searching for restaurant correspondence. Senseless to keep checking, but ties never severed as cleanly as anyone liked. There were a few messages from vendors wishing her well, but most were inquiring about unpaid invoices or confirming an order. Gino had relied on her a great deal in the last year. Oh well.

"Ivy?"

Dalton's voice sounded like it had been textured with Tar Heel sand. She looked into gray eyes honed by a dozen years and an eternal tan earned on construction sites. A thick, dark beard hinted at the rebel who'd climbed the Currituck water tower at thirteen, driven to California and back in his Jeep at sixteen, and passed on a full ride to Duke University in exchange for a navy enlistment. "Dalton."

"So you're back for a while, or is this another quick visit?" Lines creased the edges of his eyes, and more salt sprinkled his dark hair.

"Quickish?" She tucked her phone in her pocket and stood. "I'm cleaning out Ruth's house. It's going to take time, given what she's stockpiled."

He nodded slowly. "I moved it all up to the cottage. She wouldn't let go of anything that could be saved."

"I appreciate the strategic tunnels to the back deck and bathroom."

He studied her as if he, too, was reconciling a dozen years' worth of changes. "I knew it would have to be dealt with soon."

She tucked a stray strand behind her ear as she wondered how she now stacked up in his eyes. "Thanks for doing that. It'll be a pain to clean out, but if it gave Ruth some peace, then so be it. Losing the hotel was bad enough."

"Let me know if you need help hauling that stuff away."

"Thanks, but I've got it. It'll take lots of trips, but I've got the time."

"Back to New York?"

"Maybe."

He leaned forward a fraction. "New York didn't soften your North Carolina accent."

There'd been times when she'd wanted to divorce herself completely from here, but her roots ran too deep. "You can take the girl out of the South but not the South out of the girl."

Gray eyes never wavered. "I suppose so." A bell dinged, and the cashier called out order thirty-two. "That's me."

"Ruth said you and your father's construction company are doing well." Twelve years ago, it had been struggling in the wake of the mortgage-market meltdown.

"We have three dozen employees now."

"That's terrific."

He raised his coffee cup to his lips and hesitated. "Did Ruth tell you that my father bought the Seaside Resort land?"

She shook her head slowly, a little shocked and hurt Ruth hadn't told her. "She said PDD Construction."

"That's us. Peter Dalton Dani. PDD."

She pictured the freshly stripped hotel site. "I didn't realize. It was a done deal before she told me."

"Dad gave her a more-than-fair price." He spoke with authority, as if he wanted her to understand that the Manchester family had treated Ruth well.

"That's what she said." The sale had settled all Ruth's debts, which was a big comfort to her grandmother.

"Dani know you're back?" Dalton asked.

Ivy cleared her throat, not ready to face her ex–best friend. "No. I just arrived last night."

"Give her a call. She'd like to see you. No one got much of a chance to talk to you at the funeral."

"Bygones, right?" That sounded snippier than she'd intended.

He regarded her as if time should have healed that wound. "Ruth's house is full. It's an impossible task to do alone. Call me."

"I've got the van. And I'll buy a few dozen garbage bags and boxes."

"How about a construction dumpster?"

"I don't think it's necessary."

"I've done many clean-outs like Ruth's. A dumpster is a must because there's always more junk than you think."

Ruth's house was packed, but to be asking for help less than twelve hours after arrival felt like imposing. "You don't have to do that."

"Consider it a welcome-home gift. When it's full, I'll have it hauled away."

"I think I can tackle this on my own."

"Ruth could be independent like that. Stubborn at times. But even she realized she had to give a little."

"It took a hurricane," Ivy said, coming to Ruth's defense.

A slight grin tugged his lips. "It took four hurricanes in total. Her independence was what I admired about her the most. She was one of my favorite people."

"Mine too." Ruth and Ivy had spoken on the phone several times a week during her dozen years in New York. Oddly, they'd seemed to find more in common with nearly five hundred miles separating them.

"The dumpster is the only way you're going to get the job done, Ivy."

Ivy suddenly imagined Ruth standing beside her as she had when she'd been cooking in the Seaside Resort kitchen. *Right tool for the right job. Wasted time is wasted money.* "Okay, thanks."

The tension bracing his shoulders eased. "What're you doing with her house?"

"Selling it," she said. "I need the money."

"Do you have a buyer?"

"Not yet. Been in town less than twenty-four hours."

"I want to bid on it," he said. "It's a great property."

"I'm not selling it so it can be razed," she said.

"The real value is the land." Even in high school, he could be brutally practical and seemed to store little value in sentimentality. Dani had said their mother's death had changed him, driven him more inward.

"I know. But I'd like to see the house saved. It's been in the family since 1920. Besides, vintage is very fashionable, isn't it?"

"You'll get more money if you let the house go."

"No can do."

"And if no one will agree to those terms?"

It would not be an easy house to renovate. Plumbing, electrical, and HVAC dated back to the seventies. But the sanctified beams, the handlaid stone fireplace, and the deck that rimmed the entire house carried too many memories. "I'll cross that bridge when I come to it."

"Don't accept any offer until you talk to me," he said.

"All house-saving bids welcome."

"Good to know. See you around?"

"I'll be right next door."

Nodding, he grabbed his order and left the restaurant, making his way to a black pickup truck.

Ivy sat at her table, sipped her coffee, and stared out the store's front window, watching Dalton slide behind his steering wheel as he unwrapped tinfoil while a white Lab in the front seat barked and wagged its tail. Dalton removed a strip of bacon from the foil, gave half to the dog, and ate the other half.

Footsteps approached, and a waitress set down her order. "Can I get you anything else?"

"No, this should do it."

She refilled Ivy's coffee cup. "Holler if you need anything."

"Will do."

When Ivy looked out the window, Dalton was backing out of his spot. Head turned, arm resting casually over the passenger seat. Angled jawline sharp. Ivy's thoughts turned slightly lurid. "Been too long, Ivy Neale."

He maneuvered the car onto the main road and drove off in the direction of the Seaside Resort, leaving only her breakfast to tantalize her. She tore a piece of crispy bacon in half, ate it, and immediately savored the smoky, salty flavors. No wonder Dalton's dog had been wagging its tail.

She reached for her phone, reread the same ten emails she'd read before, and then set the phone facedown. The tethers pulling her back north felt as real as a phantom limb. "Let it go, Ivy. Focus. New life. Whatever that means."

She ate her breakfast, scrounged a generous five-buck tip, and made her way out. The next order of business was shopping for food and cleaning supplies.

She had enough money in savings to last her a few months. Her birthday was in exactly fifteen days, leaving her at least a month or two of cushion until she sold the cottage.

As she walked out of the store, she grabbed the local weekly paper from the stand and headed to her car. Sitting behind the wheel, she switched on the heat, sipped coffee, and thumbed through the slim edition. Not much was happening this time of year on the Outer Banks, so the articles were mostly about winterizing homes, the odd business closing or opening, and, of course, gearing up for the season, which unofficially began the week before Easter. Used to be the season stretched from June to September, but virtual work and learning had stretched it from March to December.

At the hardware store, she grabbed a cart as she entered, located the moving-supply section, and made her way down the empty aisle. One trip down, and her cart was filled with moving boxes, garbage bags, and cleaning supplies. She ran her card at the self-checkout, crossing her fingers that it would go through, and when it did, she was $161 lighter and releasing the breath she'd been holding. First priority after selling the house would be paying her landlord and then settling her credit card debt. Ruth had lived her life balancing debts, and Ivy had done the same, though she was never comfortable with paying the minimum and being one swipe away from a denied purchase.

Vincenzo's had cut back on employee salaries fourteen months ago in an effort to keep the doors open. They were slicing costs where they could, they'd announced at the nightly staff family dinner before the evening service. Being a team player, she'd gone along, but the smaller paycheck had deepened her reliance on credit. But times were supposed to get better; hang tough, and everyone would get a bonus when the restaurant paid down the bridge loans and started making money again. So far, no bonus.

She bagged up her purchases, wheeled her cart outside to her van, and tossed them in the back. She'd had little money in her pocket when she'd moved to New York twelve years ago, and she'd turned nothing into something. She'd do it again, only better.

"Ivy Neale?"

Turning, she spotted a tall man with a barrel chest, a thick shock of white hair, a gray handlebar mustache, a bulbous nose, and rosy cheeks.

The local vet, Dr. Brown, and his wife had eaten every Friday at the Seaside Resort. Seafood chowder. Bread with extra butter.

She grinned and walked toward him. "Dr. Brown."

He wrapped her in a bear hug as if the last dozen years had never happened. "Good to see you back, kid. The seafood chowder was never the same after you left."

She inhaled the scent of tobacco and dog. "Thanks."

He stepped back, regarding her. "You look great. The years have been good to you."

"I could say the same for you."

He laughed. "And you would be lying. But I'll take it." The smile dimmed. "Real sorry about Ruth. She was a pistol."

"She was," Ivy said. "Thank you. Good to see you."

"You too."

As Ivy drove back to the cottage, it struck her that Ruth had gotten along with everybody except Ivy. When they were in the same room, sparks flew along with terse words. Ruth often said it was because they were so alike. "Can't have two she-wolves in the same kitchen and not expect trouble."

Ivy had always claimed she and her grandmother were not alike. However, in the last few years, the Ruthisms, which always began with *Hard work never hurt anyone*, had crossed her lips more frequently. Other gems included *Enjoy the good times while they last*, *Actions have consequences*, and *Always room at my table*.

In her mind, she heard her mother's voice. "Ivy, sit up straight," Mama had said.

Four-year-old Ivy rolled her shoulders back and glanced over at her mother as she shifted gears. As her mother drove down the beach road, the cold winter air leaked in around the edges of the window. So far, they had passed seven green mile markers, one mini golf course, and more houses on pillars than Ivy could count.

The back of their car was packed with eleven green garbage bags filled with her and her mother's clothes. Ivy also had her favorite quilt, a stuffed bear with one eye, and a baggie filled with the three last Goldfish. "Are you sure we'll be back home in time for Christmas? Santa won't be able to find me down here."

The rearview mirror caught her mother's nervous smile. "Don't worry. Santa will find you."

Mama ran long fingers through her thick, straight black hair, which elongated her narrow face. Even at age four, Ivy envied her mother's slim lines and hoped her stout legs would grow as long and her dark, curly hair would magically straighten.

Ivy wiggled out of her car seat straps, leaned forward between the seats, and pushed the scan button on the radio dial, searching for music. For the last two hours, none of the radio stations had matched the ones in Richmond. She pressed again. And again.

Finally, she found a hazy "Always Be My Baby." Some of the day care moms weren't a fan of Mariah, but Mama didn't care.

Ivy settled back in her car seat but didn't slip her arms into the straps. "Will we be back in time for Jessica's birthday party on Saturday?"

"I don't see why not."

Ivy watched the rearview mirror, waiting for her mother to meet her gaze. "That's five days from now."

"I can count." She pressed the radio button several times, returning to the original station.

When Mama lied, she always found something to fiddle with or do with her hands. But Mama had once said her lies were kindness more than a sin. Telling people what they wanted to hear kept the peace. And it worked, until Mama couldn't take it anymore and broke up with a boyfriend, moved them out of an apartment, or quit a job.

"How many more miles?" Ivy asked.

This time the mirror reflected her gaze. "Just a couple."

"What's the emergency?" Ivy asked.

"What do you mean?"

"You told Jessica's mom that you had a family emergency. You never told me."

Mama fished dark sunglasses out of her purse and slid them on. "It's nothing."

"How can it be nothing? All our stuff is in the back seat, and we're going to see Ruth. We never go to see Ruth except in summer."

"We need to see more of her. You need to get to know your grandmother."

"Why now?"

"It's Christmas, Ivy. Families see each other at Christmas." She adjusted her sunglasses, which hid most of her face.

"But you two never talk."

"We talk."

Ivy recognized the cautious tone in her mother's voice. "When?"

"Lots of times."

"But we never visit except in the summer."

"You just pointed that out. Now we're visiting Ruth."

Ivy looked out her window at the shuttered business windows and signs that read: SEE YOU IN THE SPRING. "Santa's not going to find us, is he?"

"Stop asking so many questions, Ivy. It's giving me a headache."

Mama had headaches a lot these days, and once one started, she got unhappy very fast. So Ivy folded her arms, slumped her shoulders, and counted the cottages as they rolled past.

Mama drove past the Seaside Resort, and Ivy thought for a moment she had changed her mind and they were going back home. Mama changed her mind a lot. But being home meant Santa would find her and she could go to Jessica's birthday party.

But Mama muttered a curse, pulled into a parking lot, and turned the car north again. This time when they approached the hotel's empty parking lot, Mama flicked on her blinker.

"Home sweet home," Mama said as car tires rumbled over the rough pavement.

Ivy sat a little straighter, curious about the place that only existed for her in summer. The lot was empty, and the collection of small aqua bungalows was the lone source of color now under the slate-gray sky.

Parking, Mama shut off the engine. "Ready?"

Ivy was wary of the grandmother she knew so little about. "I guess."

Mama got out of the car, adjusted her sunglasses, and straightened her back. Ivy came around, tugging her quilt around her shoulders, and together they crossed the lot as an ocean gust rushed them.

Inside the lobby, Mama hesitated, removed her glasses as she walked to the front desk, and rang the bell.

"Be right out!" a voice rattled from a back room.

"I always know where to find Ruth," Mama said. "She's a fixture behind that registration desk, just like I was as a teenager."

The door swung open, and a woman in her late fifties appeared. She wasn't tall, but a sharp stare made her seem like a giant. A thick shock of silvering curly hair was skimmed back in a ponytail and framed a deeply tanned face lined around her eyes and mouth. Her smile was automatic, practiced, but it froze when she saw her daughter and granddaughter.

Mama squared her shoulders again as if the first time hadn't worked too well and walked toward the desk. "Mom."

Ruth's smile melted as she came around the reception desk and hugged Mama, who wrapped her arms around her mother's sturdy, square shoulders. Ivy sensed that all the tension chasing her mother had been stopped dead in its tracks.

"It's good to have you home," Ruth said. "I've cleared out the spare room at the cottage for you and Ivy."

"Thanks, Mama." Mama swiped her fingers over her moist cheek. "Have a look at Ivy. She's grown three inches since you saw her in June."

The sound of her name prompted Ivy forward a step. "Hello."

Ruth swallowed Ivy with her stare. "Last time I saw you, you barely came up to my knees."

"I'm almost five."

"Well, you were three when I saw you."

"It's been two summers?" Mama asked, more to herself. "Time's gotten away from me."

Staring at Ruth, Ivy saw her own stocky frame and thick dark hair mirrored back. Would her hair turn silver one day too? "Mama said I was four when we came last."

"You were three. I have a head for numbers," Ruth said.

"I can count to one hundred." Ivy didn't mention that she sometimes lost track in the middle and had to start over.

Ruth regarded Ivy's quilt covering a short-sleeved T-shirt. "Hope you packed sweaters. It's going to be cold for a few weeks."

"I thought it was going to be hot here," Ivy said.

"In the summer, it can get hotter than a fritter. By winter, it's mighty cold."

"I have a birthday party on Saturday," Ivy said.

Ruth looked at Mama, who quickly wiped a tear from her cheek. "You didn't tell her?"

"No. I thought I would say something after we arrived."

"What's that mean?" Ivy asked.

"We're moving to Nags Head," Mama said. "This is our new home."

"I can't go to the birthday party?" Ivy thought about the friends she'd left behind in Richmond, her room painted purple and yellow, and her preschool. "We're never going back home?"

"No," Mama said, turning away. "Richmond wasn't working out for us, and we need a new start."

Another new start. "I liked it."

"You'll like this place better." The tones in Mama's voice pitched a little higher.

"But what if I don't?" Ivy asked.

"Then you don't," Ruth said. "And you'll have to make the best of it, just like the rest of us."

"That's not fair," Ivy grumbled.

"Life's not fair," Ruth said.

Ruth's gaze held an iron resolve that wasn't muddled by emotion or tears. She traded only in facts. Santa wouldn't find Ivy. She wasn't going to Jessica's birthday party. The beach was home for now.

CHAPTER THREE

IVY

Tuesday, January 18, 2022, 8:30 a.m.

At the grocery store, Ivy made her way to the seafood department, knowing even in the off-season the offerings would be fresh. When she'd worked in the Seaside Resort kitchen, she'd made gallons of fish chowder, mountains of corn bread, and thousands of fig cakes. Suddenly, she had a taste for the seafood stew and Ruth's fried chicken.

She bought clams, Old Bay, clam juice, and, from the meat department, fatback and organic chicken legs. From produce she scooped up bags of potatoes, onions, carrots, preserved figs, and nuts. On the baking aisle she found bread crumbs and all the fixings for a cake, and finally from dairy, she bought butter and buttermilk. It had been twelve years since she'd cooked the Seaside Resort menu, but much like a forgotten toy that had been retrieved from the attic, the idea of cooking Ruth's recipes again was fresh and new.

Remembering the cluttered interior of the cottage, she nabbed more green plastic trash bags (twenty boxes in all) and tossed them in with the groceries. Checkout took less than five minutes (in the summer that time quadrupled), and her credit card cleared yet again. Within fifteen minutes she was driving on the beach road back to Ruth's.

She balanced all six grocery bags between her hands and climbed the stairs to the porch. Each gust of northern wind cut through her jacket.

After wrestling with the front door lock, Ivy shoved inside the cottage and moved to the small, dark, L-shaped kitchen. She opened the refrigerator, bracing for a mess, but found it cleaned out. Her fairy godmother had struck again. She put the groceries away, then rummaged through the spice cabinet, tossing several bottles of outdated cinnamon, oregano, and basil. Normally, Ruth had kept her spice cabinet up to date, but like everything else, age or shifting priorities had diminished the importance of the task.

Ivy walked into the main room and wove amid the clutter, conceding Dalton's idea of the dumpster was a good one. She unlocked the door to the sleeping porch, tugged a few times at the swollen wood, and opened it.

The moist breeze off the ocean whistled past her into the cottage's rafters. The winds had churned up the water, and the waves crashed onto the shore in their timeless way. She stepped out onto the porch, the only clutter-free spot in the house. The screened walls flapped, and sandy grit crunched under her feet as she stared out over the swaying sea oats. As welcoming and beautiful as this land could be, it was just as ungracious and forbidding. The barrier islands expected much of their inhabitants, but their promises of a good life extended only until the next storm.

Returning inside, she closed the door and turned toward the papers piled on the dining room table. Most appeared to be junk mail, bills, and newspapers that someone had dutifully collected and placed on the table in the last few weeks. She grabbed the garbage bag rattling with old spice jars and began sorting the top layer, tossing all junk mail into a bag while creating a pile for papers that needed her attention. If she had learned anything in the last few weeks, it was that death generated lots of paperwork.

It took nearly a half hour before she had cleared the top layer and reached what appeared to be a hotel-registration book spanning the 1930s. Opening it, she skimmed her fingers over signatures written in bold black ink, leafed through the yellowing pages, and studied the unfamiliar names written in a careful penmanship that seemed to have been the norm in those days. Her own handwriting had been described as a scrawl only a doctor or cryptographer could love.

Beyond knowing Ruth had been born on January 2, 1938, Ivy knew Ruth's mother, Edna Wheeler, had been in her midthirties at the time. Not so remarkable now, but that was considered an advanced age for baby making in the 1930s.

Ruth was the only child of Edna and Jake Wheeler. From what Ruth had said, Edna had been a bit of a rebel. Though she had been born in 1902 in western North Carolina's Appalachian Mountains to a large family, she had moved east to the Outer Banks in 1920 to find work. She had met Jake Wheeler, he'd hired her on the spot, and the two had married within a year of her arrival.

Ruth married around 1960, but her husband, as the story went, died in a fishing accident. And when Jake Wheeler died months later, Ruth, a new mother now herself, stepped up and, with Edna, took over the hotel's operation.

Next to the register was a leather-bound address book. Filled out in Ruth's block letters, the names meant nothing to Ivy. Ruth had raised Ivy, and yet Ivy knew very little about her.

"Maybe this is our time to get acquainted, Ruth."

A knock at the front door had her crossing the room. She opened the door, half expecting to see Dalton.

Instead, it was his younger sister, Dani Manchester, who stood on the front porch, holding up two bottles of wine and wearing the grin she defaulted to when she wanted to make peace. "Welcome home!"

Ivy tensed, searching for words as she stared at Dani's long-limbed body and angled face, which were a little fuller since high school.

Her blonde hair remained thick, and her makeup was still expertly applied. She wore a heavy emerald-green overcoat, tortoiseshell-framed glasses, black jeans, a sweater, and red Chucks. If Ivy had put that outfit together, she'd look ridiculous, but Dani made it all work.

Twelve years since Ivy had called home to Ruth, homesick and ready to return after four months in the Big Apple. Twelve years since she'd wanted to beg Dani and Matthew for forgiveness. "How's Dani? I've been meaning to call her, but I haven't screwed up the nerve."

"Well, things aren't like you left them," Ruth had said.

"They were pretty bad when I last saw her."

"Well, there's more."

"What do you mean?" Ivy huddled in the corner of the tiny room she rented on Staten Island. Outside, traffic horns and police sirens wailed. A yellow neon **BAIL BONDS** sign blinked outside her window.

"Dani and Matthew. They got married."

"What?"

"She's pregnant."

Ivy quickly counted backward. "How pregnant?"

"Two months."

Tears clogged her throat. "Did they even wait for me to clear the North Carolina state line before they hooked up?"

"You'd been in New York at least two months," Ruth said dryly. "It wasn't like they betrayed you. *You* left *them*."

The truth of Ruth's words didn't ease the sting. "Isn't there a code prohibiting ex-boyfriends and friends from hooking up?" She was fairly certain the universe required at least five, maybe six years before exes could move on.

"Life never stops, kid, whether you like it or not. Your leaving created a hole in their lives, and they filled it."

"They were my backup plan," she said, more to herself.

"You were their plan," Ruth said. "The funding for Matthew's restaurant fell through without you. And Dani's back working for her dad."

"I didn't mean to hurt them," she said.

"I know. But you did."

And now, just like that, it was twelve years later.

"Aren't you going to invite me in?" Dani asked.

Ivy stepped aside. "Dani, you look great."

As Dani moved past Ivy, her gaze wantonly roamed the cottage's interior. Her smile always widened when she was nervous or mad. "I haven't been here since Ruth passed. I'd forgotten how determined Ruth was to save what she could."

No one had seen Ruth's heart attack coming. "She told me you two talked a lot."

"We single mothers stick together." Dani held out the wine bottles. "You didn't drink wine in high school, but I figured you acquired a taste while in New York."

Ivy accepted the bottles, read the labels, and was impressed. Both cabernets came with a hundred-dollar-plus price tag, and as far as peace offerings or welcome-home gifts went, they were extravagant. Dani wasn't showing off her money, but as with her brother, money had never been a problem, except for the few years Dani was supposed to attend art school. "Thank you."

"The Manchesters can do better than a construction dumpster. Though now that I'm here, Dalton might be onto something."

"Both are welcome." Ivy set the bottles on the kitchen counter. "How is Bella?"

Dani's grin widened. "She's great. Would you like to see a picture?"

"Sure."

She scrolled through the images on her phone and picked one that looked recent. "I took this yesterday."

Ivy studied the image of the young girl with her father's dark hair, her mother's blue eyes, and an enviable peaches-and-cream complexion. If she'd stayed in Nags Head, would Matthew and she have really married and had children? Would their child be as lovely as Bella? "She looks like both you and Matthew."

"She has my creative energy and his mind for business. We're convinced she'll go far."

"I'm sure she will."

Dani slid the phone into the back pocket of her designer jeans. "It's dark in here."

"I've not had time to open the windows and let the light in. Whoever buys the house will have to consider better lighting."

"Ruth always had the shades open when we were kids." Dani carefully wove around boxes and stacked chairs toward a row of curtains covering north-facing windows. She opened each, allowing what little sunshine the gray clouds would let pass inside. "That's better. As I get older, I don't like the dismal days. Give me bright sunshine twenty-four seven."

"I'm looking forward to a few sunny days. There haven't been many in New York this winter."

Dani traced a dusty PLEASE WAIT TO BE SEATED sign with her fingertip. "How is New York? You still setting the culinary world on fire?"

"That fire has been put out. I'm looking for other adventures."

Dani raised a brow. "You're leaving New York?"

"Taking a break."

"Restaurant work is grueling. Matthew has had his share of ups and downs in the business."

Ruth had said later that Matthew eventually found new backers and opened a place. He'd had limited success, and none of his three subsequent ventures hit it out of the park.

"Enough about Matthew," Dani said. "Have you seen Ruth's paintings? She told me she stored them all away in her spare room."

"Paintings?"

"The spare room was her art studio."

"I didn't realize she was painting." Ruth had always doodled on random blank pages or in the margins of budgets and registration lists, but she'd never painted.

"Became very prolific after you left."

Ruth had never told Ivy. And it stung a little to know she'd told Ruth everything, but her grandmother had held back this detail. *Life moves on.* "I haven't had the chance to tackle anything yet. I'll have to clear out this room first so I have room to move."

"I can help."

Accepting the dumpster and this polite reunion had been easy enough. But working side by side with Dani was too much, too fast. "This is something I need to do alone."

A pained sigh escaped on Dani's exhale. "Okay, I'm going to slay the elephant in the room, Ivy."

"Me ditching you or the you-sleeping-with-Matthew elephant?"

"Twelve years ago," Dani pointed out. "And Matthew and I happened two months after you abandoned us for New York."

"I never thought you liked him romantically."

"When the bridge behind you collapses, the only choice is to move forward," Dani said.

"I didn't want to be everyone's bridge to the future. I didn't even know what I wanted."

"You did a good imitation of someone who did." Dani paused, drew in a breath. "My one night with Matthew was the result of too many beers and hurt feelings too raw to express. I was ready to forget Matthew had happened, and then I found out that flu bug I had was a baby. And my plans for art school evaporated just as money started to roll in for Dad." She sounded annoyed. "Don't feel sorry for me. You made your choice. I made mine, and I took responsibility for it."

Ivy couldn't say the same. She'd never called Dani or talked to her about leaving. "That's why you married Matthew?"

"We got married because of the baby. And I'm glad we did at least try for Bella's sake. The marriage didn't last two years, but we've stayed friends and have done a good job of coparenting. Matthew and I made the best of it. And I'd like us to do the same."

Ivy rolled her head from side to side, waiting for anger to spark. However, the embers had long grown cold and couldn't muster a puff of smoke, much less a flame.

"You did me a kindness," Dani said. "My kid is the best thing that ever happened to me."

"But no art school."

"No."

"None of us ever gets everything we want," Ivy said.

"I'm proposing a truce. No more grand expectations of each other. No pressure," Dani said.

"Sounds simple." Mama Leoni's rejection still stung, and Ivy wondered if she could be as reasonable as Dani if the shoe were on the other foot.

"No fight. No drama. Though we could at least shout a few *bitch*es at each other if it'll make you feel better."

Christ, why was it so hard to be mad at Dani? "We'll drink that wine you brought some evening. Then the gloves will really come off."

Dani regarded her and then grinned. "I think it's best we keep the gloves on. No sense opening old wounds."

CHAPTER FOUR
RUTH

Saturday, June 17, 1950, 11:00 a.m.

Mama was in a mood. She'd been up for the last couple of nights making sure all the rooms at the Seaside Resort were ready. Stocking the kitchen, unpacking the new order of sheets and towels, cleaning the pool one more time, and sweeping the carport in front of the registration office.

She was always nervous on the opening day of the summer tourist season. The money the hotel earned over the next three months would sustain them through the slowing days of the fall and the dead ones of winter. The hotel was booked solid for the summer, but a turn in the weather could chase away customers and cause more damage than Mama and Daddy could afford to fix. Because it could all be gone in a blink, Mama didn't exhale until after the Labor Day weekend.

Ruth hated this time of year. She considered the tourists' arrival a yearly trial to be endured. Strangers confiscated her quiet life, filling the hotel with too much noise and endless cackling laughter. And spare time became infinite hours in the kitchen peeling peaches and figs, shucking corn, or descaling fish to feed hungry vacationers, who, as far as Ruth was concerned, ate more than a normal person should.

For the mainlanders, opening day meant giddy excitement, beginning when they packed their suitcases, loaded automobiles, and stopped at Nettie Pearl's on the other side of the Currituck Sound to eat their fill of dumplings and fried seafood.

"Ruth!" Mama called.

Ruth wiped the charcoal pen from her hands and set her sketchbook down. "Coming."

"Time to greet the guests. Put those drawings away."

"I am." Ruth tucked her pencils and pad in the back corner of the kitchen pantry and rose up off her stool.

Her mother stood by her father, who was stirring a large pot of fish-chowder stock, which, along with corn bread and peach pie, would serve as the welcome dinner many regulars expected. Daddy was particular about his seafood, only bought from people he trusted, and he never used a recipe.

Ruth paused by the simmering pot. If she had a nickel for all the bowls of chowder she'd eaten or stirred in her twelve years, she'd be the richest girl in North Carolina. She swore a few times her parents had filled her baby bottle with it. "Looks good, Daddy."

"Thanks, baby girl." Daddy was older than all the other fathers. Though he never said, she guessed he had to be at least sixty. Muscled forearms and a lean frame belied the graying hair and skin wrinkled by a lifetime of working in the sun, first as a fisherman, then as a navy man, and finally as a hotel owner. The tattoos along his arms chronicled years served in World War I, and his wooden right leg was a reminder of the onboard ship explosion near France that had forced him to retire.

He'd returned to the Outer Banks in 1920 with a wooden leg, a limp, sizable savings, and a grim determination to rebuild his life.

After an all-night poker game, he took possession of Roy's Folly, a collection of small bungalows housing winter duck hunters and summer fishermen.

Roy's Folly had no luxuries in the rooms and no central meeting place where guests could gather in the evenings. Daddy's first order of business was constructing the center building that still housed a bar, kitchen, and dining room. Back then, men gathered at night to smoke cigars, drink, and play cards, so he saw no need to furnish the space beyond the bare necessities.

When Mama moved to Nags Head in 1920, her first stop was Roy's Folly. Daddy said he'd hired Mama on the spot to waitress because he'd fallen head over heels in love with her the instant he'd laid eyes on the tall blonde with alabaster skin. She said he'd been drinking and couldn't possibly remember their first meeting. Either way, the two were married in 1921. He was thirty-one, and she was nineteen. It would be seventeen years before Ruth came along.

When Mama wasn't fretting about opening day, Ruth liked to hear the story about the day Mama had found Ruth wrapped in the pink blanket in Bungalow 28. Mama would get really quiet, as if the retelling were a solemn occasion, and start by describing the screaming winds of a nor'easter and how it was pure luck she'd decided to check the cottages for storm damage. Mama said that, despite fifty-mile-an-hour gusts, a woman must have sneaked into the bungalow and given birth before running away. Edna had heard Ruth hollering for attention. When she opened the door to 28, she thought at first a cat had gotten into the room, and then she saw the wiggling pink blanket. She saw no signs of the mother, so she scooped up the baby and took her home.

While she wicked canned milk on a twisted piece of muslin so Ruth could suckle, she sent Jake to the nearest neighbor for a bottle and then to the sheriff. After thirty days, when no one came forward to claim the baby, Jake and Edna decided enough was enough and declared they were keeping the child. Since no one had a better idea, no fuss was made, and the baby, named Ruth after Jake's mother, became a Wheeler.

Mama brushed imaginary dust from her starched blue linen dress and adjusted the red silk scarf, reserved for opening day, and moistened red lips made brighter by a peaches-and-cream complexion. Mama didn't wear makeup as a general rule but made an exception the first day of the season.

Mama turned to Ruth and slipped an unruly dark strand behind a cinnamon ear already tanning in the sun.

"I'm not a baby," Ruth complained. "And why can't I wear lipstick?"

Mama licked her thumb and dragged the damp edge over a smudge of charcoal above Ruth's right eyebrow. "You're not a baby," she said with some regret. "But still too young for lipstick."

"Just a little?"

"No."

"When will I be old enough?"

A half smile tweaked her lips, as if she were recalling a conversation she'd had with her own mother once. "Not this year."

"I bet the other girls will be wearing it."

Ruth was referring to Dora, Jessie, and Bonnie, three girls who had been vacationing at the Seaside Resort since the war had ended. The girls and Ruth had all been about seven years old when they'd first met, but Mama had been careful to keep distance between her daughter and the other girls.

"Remember what I said about the line separating guests and staff. They're on one side, and Daddy, you, and I are on the other."

"Do you think they've forgotten me?" Ruth asked.

"You're a hard one to forget," Mama said. "Now go and find Talley and see if she needs help around the pool. Check-in time isn't for another hour."

"Okay."

Talley Jones was a cousin Ruth had learned about weeks ago, when Mama announced she'd be working here for the summer. Talley had arrived yesterday on the Greyhound bus that stopped in Great Bridge. Ruth and her father had driven the hour and a half to pick her up, and when Talley stepped off the bus, her brown suitcase clutched in her right hand, her expression was a mixture of fear and excitement. Ruth pegged her as Mama's kin, given her fair skin and light hair. When Talley saw Ruth coming toward her, calling out her name, the tension eased from her shoulders.

Talley was bunking in Ruth's room, sleeping in the twin bed across from hers. When Talley had climbed to the top floor of the cottage, she'd stared out at the ocean dumbstruck for a good ten minutes. So far, she was still afraid of the waves and hadn't let the water roll up to her bare toes.

Ruth cut through the lobby out the back door to the large rectangular pool that Daddy had put in at the end of the war. The pool was a risk, but Daddy bet it would be the extra attraction to set the Seaside Resort apart from the growing number of hotels on the barrier islands.

Talley stood beside the tiki bar, carefully folding a stack of freshly bleached towels. The towels not carted off by guests would be washed thousands of times in the next twelve weeks. The few that survived the season rarely made it through the next.

Talley was tall and thin and wore her thick blonde hair, so like Mama's, in a ponytail. She was the youngest of eight, and her kin—their kin—were from the mountains of western North Carolina, near Asheville. Mama and Talley's mama, Jolene, were sisters. Mama also had a twin named Patsy and another sister, Beth Ann.

Ruth had never met any of her extended family, but Talley said her mama exchanged regular letters with her sisters back home. Sometime last winter, during the course of a few letters, Mama and Jolene had decided Talley should work at the Seaside Resort for the summer.

Not only was Talley afraid of the ocean, but she didn't like sand between her toes. When they'd returned from the beach last night, she'd washed her feet twice and then fished two worn paperbacks from her suitcase and started reading. She'd declined Ruth's offer to go for a walk early this morning.

Ruth glared at the stack of unfolded white towels. "I swear they grow whenever your back is turned."

"What, the towels?" Talley regarded the stack. "Towels don't grow."

Ruth reached for a fresh terry cloth rectangle, folded it in half once and then again. "Just you wait and see. You'll have a full stack of folded towels; turn your back, and a pile of dirty ones will have taken its place in a blink."

"I don't mind folding," Talley said. "It's relaxing."

"If I had a nickel for all the towels I've folded, I'd be rich."

Beyond the pool, the waves of the Atlantic crashed against the shore, chasing off a flock of gulls rooting for tiny crabs bubbling below the moist sand. "What's it like growing up by the ocean? I mean, it's a sight to behold, but it scares me."

Ruth looked past Talley to the smooth-as-glass ocean. "It's calm today. Has been since you arrived." Ruth grinned. "Mama don't tolerate storms on opening day."

"She can't control the weather."

"Daddy swears she can," Ruth said.

"I'd like to collect some shells," she said.

"I thought you were afraid."

"I am, but my curiosity is getting the better of me."

"You'll have a million of them by the end of summer." Ruth still collected shells, but as she'd grown up by the ocean, selectivity was key if she didn't want to be overrun. The half clamshell or conch needed smooth, clean lines, or she placed it back in the sand. "Is the ocean as pretty as the mountains? I've only seen pictures."

"The hills and valley got their own beauty," Talley said, stacking another towel on the growing pile. "But they're as still as they can be. The world moves around them."

"Not like that here. We move around the ocean."

"Creates the sense of coming and going," Talley said, nodding. "I saw a ship out there last night. It was lit up like a Christmas tree."

"The fishing ships drop anchor off the shore in the evening so they have their lines in the water before sunrise, when the fish bite best. I bet the boat you saw belonged to my uncle Henry."

"Have you been out on a ship?"

"Sure. Hundreds of times. I caught ten spot fish last month with Uncle Henry."

"I've caught fish in the river. I don't suppose they're that different."

"No, I suppose they're not, though I'd have to see both fried up on a plate and taste each to be sure." Ruth's stack of towels teetered slightly, so she started a new pile. "Friday nights are always the fish fries, so you'll have more than your share of ocean fish by the end of the summer."

"Aunt Edna was telling me about the daily menus."

"Chowder on Saturday, fried chicken on Sunday, barbecue on Monday, spaghetti on Tuesday . . ." Ruth rattled off the entire list. "Never changes. Daddy said he can budget better if he knows what to buy, and he said folks like something they can depend on in this crazy world."

"I never get tired of a hot meal." Talley spoke as if it were an oddity.

"What does your daddy do?" Ruth asked.

"He's a minister, and he farms, hunts, makes wicker baskets in the winter. He stays busy, but with all of us to feed, it's always a stretch."

"And your mama?"

"She keeps the house, does some mending. She's not like Aunt Edna. She doesn't know how to run a business or anything."

"You'd think sisters would be the same."

"As different as night and day, according to my mama," Talley said.

Ruth had never met her extended family. There was Uncle Henry, who was really Daddy's cousin, but she'd never met anyone from Mama's side. "How many cousins are there?"

"Well, you're one. Patsy, her twin, has four. Mama has eight. No one knows about Beth Ann. She run off with Cousin Carol years ago."

"Where'd Carol and Beth Ann run off to?" Ruth asked.

"Don't know. Mama says those two girls was the prettiest of the lot and likely found themselves rich husbands."

Ruth added up the numbers in her head. "I got at least twelve first cousins."

"Likely more, considering Beth Ann."

"Mama doesn't talk much about her family."

"We all know about Aunt Edna. Mama and Aunt Patsy always enjoy talking about her letters."

"What do you know about Mama?"

Talley smoothed out wrinkled terry cloth. "She was the first to leave town, and Grandma used to say Edna was the one who gave Carol and Beth Ann the idea to run. But when Aunt Patsy and Mama gossip about Aunt Edna's leaving, their gripes always end with how much they miss her."

Ruth couldn't imagine her mother being a trailblazer. She was as steady as the cycles of the moon. "Your family gatherings must be something to see at Christmas."

"Loud is what it's like," Talley said. "Can barely hear yourself think."

"Daddy barbecues a hog each Christmas and invites everyone to a big potluck meal. Like the restaurant, Daddy flavors his pig the exact same way each time, and he always serves sweet potatoes, collards, and fig pies."

"No turkey?"

"He's not fond of turkey. And he'd have to shoot a lot of ducks to feed the crowds he gets."

"Girls, how are those towels coming?" Mama shouted.

"Almost finished," Ruth said.

"We had our first guest pull up," Mama said.

"They're early," Ruth said. "Check-in isn't until one p.m."

Mama always tried to work with guests. If the room was ready, she let them check in. Making a customer feel special didn't cost much.

Ruth and Talley stacked the towels in the pool cabana and hurried out to the lobby. Both came to a halt when they saw the powder-blue car with the white convertible top. The paint glinted in the late-morning light, sparkling like a polished gem.

The woman behind the wheel was new to the Seaside Resort and didn't look anything like the summertime guests. She wore a white scarf on her head tied at her chin, big dark sunglasses, and a bright-blue dress peppered with white polka dots.

"Is that one of the families?" Talley asked.

"She can't be." The mothers were always dressed nicely when they arrived, but they wore soft pastels and drove wood-paneled station wagons filled with children and suitcases.

"She looks like a movie star," Talley said.

"She sure does."

Mama stood behind Ruth close enough for her to feel the strain tightening her body. "She's going to be the singer here for the next two weeks."

"A singer?" Ruth asked. "You never said we were going to have a singer." Most evenings, the music was either one of the local boys playing guitar or Daddy putting a record on the phonograph.

"I wasn't sure if she could make it," Mama said. "You never know with show people."

The woman opened her car door, placed a high-heeled shoe on the ground, and, with a little white dog tucked under her arm, rose out of the car. The dog wore a blue polka-dotted bow on its head and a sparkly collar around its neck. The woman pulled her shoulders back, brushed the wrinkles from her skirt, and closed the door with enough force that it didn't go unnoticed.

Mama's smile tightened as she moved past Ruth to the woman. "I'm glad you could make it."

The woman regarded Mama behind her dark glasses, and then her red lips spread into a wide grin. "I'm sorry I'm late. There were more repair details to take care of at the *Maisy Adams*."

"The spring storm caught us all off guard," Mama said. "I'm glad you were close enough by to visit."

"What's a *Maisy Adams*?" Ruth asked.

Mama laid her hand on Ruth's shoulder. "This is my daughter, Ruth. She's twelve. Ruth, this is Miss Carlotta DiSalvo. She's going to be singing for us each night. Normally she's on the showboat *Maisy Adams*, but it's in for repairs in Coinjock. Got hit by that storm that rolled through here in May."

Miss Carlotta extended a white-gloved hand. "It's a pleasure, Ruth."

Ruth wiped her hand on her skirt before taking Miss Carlotta's hand. "Nice to meet you, Miss DiSalvo."

"Call me Carlotta. Everyone does."

Mama wasn't fond of using first names. Said it was never a good idea to get too well acquainted with the guests and summer staff. "And this is my niece Talley Jones," Mama said. "She'll be with us for the summer."

"Talley," Carlotta said. "A pleasure."

Talley curtsied. "Yes, ma'am."

"What's the dog's name?" Ruth asked.

Carlotta scratched the little white dog between the ears, and the pup's eyes drifted closed. "Her name is Whiskey. You'll have to excuse her. She's a little old and sometimes drifts off to sleep."

"She's so tiny," Ruth said. "She looks like a puppy."

"She's twelve," Carlotta said.

"Like me."

"Yes," Carlotta said.

"Carlotta, why don't you let me show you to your cottage?" Mama said. Beside the hotel were three small cottages that the Wheelers had bought cheap during the war. One was their home, and the other two they saved for guests who stayed more than a month.

Talley stared at the woman with a mixture of shock and awe.

"What do you sing?"

"Show tunes, mostly. Come and see. I open tonight."

"Carlotta," Mama said. "Your cottage is the gray one with the blue shutters." Mama pointed, and Carlotta tipped her sunglasses down a fraction, exposing vibrant green eyes that tracked Mama's outstretched hand.

"Lovely. Is there parking there?"

"Under the house," Mama said. "I'll meet you over there."

"You can ride with me."

Mama slid her hands over her blue dress, which had lost some of its luster. Her red lipstick had also dimmed, and the lines feathering around her eyes had deepened. "Be quicker if I walk."

"Are you sure?" Carlotta asked. "I promise not to drive too fast."

"Best I walk."

"Can I ride with her?" Ruth asked.

"Maybe some other time," Mama said. "You need to be ready for the guests."

Carlotta's green eyes vanished back behind the dark glasses. "There's plenty of time for a ride for Ruth and Talley."

Talley looked up, her face full of awe, as if she were standing next to a real movie star. "I'd like that."

"Then the three of us will all go for a ride."

Talley clapped her hands together. "That really would be swell."

"On second thought, Ruth, could you do me a favor?" Carlotta said. "Can you give Whiskey a cup of water and then walk her to the cottage? I'll have her blanket ready for her."

"Sure."

Carlotta leaned closer, her spicy perfume summoning a bigger world that hovered beyond the waters of the sound. "I promise I'll take you for a ride soon."

Ruth accepted the little dog, who fit neatly in the crook of her arm. She held the pup close, afraid she might drop her. Whiskey looked up at her and licked her chin. "I think she likes me."

"I think she does," Carlotta said.

"I'll take good care of her," Ruth promised.

"I know you will."

"Girls, take care of the dog and deliver her to Carlotta," Mama said. "We have an army of guests showing up soon."

"Yes, Mama." Any thoughts of a ride abandoned, Ruth and Talley hurried off, each cooing over the dog as if it were a child.

"Have you ever seen a woman so glamorous?" Talley asked Ruth.

"We've had some fancy folks here, but nothing like her," Ruth admitted. "I've never seen hair that blonde."

"And did you see her nails? They were painted bright red." Talley looked at her own nails, cut short with rough cuticles. "I swear I'll stop chewing my nails if my mama will let me paint mine red."

Ruth cradled the dog closer, inhaling the hints of Carlotta's perfume as she ran her finger over the rhinestone-studded collar.

"Are the summers always this exciting?" Talley asked as they entered the kitchen.

"Never. Same old people, year after year." She grinned as they crossed to the clean stack of dishes.

Talley took a bowl, filled it with cool water, and carefully set it down. "If Carlotta is 'same old,' it's going to be interesting."

When Ruth set Whiskey down, the dog sniffed the water and then lapped it up. "This isn't going to be like all the other summers."

And it wouldn't be.

CHAPTER FIVE
IVY

Tuesday, January 18, 2022, 3:00 p.m.

Ivy had filled her eighth garbage bag, but she had only made a dent in Ruth's downstairs bedroom closet. The woman had a secret weakness for sensible shoes, fanny packs, and sweaters, and Ivy was fairly certain her grandmother hadn't thrown out anything since the 1960s. She dragged each bag down the cottage's wooden stairs, thumping her way one step at a time toward her van, which was already full. She pushed and shoved the last bag in the front passenger seat next to the boxes of stoneware dishes.

As she slammed the door closed, the sound of a large truck downshifting turned her attention to the main road. The truck was a flatbed with a construction dumpster. She watched as it stopped at her house and then backed into the spot next to her car.

She strolled to the window, surprised to see Dalton behind the wheel. "Are you sure I'll need one this big?"

"Better safe than sorry." He put the truck in park and pressed a button, and the bed tipped slowly.

Ivy stepped back. "It's the perfect welcome gift."

He watched in the side mirror as the dumpster slowly lowered to the concrete driveway. "You didn't strike me as the flowers type."

That coaxed a smile. "I wouldn't go that far. But this morning, that dumpster really makes me go weak in the knees."

He shut off the engine and climbed out of the cab. "Ruth wanted to save everything."

"If all this gave Ruth comfort, then it's worth the trouble. Don't suppose you know anyone who wants ten sets of white stoneware dishes?" She'd found the stacks on the dresser in Ruth's bedroom.

"The thrift store at Milepost 5. They'll take whatever you got."

"I was hoping they were still in business."

"Offer still stands. If you need help, call me."

"You've already been a big help. I was kidding myself when I bought the garbage bags and a dozen moving boxes. A serious case of denial."

"I've never had a job that went completely to plan. Always a glitch."

The dog peered out the cab window and barked.

"Your partner in crime?" she asked.

"Sailor's getting old, but he won't hear of me leaving him at home. He's my official shadow."

Ivy climbed up on the truck running board and petted Sailor. He nudged her hand until she was scratching him directly between the ears. "Dani came by this morning. Brought a couple of nice bottles of wine."

"Moss never grows under my sister's feet."

Ivy drew in a breath as she climbed down. "It was always hard to stay mad at her."

He shrugged. "She can be charming."

"Yeah."

"For what it's worth, if not for Bella, she would erase her entire history with Matthew."

"I wish I could rewrite a little history. But it's written in stone."

Three larger flatbed trucks carrying land excavators arrived at the barren site next to the cottage. The traffic noises from New York had found her.

"You really did pick the best spot," Ivy said. "Ruth said her father fell in love with this location the first time he saw it."

"A visionary."

"Ruth said that many times." The rumble of trucks grew louder. Home sweet home. "How long will you be in the construction phase?"

"The heavy equipment will be around a week or so. Then the noise should be more manageable. We're aiming to be under roof in a month. Cottages could be ready by midseason this year. Keep your fingers crossed we don't get a lot of rain and the construction materials arrive on time."

Whereas Matthew could be cocky, Dalton had a quiet confidence. She doubted even a hurricane would stop him from having those cottages ready.

"You've got your work cut out for you," she said.

"We both do. I do want to bid on Ruth's place," he said.

"When's the last time you were inside?" she asked.

"December after the storm. Though I was just moving in boxes and items from the hotel."

"You didn't get a great look at the place."

"No."

"I thought you just wanted the land."

"Maybe I want the house."

"Okay, but I'll warn you it's going to require a big influx of cash to drag it into this century."

"Do you have time to give me a tour now?"

"It's still a bit of an obstacle course in there, but I've cleared a few more navigable paths."

"I'm game." He told Sailor he'd soon return. The dog barked and settled in his seat.

"Follow me." As she climbed the stairs, his steady footfalls followed close behind. She opened the door. "Welcome to the jungle."

Inside, he wiped his feet on the mat and removed his hat before he surveyed the dark interior crammed full of boxes and rescued hotel furniture. He turned first to the kitchen, with the avocado-green appliances. "This would be a gut job."

Ivy stared at the stove with the cracked knob and broken clock. She was ten when she'd grabbed a thin towel, reached for the handle of a hot cast-iron pan, and lifted it toward the cooktop. The heat seared through the fabric and burned her fingers. She dropped the pan, and it hit the knob. Ruth immediately pulled her toward the sink and ran cold water on her blistering fingers.

"Wish I had a nickel for all the times I burned my hands in the kitchen," Ruth said. "I was about your age when I started helping my daddy cook at the Seaside Resort."

Ivy hissed in a breath. "What was your dad like?"

"He was a quiet soul," she said. "In the summers he was working in the kitchen, and in the winter, doing maintenance repairs. The man never stopped moving."

"How old were you when he died?" Ivy had become fascinated with judging the age-appropriateness of someone's death since her mother's passing five years ago. Over thirty? Sixty? Eighty? There was a line dividing too young from just right, but she hadn't decided where it was.

"I was twenty-two." Ruth shut off the water, reached for a red-and-white checkered cotton dish towel, and carefully wrapped it around Ivy's fingers.

Ivy shifted at the memory, reminding herself she didn't have the luxury of saving a forty-year-old stove, even one with memories. "The cabinets are dark, but they were made from salvaged wood from a shipwreck by my great-grandfather."

"Do you know which wreck?"

"It was a schooner that went down right after the First World War. A local guy harvested the wood and sold it to my grandfather for two dollars. That's very illegal now, but then, anything on the beach was fair game for harvesting."

He opened a cabinet door, sending a collection of plastic storage dishes tumbling down.

Ivy gathered the tubs, most of which didn't have tops. "Sorry about that."

"Safe to say these aren't heirlooms."

"If there's a market for plastic storage containers, then I'm going to be rich." She shoved the containers back inside and quickly closed the door before they tumbled out.

"The cabinets are solid, and the history is unique. They need a good cleaning and maybe rearranging so that they don't block the view of the living room and the stone fireplace."

She liked his idea, but future cottage renovations were not her business. "I leave all that to you or whoever buys the house."

"Have you thought about the rest of your life?"

"Honestly, no. I've been consumed with the destruction of the Seaside Resort, Ruth dying, and moving. Once this place is sold, I'll catch my breath."

The small U-shaped kitchen was just big enough for one person and snug for two. This close to Dalton, she could smell the blend of freshly milled wood, salt air, and his scent. The room grew warmer.

She stepped back into the entryway and made her way among the boxes to the main room with the vaulted ceiling and stone fireplace that ran from the floor to the ceiling.

He followed Ivy along the narrow path toward the back sleeping porch. With a hard tug, he opened the back door and stepped outside, inviting in a cool gust of salty air. The chilled air felt good against her flushed cheeks.

He walked to the edge of the screened porch and stared out over the crashing waves. "I love this place. So will my father. He had a lot of very nice Seaside Resort vacation memories when he was four or five."

"His family vacationed here just a few years?"

"After his father died, his mother stopped taking vacations at the Seaside Resort. But Dad's said more than a few times that the beach got in his blood, and as soon as he was old enough, he moved back."

"Ruth said she and her parents were in the business of making memories."

"Made an impression on my father."

Ivy had assumed Ruth had been friendly with the Manchesters because of her friendship with Dani.

"Your mother was young when she died," Ivy said.

"Forty-six," he said. "Taken too soon, like your mother."

Shared losses had been the basis of her relationship with Dani when they'd met in elementary school. They'd been the half-orphan duo, forming their own select club. Both had known what it felt like to miss a mother, understood there was no time limit on grief, and cried with the other on birthdays and death anniversaries.

"Ruth was always kind to Dani, and that never was lost on me or my dad," Dalton said.

"Is that why you bought the hotel land?"

Dalton worked the toe of his steel-tip boot into a bit of rot on the porch. "It was good business."

"Be careful, Dalton; I'm going to peg you and your dad as soft touches. First bacon for Sailor and now a sympathy buy."

A small smile tugged the edges of his lips. "Don't worry about us. We're good at making money."

"I have no doubt."

"I'll make you a fair offer for the cottage."

"I look forward to seeing it."

He inspected a stack of black metal chairs from the hotel's banquet room. "Not all this is sentimental."

"No. Ruth could have told you down to the penny what she paid for each item in the hotel. The woman always guarded her pennies. Maybe she thought I could sell them and make a few bucks."

"You're selling the hotel stuff?"

"Donating," she said. "It's all in good shape and will benefit someone else more than the few dollars it'll earn me."

He shook his head. "What's crammed into this house is worth more than a few dollars."

"Better karma to pass it on."

He paused a long moment, staring down at her. "Anything sentimental so far?"

"There was an old hotel registry and an address book under the mail on the dining room table. I've no idea why she saved the registration book." She made her way to the table and picked up the address book. "Maybe you'll have better luck recognizing some of the names."

He gently thumbed through the small black book. "I recognize a few names. Henry Anderson was a local craftsman and fisherman. He did cabinet work for Dad in the early days of his business."

"I remember Henry. He worked in the kitchens until I was about six or seven. Nice man." She had vague memories of Ruth dressing them for his funeral. Sitting next to Ruth on the pew in the Methodist church, she'd watched a tear trickle down her grandmother's cheek.

"Dora Bernard Walton was a friend of my mother's. So was Jessie Osborn Lee."

The women's married names were written in a different shade of blue ink, and the loops on the Os and Bs were smaller, more controlled. "She updated their addresses several times."

He thumbed through the pages. "My grandmother's or Aunt Bonnie's names are not in here."

"Makes sense that they'd lose touch after your grandmother stopped coming to the beach."

"When my aunt Bonnie died, I was about twelve. Ruth attended the funeral."

"Really? She didn't take me to that one."

"Ruth and my dad spoke in the reception line."

"Were you close to your aunt?"

Dalton frowned. "Aunt Bonnie didn't have much use for me. Never made it a secret that Dad was making a mistake adopting his wife's son."

Ivy could almost feel Ruth's outrage. Ruth didn't tolerate that way of thinking. She accepted everyone.

"There are two downstairs bedrooms. One was Ruth's bedroom. The other was her art studio and is crammed with easels and paintings. I'm leaving the art room untouched until I can clear this room out. Hopefully, I'll have one of the bedrooms cleaned out soon so I can sleep in a real bed. The couch is as uncomfortable as it looks."

He glanced toward the couch, the rumpled blanket and pillow with a fading impression of her head. "Ouch."

"Tell me about it."

"Dani's interested in seeing the paintings. She said there could be a real demand for Ruth's work. More income for you."

"Dani's seen them?"

"They used to paint together. It was good for them both."

Ivy didn't want to be jealous, but it did bother her that Dani had had a part of Ruth she'd never known about. "Maybe. We'll see. I want to really look at the paintings before I make any kind of decision."

"You haven't seen them yet?"

"Working up the nerve." She still wondered why her grandmother had never told her about painting. "Ruth guarded her sketches closely, so I can only imagine the paintings were just as personal."

He reached for the hotel registry on the table and opened the cover. "1931 to 1939."

"I have no idea why she saved the registration book."

"The records room at the Seaside Resort was a total loss. The storm tore off that portion of the roof, and the rain flooded the room. Nothing could be salvaged, so she must have kept it here."

"Wonder why?"

"Maybe she wanted you to find it."

"Why not just tell me? Why the tangled mystery?" Ivy asked.

"I don't know." He scratched his beard. "That generation didn't do open and honest too well. Or maybe it was too painful."

"She always had a reason." Ruth had lived a regimented and predictable life. Laundry on Saturday morning, fried chicken on Sundays and barbecue on Mondays, bookkeeping on Tuesdays, and grocery shopping on Wednesdays. Off-season, Ruth had spent some time with her sketch pads, but the next season had always been looming on the horizon.

"Let me know if I can help."

"The construction dumpster is a big help. I just might fill it."

A heavy sigh shuddered through him. "I suspected that when I carried all the stuff up here." He strode toward the door and paused with his hand on the doorknob. "I'll be right next door if you need anything. Plenty on my crew to haul out the heavy stuff."

"I'll take you up on that."

"Good." He twisted the rusted knob, descended the stairs, and strode toward the running truck, where Sailor was waiting in the front passenger seat.

Thunder cracked in the night sky and vibrated through the house, waking Ivy out of a quasi-sound sleep. She was still on the couch, huddled under one of the three dozen rose quilts salvaged from the hotel. She'd stopped cleaning out Ruth's room about six, when she'd seen the rain-plump black clouds gathering above the dumpster. Her phone's weather app had made no mention of a storm.

Ruth had never been a fan of television, so there wasn't one in the cottage. And Dalton would have warned her if this was a big one. Impending storms were always the talk in town, and no one at the breakfast diner had said a word yesterday. But gales did pivot and surprise everyone.

She shifted off the bruising pressure on her right hip, looked out a window as lightning flashed in a starless sky. The winds howled, punching the cottage with twenty- or thirty-mile-an-hour gusts. Old timbers rattled, the eight-foot pylons under the house swayed, and the walls creaked.

She rose, wrapped the quilt around her shoulders, and padded in red Wonder Woman socks to the window. Drawing back the curtain, she squinted through the porch and the blackness toward the dunes and the beach. Thunder roared, and a bolt of lightning cracked the sky over churning waters.

Ivy tightened the folds of her blanket. Ocean waves rushed over the shore, up under the dune stairs, splashing white foam on the beach grass.

How many times had she weathered storms with Ruth, who had taken them all in stride? When other families had evacuated, Ruth sent Ivy with the Manchesters and always promised to follow. But she never had. She'd stayed in this cottage, keeping a watchful eye on her hotel. Her stubbornness had confounded local authorities, who'd reminded her repeatedly that if it got really bad, they couldn't save her. She understood, but she'd held her ground right up until that last December night, when the sheriff had threatened to arrest her if she didn't leave.

The curtains slid from Ivy's fingers as she retreated back to her couch. She slipped on her shoes and set her purse and keys beside her just in case. Cell phone in hand, she switched her pillow to the opposite end of the couch, lay on her other side, and stared out the window toward the storm. Driving now would be more dangerous, but if the storm worsened and the house became unstable, she would leave.

Leave. Right. Who was she kidding? If the storm grew in intensity, the road would not be drivable. Hell, the bridge might be closed. And she would be screwed.

"Wouldn't that be the perfect ending?" Ivy muttered. "The cottage and I get taken out in the storm." The dark rafters exploded with another jab of lightning sizzling through the room. Rain pelted the gabled roof, tumbled down the chimney, and seeped through the closed flue onto the fire grate.

"Ruth, if you're there and this is a test, it's really not funny. It's been a hell of a year already, and I don't need this." She drew her knees up into a fetal position. "And if this isn't you and you have some pull wherever you are, I could use a little help here."

CHAPTER SIX
IVY

Wednesday, January 19, 2022, 7:00 a.m.

Sleep came and went with each crack of thunder, which did not ease up until four o'clock in the morning. By then Ivy was so tired of worrying if the cottage would fall down that she fell into a deep, dreamless sleep—a rarity for her.

She might have slept the morning away if not for the bright light streaming through the open curtains of the sleeping porch. She opened an eye and glanced at her phone. Seven a.m.

"Too early. More sleep." She yanked the covers over her head, determined to stay hidden until she'd logged at least three more hours. She would make up the lost cleaning time in the afternoon. It had been years since she'd slept late. No harm, no foul.

The engine of a dozer, no, two, roared outside her window. Their engines groaned as their metal belts dug into dirt and rolled forward, while another vehicle's beep, beep signaled it was backing up. "Of course. The construction site."

Ivy rose up off the couch. The air in the cottage was cold, so she moved to the thermostat and realized the room was fifty degrees. "Please tell me I have electricity."

She tried several lamps, and none worked. "It gets better and better." Slipping on her jacket, she went outside and hurried down to the circuit breaker box. She checked, saw that the main breaker had popped. She flipped it back on and heard the heating unit rumble to life.

Glancing over at the construction site, she saw Dalton standing next to a truck, giving instructions to the driver, who was surveying the muddy puddles covering the lot. She appreciated his confidence and how he moved around the site as if it were his kingdom. She'd been just like that in Vincenzo's kitchen. No problem was too big or small for her in that world. She'd been a master and enjoyed her life. Even when the problems had mounted one on top of another, she'd never once doubted herself. And now she was here, with no job or plans for the future. Should have been freeing, but it felt a little like being on a high-wire act without a net.

She climbed the stairs, pushed through the front door, and made a pot of coffee. The machine quickly gurgled, and when the pot was a third full, she filled a blue OBX mug. Cradling the cup, she tunneled through the stacked chairs, tables, lamps, and nightstands to the porch. The sun splashed yellow light over now-calm waters touching the horizon. The fickle weather at the end of the earth could be as breathtakingly beautiful as it could be dangerous.

Her gaze drifted to the ribs of what looked like an old ship jutting out of the sand. It wasn't unheard of for storms to unearth the bones of sunken vessels. The area offshore was known as the Graveyard of the Atlantic because hundreds of vessels like this one had sunk off the shore over the centuries.

When Ivy was in elementary school, a clipper ship had risen from the sand near Hatteras and had remained above ground long enough for her fourth-grade class to take a field trip to see it. Her teacher had explained that off the coast, there were two great landmasses that butted against each other. Natural currents were constantly shifting underwater sandbars that could easily beach or sink a vessel.

Curious, Ivy took a swig of coffee, set it down, and then crossed the sleeping porch, opened the squeaking screened door, and descended the stairs to the moist sand. She zipped up her jacket and jammed her hands in her pockets as she crossed to the wreckage.

The vessel's hull was gone, and what remained were the ribbed support beams curving out from the ship's keel or backbone of the ship. The wood was darkened and petrified by decades in the salt water.

Ruth had never mentioned a shipwreck near her back porch, but decades if not centuries could pass before the sands divulged one of their secrets.

A dog's bark had her turning, and on the dune, she saw an Irish wolfhound. The dog looked more like a beast than any domesticated canine she had ever seen. Its deep woof rumbled along the ridge of the dunes and caught the wind. The rising sun to her back, she watched it vanish behind the tall beach grass.

Ivy looked up and down the deserted beach for signs that the hound's owner was walking nearby. When she didn't see anyone, she followed the dog and spotted it darting under a cottage with shuttered windows and an empty driveway. This time of year, this entire stretch of beach was deserted, so surely the dog didn't belong to anyone at the cottage.

Interested, she followed the boardwalk down the dune and then cut across the sandy soil to the beach house. The cottage, built in the 1970s, was a long rectangular box resting on eight-foot stilts with a shingled asphalt roof and shutters. The deck ran along the ocean side, and there were two sets of stairs, one in the front and another in the back.

Ivy made her way through the weeds and sand and came around the front of the house to a concrete driveway. She walked under the house but didn't see the dog. Entirely possible it had dashed across the beach road to another home.

She wasn't sure why the dog had captured her curiosity. It appeared to be in good health, and its lean, wolflike body moved with a native's confidence. She walked past two plastic garbage cans and toward a small utility room.

There was no sign of the animal. Her stomach growled. "Okay, back to real life."

As she turned, she heard a very faint whimper coming from the other side of the utility room. It couldn't be her wolfhound, but her curiosity nudged her around the back of the house.

The instant she rounded the corner, she saw a small dog burrowed into a beach grass nest. Ivy could see her very swollen pregnant belly.

Ivy approached slowly and knelt by the mother dog, who looked up at her and wagged her tail. "Ah, mama. You're alone, aren't you?" She scratched the dog between the ears. "You can't have your pups here. I need to get you out of the cold."

The dog drew back slightly as she shrugged off her jacket and laid it over the dog's tense body. "It's okay. It's okay."

The dog couldn't have weighed more than twenty pounds and looked like she was a mix of dachshund and who knew what. "I'm picking you up, so please don't bite me."

Another contraction tightened the dog's belly, so Ivy waited until it passed before she scooped up the creature. She cradled her close and hurried along the beach road until she arrived at her driveway. Up the cottage stairs, she pushed open the door.

She grabbed the comforter she'd used last night and piled it in a corner of the room behind boxes, which she hoped would give the mama dog a sense of privacy and security. The dog looked up at her and tried to rise before another contraction sent her back to the quilt's folds. "You're safe. Just relax, if that's possible at a time like this. I'll get hot water or clean towels or something. That's the beauty of being here with me now. We have hundreds of towels and dozens of comforters, so don't worry about a mess."

Ivy hurried to the kitchen, filled a bowl with water, and grabbed a handful of towels on the way back. When she arrived, the dog was licking what looked like a puppy. "My goodness, you are a fast one."

She considered sitting and helping but decided the dog would fare better without her looming. She had no children but suspected she wouldn't want anyone staring at her business end while she pushed out a baby.

She searched online for Dr. Brown's vet hospital and dialed the number. She landed in voice mail. "Hey, Dr. Brown. This is Ivy Neale. I found a stray dog, and she's giving birth as I speak. Any advice would be most welcome." She left her number.

After pouring a fresh cup of coffee, she paced the kitchen. Seconds and then minutes passed. Sensing that her constant movement was not helpful, she sat at the dining room table and opened the hotel register from the 1930s. The handwriting was as varied as the guests, and she was surprised to see the hotel had done such a steady business in the Depression. Most were men and listed their occupation as hunter or salesman.

She wondered how her great-grandmother had fared about that time. She would have been very pregnant with Ruth and ready to deliver herself.

Another whimper from the dog drew Ivy's attention to the corner. She rose slowly and peered behind the boxes. Mama Dog now had three puppies.

"I hope for your sake that you're finished. Triplets are a handful."

The dog licked the amniotic sac off the last puppy as the contractions eased their grip on her belly. The puppies, sightless and small, wriggled close to their mother as they rooted for a teat.

Ivy held the water bowl to the mother dog's mouth. The dog sniffed and lapped up several licks. Ivy dampened a rag with warm water and carefully wiped down the mother dog and pups.

Her phone rang. "Hello."

"Ivy, this is Dr. Brown."

"I now have three puppies."

"That was fast."

"It sure was. What do I do now?"

"I'm on my way into the office, so I'll swing by in a few minutes. You're at Ruth's, right?"

"I am. See you soon."

When the bell rang minutes later, Mama Dog had cleaned her puppies, who were already rooting at her nipples. She opened the door to find Dr. Brown. "Thanks for coming."

"Sure thing. Where is the new mother?"

"Follow the trail through the boxes on the right. She's behind them."

Dr. Brown's mouth opened when he saw the room. "My word."

"If you're short on hotel supplies, help yourself."

"I should be set on all that." His gaze wandered the room as he made his way through Box Canyon.

He knelt, spoke softly to the dog, inspected each of her puppies, and then rose. "They all look healthy."

"That's good."

"Do you want me to call animal control for you? They can come get them."

It would be the easy solution. "No, Mama Dog and the kids can stay. I'm here for at least six or seven weeks, so we'll have time to figure this out."

"All right. Call me if you need me." He paused by a box marked *pencils* and peered inside. "We can always use office supplies at the clinic."

"Then today is your lucky day. Take them all."

He hefted the box. "I've never been paid in pencils and pens before."

"If you'll bill me, I'll cover the visit with real money."

"Wouldn't hear of it. My pleasure."

She walked him to the door. "Tell your friends I have hotel equipment and puppies. All free to a good home."

"Will do." He reached in his coat pocket and pulled out two cans of dog food. "Mama Dog might be hungry. Give her a little now and let her drink water. More in a couple of hours."

"Will do. Thanks, Doc."

"Pleasure."

"Doc, do you know of an Irish wolfhound living around here? I saw one today."

He shook his head. "I've not seen one in years."

"I was just wondering if you knew who the owner might be."

"I'll keep an eye out."

"Thanks."

She closed the door, and back in the kitchen, she pulled a white plate from the cabinet, opened the can, and carefully spooned a small portion of dog food on the plate. After reaching for a paper towel, she wiped the edges clean, as she'd done with every dish at Vincenzo's. Behind the boxes, she knelt, dipped her fingers in the food, and held them out to Mama Dog. The dog licked her fingers clean several times and then accepted more water from the bowl.

Ivy washed her hands and then laid a clean bedspread on the floor and carefully moved each puppy to the fresh bedding, sensing the mother dog would follow. She did. Once the four were settled, Ivy gathered up the old blanket and carried it outside to the dumpster.

Returning to the cottage, she refueled on fresh coffee and then looked around the great room. She started with the stacked chairs, which she carried quietly down the front stairs two at a time. Though it would have been easy to toss them in the dumpster, they were still in decent shape. Instead she stacked them at the end of her driveway and put a sign on them that read FREE.

With the maze of chairs gone, the room already looked lighter. Next, the folded round banquet tables ended up at the end of her driveway with another scribbled **FREE** sign taped to them.

The day became a series of monotonous trips up and down the stairs (fifty-six total). Every hour she checked on Mama Dog, and she was glad to see the dog sleeping. Finally, around one, she picked up Mama Dog. "Time to go pee-pee. The kids will be fine. I promise."

She carried Mama Dog outside, but her body tensed, and she kept looking over her shoulder and whimpering. "They aren't going anywhere, I promise."

Ivy set the dog in a soft patch of grass and waited but was careful not to stare. Again, it was one of those moments when a girl did not need an audience. Finally, the dog peed, and Ivy scooped her up and carried her back to her puppies. The dog meticulously checked each one. Satisfied all were present and accounted for, Mama Dog drank more water and went to sleep.

Twenty minutes later, a knock at the front door distracted Ivy from a box filled with cloth napkins and tablecloths. Ivy opened her door.

Dani stood on her doorstep. Smiling. "Looks like you're having a yard sale."

"Trying to get rid of all the less-than-charming stuff Ruth saved," Ivy said.

Dani paused. "What's that smell? Dog?"

Ivy stepped aside and, as Dani passed, closed the door. "I found a pregnant dog this morning, and she gave birth behind those boxes over there."

Dani grinned. "Can I see?"

"Go easy. She's still nervous."

"I was a wreck after Bella was born." Dani moved slowly and then peeked behind the boxes. Her expression softened. She snapped a couple of pictures with her phone. "Don't let Bella see the puppies. She'll fall in love."

"In seven or eight weeks, they'll need homes. You and Bella can have the pick of the litter."

"Puppies are like having babies. I'm saving all my two o'clock in the mornings for sleeping, Bella, and maybe a hot date."

"Two a.m. was about the time I used to get off work."

"In New York. This is Nags Head. This time of year, we roll up the streets at ten p.m."

"That's got to cramp your style."

She shrugged. "Not anymore. I'm a day person."

"Since when?" Ivy remembered more than a few late nights the two had spent out at a party or drinking (when they weren't legal) on the beach.

"We all evolve." Dani looked around the room. "You've made progress."

"All the big items appear to be in this room. I'm afraid the bedrooms are going to be more time consuming. I cleaned out Ruth's closet, but there's so much to go through in her room I decided to focus on the big stuff first."

Dani held up a bag. "I brought doughnuts."

"Doughnuts?"

"Unless you've evolved beyond your sweet tooth."

"I have not." Ivy accepted the box and looked inside at the three chocolate-bacon doughnuts and the three vanilla glazed with sprinkles. "I wish I had the metabolism of a teenager."

Dani chuckled. "Don't we all."

Ivy selected a chocolate doughnut. "Can I pour you a coffee?"

"God, yes."

Dani sat at the dining room table as Ivy made a fresh pot and then filled two stoneware mugs. She glanced at the hotel register. "It's from the Seaside Resort."

"Ruth saved the years 1931 to 1939."

Dani's eyes narrowed as she scanned the names. "Mr. Edward W. Trainer, of New York. Duck hunter."

Ivy set the doughnuts on the table and sat across from Dani. How many years had she been pissed at Dani? And now they were sitting together as if time or drama had not passed between them.

"Mr. James T. Kelce, of Wilmington, Delaware, duck hunter," Dani said.

"January is still duck-hunting season."

"A lot of men and hunters." She scanned the list and turned the pages. She paused. "A woman, traveling alone. That's not that common."

Ivy leaned forward. "Mrs. Janet Irvington."

"A common enough name."

"Mrs. Irvington doesn't say why she's traveled to Nags Head in mid-January."

"Women hunted too," Dani said.

"I'd like to think her story has a bit more flavor to it. Woman on the run hiding from the mob. Far more interesting."

"I didn't come here to talk about this register." Dani sipped her coffee. "I came to warn you that Matthew knows you're back, and he's determined to see you."

Ivy shifted in her seat. "Why would he care one way or the other?"

Dani shrugged. "He was picking up Bella for the day, so I didn't get into it with him. I think he is crazy or desperate enough to offer you a business proposal."

Ivy had never pictured Dani or Matthew as parents. It still didn't quite jibe with the lingering mental pictures of two teenagers hopeful for a different future Ivy had abandoned.

"Who would have thought the hound dog in high school would end up head over heels in love with a daughter. He's forever torn between work and spending time with her."

"He was always ambitious." He'd talked to Ivy often enough about his dream to open a restaurant. She would run the kitchen, and he would manage the front-end operations. He'd been thrilled, but each time he'd spoken about his dream, she could feel hers shrinking.

"That has not changed. And now that you've cooked in New York for over a decade and you'll soon be flush with cash, he sees an opportunity. Though I suspect this time he'll have you sign a contract sooner rather than later."

"I can save him the trouble. I'm not sticking around. I'm staying long enough to sell this place and find homes for the pups."

A shadow of annoyance drifted behind Dani's expression. "And when you get to this unknown place, what will you do?"

"I don't know."

"Of course you do. You just don't want to say it out loud. It'll be some kind of restaurant. You and Ruth were cut from the same bolt of cloth."

"The risk is tremendous. And if I lose whatever money I get from the sale of this house, then I got nothing."

"You're assuming you'll fail. I don't think you will. Run the numbers. I know you love numbers."

"I don't have a net under me, Dani. You do."

"Money isn't everything."

"It's a soft place to fall." She looked around the room. "Ruth understood the value of a dollar; otherwise she wouldn't have saved all this."

"The only time Ruth was really relaxed was when she was painting," Dani said. "She was happy. She had a wicked sense of humor."

"I never saw her paint once. She doodled but never painted."

"She had the hotel, your mother's illness to manage, you to raise, and then I started hanging around all the time. She barely had a minute to herself." Dani held up her hand. "And don't get all twisted up about that. She loved you and was happy to give you a home."

Ivy looked around the house, wondering if Ruth would have been happier if she'd just sold the cottage and found a more accessible home. "You were with her when she died."

A silence settled between them. "I'd come to see her latest painting. I could see right off she wasn't feeling well, and her left hand was shaking. She didn't want me to fuss, but I called 911. When the rescue squad arrived, she had a heart attack just as they were loading her on the stretcher. They worked on her all the way to the clinic, but she was gone before they arrived."

Sadness tangled with guilt and lodged in her throat. "Thank you for being with her."

"Of course. She was a second mother to me."

Nestled under Ivy's gratitude, flickers of resentment flared. Dani had again stepped into a role that Ivy could have had if she'd stayed in Nags Head. But leaving was her own mistake.

"She was glad you went to New York," Dani said. "She said you needed the time away."

"Why would she say that? She never left the shore."

"I'm not so sure about that."

"What do you mean?" Ivy asked.

"My father once mentioned Ruth wasn't living in the area when her father died."

"Did your father know where Ruth went?"

"No, but I'll be sure to ask." Dani's gaze roamed the cluttered room. "I think Ruth has more to say."

CHAPTER SEVEN

RUTH

Saturday, June 17, 1950, 12:00 noon

Whiskey was stubborn. She glanced up at Ruth and Talley, her gaze defiant. She sniffed the ground, looked as if she'd squat, and then didn't. Choosing another spot, she changed her mind again. And again.

"Can't you just pee? We want to see that lady. Don't you want to see her too?" Ruth asked. "She's about the most interesting person I've met ever."

"Me too," Talley said.

The dog grunted out a breath. Pawed at the ground as if solid soil deserved suspicion. Finally, finally she dropped down and peed.

"About time," Ruth said. "You really are a spoiled thing, aren't you?"

Whiskey yawned.

Ruth scooped up the dog, and the two girls pivoted toward the cottage where Carlotta was staying. Squinting against the sun, they moved across the pale sand, past the scrub bushes and bramble. The day's heat gathered in the humid air, and within a few steps, sweat dampened the slender alley between Ruth's shoulder blades.

"The sun's hot," Talley said.

Her cousin, like Mama, was turning bright pink, and soon her skin would burn. Ruth soaked up the sun with the ease of a sponge. She cupped her hand over Whiskey's eyes just to be on the safe side. "We need to get you a hat from the lost and found."

"I won't say no," Talley said. "Do you get entertainers a lot?"

"Mama has had performers in before, but they rarely stay more than a night or two. And none have been as glamorous as Carlotta DiSalvo." Her every detail sparkled. Even her hair was unique.

Ruth ran her fingers over her own tempestuous black curls, barely contained by the rubber band, wondering if she could straighten the strands and twist them up into a smooth updo.

When they approached the cottage, she could see through the opened screened windows that Mama was giving Miss Carlotta the tour.

The house had sat empty since last summer, so Mama had collected her buckets and mops, and three days ago she and Ruth had mopped the wooden floors, wiped the kitchen countertops, swept the porch that wrapped the entire house, and wiped each window with a clean rag damp with white vinegar. By the time they were finished, all traces of dank mildew had been replaced by the clean scent of linseed oil.

Now, the windows were open, and the soft ocean breeze made the porch swing creak against rusting chains as it teased the edges of new floral curtains. The main room was sizable by Outer Banks standards, but there'd been a guest or two from the mainland who'd complained it would have been too small if not for the stone fireplace stretching up to the vaulted roofline.

The furniture—a couch; two chairs; coffee, end, and dining tables; plus the four headboards—had all been handmade by Daddy and Uncle Henry. Each piece was solid and set low with thick armrests like the furniture Daddy had seen when his navy ship sailed the South Pacific. Instead of carving tikis and turtles into the oak, Daddy had etched the reclaimed wood with ospreys, sanderlings, and gulls. Mama had sewn thick cotton sailboat fabric into cushions and pillows.

Ruth had helped Mama make up the double-framed bed on the first floor with a spread of bright green, red, and blue sailboats. She'd also been tasked with dusting the dresser, the mirror, and a small chair in the corner. She had helped Mama clean her share of bungalow rooms but wished this time she'd taken more care and not swept a dust pile under the bedroom's braided rug.

Mama's voice drifted through the screened walls of the sleeping porch. "There's two other rooms upstairs. The cottage can sleep eight, but let me know if you host any overnight guests. I like to know who's on my property."

"I won't be having guests," Carlotta said. "I'm looking forward to a little privacy and space of my own after years of living on the boat."

"You've been on that boat for a long time." Mama's statement held hints of an unasked question.

"Fourteen years," Carlotta said.

"How have you found it, the boat, I mean? All the traveling?"

A sensation curled in Ruth's chest as she stood at the bottom of the stairs, drawn to their conversation as if a truth would be whispered.

"I like it," Carlotta said. "We're in a different port every day or two."

"You don't get tired of moving around?" Mama asked.

"No. I spent the first fifteen years of my life in one very small town."

"Do you miss home?"

"No. You?"

Whiskey barked, wriggled her small furry body against Ruth.

Ruth glared at the dog and rolled her eyes, and she and Talley climbed the stairs. "We were just getting to the good part."

"Probably best not to eavesdrop," Talley said.

"That's all anyone does who works in a hotel."

Whiskey yawned.

Ruth, Talley, and Whiskey found the two women moving from the porch to the living room.

"That was quick," Carlotta said. "Whiskey usually takes her time."

"She's mighty particular about where she does her business," Ruth said. "Took longer than I expected."

A silver charm bracelet jangled on Carlotta's wrist as she accepted the dog. "She's not used to dry land. She's grown up on the boat."

"The *Maisy Adams*?" Ruth asked.

"That's right."

"You must have been to a lot of places." Ruth had been as far west as Elizabeth City and as far north as Norfolk. All the trips had been with Daddy, who was picking up either lumber or a part for his boat. He didn't like traveling far because he liked to sleep in his own bed at night. But Ruth loved crossing the bridge, seeing what was beyond, and stopping at a five-and-dime for a fountain drink.

"The *Maisy Adams* travels the inland waterways and up and down the East Coast," Mama said.

"Have you ever come across the sound to the Outer Banks?" Ruth asked.

"We try to stop in cities that have larger populations," Carlotta said. "There's just not enough people here."

"Maybe not in the spring and the fall, but in summer we're packed to the gills," Ruth said. "Isn't that right, Mama?"

"That's right, Ruth." Mama sounded formal, serious, not her first-day-of-the-season happy-to-see-you self.

Carlotta smiled. "I shall keep that in mind when we get back up and running."

"When's that going to be?" Ruth asked.

"A month, maybe a little less."

"And you'll be here the entire time?" Ruth asked.

"Your parents were kind enough to give me a two-week job while the boat is dry-docked. Whiskey and I are looking forward to having dry land under our feet for a while."

"Well, we got plenty of that." Ruth couldn't hide her excitement.

"Ruth and Talley, time to get back to the hotel and see to the guests," Mama said. "We'll let Carlotta and Whiskey get settled."

"Maybe I could help her," Ruth said.

"The guests always come first," Carlotta said. "It's the number one rule in entertainment."

Ruth's grin faded. She wasn't interested in seeing the same old people and playing the same old games they repeated year after year.

Carlotta grinned and added, "The show must go on."

"Come on, Ruth." Mama's words rushed out like an impatient gust. "I'm sure you and Talley will enjoy talking to the girls your age."

"You said yourself we can't be friends with the guests."

Mama, always a bundle of nerves on the first day of summer, was wound tighter than normal. "Say goodbye to Carlotta."

"See you soon," Ruth said.

"Bye, Miss Carlotta," Talley said.

"I look forward to seeing you both soon, girls." Carlotta's gaze warmed with a smile.

Ruth and Talley followed her mother outside, and as they walked across the sand, already growing hot in the late-morning sun, all her questions about the singer boiled inside her. "How did Miss Carlotta find us?"

Mama checked the small, slim gold watch on her wrist. "She wrote to me and told me her ship would be moored in Coinjock."

"But how did she find us? I've never heard of the *Maisy Adams*. The only people that know about us have been coming for years!"

"I suspect she wrote to several hotels. When I received her letter, I thought she would be a nice addition to the summer entertainment.

That new hotel is going to be competition. Always good to stay a step ahead."

"She's so pretty," Ruth said.

"Her hair is so blonde," Talley said.

Mama kept walking, her gaze on the hotel.

"Do you think she's ever been to Hollywood? I mean, she could be a movie actress."

"She is very pretty."

"How old do you think she is?" Ruth asked.

Mama's eyes squinted against the sun. "I'd say thirty."

"She looks younger."

"She's not."

"How do you know?"

"I know."

"And she just wrote you out of the blue?" Ruth asked.

"As I said, she wrote to hotels near Coinjock."

"I'm glad you said yes to her. I bet she's going to be a big hit."

Talley nodded.

Mama looked down at the girls, her fading red lips curling slightly. "Me too."

When they arrived back at the registration desk, it was less than a half hour before the first wood-paneled wagon pulled up under the carport by the main entrance. The woman behind the wheel wore brown-tinted sunglasses and a white kerchief over her blonde hair, an eyelet dress, and small pearl earrings. In the front seat was a little boy with flaxen hair, and in the back seat a girl cut from the same pale cloth.

Ruth recognized Mrs. Manchester and her two children, who had been regulars at the Seaside Resort since the war ended. Mr. Manchester, who worked in a lumber mill in Elizabeth City, never joined his family the first week of their two-week vacation.

Mrs. Manchester rose out of the car, clutching her red purse, which matched a sash tightly cinching her waist. She ran a finger under a strand of pearls encircling her slim neck and looked at the hotel with a mixture of tenuous relief and worry.

Her daughter, Bonnie, and her son, Pete, both long limbed, winter pale, and trim, piled out of the car. Bonnie, wearing sunglasses like her mother's, was a year younger than Ruth, but she was two inches taller, and her breasts—good Lord, her breasts had grown twofold over the winter and now filled out her pink sheath dress. Pete, five or six now, wore khaki shorts and a half-tucked white shirt. He rubbed his nose, already looking toward the ocean.

Ruth shifted, glanced at her flat chest, and drew in her breath, hoping to add a little volume. Nothing.

Mama nudged Ruth forward as she found a wide grin and walked up to Mrs. Manchester. "It's wonderful to have you back, Mrs. Manchester. It's never summer until you arrive." She greeted every regular guest with that line or a version of it. "Will Mr. Manchester be joining us at the end of the week?"

"Not likely," Mrs. Manchester said. "He's very busy with work."

"Too bad," Mama said. "We will miss him."

Bonnie peered over the tops of her glasses at the hotel and sighed, as if already bored.

"Glad to have you back, Bonnie," Ruth said tightly. "I hope you've fared well."

Bonnie regarded Ruth. "Help me with my bags, Ruth. I want to go for a swim."

Ruth stood still for a moment. "Did you have a nice winter?"

"We moved into a new house."

"You moved out of your grandparents' house?"

"Daddy said it was time we had a place of our own." She fiddled with a dog charm dangling from a silver bracelet. Her nails were neatly trimmed and painted in a clear coat. "Time to get the bags."

Ruth chose one of the three luggage carts by the front door and wheeled it toward the car as Mrs. Manchester opened the tailgate. Ruth,

Mrs. Manchester, and her mother unloaded the suitcases and stacked them carefully on the cart as Bonnie checked her nails and Pete edged toward the sign that read **POOL**.

"Peter Jr., do not go far," Mrs. Manchester warned.

"I'm not," Pete said, his gaze on the ocean.

"Let's get checked in, children," Mrs. Manchester said. "Good to see you again, Ruth. You've grown."

"A full inch," Ruth said.

Ruth pushed the cart to the glass door, paused, and opened it for Mrs. Manchester and her children. She glanced back to her mother, expecting a smile or sign of encouragement, but instead, she looked slightly stiff. What was it with Mama?

The next car rolled up under the carport, Mama's grin returned, and Talley stepped up to unload. Ruth propped open the main building's door with a rock they kept for just such a job and followed the family into the lobby. By the end of the day, they would have repeated this task over two dozen times.

Ruth opened the register and watched as Mrs. Manchester signed it while Bonnie glanced again at her nails and Pete shifted his weight from foot to foot.

"How many more days do we have left?" Pete asked.

Mrs. Manchester sighed as she signed her name and set the pen down. "Pete, we only just arrived. Don't ask me that question for several days."

"But how long?"

"Fourteen days."

Pete grinned. "Can I go swimming?"

Mrs. Manchester's voice carried whispers of fatigue and annoyance. "As soon as we get to our room and unpacked."

Ruth followed the family out the south side of the main building down a concrete sidewalk to the last bungalow. The Manchester family reserved the same end unit every year because it had two bedrooms separated by the biggest living room that opened onto the ocean.

Ruth unlocked the door, pushed it open, and dragged the luggage cart into the room. As her mother had taught her, she opened the thick aqua curtains, allowing light to rush inside.

Mrs. Manchester dropped her purse on the couch, opened the sliding door, and inhaled the salt air as she stared at the calm, smooth waters. "How's the weather supposed to be this week?"

"Daddy said clear skies." Ruth unloaded the luggage into the living room and pushed the cart to the open door.

"Good. This place can be rather bleak in bad weather," Mrs. Manchester said.

"Can I get anything else for you?" Ruth asked.

Mrs. Manchester turned, studied Ruth for a beat, and then handed her a folded dollar bill. "No, that's all, Ruth. Thank you."

Ruth nodded, closed the door, and pushed the cart toward registration, pocketing the money. The weight of the luggage gone, the front wheel wobbled as she crossed the lobby and found her mother loading luggage onto another cart.

She recognized the Osborns and their four children. Jessie, at twelve, was the oldest. Next, the twins, Gary and Grant, both boys, were ten, and the youngest, Billy, eight. Mrs. Osborn raised a cigarette to her red lips and inhaled deeply before she rose out of the car. A tap on the cigarette, and a long ash fell to the ground.

Mama's smile was more relaxed. "Now summer has begun."

"Edna, it really begins when I'm sitting by that pool with a cold gin and tonic in my hand," Mrs. Osborn said.

"Well, the bar is always open," Mama said, smiling. "Let's get you signed in, find your keys, and you can head to your room. The pool is waiting, and today is one of the prettiest days we've had in weeks."

"Bless you, Edna. I've been dreaming about this place for weeks," Mrs. Osborn said.

"I'm glad to hear it."

To Ruth's disappointment, Jessie had grown taller, and her breasts also filled out her short-sleeved navy-blue top. "Hey, Ruth."

Ruth tugged on the hem of her shirt. "Jessie. Good to see you. Bonnie is here."

"Great. I'm getting changed and going swimming right now."

A breeze caught her copper bangs and brushed them off her freckled face, already turning pink in the sun. "Well, I'll see you later."

"Sure." Ruth watched the girl hurry inside, not sure if she was glad or disappointed that they'd never been friends.

The cars kept rolling in. Dora Bernard, a tall, thin girl with brown hair, arrived with her family just after one. She still wore wire-rimmed glasses, though she had a sleeker, more stylish pair than last year, and thankfully, her breasts had not exploded off her chest. Her green dress and smooth summer sandals looked new. But all these girls had new outfits and swimwear for the summer.

It was past three o'clock when Ruth and Talley had a break. They went to the kitchen to find her father scraping cooking scraps into a bucket that he'd give to the crabmen to bait their pots.

Ruth poured glasses of lemonade for Talley and herself, and both drank greedily. Her father set a fresh bowl of chowder, coleslaw, and corn bread in front of each girl.

"Thanks, Daddy."

"Eat up, kids. It's going to be a busy afternoon."

Ruth tore off a piece of crispy bread and popped it in her mouth. "Did you see that new lady? She's going to be a singer."

"She's real pretty," Talley said.

He crossed to the sink, his limp noticeable, a sign he was tired. "Your mom told me about her. We haven't met."

"She's pretty different. I have never seen anyone like her."

Talley buttered a square of corn bread. "Me either."

"What's so special about her?" The faded anchor tattoo on his right bicep peeked out from under his white T-shirt as he rinsed dishes.

"The way she dresses, her hair, her painted nails," she said as she looked down at her own fingers. "Mama says I can't wear lipstick, but I swear Bonnie Manchester was wearing it today. And I think there was polish on her fingertips."

The lines over his brow deepened. "Bonnie is about your age?"

"A year *younger*. But she looks so much older this year."

Steam from the hot water rose from the sink. "Some girls grow faster than others. You'll get there sooner or later. And no matter how you turn out, you're going to be very pretty just as you are."

"I am not."

"Yes, you are," he said clearly.

She reached for the butter and slathered it on her corn bread. "You sure?"

"Yes," Daddy said.

Talley giggled. "My mama says it's a blessing when it comes later than sooner."

"Talley's mama is right," Daddy said. "No need to rush life."

"Why?" Ruth pressed.

Daddy glanced toward the ceiling, shook his head, and mumbled something about payback.

"Payback for what?" Ruth asked.

Daddy cleared his throat. "Never mind. Just take my word for it. Later is better."

Ruth sat in silence for several minutes as she ate her chowder. The sounds of laughter, splashing water, and a radio blaring "Don't Fence Me In" by Bing Crosby drifted through the screened door.

"I know it's hard, girls," Daddy said. "But you're old enough to understand that it takes hard work to keep this place working smoothly. All hands on deck."

"I don't mind hard work," Ruth said.

"You don't see half of what your mother does for this place."

No matter how late Ruth went to bed or how early she rose, her mother was wearing her starched dress and making chore lists, setting tables, or pushing a broom.

"I know," Ruth said. "Sometimes I wish she'd slow down a little."

Daddy set a clean, damp plate on a drying rack. "I don't think she knows how."

Ruth grabbed a towel and began drying the white stoneware dish. "Think Carlotta might need a plate of food? I didn't see her during the lunch service. She must be hungry."

"I imagine she is."

"I can take her something to eat."

He was silent for a moment. "That might be nice. Go on and make her a plate and run it over to her. But don't linger too long."

"Can Talley come?"

"I don't see why not."

Talley ate the last of her chowder and brought her plate to the sink. "Thank you, Uncle Jake."

"I'll need you girls back in a half hour so you can work the drink hut by the pool. Henry's running late and won't make it today."

"We can do that." Ruth took a clean plate and bowl. At the stove she selected a neat square of corn bread, coleslaw, and a big slice of butter and filled the bowl with soup, which she covered with an inverted plate. She carefully wrapped up clean utensils in an aqua cloth napkin and grabbed a bottle of soda from the refrigerator. "Be back soon, Daddy."

As Ruth and Talley headed out the side door, Mama came into the kitchen. "Where are you girls headed, Ruth?"

"Daddy said we could take a plate to Carlotta."

"Daddy said that?" Mama was quiet for a moment. "Don't be away too long."

"He already said." As the girls crossed the hot sand, Ruth, mindful the soup didn't slosh over the bowl's sides, moved as fast as she dared.

As they approached the cottage, music drifted out of the open windows. She could hear a woman singing, and as she grew closer, she peered in the window to see Carlotta standing in front of the mirror singing.

Her voice had a slight raspy sound as she sang "A Little Bird Told Me." She swayed her hips back and forth, snapped her fingers, and tapped her bare foot.

"Her voice is so pretty," Talley whispered.

"I know." Balancing the plates, Ruth moved her hips back and forth, trying to mimic Carlotta. However, her movements weren't as smooth and looked a little jerky. Talley giggled.

Whiskey barked and trotted toward the window where Ruth was standing.

Carlotta turned, her gaze locking on Ruth before she switched off the record and moved toward the door. "Ruth and Talley."

Ruth held up the plate and the soda. "We brought you something to eat. Mama and Daddy thought you might be hungry."

"They thought I'd be hungry?"

"Well, I did. And Daddy and Mama said to go on and drop off a plate. He makes the best fish chowder in the state."

Carlotta smiled and pushed open the screen door. She accepted the plate and the soda and set both on the counter. "I do appreciate the meal, girls. I normally don't eat a big dinner before I sing, but the soda will be a nice treat."

"The chowder tastes good cold," Ruth said. "But that butter might melt."

"Then I best put it in the icebox. Come on in, girls."

Whiskey came up to Ruth, sniffed her feet, and licked her fingers as she extended them. A grumbling bark rumbling in her throat, she retired back to a pink cushion Carlotta had set out.

"How do you like the house?" Ruth asked.

"It's nice. More space than I'm used to."

"I guess it must be huge compared to a boat," Talley said.

"A showboat. And you might be surprised. I have one of the larger rooms, but it's nowhere near this size. It's nice to have the space to spread out."

"Do you like living on the boat?" Ruth asked.

"I enjoy seeing all the different towns, and if I want to sing, I must find the audiences."

"You have a real pretty voice," Talley said.

"Thank you. Do either of you sing?"

Talley shook her head as Ruth giggled. "I'm the worst. Terrible. But I like to draw."

"What do you draw?"

"Anything. I don't have much time for it in the summer, but when the weather turns cold and the guests leave, I have plenty of time. Mama sews together the unused paper place mats, makes a book, and I draw on the blank sides. On my birthday my parents gave me colored pencils."

"When is your birthday?"

"January second, 1938."

"You're twelve."

"Yes, that's right. Talley is fourteen. How old are you?"

Carlotta grinned. "Old beyond my years."

"What's that mean?"

A slight shrug lifted Carlotta's shoulders. "It means I'm not going to answer that question. A lady doesn't tell her real age."

"Mama is forty-eight. She told me," Ruth said.

"My mother is forty-six," Talley offered.

"Are you two always this bold?" Carlotta asked.

"Yes," Ruth said.

"Mama says I speak just about every thought that hits my brain," Talley said.

"Sounds like your mothers know you both very well."

"I guess," Ruth said.

"Ladies, I have to get ready for my show tonight, which means I have to rest. But feel free to come back. And Ruth, show me some of your sketches. I'm very curious."

"Really?" Ruth asked.

"Of course."

CHAPTER EIGHT

IVY

Wednesday, January 19, 2022, 11:00 a.m.

"Did you see the shipwreck?" Ivy asked Dani.

"What shipwreck?"

"Have a look outside. It appeared last night."

Dani moved onto the back porch, the cool breeze feathering through the screens and drawing her outside. She crossed her arms and huddled deeper into her jacket as she stared at the vessel's exposed ribs. "You've heard the story about this one, haven't you?"

Ivy moved onto the porch. "No. How do you know about this one?"

"My dad told me about it. The first time the wreck appeared, he was about five or six. He remembers playing on it. Though, based on his description, more of the ship was exposed in those days."

"What year was that?"

"1950. Dad kind of became obsessed with the wreck and in his teens began reading all he could about it. He became an expert on the shipwrecks along this stretch of beach and was able to identify this wreck."

"Really. What's its story?"

"It was called the *Liberty T. Mitchell* and was a wooden sloop that sailed these waters in 1870. It was traveling from South Carolina to New York and got caught in a storm. The winds and high waves swamped the ship and capsized it."

"Wow."

"According to Dad, all eight crewmen were killed, along with two passengers."

When Ivy was nine, she was swimming in the surf and was blind-sided by a large wave. She'd tumbled over and over, her shoulder and back scraping against the sand as salt water filled her mouth. She struggled to regain her bearings and in the process swallowed water. She thought she was going to die. And just like that, a hand reached in and pulled her out of the surf. She looked up to see Ruth staring down at her, her expression a blend of fury and fear. The moment had left her with a healthy respect for the ocean. She imagined those ten people and their terror as the Atlantic sucked them under its surface.

"Does he know any more about the people who died?" Ivy asked.

"I don't remember all the details. You'll have to ask him. But be warned, if you do ask him about the *Liberty T. Mitchell*, he'll bend your ear for hours. He even remembers the name of the ship's Irish wolfhound. Boris."

Ivy stared at the arched, blackened wood. "An Irish wolfhound? I saw a dog like that on the dunes early this morning. If it wasn't for him, I wouldn't have found Mama Dog."

"Mama Dog?"

"Until I can come up with a name."

Dani waved Ivy's words away. "Don't give her a name. I know you. You're a soft touch, and you won't be able to let her go."

"I'm not a soft touch." She'd upended her life and professionally thrived in New York's tough culinary scene for a dozen years, and now she'd overturned her life again. That took stones.

Dani laughed. "If you say so. But a dog means roots, responsibility beyond the job and this old house, which will soon be sold."

Hearing Dani speak about the dog so bluntly was a reminder that Ivy's disappearing act twelve years ago wasn't forgotten. "What else can you tell me about the *Liberty T. Mitchell*?"

Her eyes twinkled. "While the ship is exposed to the sunlight, it's said the lost souls roam these shores and stir up trouble for the living."

"Seriously? You really believe that?"

"Well, the wolfhound did lead you to Mama Dog, and now you're responsible for four dogs. That's trouble."

"I'm not responsible for anyone but myself."

Dani laughed. "I'm calling bullshit on that one. I mean, two months ago, did you imagine this moment?"

"I was here before the wreck."

"Dad says bits of it appeared after the hurricane that took the Seaside Resort." She shrugged. "The spirits were being stirred, and now that a chunk of the wreck has appeared, who knows what they'll do."

Ivy shook her head. "Unless that wolfhound leads me to another pregnant dog, then I should be fine. I've made good progress today, and it's a matter of time before this place is cleaned out, sold, and I'm on to greener pastures." It was a simple plan, even if it was tangled with regret and sadness.

"You really think you can leave this place again?"

"I know I will."

Dani arched a brow. "Where are you going?"

"Destination unknown."

"Here's as good as anywhere," Dani said. "You've not experienced the Outer Banks as an adult."

"Too much past here." Her mother's and grandmother's deaths had tainted the house with a sense of loss.

"And you think you living somewhere else erases it? It follows you. I know."

"And you're suggesting?"

"You confront it."

"I am. I'm here."

"You're ignoring it. Take me, for example."

"What about you?"

"You've been nothing but polite ever since I arrived on your doorstep. Shoe on the other foot, I would have been pissed at you."

"I've already promised you a good fight. Eventually."

"You won't. You're too nice to do anything about it. Too many years of smiling at undeserving Seaside Resort guests and Vincenzo's patrons has trained you well. Nonconflict is so ingrained in you that you don't know how to fight."

"I fight. Ask the vendors in the New York food markets, the restaurant distributors, or reviewers."

"That's the easy kind of conflict that doesn't scrape any skin off your nose. The emotional stuff like losing a mother, grandmother, seeing your family legacy wiped out in a hurricane, having your best friend sleep with your ex . . . that shit stings."

"Maybe I'm keeping it classy. Mom died when I was five. Ruth lived a great life. The Seaside Resort's doors were open a century. And I'd been in New York two months before you and Matthew hooked up."

Dani shrugged. "Logic works great until your head explodes from rage."

Tightness fisted in Ivy's chest. "You're being dramatic. And I don't have time for drama. I have to get started on the bedrooms."

"Okay, suit yourself. But if you ever get furious and want to rage at the moon, come sit next to me. I'm an expert."

"Why would you be angry? You have a daughter, a business, and you've moved on from your ex-husband, correct?"

"Life's full of all kinds of pitfalls, Ivy."

"What aren't you telling me?" Ivy's eyes narrowed as she stared at Dani. "Are you dying?"

"No, I'm not dying."

Relief washed through Ivy. "Is Bella okay?"

"Yes."

"Your father? Dalton?"

"All well."

"What aren't you saying?"

"Nothing to report here," Dani said. "I'll live to be one hundred. Besides, you've been the villainess in too many of my recollections. I would miss getting annoyed with you when I have no one else to blame but myself."

"I'm not a villain," Ivy said quickly. "Stupid, weak, immature twelve years ago, but not a villain."

"The heavy never see themselves as evil. Some are quite charming and cute. That's what makes them so likable."

"I'm not sure if that's a compliment or an insult," Ivy said. She'd not cast Dani as the architect of her troubles for a long time, and she'd just assumed Dani felt the same way.

For a moment, neither spoke as the surf crashed around the ruins of the ship.

"Inside thought. And an old one at that."

"The spirits are stirring up trouble," Ivy said.

"No, it's this conversation about feelings. Those kinds of talks have never ended well for me." Dani smiled. "Look at me. I sound so much like Ruth."

Work harder. Nose to the grindstone. No one said life was supposed to be fair. Ruthisms. "She was smarter than I gave her credit for."

"She was smart in so many ways. She also gave up so many opportunities to be happy," Dani said.

"Whose idea was it for her to paint?" Ivy asked.

"Hers, but she said she was doing it for my sake. Bella was only a couple of months old, Matthew was working all the time, and I was pretty lost. She told me to pack up the kid and come here. We would paint together."

"I'm glad she found the thing that made you both happy."

"She'd wanted to be an artist since she was a kid. She finally felt like she was on the inside, if that makes sense," Dani said.

Annoyance snapped. "How would you know about living on the outside? You were born at the very center of the inside. Christ, you were baby Virginia Dare in the *Lost Colony* play."

"Like I've said, money doesn't fix everything, Ivy."

Ivy felt a little pleased that she'd ruffled Dani's feathers and then just as quickly was disappointed in herself. "You keep saying that. But it sure doesn't hurt."

Dani's demeanor shifted from playful to exasperated. "This is getting too deep for me. I have to be drunk to have a conversation like this. I better get going. Call me if you need anything. Or want to get drunk."

"I will."

"You won't. But I'll be stopping by again. Bella would love to see the puppies. Who knows—we might take one."

"Seriously? I thought you said you didn't want a puppy."

"My kid's been after me to get a dog. And now the spirits have delivered three puppies, so who am I to argue? Are you here tomorrow?"

Ivy was now sorry to see Dani leave. When they were growing up, Dani had been the one person she could fight with in one moment and then ask to borrow a quarter from in the next. "I'm here every day for the duration."

"Good." Dani looked around the room. "Have you seen my purse?" she asked.

"On the dining room table."

Eyes thinning, she spotted it. "Right."

"If it were a snake, it would have bitten you."

Outside, Dani stared up at a cobalt sky. "The most beautiful blue."

"It's lovely."

"They're all one of a kind. I'd bottle them all up if I could." Down the stairs, Dani got into her car and slowly backed out of the driveway onto the road. She used to drive like a bat out of hell. Motherhood had mellowed her. The spark was still there. The nosiness remained. But her energy was more subdued.

Ruth, never one to share feelings, had never shared these paintings with anyone. She'd likely say they were "too personal." Would Ruth be annoyed she was looking at them now? The last thing Ivy needed was to have Ruth's annoyed spirit join the gaggle of ghosts from the ship.

She glanced to the curb and noticed that all the chairs and tables she'd left were gone. Score one for the free market.

Ivy closed the door, and as she turned, she heard the puppies mewing. She peeked behind the box and saw that Mama Dog had stood. "Need to pee?"

She carefully scooped up Mama Dog, they went out the back porch, and she set the dog in the sand. Thankfully, Mama Dog took care of business, and they were out of the cold quickly. "I'm going to have to stop calling you Mama Dog. Giving you a name is not bonding. Everyone deserves a name."

The dog licked her face.

"Yeah, yeah. I kind of like you too." She scratched the dog between the ears.

Back inside, Mama Dog drank water, ate a half bowl of dog food, and then settled back down with her puppies, who quickly wriggled toward her nipples as they mewed complaints of her absence.

"What's your name, Mama Dog?" Ivy asked.

The dog looked up at her.

"The *Liberty T. Mitchell* brought us together. What about Liberty?" It had a ring. "Libby?"

Libby closed her eyes, unimpressed.

"If you don't like it, I'm open to suggestions. And be thinking about names for the puppies. We can't call them Thing One, Two, and Three for the duration."

Ivy opened the door to Ruth's art studio and flipped the switch. The overhead bulb spit out a paltry amount of light, which cast shadows on at least fifty paintings wrapped in brown paper and leaning against the walls. In the corner was a paint-splattered easel standing on a canvas drop cloth, as well as a folding table covered with brushes, paints, thinners, and rags. In the other corner was a crate packed with filled sketch pads.

She reached for a small painting and carried it into the living room. After laying it on the table, she unwrapped the brown paper and discovered a rendering of the Seaside Resort with a 1950s vibe.

The painting was a bold blend of blues, whites, and aquas splashed on the canvas in a haphazard way that somehow came together to create a festive feel. Parked in front of the triangular Seaside Resort sign (NO VACANCY) was a powder-blue Buick with a white convertible top.

Ivy could see why Dani wanted to examine the paintings. "I had no idea, Ruth. I wish you'd told me."

She felt Ruth so closely she turned to double-check and make sure her grandmother wasn't standing there. "I'm sorry. I shouldn't have left you."

Outside the ocean crashed against the shore. Tears glistened in her eyes, and she blinked twice to stop the flow. Refusing to feel sorry for herself, she shifted back to the decluttering job at hand. Stepping away from the painting, she glanced up the stairs and then began to climb. She opened the door to her old room. Like every other corner of the house, it was filled with salvage from the Seaside Resort. But beyond the clutter, she could see hints of her old life here.

"This is going to be your room," Ruth had said to Ivy years ago as they'd entered the room.

"Why don't you sleep upstairs?" Ivy asked.

"I like my feet closer to the ground," Ruth said. "But you should love this room. It's the best in the house. You can see the entire length of the beach from your window. Not many girls have that kind of view." The room had twin beds, one covered in a green comforter and the other in blue, and between them a large window that overlooked the beach and ocean.

The floorboards creaked as a wind pressed against the house. "Is it scary at night up here?"

"When I was a girl, I lived in this room alone most of the time. Your mother also slept up here when she was your age. And now it's your turn."

"Why is she downstairs now?" Ivy asked.

"It'll be better if she's closer to me."

"Does she get scared?"

"Sometimes."

A frown furrowed in the center of Ivy's forehead. "And if I get scared at night?" She stared out over the stretch of beach toward the crashing waves.

"You won't get scared."

"Why does Mom?"

"You're different than your mother. She's more like her daddy, and you're more like me."

"What was my grandfather like?" Ivy walked into the room and skimmed her fingers over the blue comforter.

"He wasn't the bravest of men, but he tried to be the best he could." Ruth shrugged as if knocking off an old weight trying to resettle on her shoulders.

"Where is he?"

"He died in an accident."

"Like my dad?"

"Yes. Like your father. We Wheeler women don't have the best luck with men."

"Does that mean I'll have bad luck?"

"No, you're better than your mother and me put together."

"What if I don't want to live here?" she asked Ruth.

Ruth grinned. "I'd bet good money when you come full circle, this is where you'll end up."

The words had echoed in Ivy's head for years, and whenever she remembered them, she always laughed, certain Ruth was wrong. Now, to prove a point, she said aloud, "This is a U-turn, not a circle back, Ruth."

She spent the next hour carrying boxes of utensils, Bibles, napkins, and bowls out to her "free" spot at the end of the driveway. Then, when she could actually see the wood-paneled floor, she began sweeping in the far-right corner, corralling dust toward the door. When she came around the bed, she lifted the end and carefully moved the frame several feet to the left.

The shift exposed a collection of boxes under the bed, including what looked like homemade and store-bought sketch pads and a black box.

Ivy collected the items, carried them to the living room, and set them all beside the hotel-registration and address books. Her gaze was drawn to the older makeshift sketchbooks, which were a collection of paper place mats from the Seaside Resort stitched together. Judging by the images, the sketches dated back to the late 1940s or early 1950s.

Every square inch of white space was covered with drawings of the ocean, this house, and the bungalows. All were signed with an *RW* in the bottom-right corner. Ruth Wheeler. Given the dates, Ruth would have been about eight to twelve.

Ruth's sense of perspective, shading, and detail would have shown remarkable talent for an adult, let alone a child. But it was her eye for shape and movement that infused the images with emotion.

Ruth had had no formal art training, though she'd once said she would have studied art if she'd made better choices. Ivy assumed the bad choices were the marriage and daughter at a young age and then the decision to join her mother and run the Seaside Resort.

She opened the black box and found brittle tissue paper that broke apart as she lifted it. Underneath was an old 35 mm Leica camera. This German camera's sharp images had been used by the best photographers covering fashion, war, and life.

On the silver metal bottom were scratched the initials *CD*. "Who are you, CD?" she asked. Ivy thumbed through the address book, running her gaze over all names in the *D* section. No one with a *D* surname paired with a *C* first name.

As tempted as she was to open the back of the camera, a glance at the photo counter indicated that there was film inside and the user had taken ten pictures. Opening the camera would expose the film and ruin the photos. Ivy set the camera aside. Photo-developing stores weren't as common as they used to be, but there had to be someone in the area who could safely check the film.

She traced the engraved *CD*. Ruth could have bought the camera secondhand, or it could have been left behind by a guest years ago. It amazed her what people forgot. But it wasn't like Ruth to have a camera as nice as this and just stow it away. Ruth had kept a lot of stuff, but all of it had been connected to her on some emotional level.

That meant that CD must have meant something to Ruth.

CHAPTER NINE
RUTH

Saturday, June 17, 1950, 4:00 p.m.

Ruth now stood in the towel shack by the drink hut, staring at the kids splashing in the cool water. She shifted from her left foot to her right and leaned back away from the sun's heat. Mama had said she could swim later, when the guests were eating dinner, but for now, her job was to hand out towels and answer questions about bathroom locations, dinner hours, evening tide schedules, phases of the moon, or whatever information a guest might want. And if she could sell them a cola or a cocktail from the drink hut, then all the better.

Talley stepped out of the restaurant, balancing a tray of iced glasses, which she carried to a collection of mothers sitting by the pool under their large aqua umbrella. Mmes Manchester, Osborn, and Bernard were all sitting together at the same table in the same order, just as they had last year and the year before. Each was on her third cocktail.

Talley set the drinks on the table, but none of the three women looked up. Mrs. Manchester reached for a red packet of Pall Mall cigarettes, snapped open a silver lighter, and held the flame to the tip. She inhaled and exhaled rings of smoke.

Talley came over to the hut with her tray, still sporting two bottles of Coke. "Aunt Edna said we could have a soda."

Never one for soft words or hugs, Mama did her communicating through cold sodas, new art pencils, and trips to Elizabeth City. "Thanks."

Water droplets rippled down the side of Ruth's misty cold bottle as she took a long drink, draining nearly half the soda as Talley sipped hers.

Talley wrinkled her nose, and her face softened with pure pleasure. "Wow, this tastes really good."

"You ever had a cola before?" Ruth asked.

"Once when I was twelve, my cousin let me take a sip of his. But I never had a whole bottle to myself."

"Mama always lets us have one on Saturdays during the summer. It's the busiest day of the week."

"Aunt Edna's been really nice."

"We only have about another half hour here," Ruth said. "Then we help Mama set up the dining room for dinner."

"You think we can watch when that lady sings after dinner?" Talley asked.

"We got to be around to wait on the guests, so there's no reason why we can't listen to the songs in between fetching drinks."

"I've never seen a woman like her," Talley said, a little breathless.

"You ever been to the movies?"

"No."

"Mama took me to see *Melody Time* last year. Full of all kinds of songs and ladies who look like Carlotta."

"I read for fun mostly."

When Talley arrived, she had carefully unpacked three worn paperback novels and arranged them on her nightstand. "What do you like to read?"

"I like Nancy Drew. I'm partial to the mysteries," Talley said.

"Who is Nancy Drew?"

"She's a girl like us who solves crimes."

"Why would she want to do that?" Ruth asked.

The Manchester boy cannonballed right into the center of several girls, including his older sister, and splashed water over the edge of the pool toward Ruth. The girls screamed and called for their mothers, but Ruth enjoyed the cool spray of water droplets on her face. Pete dived under the water when his mother called his name.

"I don't know," Talley said. "Nancy's smart, and she likes to figure things out."

"Nancy," Ruth said, smiling as she raised the soda bottle to her lips. "You say her name like you two are friends."

"It feels that way sometimes."

Ruth stared into her cola bottle and wished there was more than a swallow left. She had no book friends, but when she drew her sketches, she never felt alone as she shaded more here, drew the lines darker there, or just left the space white.

"Be on the lookout for books this summer. These folks leave all kinds of things in their bungalows after they check out. In fact, Mama might still have a big box of books from last year in the storage room."

"Really?" Talley asked. "What kind of books?"

"I never gave 'em much notice." She always collected the abandoned crayons, pencils, and pens to use over the winter. "We can go to the storage shed between dinner and the show and see what we can find."

"I'd like that."

Ruth drained the last of her cola. It felt good to have someone to talk to.

The Saturday-night dinner was a big success. Everyone loved Daddy's seafood chowder, and because it was the first night, many came up for seconds and thirds. By next Saturday, they would all be sluggish and bloated and ready to cut back on the eating, but for now their bellies were primed to consume as much as their eyes could see.

Once the plates had been cleared and the folks had retreated to their rooms for regrouping before the evening entertainment, Ruth nudged Talley as they stacked the last of the clean dishes on the long prep table in the kitchen. "Daddy, can we look in the storeroom for old books? Talley likes to read."

"Be quick," he said. "Your mama will be looking for you soon to serve drinks during the entertainment."

She guessed they had twenty, maybe thirty minutes tops before Mama came looking. Fact, she'd known better than to ask Mama for a break on opening night. But Daddy was the softer touch, and he wasn't good at saying no to reasonable requests.

Ruth dried her hands. "I'm going to need the key."

"There's a spare hidden under the rock by the front door. I know you've been in there scavenging before."

Ruth kissed her father on his cheek. "We'll be right back."

"Hurry," he said easily. "Or we'll all have hell to pay."

Ruth took Talley by the hand and pulled her from the kitchen. "The shed is behind our house," she said.

The two dashed across the sand toward her parents' house, cooling in the softening light. Behind the house was a ten-by-ten storage shed, the front door fastened with a padlock. Ruth found the key under the rock and undid the lock. Hinges squeaked as she opened the door and pulled a single string dangling next to it, and a light bulb clicked on.

The room's wooden walls trapped the heat and humidity, creating a stale, musty smell. A dim light splashed over brown boxes stacked one on top of another and caught dust particles dancing in the air. Each brown box was dated with a year. "Mama lets me go through what's left behind at the end of each summer. She used to take the extras to the Methodist church, but she's not been to church since the war, so the boxes are still here."

"Why'd Aunt Edna stop going to church?" Talley asked.

"Mad at the preacher. But she never would say why. Daddy says when Mama gets an idea in her head, she never lets it go."

"Does Uncle Jake go to church?"

"No. He never was one for the Sunday service, so when Mama quit, he didn't press."

Talley walked into the room and skimmed her fingers over the boxes. "And this is full of things people just forgot?"

Ruth reached for the box labeled *1946*. Four years seemed enough time for someone to completely forget what had been lost. She set the box under the light bulb and removed the top. She pulled out a few blouses, hats, a pair of sunglasses, and a toy soldier.

Talley held up a pink-and-white checkered top. "Someone forgot this? It's so nice."

"Yeah. If you see anything you want, take it. Mama won't mind."

"You sure? Someone might see me wearing it and claim I'm stealing."

"How can you steal what was left behind? If they cared, they'd have come for it by now, the way I see it."

The box didn't have any books, so she reached for the next container. There was a straw hat with a slightly frayed edge that Ruth insisted Talley would need for walks on the beach. As Talley settled the hat on her head, she spotted Georgette Heyer's *Penhallow*.

Talley's eyes lit up. "It's nearly perfect, barely a page bent. I've read my books so many times I need a rubber band to keep the pages from falling out."

Finding no more books, Ruth closed up the box and reached for another. "What's that book about?"

"It's a mystery."

"Like your pal Nancy?"

Talley carefully thumbed through the yellowed pages. "I don't know."

Ruth opened another box from 1949 and dug her hands into a sea of fabric, hats, and scarves, until her fingers skimmed the binding of another book. She handed the well-used paperback to Talley.

"*Forever Amber*," she said as she marveled at the gowned woman on the cover. Several corners were dog-eared, and the pages in the bottom-right corner rippled as if they had gotten splashed by the pool.

Ruth closed up the box and in another found a detective story with a scowling man holding a gun on the cover. "Maybe you shouldn't show Mama this book until after you've read it. She might take exception to the gun."

Talley held the three books close. "I'll give them back as soon as they're read."

"Read them as much as you want. Just don't tell Mama about the one with the gun."

"Is not telling lying, or is it just not telling?"

"You can tell Mama anything you want, but if I was you, I'd wait until I read those books."

Talley looked thoughtful. "Better late than never." She held up the blouse. "Should I put this back? Your mama might not like seeing me wear it."

"No, she won't worry about that. But she might worry about a book putting an idea in your head."

"What kind of an idea?" Talley asked.

The two stepped out of the shed. Ruth shut off the light, closed the door, and replaced the padlock and key. "I don't know. She says that to me when I draw. She says it might put ideas in my head. Makes me dream for what I can't have. Which it does. It stuffs my head so full of ideas and dreams they barely have elbow room."

"What kind of ideas?"

"Like going to school to study art. Like one day getting paid to just draw pictures. Can you imagine? It would be like you getting paid to read."

Talley giggled. "Those aren't bad ideas."

"Mama just doesn't want me to forget that the Seaside Resort puts food on the table and keeps a roof over our head. Not everyone has that, she says."

"She's right. There's plenty of people going hungry back home."

"That's why you came here?"

"That, and my mama wanted me to see the world."

"Don't know how big our world is here, but there's plenty of work."

"Better than working in the fields like your mama and mine did."

"Mama worked in the fields?"

"Our grandfather owns a farm. Now our uncle Rich, the oldest boy, runs it. He grows melons, sweet potatoes, corn, and wheat. After the harvest last year, my back hurt and my arms felt like they'd been lined with lead."

"When'd you start picking crops?"

"I was about ten."

When it came to her life before here, Ruth's mother had always skirted the questions or distracted her with a question about her drawings. "Mama works harder than anyone I know."

"Your mama must be doing something right. This place is so pretty, and the guests look happy to me."

"She keeps the hotel very clean. And as far as the guests, it's the first night," Ruth said. "As the week goes on, they find things they don't like. Just wait; you'll see."

The girls rushed back to the room they now shared. It was strange having someone else in her room. Talley had tossed and turned during the night, but it was oddly comforting to have another body nearby.

Talley tucked her books under her mattress, hung her blouse carefully in the small closet, and hooked her hat on the headpost. The two girls hurried back toward the pool, now surrounded by laughter, the clink of glasses, and soft music from the phonograph playing Frank Sinatra's "Fools Rush In." Mama had heard it on the radio a few years ago and liked it so much she'd made a point to search it out in a Norfolk record store.

The guests, mostly women, all had drinks in their hands. The younger children were swimming in the shallow end, and Dora, Jessie, and Bonnie, all sporting beet-red shoulders and noses, had changed into cotton sundresses. They leaned close, talking, their giggles drifting above the adult voices.

"They're as thick as thieves," Talley said.

"Yeah."

"You know them, right?"

"They been coming since the war."

"And you aren't friends?"

Ruth rubbed her belly, unconsciously uncoiling an unnamed tightness. "No mixing with the guests."

"They look a little stuck up to me," Talley whispered.

"I think it's because they have breasts now," Ruth said.

Laughter tumbled over Talley's lips. "I have breasts, and I'm not stuck up."

Ruth jutted out her chin. "And when I get mine, I won't be either."

"This winter if you write to me, I'll write back. There's nothing I like better than a letter."

Mention of the winter reminded Ruth that summer was fleeting and soon Talley would leave, and she'd be alone again. "I do write a good letter."

"Make sure you include sketches."

Her mood lifted. "Okay."

They moved to the refreshment tent, where Mama was setting iced glasses with a green slushy drink topped with a red cherry. "Girls, where have you been?"

"We went to the shed," Ruth said. "We went looking for a beach hat for Talley. Her skin's going to get pretty pink if she doesn't wear a hat."

"That's a good idea, Ruth," Mama said. "Each of you girls take a tray and ask the guests if they'd like a drink. Just one per customer."

"It's the welcome drink," Ruth said. "After this one they're going to have to pay."

"Make sure you girls don't have any of it. This batch is stronger than the last."

Ruth and Talley carried trays toward the women, who happily collected their complimentary drinks. As Ruth passed the pool, Bonnie said as she glanced at Dora and Jessie, "Ruth, don't forget our drinks."

The girls giggled.

"They're only for the grown-ups," Ruth said.

"Then bring us each a cold soda," Bonnie said. "With straws. You can charge it to our rooms."

If Bonnie weren't a guest, Ruth would have told her to go pound sand. But the bottled drinks, according to her daddy, were moneymakers. "Sure. Be right up."

She handed out the last of her drinks and returned to her mother. "Three colas for the girls. They said to charge it to their rooms."

Mama raised a brow as she fished three bottled colas from the ice bin. "Aren't they all grown up?"

"I guess so. I mean, look at them."

"Don't worry. Your time will come." Mama dropped her voice a fraction. "Before it's all said and done, you'll have bigger breasts than they do."

Ruth's eyes widened. "How do you know?"

"Daddy told me," Mama said.

"But how can you be sure? No one knows what *she* looks like."

"I suspect you'll have all the curves you want one day."

Ruth wished her chest could sprout this summer before those girls left. Still, just the idea that her body would change buoyed her spirits. She carried the bottles over to the girls and handed each a cold cola.

Bonnie sipped from the straw. "Mmmm. So good. Aren't you going to have one, Ruth?"

"Not right now. I'm working."

"I noticed the little uniform you were wearing when we arrived. Very cute."

"It's just a new dress. Not a uniform."

"Oh, my mistake."

Ruth shook her head and turned.

"Don't go far," Bonnie said. "We might want another drink."

"Sure."

The phonograph stopped, and Mama walked up to the small stage that Daddy had built just last week. Mama's smile was always bright and friendly during the season, and even if it wasn't exactly real, it had an infectious quality that made it hard not to feel good when she was like this.

"Ladies and gentlemen." The microphone squealed, forcing Mama to tap it a few times. "I have a rare treat for you this week." The guests' chatter continued a beat before thinning to silence. "Any minute now, the very talented Miss Carlotta DiSalvo is going to sing for you. She's the headliner on the *Maisy Adams*, currently dry-docked in Coinjock. If any of you have had the chance to see a show on the *Maisy Adams*, then you know the treat that's in store for you tonight."

The side door leading to the lobby opened, and out stepped Carlotta as if she had just arrived on a grand stage in front of thousands of people. Didn't seem to matter that the stage was made of reclaimed wood and there were only about twenty people gathered around the pool.

Her dress was emerald green, and when she moved, her flared skirt sparkled slightly as the fabric floated around her swaying hips. The dress nipped a narrow waist and molded her full breasts displayed by a low neckline. The few men there stood taller, and the women shifted a little uncomfortably. Even Bonnie, Dora, and Jessie seemed to notice they'd been outbreasted by Miss Carlotta DiSalvo.

Carlotta had teased her blonde hair and twisted the ends into a chignon, displaying diamonds dangling from her ears. High-heeled shoes glinted. Cherry-red lips widened into a grin, flashing white teeth that were slightly crooked. The imperfection didn't detract from her glamour but only added to it. She wasn't shy about her flaws.

Ruth ran her tongue over her teeth, noting the slight twist of her front tooth.

"Good evening, ladies and gentlemen," Carlotta said. Her voice was clear and bright and silenced the remaining chatter. She wasn't the kind of woman anyone ignored. Men liked the look of her, and a part of all the women wondered how different their lives would be if only they were her.

A smile tugged at the edges of Carlotta's lips, as if she knew a naughty secret no one else did. She lowered her hand to her side, and she began to snap her fingers as her hips gently rocked to an orchestra only she could hear.

Billie Holiday's "It Had to Be You" glided easily over her lips.

Many in the crowd clapped, each recognizing the song.

She looked left, then right, her grin widening before she began to sing.

Her voice was as smooth as the ocean on a windless day and effortlessly slid over the notes. She began to clap, encouraging the audience to follow along. The men remained entranced, and the women who'd initially looked a bit green eyed started smiling.

Ruth glanced over at a grinning Talley. "She's amazing."

"She's right out of a storybook," Talley said.

Mama had been so certain that Ruth's figure would bloom and blossom, suggesting that one day she would be more exciting than the mainland girls. As she watched Carlotta sing, a kernel of knowing sprouted in her belly. Was her mama trying to tell her something?

Ruth often searched for pieces of herself in other women. A crooked smile, a mannerism, even a talent for drawing. But now as she ran her tongue again over her crooked tooth, her heart scurried into her throat. It sure made sense that a woman working and traveling on a showboat wouldn't have time for a little bitty baby.

This wasn't the first time she'd ever wondered if a guest could be *the* woman who'd arrived in a storm, given birth to her alone in Bungalow 28, wrapped her in pink flannel, and then vanished.

But this was the first time that little voice inside her said Miss Carlotta DiSalvo had to be her real mama.

CHAPTER TEN
IVY

Thursday, January 20, 2022, 3:45 p.m.

By the early afternoon, Ivy had cabin fever. She had tended to Libby and the pups, cleaned out the closet in her old bedroom, and carried a dozen stackable end tables, four PLEASE WAIT TO BE SEATED signs, and six beach landscapes bordered in tarnished gold frames to the curb. She taped a new FREE sign on them and hoped it would bring magic her way.

With the Leica camera tucked in her purse, she slid behind the wheel of her van, now fully packed with items for the thrift store. Ten minutes later, she pulled into the parking lot of the one-story cinder block building and opened the back of her van. The first garbage bag she hefted from the back was overstuffed with hotel sheets and towels. She waddled to the front door, balanced the bag on her knee, and opened the door. Bells jingled above her head. A gray-haired woman behind the long front counter came around. "Honey, you can put that right over here."

"Thanks." She let the weight drop. "I've got a few more."

"Getting ready for a renovation?" the woman asked.

"Selling the house," she said.

"Well, this is the time to do it. It's a buyer's market. Where's your property?"

"Remember the Seaside Resort?"

Her eyes grew wistful. "Sure. Ruth's place."

"I'm her granddaughter. I'm selling her cottage."

"Ivy Neale?"

"Yes."

"The last time I saw you, you were in high school."

Ivy searched her memory and conjured vague recollections of working a charity fundraiser at the Seaside Resort. "We were raising money for this store."

"That's right. Ruth didn't charge us a dime for the rental and refreshments."

"Wow. That was kind of her."

"She did that a lot. Hated it when people made a fuss."

Ivy remembered now. Ruth had paid Ivy for working the event. "I didn't realize."

"My husband and I loved the Seaside Resort. We celebrated our anniversary there right up until last year. He loved the fried chicken."

"Mrs. Cooper, right?"

The woman smiled. "Good memory."

"You always asked for a table by the window."

"We loved the view. Best in the area." She leaned forward a fraction. "I thought the food was never the same after you left. Ruth was always bragging on your cooking. In New York City, right?"

She had assumed no one had noticed when she left the hotel kitchen. "That's right."

"Well, from what I remember of your cooking, you won't have any trouble getting work. Maybe you should open a place here."

"That's an idea," she said out of politeness.

When Mrs. Cooper began to speak, Ivy held up a hand. "Hold that thought. Be right back with more stuff." She was out the door and soon back with two more bags. By the time she was finished, ten bags clustered around the desk.

The woman came around the corner. "What do you have here?"

"Lots of towels, table linens, and sheets from the Seaside Resort. They're all in great shape. Some clothes. My grandmother saved everything."

"Do you want a receipt?" Mrs. Cooper asked.

"No, thanks. Just hope they're of some use. Ruth would have been glad to know they helped someone."

"I'm not surprised she held on to all this. The Seaside Resort was her home. All this was her last connection to it. They'll get good use at several of the shelters."

Many of the items conjured up memories for Ivy. The napkins she'd folded each day before and after school, the bedspreads she'd smoothed with her hands when there was no one else to clean a bungalow room, and the banquet tablecloths she'd fluffed over round tables before a wedding or family reunion. All the stuffing, dragging, and hefting had been a walk down memory lane. "Is there a camera shop in the area?"

"Sure. It's Bob's Small Appliance Repair. No one really wants cameras anymore, but a few still get appliances repaired. He considers cameras small appliances. He's at Milepost 10."

"Just a few miles from here. Perfect."

"You need a camera? I've plenty of used ones here."

"Thanks, but no. I have one that belonged to Ruth. I think there's film inside."

Mrs. Cooper nodded. "A mystery. Keep me posted."

"I'm sure I'll be back. This only represents my old bedroom and part of Ruth's room."

"Ruth never did like anything to go to waste."

Ivy thanked the woman and drove south the five miles until she spotted the small store in the strip mall. A red neon **OPEN** sign blinked in the window.

Out of the car, she stepped into the small shop filled with toasters, fans, microwaves, and leaf blowers all crammed together on the floor and shelves that lined the walls. She moved to a glass display case filled with cameras, watches, and decorative clocks. Behind it was a register and a curtained-off room.

She rang the small bell on the counter, and a stocky man with thinning black hair appeared from behind the curtain.

"What can I do for you?" he asked.

"Hey, hoping you can help me. I'm Ivy Neale. Ruth Wheeler's granddaughter." She set the camera on the display case.

"Ruth. Sorry for your loss."

"Thanks."

"I'm Bob. Need the camera fixed?"

"I don't know. I found this camera in her house."

His gaze dropped to the camera. "A Leica? Looks old school."

"I think so. I'm not sure if it's broken, but I think there's film inside."

Accepting the camera, he inspected the photo counter on the top. "Ten pictures taken by the looks."

"It was stashed under a bed. Not sure if the film inside is any good, but it's gone this long without being developed; it's worth a try."

"I can do it. I have a makeshift darkroom. Still get the rare request to develop film."

"That would be terrific."

He turned the camera over and traced a calloused finger over the CD scratched in the metal. "Think maybe a guest left it behind?"

"No idea who CD is. But maybe if the pictures are salvageable, then I can figure it out."

"We shall see," he said with a grin. "You know if this camera was opened at any time, the film is ruined."

"I know, but still worth a try. Do you need a deposit or a credit card?"

He removed scratch paper and a pen from a drawer. "Just write down your contact information, and I'll call you when I have something."

She wrote her name and number on the slip. "I appreciate it."

"Anything for Ruth. Hell of a lady. When my house flooded in the winter of 2005, she let me stay in a bungalow for three weeks. Never charged me a dime."

Ivy remembered the winter. Half their bungalows were full of local residents who'd also been flooded out. "Yes, she was."

When she left the shop, it was four. She'd been gone less than an hour, so she had enough time to stop by the grocery store and get a few more provisions to replace the chucked cinnamon, oregano, and basil and also buy new paprika and red pepper flakes. If she was going to fry chicken, it needed a twist.

When she arrived at the market, she gathered the spices, two more bags of coffee, chew sticks for Libby, and two pounds of butter.

Once she reached the checkout, she got in line behind a tall, broad-shouldered man with dark-brown hair that curled over his shirt collar. He was buying a steak, potatoes, handfuls of fresh parsley and rosemary, and fixings for a salad. From her experience, men generally reached for the prepackaged goods, so she had to give him props.

She placed her groceries on the belt as the man stepped up to the register. When he turned, his profile shifted into full view. Her stomach knotted. It was Matthew Peterson, the high school boyfriend. Dani's ex-husband. Shit. What were the chances?

She ran fingers through her hair, wishing she'd washed it, and considered backing up slowly and returning to the aisles as if she had forgotten something. Instead, she said, "Matthew?"

The man turned. At first, his eyes didn't register any recognition, and then he grinned, shaking his head. There was no sign of bitterness or anger, but Matthew always found a smile when he wanted something. He'd have hugged her if her cart weren't separating them. And considering she hadn't showered today, no contact was a good thing.

Matthew had stayed in shape, not even a dad-bod paunch, and he was dressed in neat jeans, a gray sweater, and a leather jacket with the collar turned up. He had always rocked the bad-boy image.

"Ivy, I heard you were back. How the hell are you doing?"

"Doing great."

"I almost didn't recognize you. You have a very New York vibe. Edgy."

"Or maybe grungy?"

"No. Not at all. You're wearing the years well." The checker tallied up his order, and he shoved his credit card into the machine. "I hear you're selling Ruth's place."

"It has to be done."

"The end of an era."

"Life moves on." She could not have dreamed up a better understatement if she'd practiced.

As the cashier bagged the items, Matthew's full attention settled on her. "You look great."

"Nice of you to say." The years fell away, and she was right back in 2010. Crop tops, elastic bands to hold up her curly hair, and purple flip-flops summed up that decade, also known as the awkward years.

But in those days Matthew had had a way of making her feel good about herself. Ironically, his positive outlook had given her the courage to leave not only OBX but him as well. This return home was starting to feel like a study in past mistakes.

"I bet you have your hands full cleaning out the cottage," he said. "Ruth squirreled away everything she could from the hotel."

His description hinted that Ruth had somehow lost some of her faculties toward the end. "She was a Depression-era kid. She always hated throwing anything away."

"I'm placing no blame. It's hard losing what you love."

The words carried unspoken pain Ivy didn't like acknowledging. "Right."

He loaded his bags into his cart as she stepped up to the cashier. As the items zinged past the scanner, she swiped her credit card. "What are you making?"

"Would you believe Ruth's fried chicken?" she asked.

"Right before graduation, you swore you'd never fry up another piece of chicken again." Matthew had endured her complaints of grease-spatter burns on her arms.

"At least I'm making the Sunday-night fried chicken on Thursday. A small but meaningful departure."

He chuckled. "The spirit of the girl who packed up her car and drove to New York without a plan lives."

That eighteen-year-old had been part pioneer, part fool, and mostly selfish. She would need that girl to resist setting down roots here and make the leap into the future. "I live dangerously. What can I say?"

"Think you remember how to make the chicken?"

"The recipe is burned in my brain."

"You ever going to share it with me?"

She grabbed the grocery bag. "Ruth swore me to secrecy."

"She never would tell me, no matter how much I asked. And I can be quite charming."

Matthew's smoothness had never sat well with Ruth. She'd never voiced her disapproval to Ivy, but the occasional side-eye had said more than any words. "And I'll not be sharing the recipe either." In less than a minute, they'd tripped easily into the comradery they'd enjoyed in high school. "I saw Dani. She came by the house. She looks great as always."

117

A subtle tension tightened his jaw before it vanished. "She's always pulled together. Always perfect."

Was there some recrimination wrapped around the compliment? Matthew came from a family that had made lots of money in furniture sales. Ivy had been aware of their different backgrounds but had convinced herself it didn't matter. She shouldn't have been surprised he'd ended up with, at least for a while, the very polished Dani.

"We can all aspire," Ivy said.

"How would you like to get together for dinner? I'd love to catch up."

"I'm pretty slammed right now." The idea of getting cleaned up, even for herself, was too much. And slipping on heels for Matthew was a bridge too far.

A smile tugged the edges of his lips. "It'll be strictly casual."

"Nice of you to ask, Matthew. Really." He followed her out to the sidewalk. "But with the house and the dogs . . ."

"Dogs?"

"Long story. I have a mother dog and three puppies."

"Don't let Bella see them." Warm laughter drifted up. "She's been after Dani and me to get a dog for months." His tenderness for Bella stripped away his bad-boy veneer, making him more attractive.

"So I hear."

"We really do need to have dinner, Ivy. It's crazy not to catch up." His grin was too charming.

"Sure, why not. How about tomorrow night?"

"I'm looking at new retail space tomorrow, but I'll be finished in time. Let's plan on it."

Her empty dance card made it hard to say no. And if she was honest, she was a little flattered when he looked at her with that raw delight in his eyes. "Sure."

"I'll pick you up at six."

"Sounds like a plan."

"It's good to have you back." His hand rose as if he'd touch her, but instead, he curled his fingers into a loose fist. "OBX was never the same after you left."

"Thanks."

She loaded her groceries and drove back to the cottage. When she arrived, the pups mewed as they greedily nursed. Libby lay on her side, allowing her brood to feast.

In the kitchen Ivy rummaged through the cabinets, looking for a large skillet. Instead of one, she found dozens that were rescues from the Seaside Resort. She chose a cast-iron skillet, blackened and seasoned by the years, that she'd used more times than she could count. She hefted the pan, gripping the handle as she would the hand of an old friend. She set it on the front burner and turned it on to high, remembering an old conversation with Ruth.

"Why do we use the same pan all the time?" Ivy had asked Ruth as she wrapped an apron around her narrow waist. She was in fifth grade and working her first shift in the kitchen as an assistant.

"It's never failed me or my mama or daddy," Ruth said. "It won't fail you, if you take care of it."

"Do you do everything they did?" Ivy asked.

A smile tugged at Ruth's lips. "My mother would have a good laugh at that one. She often said I was hardheaded."

"You've said that about me."

"Apple doesn't fall far from the tree." She poured a liberal amount of oil in the skillet, turned on the burner, and then reached for a bag of flour, which she shook into a bowl. "We'll salt and pepper it. No one likes a bland piece of chicken."

Normally Ruth brought fried chicken home after she closed the hotel kitchens on Sunday nights, but this was the first time they had made it together.

Next she poured buttermilk into a bowl, and then she washed and patted dry several room-temp chicken legs. The crackle and pop of the oil sounded extra loud without her mother's background chatter. Her mother had been gone five years now, and the house was still too quiet.

Ruth carefully dredged the chicken in the buttermilk and then the flour. She coated all the pieces, and as they rested, she plunged the handle of a wooden spoon into the oil and watched as the liquid bubbled around it. "When you see that, you know the oil is just right." Carefully she lowered a piece into the oil. It hissed and snapped. "Now you do a piece."

Ivy picked up a leg and hovered over the pan, and then, like her grandmother, she dipped it slowly into the spitting-hot bath. Oil popped up and bit her skin.

"Ouch," Ivy complained.

Ruth handed her a damp towel. "That's a part of cooking."

Ivy studied the red welt. "Maybe I'm not any good at this."

"Don't worry about it," Ruth said. "You're a natural."

"Can I work in the Seaside Resort kitchen as a cook?"

"I don't see why not."

Ivy started work in the kitchens after school the next day. At first, she was strictly an assistant, and mostly in the early days she sat at a table, did homework, ate a snack, and then folded napkins. She fetched items for Ruth and Mr. Anderson, who, at ninety-two, still cooked beside her grandmother from time to time. By age eleven, she was chopping cabbage for the coleslaw, dicing onions for the Wednesday-night seafood stew, and by the end of middle school she was at the ovens, standing on a step stool, cooking.

The pay wasn't much. The way Ruth saw it, running the Seaside Resort was a family business, and family was paid the least, including Ruth, who sometimes didn't draw a paycheck.

As Ivy's skills grew in the kitchen, so did her confidence, and when many of her friends were floundering in high school, she found her purpose. No matter what, she knew she would be a chef.

Ivy set the ingredients up just as Ruth had taught her nearly twenty years ago. She no longer tested the oil with a spoon because thousands of hours in kitchens had honed her senses, so she knew when the oil was just right or when the chicken needed to be turned or removed.

Forty-five minutes later, the aroma of frying chicken filled the old cottage, stuffing the air with as many memories as scents. Libby rose from her bed and came into the kitchen, her ears perked.

"It has that effect on people," Ivy said. She made a bowl of dog food and sprinkled a few bits of crispy chicken skin on top. "I'm creating a very bad habit, but a new mother deserves to treat herself."

Ivy set the bowl down, and the dog gobbled it up. There was something satisfying about watching someone enjoy the food she'd created.

She picked up a leg, blew on it, and held it up to her nose. For her, smell was the strongest conductor of memories. And smelling Ruth's fried chicken again reminded her of the life she could have had.

CHAPTER ELEVEN
IVY

Ivy woke up to the sounds of bulldozers grating against sand and soil. "Good morning, Dalton."

She sat up in her old twin bed and looked out her window toward the ginger sun peeking over the horizon and glittering fresh light on the Atlantic's waters. She swung her legs around and stretched the lingering tightness from her back. As the machines ground over the lot next door, she rubbed her eyes and padded down the stairs into the kitchen. She turned on her coffeepot, then glanced around the boxes at Libby and the sleeping puppies. Libby looked ready for a break.

She took the dog out the back door and toward the dune. As the dog sniffed and considered her options, Ivy was glad to see the wreck was still visible. If the veil between the living and dead truly had thinned, Ruth had to be close. And that gave her comfort.

She took Libby back in the house, fed her, and refreshed her water bowl as her coffeepot gurgled. She filled a large earthenware mug, walked back, descended the stairs, scaled the dune, and crossed the sand to the old vessel. She skimmed fingertips over the damp, darkened petrified wood, now harder than steel.

Dani had texted last night and asked if her father could stop by midday and see the wreck from the sleeping porch, which had the best view. Ivy had quickly agreed, and they'd settled on 11:00 a.m. Enough time to drink coffee and shower.

She glanced around for signs of the wolfhound, but there'd been no sighting since the day after the storm. And thankfully no evidence of wandering spirits waiting anxiously for the vessel to return below the ocean waters.

Ivy sipped her coffee, now already too cold for her taste. "For the record with all the spirits. I never plundered your ship, so don't take your frustration out on me."

Wind whistled over the tops of the beach grass and skimmed over the beach, carrying sand with it. "And Ruth, if you're lurking about, any guidance regarding the cottage would be greatly appreciated. I miss you."

Another half hour passed as she stood inhaling the salt air and listening to the sounds of the ocean. This place did have a wild lure, and today's gentle breezes were trying to seduce her into staying.

The grind of machines scraping earth drew her attention back to what had once been the Seaside Resort. "I won't be fooled. I know how this can all turn on a dime."

She poured the dregs of her coffee out into the sand and returned to the house. Dani and her father would be here in a few hours, and she wanted to get a little more cleaning done. She shouldn't care that Dani had seen the house at its worst, but it would have bothered Ruth if Pete saw it in disarray.

She climbed to the second floor and started clearing out the second upstairs bedroom. She carted off old banquet chairs, obsolete printers, a cash register, and what had been a modern computer fifteen years ago.

It was after 10:00 a.m. when Ivy's phone rang, pulling her out of a closet crammed full of more Bibles. She reached in her back pocket for her phone. "Ivy Neale."

"Ms. Neale, this is Bob from the photography shop."

She brushed back her bangs. "Yes, sir. Any luck with that film?"

"Film was in excellent shape. I was able to develop all ten of the exposed negatives. I've just finished the prints."

She sat back on her heels and swiped a strand of hair from her face. "And what did you find?"

"Looks like vintage Seaside Resort from the early 1950s. The photographer took an image of a showboat, the Seaside Resort, a little white dog, a very lovely woman who reminds me of Lana Turner, a group of young girls, several women in their thirties, and I think there's a picture of Ruth."

"Really?" She stretched the tension from her back. "Are they ready to be picked up?"

"They are. I'm here all morning. I'm closing at noon and taking the afternoon off to go fishing."

"I'll be right over."

"See you soon."

Ivy ended the call, excited. She checked on Libby, ran her outside for a quick pee break, and inspected the pups. They all looked like sightless little creatures, but already their personalities were developing. The biggest pup wiggled away as soon as he'd eaten because he seemed to get hot. The light-brown female was the most laid back, and the little black-and-white female was the most vocal. They all were gaining weight and growing. Once the kids really got mobile, it was going to be bedlam.

She grabbed her purse, and as she locked the front door, she noted surveyors had arrived on the neighboring property and were staking out what must have been the new homes. Judging by the number of stakes, this cottage would have plenty of new neighbors next year.

Dalton stood in the center of the activity, wearing a heavy jacket, a skullcap, jeans, and work boots. He moved among the workers, walking with long, decisive strides. He was a man comfortable in his universe, and if Ivy was honest, she was jealous. For a time in New York, sandwiched between adolescence and adulthood, she'd thought she had found her sweet spot.

When she'd packed up her apartment, she'd assumed an older, wiser Ivy would know instinctively what would come next. But so far, she had no clue.

In her car, she backed out of the driveway, noticing the items she'd left with the FREE sign were again gone. "Bless you."

Out on the beach road, she drove north and, five minutes later, pulled into the repair shop's parking lot and made her way inside.

Bob stood behind the counter and was wearing large magnifying eyeglasses and examining the interior of a clock.

"Hello." He put down the small screwdriver and removed his glasses. "I have your order."

"I can't wait to see them. There aren't many pictures remaining of the Seaside Resort. Most were lost in the last storm."

"Salt water ruins just about everything."

Ruth had been heartsick after the December storm. Ivy had begged Ruth to come back to New York with her. She'd promised trips to the Met, great restaurants, and walks in Central Park. But Ruth had refused. Ivy had promised to return in a few weeks, but it had been too late.

Bob opened a manila folder that contained a strip of ten negatives in a clear plastic sleeve. "Like I said, the film was in surprisingly good shape. Developed it without issue."

Ivy held up the negatives, trying to reverse engineer them into positives. She set the sheet aside and reached for the stack of prints, which were cool to the touch and smelled of developing chemicals. "It's a miracle I found you, given all the digital photography these days."

"Everybody uses their phones. No one asks for a camera when they take a picture. They ask for their phone."

Ivy dropped her gaze to the first image of a large boat moored on a dock. The ship, named the *Maisy Adams*, had a flat bottom and three levels outfitted with white railings and ornamental trim. On the top tier was an awning that stretched over the back half of the vessel, and under the cover were a dozen people at the railing, all waving to the photographer. Twin black smokestacks stood silent, with no trace of smoke rising.

"A showboat?" Ivy asked.

"They were popular on the intracoastal waterways from about 1900 to the late 1960s. I called a friend and asked about the *Maisy Adams*, and she told me the showboat did a good book of business until the mid-1960s." The inland waterways stretched from the southern tip of Florida up into Boston. The route, a collection of canals, rivers, inlets, bays, and sounds, had been used to move goods and services for over a century.

"Basically, a traveling show or circus," Ivy said.

"That's about right. They'd have had singers, actors, magicians, jugglers. Anything that they thought would sell tickets found its way into an act."

"So why does Ruth have a camera with a picture of the *Maisy Adams*? Did her parents take her to a show?"

"Maybe, but this camera was not cheap back in the day. The Wheelers were known to squeeze every penny they could out of a buck. This doesn't seem their style."

Ivy flipped to the next picture, which captured a light-colored Buick with a white convertible top. It was the blue car in one of Ruth's paintings. "They weren't the kind to drive a car like this."

"That Buick dates back to the late 1940s. The kind of car driven for fun, not function."

The next picture featured a woman with bottle-blonde hair twisted into a chignon. Pencil-dark eyebrows accentuated light eyes and grinning painted lips. Her smile was wide and infectious. Her light-colored top rested on the edges of her shoulders and dipped just below the crest of full breasts. "That certainly was not Ruth's mother." From what Ruth had said about Edna Wheeler, she'd been loving, dedicated to the hotel, and a bit dour. "She has to belong with the car and the showboat."

The next image was of the Seaside Resort. In those days the bungalows had been painted limestone white and flanked the main building, which had housed the dining hall. On the other side of the central building would have been the pool. It all looked so new, nothing like the tired, careworn place she remembered. The SEASIDE RESORT sign appeared newly installed, and NO VACANCY was lit up. Again, like the painting. "The place stayed booked solid for a couple of decades' worth of summers."

"It was the place in its day," Bob said.

The next image was of a young girl grinning with the sun shining on her face. Immediately, she recognized the dark eyes and the wide smile. "That's Ruth."

In Ivy's mind, Ruth had always been old. She'd rarely done anything beyond caring for her hotel and then Ivy's mother and later Ivy.

Other than the physical features, there were no hints of the woman Ruth would become. This girl looked as if everything was exciting and work was the last thing on her mind. Ivy guessed Ruth was about twelve in the picture, which would put this circa 1950.

The next picture captured the ocean, and judging by the vantage point, it had been taken from the cottage she now owned. The centerpiece of the picture was the very shipwreck that had rematerialized yesterday.

"That ship's resurfaced again, hasn't it?" Bob said.

"It has. And it's still there as of this morning. Pete Manchester is coming by soon to see it. I hear he's a bit of an expert."

"He is. Hopefully, he'll bring some of his photos of the wreck. One dates back to 1870, the year the vessel came ashore."

"I'm looking forward to it."

"Watch out for the ghosts and goblins," Bob said with a grin. "They'll be stirring up trouble."

"Let's hope they give me a pass," she said as she thumbed through more pictures of the Seaside Resort and the people vacationing there. "How much do I owe you?"

"Not a thing," he said.

"You sure?"

"Ruth's granddaughter will never owe me a dime." He slid her pictures into a white plastic bag that read BOB'S SMALL APPLIANCE REPAIR.

"Thanks again."

"You bet."

In her car she was no closer to identifying the owner of the camera, but maybe Mr. Manchester would know. He could have been on scene the summer the pictures were taken.

When she arrived at the cottage, Dani's car was in the driveway, and she and her father were staring up at the cottage. Mr. Manchester was tall with a thick shock of gray hair and shoulders that remained broad and straight.

"Ivy," Dani said, grinning. She wore designer boots, boot-cut jeans, and a thick fur-lined leather jacket that hit her midwaist.

Again, Ivy's tried-and-true gray sweats left her feeling lacking. "Dani."

"You remember my dad, right?" Dani asked.

Ivy extended her hand. "Good to see you again, Mr. Manchester." When she was leaving Ruth's funeral, he'd shaken her hand, said something kind about Ruth. But all the people and their words had melted into an unrecognizable collage.

"Glad you're back," he said. "We've all missed you."

"Nice to see Dani, you, the old place again."

"The cottage hasn't changed," he said. "A rarity these days."

But everything else had. "Here to see the wreck?"

"Can't wait." He rubbed his long, calloused hands together. "Dani tell you I'm a bit of a history buff?"

Ivy climbed the cottage stairs. "She did. And lucky for me you are. The wreck is remarkable."

Ivy opened the front door, and Libby, who'd been rather quiet up until now, barked as she peeked around her box wall. "Just me. You and the kids are safe."

"Bella would be here now, if not for school," Dani said. "She's dying to see the puppies."

"She's welcome to visit anytime."

She set her folder of pictures on the table by the hotel-registration book and led Dani and Pete to the back door and over the dunes. The minute Pete saw the shipwreck, he pulled out his phone and began snapping pictures.

"You've become quite the talk of our family," Dani said. "Bella and puppies, Dad and the wreck and Dalton and . . ."

Her cheeks warmed. "Dalton and what?"

"Let's just say you're a welcome addition to the Outer Banks as far as he's concerned. Has he been by much?"

"Not really. Looks like he has his hands full with the jobsite."

"It's a big project for the company. Ten houses," Pete said. "He's under pressure to get them sold and built."

"Business must be booming," Ivy said.

"Beachfront land like this is a rare thing. Dalton's already sold half the lots." No missing the pride in Pete's voice.

Pete walked up to the wreck and traced his hand along the beams. "She was transporting goods from South Carolina to New York," he said. "Along with the crewmen, there was a woman and her two-month-old baby aboard. The woman was Francesca Wentworth, and the baby's name was Sarah. Francesca was a young socialite who was traveling to join her husband. I found several articles in the New York papers with her picture. Her death was big news for a couple of days. She was only twenty-one. Of the twelve souls on the ship, all the bodies were recovered but the baby's and hers."

"What happened to their bodies?" Ivy asked.

"Best guess is Francesca's heavy skirts pulled her under and kept her weighted on the ocean floor. Many theorized she was holding Sarah to the end."

A cold breeze blew from the ocean, chilling Ivy's skin. "That's terrible."

"I can't imagine," Dani said softly.

"Some say they've seen her ghost," Pete said. "She's wearing a black dress, and her curly blonde hair frames her pale face like a halo."

"Wow, you have done your research." Ivy ran her hands together, trying to generate warmth.

"I can tell you something about all the sailors who were on the manifest as well as the cargo. The ship was a bit of an obsession." He pulled his phone from his pocket and brought up a black-and-white image of the ship, its sails furled and its lines clean as it docked in the port of Charleston.

The chilled air settled in Ivy's bones. "I also have found something that might be of interest."

Inside and out of the wind, warmth wrapped around the trio. Ivy went to the dining table and removed color photographs from the folder. "Have a look at these. I recognized pictures of Ruth, the hotel, and the wreck, but there are several people I don't know."

She laid out the ten pictures side by side along the length of the table. Pete came behind her, his eyes sparking with recognition. "That sure is Ruth," he said, pointing to the young girl. "And these five girls, one is Ruth, the other is Talley, and that's my sister, Bonnie, and her two friends Jessie and Dora."

Ruth's smile appeared brittle, forced even. Ivy shifted to the collection of women dressed in bathing suits, straw hats, and cat-eye sunglasses. All were holding cigarettes, and their table was filled with empty cocktail glasses. "And those three women sitting by the pool . . ."

"The woman on the far right is my mother, Ann Manchester," Pete said.

Dani leaned forward, studying the lean blonde. "That's Grandma? She looks like Grace Kelly."

"She was quite striking in her younger years," he said. "She used to say my father fell head over heels in love with her the minute he saw her. He shipped off to boot camp, and when he returned in the spring, they married. My father's family wasn't happy, but what was done was done." Pete drew in a slow breath.

Dani rubbed him between the shoulder blades. "It's nice to see her before she got sick."

Pete cleared his throat. "The women with her are Mrs. Osborn and Mrs. Bernard. Their daughters played with my sister, Bonnie."

"They would have all been about Ruth's age," Ivy said.

"Ruth was a year older. Ruth was always nice to the girls, but they didn't really give Ruth the time of day."

"Why not?" Ivy's outrage for the young Ruth boiled her blood.

Pete looked a little abashed. "My mother was very aware of the lines between the classes. Ruth was staff. My mother, her friends, and their children were guests."

Ivy understood the life of a service employee. Customers didn't always make eye contact, could be rude, and often said things to her they'd never say to a peer. Many spoke around her as if she were invisible or she couldn't hear. In high school, that line had never kept Ivy and Dani from hanging out, but she'd always been aware that folks with money had a different set of problems than she did.

Dani picked up another picture. "Who is that?"

"That's Carlotta," Pete said.

"Carlotta?" Ivy asked.

Pete appeared to rummage in his mind for a detail. "DiSalvo. Carlotta DiSalvo. She was the singer that summer."

"Singer?" Ivy asked.

He tapped the picture of the showboat. "She worked on the *Maisy Adams*. The vessel was damaged in a spring storm, and the cast and crew were stranded nearby. The entertainers fanned out, looking for work at the resorts and hotels. Carlotta came to the Seaside Resort."

"Do you remember her?" Ivy asked.

"Oh, I sure do. She was impossible to miss. A larger-than-life personality who took the stage as soon as she walked into the room. Women envied her, and the men, well, they desired her. I remember hearing her sing and thinking that I just might be in love."

Dani laughed. "How old were you, Dad?"

"Six." He shrugged. "Hard not to appreciate her."

Dani gently jabbed her dad in the shoulder with her fist. "Dad, you have never mentioned her."

"I forgot about her until now."

Ivy pointed to Talley. "Ruth never spoke about her."

"They were great friends for years, but they'd had a falling-out. Last I heard, Talley was living in Elizabeth City in an assisted-living home. I didn't see her at the funeral, but she's been ill recently."

Ivy reached for the address book but spotted no Talley. "Another mystery."

"She was sweet. A little nervous. She and Ruth were best buddies that summer. But I was more interested in swimming in the pool and playing with my friends. Then things turned sideways that summer, and I forgot all about the Seaside Resort for the next decade."

CHAPTER TWELVE

ANN

Sunday, June 18, 1950, 12:00 noon

Ann Manchester held her gin and tonic in her left hand and a cigarette in her right as she huddled her already red body under the shade of the poolside umbrella. This was her third drink in the last hour, and as much as she wanted a fourth, she needed to slow up. It was barely noon, and at the rate she was going, she'd be flat on her fanny by dinner. And she would be damned if she would waste any of this vacation time passed out. She was aiming for pleasantly drunk—that delicate haze that softened life's angers and frustrations always nipping at her heels.

"What do you think about the singer?" Kate Bernard drew out the words in her Georgia drawl. "She's certainly very attractive. And her voice is quite good."

Closing her eyes, Ann took a drag of her cigarette as she imagined the singer's bold green eyes and wide, expressive smile. The woman lived outside the bounds of decent society, and Ann couldn't decide if she was envious or resentful of her daring choices.

Ann had seen Carlotta perform years ago, shortly after she and Peter had been married. He was enthralled, talked about her endlessly after the show, and she'd assumed he'd simply enjoyed the performance.

She was nervous and on edge, fearing Carlotta would recognize her and she would have to admit to a time she no longer acknowledged. Turned out Peter had barely noticed Ann's mood that night.

"As long as she keeps her act on the stage, then I suppose she's fine," Ann said, more to herself.

Kate looked at Maggie Osborn, and they both raised their brows. Neither dared to laugh or comment. Peter Manchester's wandering eye was no secret. "How do you think Edna was able to get her? The Seaside Resort is lovely, but it's hardly the kind of place performers flock to."

"Edna is very clever," Maggie said. "Financing a pool and redecorating the main building was no easy feat after the war."

Edna was no shrinking violet. Behind her smiles was an inflexible steel similar to Ann's that had gotten them both this far in life. Still, Ann also wondered how she'd enticed Carlotta here now of all times.

"I hope she sings 'Blue Moon,'" Kate said.

"Ask her," Maggie said.

"Is her showboat really in for repairs?" Ann asked. "Or did Edna spin that tale too?"

Maggie and Kate exchanged looks. "What other tales has Edna told?"

The gin was loosening her tongue. "Edna's always selling something." She rattled the melting ice in her glass, knowing she should shut up. "Carlotta could have gone to Norfolk or Raleigh. Bigger audiences."

"Who cares," Maggie said. "I'm glad she's here. It adds interest in an otherwise mildly pleasant and predictable vacation."

Maggie's and Kate's families came from lumber and big farming money. They had toured Europe before the war and often traveled to New York. This getaway wasn't remarkable for Maggie or Kate, but they all agreed it kept the children entertained.

Ann's marriage to Peter had placed her in their social circle, but she'd spent every day wondering if she measured up. She'd first proposed this getaway during the war, and they'd all had such a hunger for fun that they'd decided to make it an annual event. The husbands had begun traveling with their families after the war.

Peter never joined his wife and children because of work, he always said. But Ann wasn't so naive. In fact, she often wondered if he even bothered to go into the office while they were away. Given how tense and withdrawn he'd been after their last argument, she was glad to have this break.

"The girls seem to be having a lovely time," Maggie said.

Ann peered over the tops of her sunglasses at the three girls sitting at their own table. She had been disappointed when Bonnie announced that she and her friends would be going their own way this year. Now Bonnie, Jessie, and Dora all sat by the pool, posturing and doing their best to imitate their mothers.

She glanced around the pool and realized she didn't see Pete Jr. Likely on the beach. The boy was always searching for buried treasure.

She was considering going in search of him just as he sauntered onto the pool deck from the beach, his hair damp and tousled and sand covering his feet. He dropped his towel and jumped in the pool.

Ann raised her hand and waved until Ruth looked her way. It was Ruth's first year working in the drink hut, but she was well suited for her role. When the girl looked her way, Ann held up her empty glass and rattled it.

Ruth nodded and dashed inside to get a gin and tonic. Whoever was making the drinks this year was a little heavy handed on the gin, but Peter wasn't here, and who did it hurt in the end?

"Odd to have a twelve-year-old serving your drink," Maggie said.

"She's not drinking it," Ann said. "And she appears mature beyond her years."

"Where's Henry? He's always been the bartender," Maggie asked.

Henry Anderson, tall and lean, with tanned skin that set off his blue eyes, had worked at the hotel for fifteen years. He was an attractive guy, in a working man's kind of way. He kept his distance from the mothers no matter how much they flirted with him.

"I don't know," Ann said. "He's never been totally reliable."

The girl returned with a tray sporting a stout glass with ice floating in a fizzy liquid. She set the drink in front of Ann. "Can I get anyone anything else?"

"No, thank you, dear." The girl's skin was darker than she remembered. Brown as a berry. Still, very pretty.

"I must say you've grown over the winter," Maggie said. "You must be an inch taller."

"Yes, ma'am," Ruth said. She removed the order ticket from her apron pocket and set it on the table with a pen.

Ann's signature was barely legible. "How's your mother doing? I haven't seen much of her today."

"She's in the kitchen helping Daddy with the lunch buffet."

"Is Edna doing well?" Maggie asked.

"Yes, ma'am," Ruth said. "She's doing really well."

"How are you?" Maggie asked.

"Really good, ma'am."

Ann sipped her drink. "Still drawing?"

"Every chance I get," Ruth said.

"Good. Ruth, check with the girls and see if they'd like soda," Ann said. "It's vacation, and the girls deserve a treat."

"Yes, ma'am."

"Treat yourself and that other girl to a soda as well," Ann said. "Put it on my account."

Ruth looked at Ann. "You want to buy soda for Talley and me?"

"Yes." The gin was doing the talking now. But it wasn't the first time it had steered her in the wrong direction.

"Thank you," Ruth said.

"Of course."

Ann watched her walk over to the table with the girls, who ignored her initially and then each ordered a soda. When Ann was Ruth's age, in the before time, she helped to raise her five younger cousins and worked in the tobacco fields. Bonnie had no idea how lucky she and her friends were.

Who knew—maybe Ruth was the lucky one. Her life would follow a predictable pattern, but she was smart, and her feet would be firmly planted in this world.

Carlotta had built her own life and didn't need a man like Peter. Ann would wager Carlotta saved her money and was planning for the day when she didn't sing. Carlotta, the planner. On many levels, Ann envied Ruth and Carlotta.

Ann's beauty had been her ticket to success, and she'd worked hard on her speech, dress, and mannerisms to cement her elite position. But one day, her beauty would fade, and Peter would reject her, and this world would close to her.

She sipped her gin. The thought was always jarring, frightening. She would fix the rift between Peter and her and find a way to hold on to this life.

EDNA

As Edna set a stack of warm plates at the end of the lunch buffet, she glanced out the picture window toward the pool and watched as Ruth served Bonnie, Jessie, and Dora another soda. A part of her was sad for Ruth, who wanted so much to grow up and be like the other girls, ordering and signing for drinks like their mothers. Playing the role of a grown woman and flirting with the power a woman had over a man was fun at first. Easy at that age to envy the freedom of adults, who all seemed to enjoy life's bounties. But those rewards were few and far between, and they would all learn that freedom came with a cost.

She didn't like that Ann Manchester had bought sodas for Ruth and Talley. "Always best not to get too well acquainted with those we serve," her father used to say. He'd been a minister and carefully tended to his flock, but he'd always remained on his side of the line.

However, it was over ninety degrees today, and she hated that Ruth had to work the drink hut. But Henry was always late arriving the first week of the season, and the budget was too tight for extra help beyond him and Talley. As tempted as she was to say a few words to Henry about his tardiness, she understood it was better that he arrived late and was in a good frame of mind.

Edna retreated to the kitchen and made two glasses of iced water that she carried out to Ruth. Perspiration dampened the girl's head, and her cheeks were flushed. Edna gave a glass of water to Ruth and set the other on the bar. Sodas were tasty, but they really didn't quench thirst. "Where's Talley?"

"Bathroom," she said between gulps.

"Why don't you go inside and finish the lunch setup? It's cooler inside."

"I don't mind being here," she said.

"It's hot, and most of these folks are all headed inside anyway in a few minutes."

Ruth glanced back toward the cottage where Carlotta was staying. "I haven't seen her today. It's nearly lunch. Do you think she's not feeling well?"

"I'm sure she slept in. Yesterday was a long day for her."

"Is she going to sing again tonight?"

"She'll perform every night," she said.

Ruth drained the glass. "What do you think she does during the day?"

"Sleeps. Sits on her deck." Edna's life had been in constant motion for so long she couldn't imagine, even feared, stillness.

"Being a singer seems like a good job to me."

"I think it's harder than it looks. She makes it appear easy."

"After lunch can I go visit her? She might be hungry or want a sandwich. And I said I'd show her my sketches."

She wasn't surprised that Ruth was fascinated by Carlotta. The singer was exciting and beautiful. "Make her a plate at the end of the lunch service. Take an hour or so to visit. But don't pester her with all your pictures. Show her the best ones."

"Really?"

Edna could think of a half dozen jobs Ruth could be doing this afternoon, but she was still a girl, and she wanted her daughter to have as much of a childhood as she could. Adulthood came fast. She brushed back Ruth's dark bangs dampened by sweat. "You've earned it."

"Thanks, Mama."

A northeastern wind cooled her skin, but as she glanced out at the clear sky, she sensed the sunshine was short lived. She'd bet money they'd get a storm tonight. "Now get yourself inside and see what Daddy needs. He'll be ringing the lunch bell soon."

"Oh, and I've been keeping track of Mrs. Manchester's drinks. She's had four so far."

"If she orders more, I'll water them down a bit."

"Okay, Mama."

"Thanks, honey."

Though drink orders were a good source of income, Ann Manchester had a tendency each year to drink too much. There'd been no trouble so far, but Edna wanted to stay ahead of the problems.

CHAPTER THIRTEEN
RUTH

Sunday, June 18, 1950, 3:00 p.m.

Ruth had never been so glad to see the dining tables clear and the overfed guests wandering back to their rooms. These quiet afternoon hours, the lull between the meals, were the best of the day. The guests retired for a shower and nap, then reappeared around five for drinks, dinner, and the show.

She stared at the tray of luncheon meats ready for repackaging, trying to decide what Carlotta liked. Ham or chicken? The cheese choices were Swiss and American. Mayo was a given, but some folks liked mustard. Lettuce, tomato, onion. In the end she put a selection of everything on a single plate, along with a couple of slices of white bread.

"Where you headed?" Daddy asked.

"Taking Carlotta a plate."

"Again?"

"She's gotta eat every day, Daddy."

He sighed like he did when he was worried about something. He'd been doing a lot of that the last few weeks. "Well, don't linger too long."

"I won't take long."

Mama came into the kitchen carrying a tray of half-empty salt- and pepper shakers. "Hurry back as soon as you can, Ruth."

Daddy shook his head. "And put your hat on, Ruth. Don't be fooled by the winds. The sun's fierce today."

"Are we getting weather, Mama?" Ruth asked. "Feels like a storm."

"We are. But it won't be until later tonight."

"Okay." Ruth snatched a floppy straw hat from the peg by the back door and, guarding her covered plate, nudged the back door open with her rump. As she turned, pots and pans clanged in the sink, and her father said to her mother, "This isn't a good idea."

"It'll be fine," Mama said.

"I know you want to do what's right . . ."

Ruth's curiosity gave her pause, but as the seconds stretched and her parents didn't speak, she knew they wouldn't talk again until they heard the sound of her feet crossing the deck. Lately, they'd had a lot of hushed conversations that ended abruptly around her.

As she hurried across the hot sand to her cottage, she was grateful for the ocean brushing the heat from her skin. Clouds huddled close to the north, but to the south it was all blue sky. Mama was right. It was going to storm.

She dashed inside her house, grabbed the sketchbook that she'd picked this morning, and hurried toward Carlotta's cottage. As she climbed the stairs, she heard humming and could see that Carlotta had opened all the windows, allowing a cross breeze through the house. Whiskey slept on a pillow, unmindful of her mistress swaying to a silent song.

Carlotta wore capri pants that hugged her curvy hips, and her narrow waist peeked out from a white cropped top. She was barefoot, her hair tied back in a reckless ponytail, and she wore no makeup. In this private moment when all the glamour was stripped off, Ruth saw an ordinary woman who reminded her a little of Mama, though not so much of herself. If she was the lady who'd given birth to her, it seemed they'd look alike, even a little, right?

Ruth knocked on the door. Carlotta didn't startle but turned slowly, her smile warming as it did when she stepped onstage. "Hello."

"I brought you lunch."

Carlotta moved toward the door in a slow, steady pace. "That was very nice of you." She pushed open the screened door. "Come inside, Ruth."

As Ruth moved across the space she'd been in hundreds of times before, she decided it was different, transformed. The dark paneled wood looked lighter with all the sunshine beaming through the windows, and Carlotta's dresses, hanging from the doorjambs, splashed vibrant greens, reds, and blues around like a carnival. Five sets of high heels lined the hearth, and Ruth wondered what it would feel like to walk in those shoes. She'd wobbled around in her mother's good shoes, but those heels were low and square.

"You look like you got some sun," Carlotta said.

"I was helping in the drink hut by the pool. The regular guy hasn't made it to the Seaside Resort yet, so Mama asked me to help." She glanced at her brown arm and compared it to Carlotta's pale skin. "I always take the sun and hang on to it well toward Christmas."

"Not me. I turn beet red." A smile tugged the side of Carlotta's lips. "Your skin is very beautiful."

"Thanks."

"Your mother lets you serve drinks?" Her gaze lightened with curiosity and some amusement.

"Sodas, mostly. And a few cocktails."

"Your mother bends the rules."

Ruth shrugged. "She says we do what we must. She never lets rules get in the way of practicality."

"Edna breaks rules?"

"She doesn't make a fuss when she does it. She said God created black, white, and gray for a reason."

"Good for her." Carlotta twisted a hoop earring between her fingers. "What kind of drinks do the ladies like?"

"The mothers like gin and tonic."

"They look like a gin crowd," she said.

"I can mix a gin and tonic." It was important that she acted older than she looked. "Henry taught me. Once he arrives at the hotel, he'll take over mixing again."

"And when did he teach you this?"

"A few weeks ago." Ruth eyed Carlotta and was relieved to see no judgment prowling behind her gaze. The mothers didn't approve of Mama letting her carry drinks, but that didn't stop them from ordering. "What does a gin crowd look like?"

"Country club ready," she said. "That's not bitterness, mind you. In my line of work, you learn to read people. Helps me determine what songs to sing." She removed the napkin covering the plate, pinched off a piece of cheese, and popped it in her mouth. "Delicious."

"I wasn't sure how you'd like your sandwich, so I brought a lot of fixings."

"I appreciate that." She tore off another piece of cheese. "So what were they saying about my show last night?"

"Big hit," she said.

"I didn't see many men last night."

"The husbands come mid- to late week. The mothers and the kids stay a few weeks, but the dads just come on the weekends."

"Very practical."

"I'm pretty sure the dads are going to love you too."

"They usually do," she said.

Ruth noted the camera sitting on the dining room table. "Do you take a lot of pictures?"

"I have a couple of rolls of film," she said. "When I see something interesting, I snap a picture."

"Have you seen anything interesting since you got here?"

"A few things. Are those your drawings?"

Butterflies wrestled in Ruth's belly as she handed over the book still tucked under her arm. "I drew these last week."

Carlotta carefully opened the book and thumbed through the pages. "These are very good, Ruth."

"You don't have to be polite." A mama would say nice things because she had to.

"I'm not," she said. "You have real talent."

Warmth rose in Ruth. "Really?"

"Really."

Carlotta's gaze rose from the penciled seascape out toward the ocean. "This area is quite beautiful. I've seen many waterways, rivers, sounds, bays, but this place is one of the prettiest."

Ruth tried to identify what was so special about the ocean. "I've always wanted to see the mountains. I've seen pictures, but I've never been there."

"I grew up in western North Carolina. There are lots of mountains there. It's very green and in the winter very white and cold."

"My mama lived in the mountains when she was a baby. How did you end up working on the showboat?"

Carlotta regarded her but didn't answer.

Ruth rushed to say, "My mother says sometimes my mouth gets ahead of my head. If you don't want to answer, that's fine."

"What made your mother move to this area?"

Ruth shrugged. "She always wanted to see the ocean, like me and the mountains. She came for a visit, met Daddy, and she said it was love at first sight."

"Is that so?"

"You ever been in love?"

Carlotta grinned. "Many, many times."

"I thought we all had one true love."

Carlotta closed the sketchbook and handed it back to Ruth. "This is the kind of conversation you should be having with your mother."

"She never likes to talk about that kind of thing."

"Ah well, I suppose she doesn't like the idea of her little girl growing up and asking such questions. No mother wants their baby to grow up."

Ruth walked toward the high heels and stared at the shiny patent leather pair on the end. "Does it hurt to wear these?"

"It can. But I've worn those so much they don't bother me anymore."

A gust of wind rushed through the screens on the sleeping porch through the house. "Mama says we're going to have a storm later tonight. I never know how she knows, but she always gets the weather just right."

"I've heard of people who can feel the weather changing. I never had a talent for it."

"I do a little," Ruth said. "But not like Mama."

"I'll be sure to close up the windows before tonight's show."

"What are you going to sing?"

"I have several ideas. Not sure yet, but I'll be different than last night."

"I'm sure it'll be good."

"Are there any songs that you would like to hear?"

"I don't know. Everything sounded real good last night. But I liked the ones about the eyes."

"'Them There Eyes'?"

"That's right," Ruth said. She liked the way Carlotta had closed her eyes and poured her feelings into the song.

"It was made famous by Billie Holiday. She's one of my favorite singers. I'll be sure to sing that one again tonight."

"Really? Thanks."

"It's the least I can do, seeing as you brought me lunch today. You're a very kind person, Ruth."

"Lunch was no big deal. Just the right thing to do."

Carlotta drew in a breath, her smile softening. "Can I take your picture?"

"Yeah, sure."

Carlotta reached for a silver camera and held it up. Ruth grinned. The camera clicked once.

"Can I take your picture?" Ruth asked.

Carlotta chuckled. "Once I have my makeup on."

"You look fine to me."

"The world does not need a reminder of my plain face."

"That's not true."

Carlotta eyed her closely. "Keep drawing. Something tells me you're very talented."

"I didn't have a teacher or fancy art schooling."

"Self-taught? I like that. I taught myself how to sing, and then when I wanted to improve my techniques, I paid attention to those better than me."

"You didn't just start singing like you do from the start?"

"Have your drawings improved over time?"

"Yeah. Sure."

"You and I aren't so different." Carlotta smiled. "Now I have to rest, Ruth. I'll see you later tonight."

She didn't want to leave. "Okay. See you later."

Outside, she felt lighter, more buoyant, as she thought about Carlotta and the way she'd looked right at her. It was like she recognized the sameness in them.

She wasn't in a rush to return to the kitchen or the dining room. When she was with Carlotta, she felt grown up, felt seen, and returning to the hotel would again render her invisible.

The beach was deserted this time. The moms, even the girls now, were resting or deciding what to wear tonight. Seemed they all were in a constant competition to look their best.

She slipped off her shoes and walked along the edge of the water, savoring the cool splashes against her feet and ankles.

The squawk of a gull drew her attention out toward the water, more unsettled and restless than it had been this morning. The condensing clouds were a shade grayer.

The gull squawked again, and this time it sounded distressed. She looked toward the sky and then along the beach but didn't see it.

Squawk.

Her gaze skimmed the choppy waters, and this time she didn't see a bird but a pair of thrashing arms. She looked back toward the hotel and pool, ready to shout, but no one was there.

The arms slapped against the water harder, their movements more frantic. The crosscurrents of the tide hinted at an undertow.

Ruth's eyes squinted, and she could make out a blond head and pink skin. "The Manchester boy."

He was stuck in a rip current and needed to swim parallel with, not toward, the shore. She cupped her hand to the side of her mouth and shouted, "Stop fighting. Swim out of it!"

The arms cut faster into the water, but his cries sounded gargled.

"Tarnation," Ruth muttered as she threw her shoes up on the shore and set her sketchbook beside them. Her mother wasn't going to appreciate her getting drenched before supper.

She moved toward the water, the waves crashing higher and higher on her body. Salt water splashed her mouth, and she spit out the brine.

Ruth was a strong swimmer. Daddy and Uncle Henry had seen to it when she wasn't more than five or six. They'd insisted she learn if she wanted to go along on a fishing trip. After her first lesson, Henry had proudly called her part fish, which had gotten her to thinking maybe her real mama might be a mermaid. Took a long time to let that idea go.

She sucked in a breath and dived into the crashing wave, letting it wash over her as she pushed her body out farther to sea until she popped up above the surface beyond the breakers.

When she rubbed the salt water from her eyes, she spotted the Manchester boy. His arms were moving slower as she swam toward him. Henry's warning about those who were drowning echoed in her head with each stroke. *They'll be desperate and will pull you down. They won't mean to kill you, but they will.*

She closed the gap to the boy, came around behind him, and grabbed him under the arms, holding him to her chest. He pushed against her, desperate to escape the water.

"Hold still, damn it." Curse words went hand in hand with Uncle Henry and Daddy's fishing trips, and she'd picked up a few. "You'll kill us both if you don't relax."

"I'm going to die!"

Better words than *damn* came to mind. "If you don't quit squirming, I'll let you go, and you'll definitely die. Breathe. I've got you."

She must have sounded more confident than she felt, because some of the tension drained from his body. She kicked her feet to keep them afloat, and her heart pattered hard in her chest.

"Kick your feet like a frog," she said. "I'm going to do the same."

"Okay."

To Pete's credit, he listened and kicked. She looked over her shoulder and steered them along the shore.

"Where are we going?" he asked, the panic rising under the words.

"To get out of the rip current, dummy."

"What?"

"I'll show you when I get us to shore." She didn't have the strength to keep them afloat and talk, so she went silent as they both kicked. It took a good five minutes before she could feel the ocean's pull lessening. "We're going for the shore now."

Pete's nod was nearly imperceptible, but he kept kicking. Soon they approached the breakers. "Close your eyes and mouth," she ordered. "Don't open until I tell you."

Just as she spoke, the first wave hit them and washed over their faces, propelling their bodies to the shore. She wanted to gulp in a breath but kept her eyes and mouth shut until the next wave shoved them toward the sand. When she felt the rough, pebbled sands scrape her back, she knew they were safe. She let go of him and pushed herself up to her knees.

One breath, and the next wave hit. She grabbed Pete by the arm and dragged him up. "Stand up."

The boy didn't complain and pushed himself up on wobbly legs. He staggered a step, but she held him tight and kept him steady until he got his land legs back. Breathless and with aching lungs, they lurched toward the beach.

On dry land, Pete dropped to his knees. He spit out a mouthful of water, his chest heaving as he looked up at her through a web of blond hair. "Thanks."

"Swimming alone is stupid," she said.

"You came in after me alone."

"Which makes us both fool headed. Get up." She scanned the beach and was relieved to see that no one had seen. "Look at the water. See the way it cuts sideways in some spots?"

Eyes narrowed. "Yeah."

"That's rip current. Promise me you'll stay out of it."

"Don't tell my mother," he begged. "She won't let me go in the water again."

"Promise you won't go in alone?" She held out her hand.

He took it. "I swear."

"Then it's our secret."

CHAPTER FOURTEEN

IVY

Friday, January 21, 2022, 11:00 a.m.

As tempted as Ivy was to ask Mr. Manchester about the summer of 1950, she didn't. Dani had said once that her grandfather died around that time, and her father's life had changed forever. Every time Dani tried to ask her father about her grandfather, he changed the subject.

"What do you remember about Ruth?" Ivy asked Mr. Manchester.

"She was a funny girl. Nice. Full of energy. Pulled my stubborn butt out of the ocean when I got in over my head."

"When was that?" Ivy asked.

"The first or second day of vacation in 1950. When Mama was napping, I sneaked out to swim in the ocean."

"Alone?" Dani asked.

Mr. Manchester shrugged. "It was a different time. Parents didn't hover like they do now."

"Grandma always did like her gin and tonic," Dani said.

Mr. Manchester didn't deny the claim. "Anyway, I was bored. I grabbed my suit and sneaked out of our bungalow."

"Where was your sister, Bonnie?"

"Getting dressed for dinner with her friends. She saw me pass Jessie's room and told me to be careful. I waved and told her not to worry."

He'd been six years old. Ivy wasn't a parent, but her skin prickled when she remembered the time that she'd been badly pummeled by the waves. "What happened?"

"I got caught in the undertow. Ruth was walking along the beach and must have seen me. She swam out and grabbed me and held me against her. Cussed like a sailor. When we got to shore, she told me I was stupid. She was right. We swore never to tell anyone about what happened. And I never did until now."

"She was always adamant that I never swim by myself," Ivy said. "And the one time I did, she had to pull me out too. I was grounded for two weeks."

"Living down here gives the locals a healthy respect for the ocean," Dani said.

"I was a mainlander at the time," he said, smiling. "I didn't think the Atlantic was any more dangerous than the pool."

"Never made that mistake again, did you?" Dani asked.

"No, ma'am." His self-deprecating tone didn't quite square with the shadows hovering behind his eyes. "Edna shot me a couple of disapproving looks over the next few days as I looked out toward the ocean."

"Do you think Ruth told?" Ivy asked.

"No. But Miss Edna noticed everything. She must have seen Ruth's wet clothes and my dazed expression. Both Ruth and Edna were good at keeping their secrets." He looked down at the picture of the five girls and tapped his sister's face. "In her last years, Bonnie and I spoke about that summer, and she regretted how she treated Ruth."

"Ruth appreciated all you did for her the last few years," Ivy said. "She said you made repairs but never charged her a dime. And you bought the land when she needed to sell."

"Least I could do," Mr. Manchester said. "It's good to see these pictures. Takes me back. If I come across anything relating to the wreck, I'll let you know."

"Thanks."

He kissed Dani on the cheek. "I'm heading out. You good to see your way home?"

Annoyance edged Dani's smile. "I'll be fine, Dad. I have to pick Bella up from school soon."

"Kiss my granddaughter for me," Mr. Manchester said. "Ivy, I'll report back on that wreck."

"Thank you. I appreciate it."

When he left, Dani remained behind. "I never knew he almost drowned. Neither he nor Ruth ever said a word to me."

"Me either."

"So much we don't know about them." For a moment Dani looked like she would say something more. Instead, she shifted her gaze to the great room. "Looks like you've made progress."

"Putting a dent in it."

"I know you've got a plan for all this. But I've been dying to see Ruth's paintings."

"Sure, why not? We can look at a few."

In the studio bedroom, it was easier to see the art stacked against the walls without the clutter.

Dani walked to a small one and unwrapped it. It was of a little girl sitting on the beach and staring at the horizon. She held it up, squinted. "Mind if I look at it in better light?"

"Sure."

Dani carried the picture into the living room and held it up to the large kitchen window. Full sunshine illuminated the bright-blue colors of the sky drifting behind the moody grays of the ocean. The little girl sat, her dark hair pulled into a ponytail, her arms wrapped around her gathered knees. She wore a white shirt and red shorts. A ship sailed in the distance.

"What do you make of it?" Ivy said. "Seems she's trying to say something."

"It's you. And you're watching a ship that's moving away from shore."

Ivy thought about all the hours she'd sat just like that on the beach, staring out, wondering what life was like somewhere else. She had been certain better was waiting for her. She'd thought she'd found it for a while, but it had slipped away as easily as that ship was moving away from the girl. She hoped—needed—to believe better was still out there.

"I love her use of color. So bright and vibrant," Dani said.

"She seems to favor aqua, which was the signature color of the Seaside Resort."

"It's a pop of color in a land that can be rather stark on cloudy days."

Most who vacationed here saw it as paradise. Many wistfully spoke of getting a place by the water. Few realized with the beauty came a savagery. Mother Nature used not only storms but corrosive salt air, bugs, and rodents to remind humans they were here at her pleasure.

"Have you ever thought about living somewhere else?" Ivy asked.

"Sure. Bella and I almost moved to Richmond about four years ago, but then I decided I didn't want to be far from family. And Bella does love her dad."

"I saw Matthew in the grocery store today."

Some of the softness in her expression vanished. "And what was he up to?"

"He asked me out to dinner. Said he wants to catch up."

"And do you believe him?" Dani asked.

"I'm not expecting more than a good meal and a few glasses of wine."

"He's a great father. And he tried to be a good husband."

"And boyfriend."

"Touché." Dani looked at Ivy.

"You know, I was ready to turn around and come back after about twelve weeks." For Ivy a dozen years fell away. "By Labor Day, I thought I'd lost my mind. I'd left all the people and friends who loved me. I'd abandoned a solid future. All I wanted to do was come home."

Dani nodded slowly. "I was so hurt and terrified. But a small part of me wished like hell I'd followed you. But I wanted you to ask me to join you. I didn't want to butt into someone else's dream."

"I was living in an apartment the size of a cardboard box in Staten Island and taking the ferry into the city for work. Mama Leoni gave me all the shit jobs and every day asked if I was ready to leave. You'd have been miserable."

"I already was." Dani shook her head. "That's why I told you to go to hell."

"When I learned about you and Matthew, I realized I'd reached a point of no return. Going backward didn't feel like an option. I had to stay."

"For what it's worth, I'm sorry," Dani said. "Booze and ovulation hormones aside, it was a shitty move to sleep with your ex."

Ivy looked down at the painting that captured the little girl sitting on the beach. "You did me a favor. If not for you, I'd have come home and spent the next decade kicking myself and wondering *what if.*"

"*What if* became my mantra. I remember the nights I was up with Bella breastfeeding. My nipples ached, I was sleep deprived, and my kid had colic. Matthew was working all the time to support us. I was alone." The light dimmed as clouds passed in front of the sun. "I loved that kid from day one, but there were times when I wished I could have delayed her birth by a decade."

"Life happens while we're trying to make plans for our future."

"I'm crazy about Bella and can't imagine a life without seeing her face every day."

"Then we both got what we wanted, sans Matthew."

Dani laughed. "Don't get me wrong. He's a good guy. But not for me."

Ivy thought about her upcoming dinner. She had been oddly excited and thrilled by the invitation. Sexual attraction had sparked when she'd seen him, but she was hoping the older, wiser Ivy wouldn't let her ovaries call the shots. "Keep the painting."

"What? No."

"Seriously. You were drawn to it right away, and you were always a good friend to Ruth. She shared her art with you, not me. Take it and hang it on your wall and think of us both fondly."

"With each passing year, she put more emotion into each painting and finally admitted there was too much of her in them to ever sell. They were an extension of her. And she was tired of losing things."

Remorse speared Ivy. "Like Mom. Like me."

"She always, always understood why you had to leave. She never once begrudged you following your dream."

"I wish she had complained. I wish she'd been a bitch about it and read me the riot act. Then I'd at least have been able to summon some righteous outrage. Always easier to work from a place of anger versus guilt."

Dani laughed. "Got to let the anger go, grasshopper. It'll eat you alive."

"What do you have to be angry about? You have a great kid, and you didn't end up with Matthew."

"We all have our shit."

She knew something was troubling Dani, but if yesterday had taught her anything, it was that Dani couldn't be pressed. "Keep the painting. Seriously. I'll go through the others another day. If this little one packs so much emotion, then I'm afraid the larger ones might knock me flat."

"You and me both. But don't wait too long. I'd wager part of the reason Ruth didn't sell was because she wanted you to have them. She has something to tell you."

All the more reason to delay.

Dani moved toward the front door. "Can I bring Bella by to see the puppies? I shouldn't be the one picking it out, seeing as it's going to be her dog."

"You seriously are taking a puppy?"

Dani rolled her eyes. "I've lost my mind. A puppy is the last thing I need right now. But Bella has looked at the puppy pictures a million times. She wants the littlest girl."

"The runt?"

"She's always been a sucker for the underdog," Dani said with some pride. "Bella's already named her Star."

"Star?"

"She's a would-be astronomer," Dani said.

"Nice."

"Did I tell you I have an art gallery?"

"No."

"It's not the biggest or the fanciest, but we hold our own just fine. You should come by and see it."

The invitation sounded tentative, as if she didn't expect Ivy to follow through. "I will come see it."

"I think we're being remarkably mature," Dani said.

Ivy smiled. "That would mean we're growing up."

"Happens to the best of us."

CHAPTER FIFTEEN
IVY

Friday, January 21, 2022, 5:00 p.m.

By the end of the day, Ivy had cleared out Ruth's bedroom enough that the clutter around the bed was clear and she could strip the stale sheets and put them into the washer. As the machine chugged, she sat with Libby and the pups, who wiggled and squirmed as they jostled for a nipple.

The diminutive black-and-white runt, Star, seemed to be having trouble finding her spot, so Ivy nudged the creature to the right until her little pink mouth clamped on. She suckled hard, kneading Libby's belly with her tiny paws. Libby looked up at Ivy, wagged her tail, and then closed her eyes.

Star had a name, and it seemed the others deserved monikers as well. "How about we call the other two pups Sunny and Moon. Very Earth Mother of me, but I've got to call them something."

Libby yawned.

"Not super inspiring but seems to go with Star."

Ivy rose and checked her watch. Time to get showered and make herself presentable for her nondate with Matthew.

She fished through her suitcase and found a pair of decent jeans, a black V-neck sweater, and snakeskin ankle boots. It was her New York "uniform" she'd worn on her rare evenings off, when she and her restaurant pals had gone out for drinks and dinner. In the restaurant circles, the sous chefs and waitstaff all knew each other. They were their own small town, and at times their relationships were as intertwined as those of any tiny community.

She turned on the hot tap, and she stepped into the stall and let the hot spray wash away the salt and sweat. She tipped her face toward the water, wondering what Dalton was doing this evening. Not that it mattered or that she cared. But still, she wondered.

Though she was tempted to linger, the hot water didn't last. Ruth had complained about the tank's heating element but hadn't fixed it. Typical Ruth. Less hot water meant less water used.

Ivy toweled off, dug her hair dryer from her suitcase, and for the first time in weeks blew out her hair. Amazing how shiny it looked when she tried. Next, she scrounged up the makeup bag containing a nearly empty concealer tube, powder and blushes reduced to slivers in their cases, and mascara that clumped. Not perfect, but it got the job done.

She pulled on the jeans, sweater, and ankle boots still covered in New York City street dust. After polishing her shoes with her towel, she dug into her makeup bag for her go-to gold hoop earrings. Classics, bought on sale at Macy's for fifty-one dollars. Earrings on, she fluffed her hair. The total effect wasn't bad and was kind of refreshing. "Welcome back to the human race."

After sliding on a leather jacket, Ivy grabbed a scarf from her suit-case, checked Libby's water and food bowls, and draped her purse on her shoulder. She was running five minutes late, but unless Matthew had changed drastically in the last twelve years, he was running later. Ten minutes was his normal lag time, but waiting twenty to thirty wasn't unheard of.

She hustled out the door and locked it behind her. There was a truck parked at the end of her driveway, and the driver was loading the freebies into the bed. In the dim light, she could see the man was too tall to be Matthew. As she moved closer to thank whoever this was, he turned. It was Dalton.

She wrapped the scarf around her neck as her heeled boots clicked against the concrete driveway. "You don't strike me as the kind of guy who needs free stuff."

As he looked up, his eyes were shadowed by the bill of his ball cap, but she could feel his gaze sharpen. His lips curled into a smile. "I drive by the thrift store on the way home. Easy for me to drop this off."

"And here I thought there was a demand for vintage hotel furniture, bedspreads, and lamps."

As he closed the back tailgate and came around the truck, he regarded her. "You're mighty dressed up."

"I used to do this on a regular basis." His appreciation warmed her skin. "But the last year has been a little hectic."

"Here's to slower times."

She grinned. "Compliments always appreciated."

"I call 'em when I see 'em." He carefully removed worn work gloves.

Sailor rose up in the truck's back seat and, when he saw Ivy, wagged his tail. She opened the back door and scratched the dog between the ears.

"Where you headed?" Dalton asked.

"Dinner with Matthew."

"My ex-brother-in-law?"

"And my ex–high school beau. He wants to talk about a new project he's working on."

"What's he up to now?" Uncertainty dripped from the words.

"I hear your doubt." She patted Sailor one last time and closed the door.

"He's owned several businesses." Dalton appeared to choose his words carefully. "Some have done better than others."

She wondered if Dani's inheritance from her mother had funded some of the enterprises. "He's always been a dreamer."

"Weren't you two talking about opening a restaurant in high school?"

"He was. Lots of planning and thinking. We even scoped out a few locations."

"Why didn't you pull the trigger?"

"I woke up in the middle of the night, and I saw myself fifty years in the future. I had spent my entire life one mile from this very spot, and the world had passed me by."

"There are worse things."

"Tell that to an eighteen-year-old. I needed to spread my wings. New York seemed the best place to do that."

"And what did your time in the Big Apple teach you?"

"I learned I can survive anywhere. Plus, the millions of hours of cooking added up to a lifetime of culinary education."

"Ruth said you won some awards."

"A few local ones."

"She was bragging on you quite a bit."

"Really? When I told her about each win, she said she expected me to be the best."

"She showed me the articles written about you. 'Best Up and Coming.' And the article featuring six local chefs most likely to win a James Beard Award one day."

"Really?" That article had boosted business at the restaurant for months.

"She was one proud grandma."

Her throat tightened, silencing her for a moment. "That's nice to hear."

"I haven't seen any pots and pans in the 'free' pile."

"Those pots and pans and I spent a lot of time together. A few of the fry pans were like an extension of my arm."

"Ruth saved them all. I carried each box up to the cottage."

"I'll thin the herd eventually, but I'll keep many for old times' sake."

"More sentimental than you thought."

"Maybe." Ready to shift the conversation away from herself, she asked, "What's your deal these days? Ruth told me you were engaged."

"I was. A few years ago. In the end, it didn't work out."

"That's all you're going to say? You're about as sparse on the details as I am."

He shoved his gloves in his coat pockets. "It's an old story, right?"

"I hear ya." Her attention had always sharpened when Ruth brought up his name. "How are the new houses coming along? You guys are going full steam."

"I know we make a lot of noise, but the grating is finished. The weather's supposed to warm up next week, so we're putting in the foundations and posts. Once they're in, it will move fast. We hope to be roofed in by late February."

"Sold out by the season?"

He crossed his fingers. "The sales lines have been ringing steadily. I think we'll have them all sold before we're under roof. That means we'll be customizing each place. Dani's been our decorator for the last year, and she's already contacted a couple of the prospective buyers."

"She said she owns a gallery."

"She does. That's where she also does her design work for us."

"She's got a great eye for color."

"And she's put together some amazing rooms."

"Good to keep it all in the family."

"We try."

A car downshifted and slowed, and a black SUV pulled up beside Dalton's truck. Matthew got out. He was dressed in jeans, a blue collared shirt, and a fitted overcoat. He looked sharp, and as she approached, the scent of his aftershave teased her nose.

"Dalton," Matthew said, extending his hand. "How goes the project?"

"Can't complain."

He looked over at the build site. "Looks very promising."

"We always hope." The humble words belied the confidence she'd seen when Dalton was working.

Matthew smiled at Ivy. "You look nice."

"Sometimes I need to prove to myself I'm more than a chef's jacket and white pants."

His gaze danced with appreciation. "You proved your point."

Matthew's appraisal reminded her of high school and the rush of hormones tangled up with youthful possibilities. Intense but short lived. "Thanks. Ready to go? I'm starving."

Dalton cleared his throat. "Enjoy your dinner."

"Dalton, thank you again for hauling this stuff away," Ivy said. "And it's going to the thrift store?"

"Yes. It'll all be put to good use."

"Good. Ruth would be rolling over in her grave if she thought it'd go to waste."

"No worries there."

She took a step toward him, had the urge to place her hand on his arm, but kept going as she moved around his truck toward Matthew's SUV.

Matthew moved to the driver's side door while she opened her own. "See you around, Dalton."

"Sure thing," Dalton said.

Ivy closed her car door, settling into the soft leather seats. The interior was plush, and the vehicle was a late model. Matthew had always liked nice cars. In high school, he'd saved his money and borrowed more from his dad to buy his first truck. It had been used but in mint condition, and the first time he'd driven to this cottage and picked her up for a date with it, he'd been more focused on how he'd looked behind the wheel than her new dress.

"I meant what I said," he said. "You look nice."

"Thank you."

He pulled out onto the beach road, and as they drove away, she glanced in the rearview mirror as Dalton angled behind the wheel of his truck. Nothing short lived or temporary about him. When he charted a course, it didn't waver.

"What was your favorite restaurant in New York? And it can't be where you worked," Matthew said.

Ivy refocused on Matthew. "There was a steak house in SoHo. Rib eyes cut like butter."

"You were a vegetarian in high school."

"You must be remembering Dani. She was the vegetarian. I'm straight-up carnivore."

He grimaced. "Sorry. Didn't mean to confuse you two. Forgetful in my old age," he quipped.

"Freudian slip."

"Ouch."

They'd never had a conversation about his pivot to Dani after she'd left Nags Head. "Don't get all twisted up about it." Not that he would. She'd never seen him sweat, except right after a near fender bender with his first truck. "It all worked out in the end."

"Glad you see it that way. I appreciate it, and so does Dani."

As far as she was concerned, losing Matthew was more of a sidebar. Her main beef for years had been with Dani. And even that righteous indignation had petered out. The world was full of too many bigger problems than a failed high school romance.

"I hear you're selling the cottage."

"That I am." She looked ahead toward a small place that was one of the few open after 4:00 p.m. in the winter. It had been the hangout of locals back in the day, and it seemed to still be. "O'Toole's. Good to see some things never change."

"It's comforting." He parked in O'Toole's lot.

"Here?"

"We had a lot of good times here."

Out of the car, she walked around, waited for Matthew as he glanced at a text. A gust of wind sent her toward the front door, and she opened it. Heat rushed toward her as she held the door for Matthew.

"Sorry about that. Work," he said.

"I get it." This was a work meeting, and it shouldn't annoy her that a business detail came first. Still, his undivided attention was flattering.

As she stared around the pub, she thought for a moment she had lost a dozen years of her life. The decor, styled as a sort of Irish pub for the seafaring type, still had dark paneling, small round tables with mismatched chairs, and pictures of old ships on the walls. It smelled of burgers, fries, and Guinness on tap. A sound system played "Whiskey in the Jar" by the Dubliners.

Joe Truitt, a tall, burly guy who had gone to high school with them, stood behind the bar. His dad had run the place then, but it seemed the generations had shifted again.

"Joe, look who I found," Matthew shouted.

Joe looked up from a frosted mug hovering under an open beer tap, and his stoic expression melted into a wide grin. He set the beer in front of a guy at the bar, came around, and wrapped Ivy in a bear hug. He leaned back, lifting her feet off the floor. "Back from the great north."

Laughter spilled out of Ivy. "Joe! Still as strong as ever."

He set her down gently and regarded her. "And you're as pretty. I was sorry to hear about Ruth. I loved that lady."

"I saw you at the funeral." That day remained a blur of faces and well-meaning comments. But she remembered Joe standing in the back of the funeral home, his blue eyes red with tears. "She was the best."

"I have one of her pictures hanging over there."

Ivy followed his gaze to a rendering of the beach across the street from Joe's bar. It captured a couple facing a sunrise spilling reds, oranges, and aquas over a calm ocean. "It's fantastic."

"She gave it to me when I took over the bar two years ago. Said it was a new day at O'Toole's, and the moment needed to be celebrated."

"She had a soft spot for you," she said. The Seaside Resort and O'Toole's had teamed up for an annual charity event to benefit the fire department each May. For several years, Ivy and Joe had worked their respective booths. He'd sold small plates of bangers and mash, and she'd served bowls of fish chowder and corn bread. There might have been some friendly competition between their booths. Okay, there was. She had won the last two years, but who was counting. "How's your dad?"

"All right. The stroke took the wind out of him, and he's never quite gotten his mobility back. He comes in here from time to time but mostly stays home and drives my mother nuts."

Ruth had been rattled by Frank's stroke. She had said over and over that she hoped the good Lord took her quick when her time came. Ivy remembered joking that Ruth would live forever. "How's business?"

"Better than last January. No one wants to be home. They'd rather sit at the bar with a few strangers."

"I get it."

Matthew shifted his gaze toward an empty table. "Joe, mind if we get a couple of menus and we take that table?"

Joe handed them two laminated menus. "You know the drill."

"The burger and fries still in the lineup?" Ivy asked.

"Would Ruth ever have taken the fried chicken off her menu?" Joe asked.

"Hell no."

"There's your answer."

"Good to know. I'll take that and a beer."

"Easy enough."

Matthew grinned. "I'll have the grilled-chicken sandwich."

"No mayo. Salad, no fries?" Joe asked.

"I don't have Ivy's metabolism," Matthew said.

"We're all working harder to keep our girlish figures," Joe teased.

Ivy laughed as she winked. "I have missed you, Joe Truitt."

"Here's hoping you're here for more than a visit," Joe said.

"I'm here for at least the next six weeks. Beyond that, no promises," she said.

"Then we'll have to change your mind," he said.

She settled in a chair, her back to the wall, and set her purse in the chair beside her. Matthew followed with their two beers.

She drank greedily, savoring the cool, malty bitterness. "I could be back in high school."

Matthew sat and sipped his beer. "I thought you'd appreciate coming here. Good memories for me too."

She and Matthew had eaten enough meals here and sketched out plans on napkins that generally included his ideas for his own restaurant. He'd always figured her into his plans, but she'd been the sidekick. In those days, she hadn't been good at voicing what she wanted because she hadn't really known. Even her decision to leave had been spurred by a nameless rebellion fortified with no concrete plans. All she'd known was that she needed to prove she could be Ivy and not Ruth's granddaughter or Matthew's girlfriend.

"I'm sorry," she said. "I shouldn't have ditched you and our plans."

"Water under the bridge."

"It's not," she said. "I walked out on everybody."

"I forgave you a long time ago. So it's really okay with me. Dani might be a different story."

"She seems fine."

He chuckled. "That's when you should be most afraid."

"I don't know what else I could do for her."

"Not much you can. We can only move forward."

"I suppose."

"If you had a time machine and could go back, would you change it?"

Yes. Maybe. "No."

"Neither would I. I have a great kid and decent restaurants. Life is what you make it."

Ivy took a long sip, wishing it were that simple. "So you have an idea for a business," she said.

He traced the rim of his iced mug. "Jumping right in?"

"Why not? What's on your mind?" The corners of her mouth twitched.

He sat back in his chair, seeming to savor her attention, which for now he had. "It'll be a fine-dining experience. I've picked a location in Duck across the street from Dani's gallery."

"Makes sense you'd want to be close to Bella."

"It's important I spend as much time with her as I can. Who knows, she might end up working for me one day."

"If she's not running the gallery."

"Right," he said carefully.

Ivy shifted directions back to business. Duck was a small town about twenty miles north of Nags Head. The town had exploded with development over the last decade, and the odds favored a good restaurant. "The bigger houses mean higher rental rates."

"And more people wanting a place to get a great meal and watch the sunset over the sound."

That was true, to a point. It was her assessment that a fancy meal was good for maybe one or two nights of a vacation. But she believed the bread and butter of her industry was casual dining. Not everyone wanted to dress up on vacation. She'd heard comments like that enough times at Vincenzo's from travelers who'd returned night after night for the hand-tossed pizza.

"It sounds great," she said as she raised her mug. "I'm sure you'll make whatever you want happen."

"It's still an idea. I haven't signed the lease on the space. Putting out feelers."

"For?"

"A chef, for one."

She sipped her beer and leaned back. "And who do you have in mind?"

"You."

She laughed. "We really have come full circle. Back at Joe's talking about me working for you."

The furrow in his brow deepened. "I don't see it that way. I see us as partners, Ivy. I'll admit I was full of myself in high school."

"Who wasn't?"

"I can't do it all myself. I've tried it a few times, and none of my ventures have hit a home run."

"And you'd trust me to work with you?"

"I'm asking, aren't I?"

If Ruth had taught her anything, it was that success came with a lot of consistent blood, sweat, and tears. Matthew was an idea man, and some were really good. But he would have to pair with a solid chef for this to work. "No."

"No?" He leaned forward, his lips tweaking in a smile as if he thought she might be teasing him.

She wasn't. "The last thing I'm going to do is jump back into the restaurant life, regret it, and then bolt in six months. I grew up in it and then spent over a decade living and breathing it. I need a break."

"It's in your blood. You won't go long without a place to cook. Better you have ownership in the joint."

Joe appeared with their platters and set them in front of them. He glanced between the two, clearly fascinated by the sight of Matthew tilting toward Ivy and her leaning back as far as the chair's cane back allowed. "Some things never change. Enjoy."

"Thanks, Joe," she said. She plucked a fry from the plate and bit into it. "This isn't about you, me, and our past. I'm burned out, Matthew. I don't have the creative energy to run a kitchen right now."

"Technically, you're one of the best."

"Takes more than technique if you want to separate from the herd," she said. She unwrapped her silverware and smoothed the creases from her paper napkin. Biting into the burger, she closed her eyes as she savored the juicy flavor and the soft buttered bun. She didn't speak for several minutes as she ate the first half of the burger. She set the rest down, knowing she would explode if she kept eating. Besides, Libby would smell the burger on her breath and want a bite or two.

Matthew inspected his grilled-chicken sandwich, then removed the bun before he sliced into the meat. When he seemed to sense her amused attention, he said, "Keto. It works."

"Is life worth living without carbs?" She bit into another fry.

"Better to be healthy."

"Right." She took another pull on her beer.

"You could name the place, set the theme, pick the menu and the staff."

Though it was flattering and a little exciting, she shook her head. "I don't mean to burst your bubble, Matthew, but we aren't going into business together."

He grinned. "I'm not so sure about that."

"I am."

His wide grin and expressive eyes had once had great sway over her. After the junior prom, he'd charmed her shirt and bra right off and coaxed her to willingly give up her virginity in an empty Seaside Resort bungalow.

Either she was now immune to his charm, or she'd learned it was better to say no than make promises to keep the peace. "I'm not a kid anymore, Matthew."

His expression turned serious. "Neither am I. I have a child to support, and my feet are firmly planted on the ground. I've made mistakes in business, and I've learned hard lessons. But a lot of solid thinking has gone into this place. I'm telling you, Ivy, with you running the kitchen and me handling the front of the house, it'll be golden."

"That might be true during the season, but what about the off-season?"

"We'll make eighty percent of our annual income during a fourteen-week period."

"And if it's a bad summer? Too bad Ruth's not here to tell us what happens during an active hurricane season." She sipped her beer. The light buzz was loosening her tongue. "She has stories of Hurricane Hazel in 1954, and I remember Hurricane Floyd in 1999, and your namesake, Hurricane Matthew in 2016, did a number on this state. And let's not forget this last nameless storm that wiped Ruth out."

"If she was younger, she would have rebounded from the storm."

"Do you want to spend a lifetime always monitoring the weather and wondering if it'll hit you directly?"

"You get that from Ruth."

"What?"

"The sense of disaster always lurking around the corner. I think that's part of the reason you left. Fixated on the downside of staying. Never saw the positive. You shot down a good many of my ideas in high school."

She cocked her head. "Do you blame me?"

"To be fair, no. But that's why we need each other. I need someone to keep me throttled back, and you need someone to push you out of first gear."

"I'm not stuck in first gear."

"You went to New York. Points for you. Then you landed a job and stayed in the same place for over twelve years. Why didn't you move around?"

"I liked it."

He raised a brow. "You didn't have any other offers?"

"Sure, but I kept getting promoted."

"Did you get any richer?"

"Not exactly. But few people in the restaurant business get rich."

"You found a safe place, and you stayed." He held up his hands.

She'd found a new family, and she'd refused to let them down like she had Matthew and Dani.

"It wasn't wasted time," he continued. "You built a fantastic reputation. You're a better chef for it."

"You're saying I was too scared to venture out."

"Not scared. But you're like Ruth. You find something that works, and then you stick with it until the bitter end."

Somewhere an arrow hit a bull's-eye. "If this is your idea of a sales job . . ."

"We could make this happen."

Even if it was only to prove him wrong, she would need to see his business plan, discuss his financing, inspect the building . . .

He grinned. "I can hear your mind turning."

She finished off her beer.

"I'll take that as a maybe," he said.

"I didn't say yes."

"You didn't say no."

She stared into her empty beer mug, reminding herself that cracking the door to this was dangerous. If she said yes to Matthew, she'd live the rest of her life right here. "Do you have anything in writing I can look at?"

His grin broadened. "I sure do."

CHAPTER SIXTEEN

DANI

Saturday, January 22, 2022, 10:00 a.m.

The text soured an already overcast day. Dani hated the grays, which drained all the color from the world and not only ruined her view of the Currituck Sound from her sunporch but always dampened her mood. Color signaled life and vitality and transformed the two dimensional into three.

She typed back a response. **No worries. I'll figure something else out.** One way or another, she'd find a ride into Norfolk.

Dani looked toward Ruth's seascape, which hung on the wall facing her desk. She had never seen this painting before but guessed Ruth had created it shortly before the big storm. She had mingled and then transferred her frustrations, emotions, and talents onto the canvas.

In those days, Ruth had talked more about Ivy and wished she'd return home. Dani had considered calling Ivy a few times to tell her, but she never could bring herself to make the call. Now, as she stared at the painting, she wished she had.

"Mom!" Bella shouted.

Dani lifted her glasses, rubbed the bridge of her nose, and turned from the view of the sound's choppy waters toward the easel holding her own half-finished painting, which she had started three months ago. It should have been finished by now but wasn't for a variety of valid reasons.

"In here, Bella!" she said.

Her daughter's feet thundered through their small house, rattling dishes in the cabinet. Bella was tall for an eleven-year-old, and if the pediatrician's prediction was correct, she would be six feet tall like Dani. She had her father's blue eyes and his dark hair, always tied back in a ponytail, and his olive skin tones, which didn't burn in the summer sun. If not for Bella's height and long limbs, no one would have pegged the kid as Dani's.

Bella stopped at the sunporch's threshold. She clutched her smartphone, which she'd held nonstop ever since Matthew had given it to her at Christmas. Dani had asked Matthew to hold off giving their daughter the phone until she was twelve, but once her ex-husband got an idea in his head, he ignored any negative input. He'd listed all the safety reasons supporting why a girl should have a phone, knowing she'd do anything to protect Bella. Now, Dani was left to deal with the daily battles over screen time.

"Can we go see the puppies today?" Bella asked.

Dani had mentioned the puppies to grab Bella's attention from her phone a few days ago. It had worked. Too well. Since then Bella had not stopped talking about the puppies or analyzing the picture of the trio.

Dani glanced toward the ashen sky. The sun promised to peek out by eleven and brighten the day. As much as she didn't want to crowd Ivy, she would have no peace until Bella saw the puppies. "Let me call Ivy."

"Can you call her now?" Bella smiled as sweetly as she had as a toddler.

Dani's heart melted. She loved those smiles, one of which now had her reaching for her phone. "You're not playing fair."

Bella's smile brightened. "I know."

Ivy's reaction to seeing Dani had been relatively good. Dani had not been sure what to expect when she'd shown up with two bottles of wine. She'd been ready to take the bull by the horns, be the bigger person, and prove to one and all that she was doing just fine.

She'd never wanted the rift between them. She'd been so hurt when Ivy had left for New York. But after she'd slept with Matthew, she'd snapped out of her funk, and she'd started figuring out what she really wanted next in her life. Art school was still off the table, so she reconsidered moving to New York. There was so much art in the Big Apple, and she could enroll in school, wait tables on the side.

But life took a hard right when the home pregnancy test turned positive pink. Her head spinning, she sat in the bathroom of her father's house and cried. When she dried her tears, her first inclination was to call Ivy, her wingwoman. They'd watched each other's backs since elementary school. But what was she going to say to her best friend? *I got knocked up by your ex-boyfriend two months after you left town.*

Her next fallback was Ruth, who'd tried in her own way to fill some of the role of mother for Dani. But again, what was she supposed to say to Ruth? *You know that boyfriend you were glad Ivy dumped? Well, the old boy knocked me up.*

She pretended for a few months that the pregnancy test and the five subsequent ones were from a bad batch at the factory. It was Dalton who'd returned home from the navy and noticed she'd gained weight and was always sipping ginger ale.

Five days after he'd joined their father's business, he grabbed her by the arm and walked her outside the company offices, far out of earshot of their father. "What's going on with you?"

The late-September wind didn't temper the sun's hot rays and sweat quickly pooled at the nape of her neck and between her growing breasts. "What do you mean?"

"I'm not stupid, Dani," he said. "Who's the father?"

"What?"

"Dani, who is he?"

Outrage thundered under his tone, signaling he was not going to let this go. Dalton was intense when it came to work, but he was fairly chillaxed in everyday life. He'd sure had his share of girlfriends. But nothing about him in this moment suggested he'd ease up until he had his answer.

Her voice failed her for nearly a minute as the two stood toe to toe. Finally, she screwed up the courage. "Matthew."

"Matthew? Peterson? As in Ivy's ex-boyfriend?"

"Yes."

"Shit, Dani. When did this happen?"

She skimmed over as many details as she could but confirmed she'd gotten pregnant eight weeks after Ivy's departure. "It wasn't planned. Please don't yell, because I swear there's nothing you can say to me that I haven't said to myself."

Concern drove away his anger. "Who knows?"

"I haven't told anyone," she said.

Dalton could pivot quickly from a problem to the solution. He never dwelled when action was required. "Have you seen a doctor?"

"No."

"That's priority number one. And next on the list is Matthew. He's going to marry you."

"Dalton, this is not the Dark Ages. And I'm not compounding one mistake with another."

Dalton's jaw set as he shook his head. "First the doctor. Then Matthew."

Matthew had been shocked, but he'd agreed to marry her, and they'd tied the knot at the courthouse three days later. Their first weeks and months of marriage had been awkward. The focus was the baby. After Bella was born, they tried to be a real couple. And for a little while, it wasn't too bad. But to expect a child to buttress a marriage wasn't fair to anyone, and they'd separated on Bella's first birthday.

Dani and Matthew had failed at marriage, but both agreed Bella was their greatest blessing, and in her humble opinion, they were good parents. Neither could imagine life without their daughter, and both would do anything for that kid.

Dani's reunion with Ivy had gone well enough. Civilized, like grown adults. She'd proved to everyone she'd moved on with her life and the past didn't matter. But this time she wasn't hitching her future to Ivy's or anyone else's.

Sitting up straighter, Dani turned her back to Bella, glanced at the gray sky, and dialed Ivy's number.

Ivy picked up on the third ring and sounded a little breathless when she answered. "It's Dani. I have an eleven-year-old that can't stop thinking about puppies."

"I have three she's welcome to have in six weeks."

Ivy had changed in the last decade. Hell, they all had. She was more grounded, pragmatic, less restless—more like Ruth every day.

"Can we come by today?" Dani felt Bella inch up behind her.

"Come anytime. The puppies are feeding now, so Libby will be ready for a break and might let Bella hold Star, Moon, or Sunny."

"You named the other two?"

"Didn't Bella name the little girl Star?"

Outside, the sun carved through fringed clouds revealing blue sky. "We'll be by in an hour."

"Here all day," Ivy said.

Dani ended the call. "Okay, kid. We're good to go. Ivy said to come now."

"Now!"

"Now."

Dani touched up her makeup, brushed her hair, grabbed her purse, and fished around for keys attached to the large key fob. Bella thundered through the house gathering her coat and hat.

She checked the time. Ten fifteen. No sign of rain. Skies clearing. "Ready?"

"Yes!"

Outside, the sunlight streamed through the trees bowed and twisted by the winds always blowing off the water. Over the sound, light spilled through cracks in the clouds drifting apart.

Dani and Bella settled in the car, and she backed out, careful to keep her eye on the reflector she had nailed to the tree she'd hit once or maybe twice. On the main road, she followed the familiar route she had been driving since she and Bella had moved into this house ten years ago.

She wove through Southern Shores and then took a left onto the beach road. Ten minutes later, she pulled into Ivy's driveway behind her van.

"Remember the deal. You'll have to take care of the dog. That means feeding, walking, and cleaning up after it." She was saying this out loud for the record, knowing many puppy duties would fall to herself during the school day. She'd already scoped out a spot for the dog at the gallery.

Bella wiggled, her excitement too charged to control. "I will. And the really good thing about a dog is that I won't be on my screen as much, remember?"

Yes, her girl had played that card several times. "That's the plan."

Out of the car, she glanced toward the construction site, where the crew was surveying the foundations of the ten homes. When their dad told Dalton and Dani that he'd bought Ruth's land, they were both taken aback. Ruth had never once mentioned her finances to Dani, but she'd always suspected the dollar amount to settle her debts was high. The hotel had been operating under slim margins for so long it was a miracle Ruth had kept the lights on. Needless to say, the land had not come cheap.

Dalton had already sold five of the ten lots before he'd started clearing and one more yesterday. The next four wouldn't be a hard sell, and as long as none of the deals fell through, which she didn't expect, PDD Construction would be fine.

Dalton had already handed out her card to several of the buyers and recommended her decorating service, her little side gig that filled the slow hours at the gallery and kept her from asking her dad or Matthew for money in the months she overspent.

As Dani approached the stairs, worry took root. She wasn't sure how Ivy would react to seeing Bella, the physical product of her night with Matthew. There was no denying who had fathered this kid. She rang the bell. DNA, she well knew, was a powerful force.

Inside a dog barked, and Bella shifted from foot to foot with excitement. "Is that a puppy?"

"Sounds more like the mama dog, Libby."

The door opened, and Ivy stood there with a small black-and-white puppy the size of her palm. She glanced at Bella, and if she saw all the traces of Matthew, she hid it well with a smile. "I understand there's a little girl interested in a puppy."

"That's me!" Bella said.

"This is my daughter," Dani said, laying her hands on Bella's shoulders. "Bella Peterson."

"Pleased to meet you, Bella. I'm Ivy, and this little gal is Star. If you come in and sit down next to Libby, I'll let you hold her."

Dani had to admit Ivy knew how to sell. "Is she still nesting behind the boxes?"

"She is. You can see her staring at us right now. She doesn't like being separated from the baby."

Ivy walked toward the wall of boxes with Bella in tow, sat on the floor, and patted the space beside her. Bella sat, and Ivy let Libby smell the puppy and confirm it was fine before she laid it in Bella's hands.

"Oh, Mommy," Bella cooed as she nuzzled her face against the puppy's small body. "She is so cute."

"She's the smallest of the litter," Ivy said. "The others are a boy and another girl."

Bella looked at the two brown puppies. "They're all so cute. Mommy, can we have them all?"

Dani was ready for the question. "Just one."

"How am I going to decide?" Bella asked. "I can't leave the others behind."

"You get first pick," Ivy said. "And I'll be sure to find good homes for the babies."

"Her eyes aren't open," Bella said as she nuzzled the dog close to her cheek.

"That's the way they're born," Ivy said. "They'll open in another week or so."

"Can I hold the boy?" Bella asked.

Ivy took the female and settled her close to Libby, who sniffed and then licked her face. Star squealed and rooted closer to a nipple.

Dani felt for Libby. Bella had always had a strong appetite, and when Dani was nursing her, her nipples were raw within the first week. Ruth had stopped by her house with a pink basket filled with baby onesies. The instant Dani saw Ruth, she had burst into tears.

"It's okay," Ruth had said, wrapping her arm around Dani's shoulders.

"I didn't think you would come. I thought you would be mad at me."

"I'm not mad, honey." Ruth sat beside her on the couch in her father's den.

"Have you told Ivy?"

"I did."

"And?"

"She was upset. It was a shock for her too."

More tears streamed down her cheeks. "I didn't mean to hurt her."

"I know that. And she didn't mean to hurt you."

"She did. I did."

Ruth smoothed her hand over Bella's head, already covered with thick black hair. "As soon as Ivy sees Bella, she'll fall in love. Just you wait and see."

And now here the two were meeting for the first time. Ivy picked up the brown dog. "That's Sunny."

"He's soooo cute," Bella said.

Ivy rose and stepped back. "They're all sweet."

"You know I'm never going to hear the end of this," Dani said.

Ivy smiled. "I know."

"All part of your evil plan?" Dani asked.

"Exactly."

"When you have your first child, remind me to fill her with sugar and give her a puppy."

"So warned."

Dani looked around the house. "How's it going?"

"Tackling the last of my old room today. I'm now down to crammed dresser drawers and remains of my childhood."

Bella set the puppy beside her mother and lay on the floor beside all the dogs, cooing, lost now in her own world.

"Hey, I was wondering if I could ask a favor?" Dani asked. This was the part that really sucked. She'd been chewing on this since she'd first seen Ivy.

"You can ask."

"I have to drive up to Norfolk on Monday for a doctor's appointment while Bella is in school. I'd arranged for a friend to take me, but she just bailed." Christ, the last thing she wanted was to need Ivy. But this was a small favor. "The doctor's office is requiring I have a driver. I know I'm asking a lot."

"What kind of doctor?" Ivy asked. "Is it serious?"

"No. Nothing serious. I need new glasses. They'll be dilating my eyes."

"I thought all the different glasses were fashion statements."

"Well, they are, but they also serve a practical purpose. I have astigmatism. Irritating but a fact of life."

"You never had trouble with your eyes when you were a kid."

"As we get older, it starts to fall apart."

"You're thirty. That's not old."

"Motherhood ages you faster."

"When's the last time you went out drinking with friends or on a date?"

"Been a while."

"Same."

"There's a winery on the other side of the bridge. We'll go before you leave." Dani didn't feel like dancing around her thoughts. "I didn't send you off in style the last time, but this go-around I will. I owe you that much. I'll take you to lunch once the house is cleared and the puppies are older."

"Sure, I'll drive you to Norfolk on Monday."

"Thanks."

"I had dinner with Matthew last night. He's still very charming."

She glanced toward Bella, who was holding a different puppy and patting Libby on the head. "Yes, he is."

"He's opening a new restaurant."

"He's been talking about that for the last few months. I don't pay too much attention."

"He's put some thought into it. Did you know he had an option on a building across from the gallery?"

"Again, it's Matthew. Lots of ideas." Dani regarded Ivy, expecting her to shoot down Matthew's entire sales pitch.

"What do you think of his idea?" Ivy asked.

"Theoretically, it could work. But you know it takes years to build up a place. I'm not sure he has the patience."

"It could fail in a year," Ivy said.

"Everything can fail, Ivy."

"He told me I'm too cautious."

"I wouldn't say that."

"Having a hard time getting jump-started, then."

"He wants you to be the chef, doesn't he?" Dani asked.

"Yes."

"And?"

"I told him once he sent over a proposal, I'd look at the numbers, but I made no promises."

"I think he means well," Dani said. "And I know the building he's talking about. It's a great location." Dani eyed Ivy. "You really interested?"

"Don't look so shocked. I've been thinking about all the things I could have done differently. I don't want to disappoint anyone again."

"If you think going into business with Matthew is going to right old wrongs, it won't."

"I'm not trying to change the past."

"Aren't you?"

"I've seen enough restaurant mistakes and successes in New York. I'm older, wiser."

"Woulda, shoulda, coulda, right?"

"Ruth used to say that," Ivy said.

"She never looked back. She learned from the past but never dwelled too long on the might-have-beens," Dani said.

"I should be so lucky."

CHAPTER SEVENTEEN
CARLOTTA

Monday, June 19, 1950, 7:00 a.m.

The storm had swept in fast from the Atlantic, bringing howling winds that slammed against the cottage, waking Carlotta sometime after 1:00 a.m. She felt trapped and small while the storm raged around her, as it had that first summer on the *Maisy Adams*. The winds had shrieked and pounded against the showboat, biting into the vessel's boards and rivets. Mother Nature had rippled her fingers over the water, churning it, reminding everyone she held the power.

After that first Atlantic storm, she had packed her bag, ready to return to solid ground. No more wind and waves for her. But there'd been a young man, as there always seemed to be, and he had convinced her to stay.

Fourteen years later, the boy was long gone, but she still lived on the *Maisy Adams*, still enjoyed traveling up and down the East Coast and along the inland waterways, rivers, sounds, and bays. When the captain blared the ship's horn, everyone near the town docks came running to see the paddle wheel arrive. Crowds always grew quickly, everyone excited for their little circus on the water.

The Seaside Resort performances had gone well. Both nights, she'd been a hit, and each time she'd stepped out onto the stage, there'd been more chairs and people. Tonight would be her third night. One more night, and she'd break her record for the longest stay in a port. She would then find out if her popularity was a novelty or if she had the staying power to keep drawing in a crowd night after night.

She and Edna had agreed to a two-week stay. Neither knew if the arrangement would work, but both were willing to try, knowing each offered something the other needed. By early July the *Maisy Adams* would be ready to sail again, and she would move on to the next port.

Suddenly restless, she sat up in her bed, listening to the heavy breeze. She missed the swaying of the boat—her home. She swung her legs over the side of the bed, petted a sleeping Whiskey, and walked into the small kitchen. She filled a teakettle with water and set it on the stove. A twist of a knob, and the burner fired to life.

Opening the refrigerator, Carlotta reached for the milk bottle and then saw the half-eaten sandwich. She would miss Ruth. The kid—Edna's child—was a pistol. She worked hard, and she had a good heart. Carlotta found herself looking forward to the kid's next visit.

Several times she'd caught Ruth staring at her. Maybe the girl was getting her first look at someone from the world outside. Maybe she saw more. Ruth was smart, and her drawings proved she was perceptive.

She walked to the sleeping porch, stared out over the clear skies and what looked like the remnants of a shipwreck. She knew the waters along this stretch of coastline were littered with wrecks, but as omens went, it was not a good one.

"And why do a collection of boards matter? Why does it matter how much Ruth stares at me?" It shouldn't. But it did.

The captain of the *Maisy Adams* didn't like lingering in any port more than three days because time led to broken heads and broken hearts, both of which were bad for business.

The teakettle whistled. She turned away from the wreck, hoping that coming here had been the right decision.

RUTH

Ruth had grown up with storms. She knew enough to respect their fury and listened when her parents told her to hunker down in the bathroom. Last night's rainstorm had been a doozy, but it wasn't the worst she had lived through. Talley had cringed under her blanket each time lightning cracked across the sky. To her credit, she'd not cried or asked Ruth to wake up and comfort her.

The smell of bacon and sweet buns drew Ruth out from under her covers, and she rose quickly. "Get up, sleepyhead! Daddy's making sweet buns."

"It's time to get up?" Talley groaned.

"Afraid so." She made her bed, dressed, and brushed her teeth and hair before dashing down the stairs to the kitchen.

Daddy was standing at the stove, fishing crisp bacon from a cast-iron pan. "Morning, peanut."

Ruth snapped up a piece of bacon from a plate. It was too hot to handle, forcing her to quickly toss it from hand to hand as she kissed her father on the cheek. "Morning. That was a storm last night."

"Not so bad," Daddy said. He was rarely thrown off by the natural rhythms of the ocean.

"Did it do any damage?"

"Washed a good bit of the beach away, but the hotel is fine. Your mama went to the hotel early, just in case any guests were rattled."

Footsteps sounded in the hallway, and Talley appeared. Her face was drawn, and her hair hung loose and limp around her shoulders.

"First storm," Ruth said. "I remember mine."

Talley smoothed her hand over her hair. She stood at the edge of the galley kitchen, her hand braced on the counter as if this were a swaying ship. "I thought the roof was going to come off."

"Nah," Ruth said. "If it was that bad, Daddy and Mama would've gotten us into the bathroom."

"What good would that do?" Talley asked.

Ruth handed her a slice of bacon, as if that would fix everything, which it nearly did, judging by the look on her face. "It's the strongest place in the house, right, Daddy?"

"That's right." He reached for a dish towel, opened the stove, and pulled out a plate of sweet buns. The fact that Daddy had risen to make a yeast bread, which took hours, meant that he'd not slept so well last night either.

"What if the storm is stronger than what a bathroom can take?" Talley asked.

"Then it's best to get to the mainland," Daddy said.

"But we couldn't have left during that storm." Talley took a bite of the bacon.

"No. We could not." Daddy drizzled honey over the hot bread.

"What would we have done?" Talley asked.

Ruth finished off her strip of bacon and went to the icebox. She grabbed the half-full milk bottle and filled two glasses. She set one in front of Talley and then replaced the bottle in the refrigerator.

"No sense in worrying about it," Daddy said. "We all did just fine. Now you two girls have a seat at the table, and let's get some breakfast into you. Days after a storm are the best for shelling. And this year, there's a surprise waiting on the beach."

"What kind of surprise?" Ruth asked.

"You'll have to wait and see."

Talley stared at Daddy, waiting for something more, but like last night's hard winds, he had moved on to other thoughts. "We'll be getting more guests today. A couple of the husbands and fathers are arriving."

The men's arrival meant there'd be more bourbon sales at the bar, more late-night poker games by the pool, and the children wouldn't get as rowdy in the dining hall. The groups of mothers would disband, and the women would join their families at their own tables during the day.

"Do we have to do anything different?" Talley asked.

"They'll use up more towels, and there'll be more cups and bottles to pick up by the pool," Daddy said. "Henry will be here today, so he'll take care of the bar, and he'll be manning the grill at lunch and this evening. Burgers and dogs at lunch and barbecue for dinner."

Talley shrugged and ate the last of her bacon. "Sounds like my brothers."

"Not too different," Daddy said. "Now you girls eat up. I'm headed to the main building to check in with Edna and get this day started."

When he left, Ruth wedged a fork under a sweet bun and dropped it on Talley's plate. "These buns are the best thing about storms. Daddy doesn't sleep well during bad weather."

"He was worried?" she asked.

Ruth tore off a piece of soft bread. "As much as he ever does."

"What if there's another storm?"

There would be. There always was. But there was something constant and steady about Daddy that softened most of her fears. "Eat up. One bite, and you'll be wishing for another storm."

Talley took a bite, and her eyes brightened with surprise. "Hmmm."

"The best ever. He said the cook on one of his ships baked those buns to soothe sailors who'd weathered their first storm."

"I guess I've weathered mine," Talley said.

"Yes, you have." She took a big bite of sweet bun and gulped down her milk. "Hurry up. I want to see what the surprise is that Daddy's talking about."

"Is it more shells?"

"Maybe. Or it could be a dead sea turtle, or a monster jellyfish."

"What's a jellyfish?" Talley asked.

Ruth grinned. "Just wait and see."

Ten minutes later Ruth and Talley were climbing the dunes and cutting through the sea oats. At the top of the sandbank, they had a clear view of the calm, smooth ocean, which belied the beach littered with seaweed, shells, and driftwood.

"What's that?" Talley asked.

Ruth followed her outstretched arm toward what looked like the ribs of an old ship. The boat ran parallel to the ocean, its bow facing north but its stern partly sunken in the sand. The large timbers, some twelve by twelve in diameter, had darkened to an inky black.

"It's a shipwreck!" Ruth said. "I heard about them, but I haven't seen one before."

As predictable as the days here could be, her daddy always warned that the ocean would surprise you when you least expected it.

"Did it sink in last night's storm?" Talley asked.

"No. This one is old, real old."

"Where are the people that were on the ship?" Talley asked.

"I figure they're long dead, even if they did survive the storm."

"But the boat made it to shore. So the passengers should have, too, right?"

Ruth started down the dune, marveling over the size of the wreck. "Not always. A lot drowned before they made it to dry land. There are millions of wrecks out there. Daddy says sailors hate to sail these waters because the sandbars are shallow and always shifting. Just when you think you're in the clear of the North Carolina shore . . . BAM!"

Talley started.

Ruth grinned. "The sandbars under the water have moved, and your ship gets stuck. If it's during a storm, then the waves can bust up your ship pretty quick." Her audience was paying close attention, and she couldn't resist adding a little spice to the story. "They call all these waters the Graveyard of the Atlantic 'cause there are so many shipwrecks and dead sailors."

Talley stared out to the waters, her eyes widening. "Do bodies wash up on shore?"

"I've heard they have," Ruth said.

"What happens to them?"

"The locals bury them. But that's usually after they've stripped them of their valuables and cleaned out what they could find at the wreck. The timbers get used for building, and the goods are sold at auction."

"Oh my." Talley approached the wreck but didn't touch it.

Ruth tugged off her shoes, moved past Talley, climbed up on the exposed beam, and walked toe to toe along it until she reached the front deck. She tested the sturdiness of the damp deck and then decided it was fit to cross. She raised her hand over her eyes, shielding them from the sun and staring out at the ocean as a long-dead sailor might.

"Be careful of splinters," Talley said.

"You sound like Mama."

"Well, I've gotten my share in the barn. They're no fun."

Ruth's bare feet skimmed across wood smoothed down by decades if not centuries of water currents. Still, she was mindful where she stepped.

Talley walked around the exposed vessel, looking around curiously but not touching anything. "What kind of ship do you think it was?"

"I don't know. But Daddy will. Or Henry. Between the two, they know all the ships that were ever made."

"Who's Henry?"

"He was in the navy like Daddy, but they fought in different wars. They're cousins, but Henry's parents died young, and he was raised by Daddy's sister. He works for the lifesaving station during the winter months and at the hotel in the summer. He also fishes when he can. He never stays in one place long."

"The devil likes idle hands," Talley said.

"That's exactly what Mama says. I suppose that's why she never stops moving. Did your mama spend any time with mine while growing up?"

"I guess. Edna was long gone by the time I was born, and I never thought to ask Mama about her."

"So many brothers and sisters in Mama's family. Imagine. Do all the families grow that large in your area?"

"Most families have five or six kids. You're the lucky one with that whole room to yourself."

"Not so lucky during storm nights." Even though Talley had kept her up, it was nice to hear her stirring, breathing, and shifting in her bed. It had made her feel a little less alone.

Talley shrugged. "I suppose being alone takes more practice than I reckoned."

Ruth jumped off the ship onto the sand and walked around the boat. The tide rolled in, splashing the sides of the timber and washing over her toes.

Talley tucked her hair behind her ears and dropped her gaze to the shells lining the edge of the tide. "There are so many."

"Mostly clam and oyster shells this time of year. The conchs show up in January." When Talley looked at her with a questioning expression, Ruth added, "Like the spirally one on my dresser."

"Do you think I'll find one of those?"

"Who knows? You never know."

"I want to take one home to Mama. She can't see so well now, but she can tell a lot about anything just by touching it."

"I'll give you one of my conchs. If she holds it up to her ear and closes her eyes, she can hear the ocean."

"You serious?"

"Not lying." Ruth checked her watch and, seeing it was nearly eight, said, "We better get up to the hotel. Time to serve breakfast."

Talley picked up another shell. "Can we come back later?"

"Sure." Though the beach would be different. The tides would be higher and likely crashing closer to the wreck. Slowly the ocean would claw back the shells and eventually reclaim the vessel's remains.

They crossed over the dunes, dropped Talley's shells off under the house, and rinsed their feet off. By 7:55, they had arrived at the Seaside Resort's main building.

When they entered the dining room, a few guests were milling around, but most wore bathrobes and carried two cups of coffee as if heading back to their rooms.

There was one man sitting by the pool. He was fully dressed in khakis, a blue Izod short-sleeved shirt, and camel deck shoes. Ink-black hair was slicked back, and a half-smoked cigarette dangled from a marble ashtray as he turned the page of the *Norfolk Journal and Guide.*

Ruth walked up to her mother, who was carrying a stack of white stoneware plates. "He's here early."

"He just arrived." Mama's clipped tone nipped the edges of each word. "See that Mr. Manchester has enough coffee," her mother said. "Talley, you come into the kitchen with me."

"Yes, Mama."

"Yes, Aunt Edna."

Ruth picked up the stainless coffee urn and walked out onto the pool deck. "More coffee?"

Mr. Manchester looked up, studying her closely. "Yes, thank you."

She filled the cup, catching the strong whiff of his Old Spice aftershave. Mr. Manchester's bold appraisal of her rattled her nerves, but she held the coffeepot steady and didn't spill a drop. "Breakfast is ready."

"Thank you, Ruth."

Hearing him speak her name was jarring. Not that he wouldn't know it. Most of the regular guests did. But he said it like her name carried more meaning than it should.

"Yes, sir."

She left him sitting by the pool, feeling his gaze follow her as she reentered the main building to find Mama standing there watching.

"Everything all right?" Mama asked.

"Sure. It's fine."

Annoyance flattened her lips. "Did Mr. Manchester say anything to you?"

"Just 'Thank you, Ruth.'"

"Did he say anything else? You look flustered."

"Just the way he said my name was kind of weird."

"How so?"

"Like it was funny."

Mama laid her hand on Ruth's shoulder. "Don't mind him."

"You sure everything is fine, Mama?"

"As right as rain." Whatever Mama was thinking slipped behind her welcome-day smile. "Now let's get that breakfast served."

CHAPTER EIGHTEEN

RUTH

Monday, June 19, 1950, 3:00 p.m.

"We should tell ghost stories tonight by the wreck," Ruth said to Talley as they picked up the empty glasses at a poolside table.

Talley's eyes widened as she dumped an ashtray into a bucket. "That's not a good idea."

"Why not?" Ruth asked. "It would be fun. I could ask Daddy to build a fire near the shipwreck, and we could roast marshmallows."

"And if you start talking to spirits, what makes you so sure that one of them might not appear?"

"We can only hope!"

"No, you shouldn't wish for things like that, Ruth Wheeler. You stir up trouble among the dead, and you'll end up with a lifetime of worry."

"How do you know that?"

Talley jutted out her chin. "I just do."

Ruth collected the remaining glasses and wiped down the table. The more she thought about the bonfire and maybe a little spirit summoning, the more she liked it. "We'll ask Mama. If she thinks it's a bad idea, then we won't do it."

"Aunt Edna is not going to like it," Talley said. "No one from back home is crazy enough to tempt the spirits."

"But she's not from there now. She's from here. And we don't mind the spirits as much."

"Anyone who leaves home always carries a piece of it with them."

Ruth hauled the tub of dirty dishes toward the kitchen while Talley dragged the trash can behind a tall utility fence. This part of the property wasn't painted in pretty colors but was a pocket of concrete grays and rusted metal.

Ruth nudged open the kitchen's screened back door with her foot and then kicked it open wide enough to get herself inside before the door slammed shut. She stepped inside and set her tub of dirty dishes down. When she turned, she saw Carlotta facing Mama. Neither was talking, but each had a strained expression that said neither one of them was enjoying each other's company.

Mama was wearing an older gray work dress and over it an apron stained from cooking and damp from dish washing. Carlotta wore blue capri pants with polka dots, a white halter top, a wide-brimmed hat, and open-toed wedge shoes. Fingernails and toes were painted a bright red.

Both turned quickly as she stared at them from behind the wooden prep table.

"Ruth," Mama said, clearing her throat. "Did you get all the dishes picked up?"

"I did, and Talley's dumping the trash." Ruth smiled at Carlotta. "Hey, how are you?"

"I was just returning a few dirty plates. Thank you again," Carlotta said.

"Oh, sure," Ruth said. "No problem."

Mama had not grumbled about Carlotta's lunch plates and today had even placed an extra wedge of cheese next to the sandwich.

"Why don't you take a few hours off, Ruth?" Mama asked. "Enjoy the day."

"Don't you want me to set up for dinner?"

"I'll take care of that."

Mama had been clear this morning she needed help with the dinner service. Ruth wasn't sure why her mother had changed her mind. Mama never changed her mind.

Seeing that she appeared in more of a flexible mind right now, Ruth figured nothing ventured, nothing gained. "Could we have a bonfire by the shipwreck? We could roast marshmallows, and when Henry comes tonight, he could tell ghost stories."

Mama's eyes widened, and Ruth imagined her vetoing the idea as fast as she was rethinking what it would take to make this happen.

Carlotta remained silent but watched their exchange closely.

"People could bring their blankets." Ruth noted the gleam in her mother's eyes and kept selling. "And it looks like it's going to be a real pretty night."

Carlotta's brow arched. "That sounds like fun. It's going to be nearly a moonless sky tonight. And I hear," she said, dropping her voice a notch, "that the veil between the living and the dead is thin on nights like this."

Ruth grinned. "And there's the shipwreck. I bet you Henry has all kinds of stories about it." She looked at her mother, summoning her most pleading expression. "What do you think? No other hotel in Nags Head is doing something like this."

"I don't mind the bonfire, but you'll have to help gather the wood," Mama said.

"I'll get Talley to help. She was all ears when I talked about ghost stories."

Carlotta chuckled. "I'll bet she was. Her kin are not fond of spirits."

"She'll be fine," Ruth said. "She's been afraid of everything since she arrived, but she's coming around."

"I can do my show by the wreck," Carlotta offered. "I can change the mood of my songs to fit any occasion. Even the summoning of ghosts."

"Talk of ghosts might scare the devil out of the guests," Mama countered. "They'll complain."

"They can leave," Ruth said. "Daddy can walk anyone back to their room."

Talley entered the back door and turned on the tap at the utility sink. She washed her hands but didn't look up, as if her presence could be an intrusion.

"Talley, will you help me get the wood for a bonfire?" Ruth asked.

Talley rinsed her fingers and turned off the tap. She was no doubt thinking about dead spirits. "Sure."

"Miss Carlotta is going to sing, and Mama said Henry could tell ghost stories."

"I did not say that Henry would tell stories," Mama said.

"You didn't say he wouldn't," Ruth countered.

Carlotta chuckled. "Ruth, you might be too clever for your own good."

Ruth saw the humor in Carlotta's eyes. "You sound like Mama," she said.

Carlotta nodded her head toward her. "I'll take that as a compliment."

Mama cleared her throat. "I'll ask Henry. And if you girls can gather enough wood, then I'll make an announcement at dinner."

Ruth grinned. "It'll be the talk of the beach. Just you wait and see, Mama."

"Well, that would be very nice," Mama said. "Anything to set the Seaside Resort apart from the competition."

Ruth clapped her hands together. "Talley, we got work to do."

Talley shook her head. "I'll collect wood, but I'm not sticking around if any spirit shows up."

"Of course you are," Ruth said. "You sure don't want to make them mad by just walking off."

Ruth held the kitchen door open for Talley and glanced back toward her mother and Carlotta. Whatever tension had been simmering between them was gone, for now.

Ruth and Talley had piled enough wood for three fires, and by dinner both were starving. Daddy fed them in the kitchen and then put them to washing dishes. Just after seven, he shooed them both out of the kitchen and followed them, shovel and ax in hand, to the woodpile on the beach near the wreck.

Daddy studied the woodpile. "We won't have to worry about running out. Good job, girls."

"We picked up every piece we could find." Talley always seemed a little amazed when Mama or Daddy said something nice to her.

"Can Talley and I light the fire?" Ruth asked.

"First, we'll have to dig a pit and then lay the wood. Then we'll see. Fire's nothing to be fooling around with."

"We'd be really careful," Ruth said. "You could stand right next to us."

Footsteps sounded on the beach behind them, and Ruth turned to see Henry moving toward them. He was freshly shaved, wearing clean khakis and a white T-shirt that showed off the navy tattoos on his arms.

He was a tall man with a lean, muscled build, and his black eye patch and rawboned, deeply tanned features created a pirate's image.

Once when Ruth had been washing dishes with Henry in the Seaside Resort kitchen, she'd asked him how he'd lost the eye. He'd plunged a greasy pan into the sink filled with hot, soapy water. "Lost it off the coast of Italy. A rocket hit the ship. Sent shrapnel flying, and I caught some in the face."

"Did it hurt?"

"Not then. All I could think about was putting out the fire on the ship's deck. And then I got to thinking that if I'd been three seconds faster, I'd have died, like the man in front of me."

"He blew up?"

"He did." His grip on the scrub brush tightened, and he dug deeper into the cooking grease still clinging to the pan.

"What happened next?" Ruth asked.

The muscle in Henry's jaw pulsed as he rinsed the now-gleaming pan. His gaze settled on her as if judging the weight of his answer. "I put the fire out. That's all I could do."

She took the dripping pan and set it on the drying rack. "Weren't you afraid?"

"Fear's a waste of time, Ruth." And then he grinned, winked with his remaining good eye as he reached for another pot.

Later she'd asked her mother about Henry and learned he talked to Daddy often late at night, when they sat on the back porch smoking cigars, sipping whiskey, and staring out toward the ocean.

"Your daddy keeps Henry centered," Mama said.

"Who keeps Daddy centered?" Ruth asked.

"You and I do," she said simply.

When a storm hit the area, there was no man more fearless than Henry. Last winter, when a vessel had radioed in a distress call, he'd realized they were close, so he took his own boat out into the surf. Word was Henry fought the high waves and winds, and when he found the boat, he climbed aboard and helped six sailors onto his vessel.

Put him side by side with ten other men in a log-chopping contest, and he'd win hands down. But there were times when Henry didn't turn up like he was supposed to. It frustrated Mama, but Daddy always defended his younger cousin. "After what the man went through, he has a right," Daddy said.

"You were in the first war," Mama said. "You don't quit on me ever."

"War hits us all differently," he said softly.

As Henry now approached, he grinned as he took in the sight of the wreck, Ruth, Talley, and Daddy.

"Henry, you made it!" Ruth said.

He wrapped Ruth in a bear hug. "I'd have been here yesterday but for the storm."

"Did you go out in the water?" Ruth asked.

"I did. Pulled a few men out of the drink."

Daddy extended his hand to Henry, and they shook. "Glad to have you."

"This is my cousin Talley," Ruth said. "She's here for the summer."

Henry extended his rough hand to Talley, and she carefully took it. He gently squeezed her hand as he shook. "Pleased to meet you. Ruth running you ragged yet?"

Talley blushed. "No, sir. She's a lot of fun."

"There's no 'sirs' here, Talley," Henry said. "Just good working men. Call me Henry. Everyone does."

Talley's frown furrowed as she released his hand, as if such familiarity wasn't common where she came from. "Okay."

"Ruth, your mama said you were looking for some ghost stories," Henry said.

"We are!" Ruth said. "Do you have some to tell?"

Warm laughter rumbled in his chest. "I have one or two that are itching to be told."

"If I don't get that bonfire set soon, Ruth is likely to set that pile of wood on fire," Daddy said.

Henry studied the collection of wood laid in careful stacks. "They'll see this fire burning all the way in England."

"I wanted it to be big," Ruth said.

"Oh, it will be." Henry's attention shifted to the wreck's ink-black wood glistening with droplets from each incoming wave. "Never thought I'd see that wreck surface again. How long has it been?"

"Thirty years," Daddy said. "Summer of 1920. I had just left the navy."

"I was ten," Henry said. "Spent the weeks it was aboveground climbing all over it. There's more of it exposed this time. The storm must have hit this part of the banks directly."

"Damn near close," Daddy said.

"The wind sounded like it wanted to rattle the house right off the pilings," Ruth said. "But Talley and I weren't scared."

"That's good to hear," Henry said. "Talley, you should be proud. You've weathered your first ocean storm."

"Do they come often?" Talley asked.

Henry was never one to tease someone like Talley. "I'd like to think the worst of it is over for the summer."

"That's good to hear," she said.

Ruth held off mentioning that the worst storms came in August and September. "What do you know about the boat?"

Henry glanced at Daddy, his lips slipping into a sly grin. "You tell her about it?"

Daddy shook his head. "Not a word. Figured I'd let you do the talking."

"Tell me what?" Ruth asked.

"You'll just have to wait and see," Henry said.

"Do you have stories to tell about this wreck?" Talley's gaze widened.

"I might have one or two."

"How do you know which one it is?" she asked.

"I know."

"Are the stories scary?" Ruth pressed.

"Depends on what you think is scary," Henry said.

Talley shifted from foot to foot. "Are there ghosts in this story?"

Henry seemed to be enjoying his audience. "Do you want ghosts in the story?"

"No!" Talley said.

"Yes!" Ruth said.

"Why don't we see how the evening goes," Henry said.

Henry liked to tell stories. Not about the war but all kinds of tales about the Outer Banks. Last year he'd spent several nights by the pool entertaining guests with his tales of pirates and lost treasures. A few of the boys had spent the rest of the week digging holes on the beach in search of lost gold. It had been amusing until one of the moms had stepped in a hole and sprained her ankle.

"Fair enough," Ruth said. "Have you met Carlotta?"

"I don't believe I've had the pleasure." Henry glanced toward Daddy, who'd dropped his gaze back toward the woodpile.

"She's the singer this summer," Ruth said. "She's going to sing by the bonfire tonight."

"Sounds like this is going to be a real party," Henry said.

Daddy surveyed the shipwreck, looked back at the dunes, and calculated the direction of the wind before he found a spot downwind from the wooden ruin. He handed Henry a shovel and set about digging a deep firepit. "If you're not going to eat, you can dig."

"Be glad to."

With the two of them working, it was done in no time flat, and then Henry went about laying the wood.

"Let's start with the kindling first," he said. "You girls set the thinnest pieces in the middle of the hole."

Henry picked up the largest log, which had demanded Ruth and Talley's combined strength to drag here, and he easily carried it over to the pit. Using the ax Daddy had brought, he chopped it into smaller pieces. Within a half hour, the wood had been arranged by size and the fire laid.

Ruth and Talley returned to the hotel and picked up the stack of quilts for guests who forgot their blankets. (Someone always forgot something.)

A few guests, including the Manchester family, appeared at the top of the dune. Pete Jr. ran ahead and came straight to the firepit, glancing quickly at Ruth before ducking his head and hurrying toward the unlighted wood. Bonnie and her friends Jessie and Dora moved more slowly, as if they were worried about looking as childish as Pete. So they sauntered, pausing to whisper something to the others as they looked toward Ruth.

Mr. and Mrs. Manchester picked up one of the blankets and spread it out next to the Osborns and sat down. Each had a drink in hand, and Mrs. Manchester's face was flushed. Safe bet it was the booze or a fight with her husband.

Bonnie, Dora, and Jessie laughed, looked toward Ruth, and then went back to whispering.

It set her teeth on edge when they acted like they knew better than everyone else. They'd been doing it a lot this week, and she was finding it harder to brush off the hurt feelings.

Talley leaned close to Ruth's ear. "We should find something to whisper about them too."

Ruth looked up at Talley, surprised to see the determination in her eyes. "Like what?"

"Maybe Bonnie has big feet. Maybe Jessie's face is too wide. And Dora's a little too tall."

When Ruth looked at the girls again, her gaze moved from Jessie's face to Bonnie's feet to Dora's legs. She giggled.

"Melons, bushels of cornstalks, and beanpoles," Talley said.

"That's mean," Ruth said.

"Where I come from, family sticks together, no matter what."

Ruth laughed, seeing more grit in Talley's expression. "I think you might be the toughest of us all."

"No, that's you, Ruth. Hands down."

Henry's gaze looked past Ruth, and for a moment his jaw dropped before he snapped it closed. Ruth turned and saw Carlotta wearing an emerald-green dress that hugged her curves. She wasn't wearing shoes, but wedge sandals dangled from her manicured fingers.

She moved slow and steady, knowing as she approached that several of the fathers had shifted their gazes to her. She never sneaked into a room. She always made sure everyone not only saw her coming but had a moment to pause and admire her as they stole second looks.

Carlotta approached Ruth and Talley, smiling. "Evening, ladies. Looks like you've built a very fine fire."

"Daddy's about to light it," Ruth said.

Henry cleared his throat.

"Carlotta, this is Mr. Henry Anderson," Ruth said. "He works here most summers."

Henry extended his hand to Carlotta. "Nice to meet you, Carlotta." His drawl deepening, he drew out her name in a slow, meandering way. Blue eyes studied Carlotta as if she were the only woman in the world. "Have we met before?"

Carlotta smiled but didn't seem flustered by his attention. "No, I don't think so. I understand you're the man with the ghost stories."

His chuckle was deep, husky. "Mostly they're tales of pirates and treasure, but I'm sure there'll be a ghost or two for Ruth's sake."

"Ruth," Daddy said. "Want to help me light the fire?"

"Yes!"

"Where's your mama?" Daddy asked.

"Still in the kitchen."

Daddy looked toward the dunes. "We best be quick about it, girls, before she catches us."

Ruth and Talley quickly followed him over to the driest kindling, and he reached in his pocket for the silver lighter engraved with another person's initials. He flipped open the top and flicked his thumb over the flint. Several times sparks snapped until finally one caught and a flame danced to life. "Get me some twigs."

Ruth bundled dried weeds with the smallest branches and held them close to the flame. The brittle ends quickly caught, and Daddy took the bundle from her and placed it on the pile. The fire hungrily bit into the wood and then licked along the branches arranged into a tripod.

Henry excused himself from Carlotta and loaded up his arms with logs. He knelt by the pit and carefully fed the flames with wood. Soon the blaze danced tall and crackled as it devoured the driftwood.

Mama came down over the dune carrying a basketful of marshmallows and long twigs sharpened at the tips. Her gaze cut to the flames and Ruth's proximity to the fire. A brow rose. Daddy shrugged, winked at his wife.

Mama shook her head as a smile tried to break free.

"Go on, girls," Daddy said. "Back away from the flames, or she'll skin all our hides."

The heat of the blaze warmed Ruth's skin like the midday sun. "You just charm her like you always do."

Daddy chuckled. "I'll do my best."

Mama had changed her dress and put on lipstick, making her look younger and less tired than earlier today. The children gathered around her asking for sticks and marshmallows. Ruth hurried toward her mother and took the basket as she handed out supplies. The girls dutifully centered their marshmallows on their twigs, whereas the boys appeared more interested in sword fights.

Ruth watched as Carlotta and Henry stood by the wreck, their bodies relaxed and their smiles easy. It didn't take much to see that they liked each other. Ruth had always wondered who her mama was but never thought much about her real daddy. She reckoned it had to be someone tall and good looking like Henry because Carlotta wouldn't settle for less.

Mama approached Carlotta and Henry, and the three spoke a moment before Mama clapped her hands and got everyone's attention.

She introduced Carlotta, and everyone applauded. Her popularity had grown each night, and tonight's performance had drawn several locals and visitors from other hotels.

Mama smiled, doing her best to look relaxed, and she welcomed everyone to the Seaside Resort beach. When it came to tasks, logistics, and hard work, Mama was in her element. But in front of everyone, she looked unsure, timid even.

"You did not come here to see me," Mama said over a few lingering conversations. "I have two special guests for you tonight. First, Carlotta DiSalvo, fresh from the showboat the *Maisy Adams*."

As Mama moved beside Ruth, Carlotta stepped forward, thanking Mama. "Let's all give Edna, Jake, Ruth, and Talley a hand. Without them, we would not be under the clear sky tonight, enjoying this lovely fire."

The guests clapped, and she waited until they grew very quiet. She set her sandals down and began to tap her foot. Her fingers snapped again to a tune only she heard. Once everyone's attention was focused on her, she began, *"Blue moon . . ."*

Her voice caught on the wind and drifted above the waves and the fire's hiss. *"Blue moon . . ."*

Henry stood by the fire, his hands shoved in his pockets, his gaze transfixed by Carlotta's voice like she was a siren come to life. He shifted from foot to foot and drew in a breath.

She finished the song on a high note and then launched into several livelier tunes. When she ended her set, the audience, now numbering over forty, clapped.

As she held up her hands, Carlotta's eyes danced with mischief as she waited for the crowd to settle down. "Are you ready for a real treat?"

"Yes" murmured over the crowd.

"I didn't hear you," Carlotta said as she cupped her ear. "Was that a yes?"

Several folks laughed and shouted louder, "Yes!"

"I'm sorry?" she said, teasing. "Are you ready for a treat?"

This time the crowd yelled a resounding "Yes!"

"Well, that's more like it. Because I'm going to introduce you to a man I think many of you already know, Mr. Henry Anderson. I've heard he's spun some tales before this crowd in years past, but this year, he has a story that's far more intriguing, perhaps even a little darker and scarier."

A ripple of laughter rumbled over the crowd.

"Mr. Anderson, would you join me up here?" Carlotta asked.

Henry pulled his hands from his pockets, moving toward her with long strides. He stood by her side, towering over her by at least five inches.

She slipped her arm around his waist, as if they were old friends. "He's going to tell you about this very shipwreck and the tale of the lost souls that were aboard."

Henry looked down at her, seeming a little surprised, either by her touch or her challenge to top her performance. If anyone knew anything about Henry Anderson, it was that he never backed down from a challenge.

Carlotta stepped aside, then picked up her shoes and moved toward the fire that blazed behind her, creating an otherworldly glow.

"This ship was called the *Liberty T. Mitchell.*" Henry looked back at the ship. "She was a proud, sleek clipper who set sail eighty years ago."

Henry ran his hand over the wood, as if petting one of the wild horses that roamed near the Currituck lighthouse to the north, then easily climbed up on the ocean-worn beams and walked along the narrow edge. He moved to the bow and paused, like the captain on the ship might have, and scanned the calm waters of the Atlantic. "The *Liberty T. Mitchell* set sail on a calm day. There was just the right amount of wind to fill her sails, and the old-timers didn't sense any storms on the horizon. The voyage from Charleston, South Carolina, to New York was expected to go quickly and smoothly."

Ruth looked at Talley, who stared at Henry as if he were about to shout *boo* at her. She nudged the older girl with her elbow and whispered, "It'll be fun. You'll see."

Talley shook her head. "I don't know."

As Mama came up behind Ruth and Talley, Henry walked around the deck and then faced the crowd. "But if you were to ask the captain about the upcoming voyage, he would've told you he was worried. He felt like the entire journey was doomed. And no matter how calm the skies, he couldn't shake the fear that his ship was cursed."

Henry grinned, but this time all traces of humor darkened into something more secretive, malevolent even. "Why was it cursed, you ask?"

His gaze scanned the crowd, which was rumbling with nervous laughter.

"The single female passenger on the *Liberty T. Mitchell* was Francesca Wentworth, and she was the greatest beauty in Charleston. Her father was Charles Wentworth, a local judge who had a plantation that was believed to be one of the most productive in the region. Every eligible man in the city courted Francesca."

He rubbed his hands together, looking toward the sky and then back at the crowd. "But the truth was the judge had a secret. He had a gambling problem, and he was in deep debt. He was facing certain ruin until an industrialist from New York, Jerrod Rathbone, offered to settle his debts in exchange for Francesca's hand in marriage." He shook his head. "Francesca didn't want to marry, but what choice did she have? So the couple were wed in a lavish ceremony and honeymooned in Charleston. No one saw the couple for six weeks, and when they reappeared, Francesca was noticeably thinner and paler. She was supposed to leave with her husband on the next voyage, but her mother, believing Francesca was pregnant, begged Jerrod to let her remain until the baby was born. He agreed."

Ruth leaned close to Talley. "The bad guys in Henry's stories are always rich."

"Why?"

Ruth shrugged. "He has no use for them, I guess."

"Francesca improved immediately after her husband left, and seven months later, she delivered a baby girl. Francesca wanted to stay with her parents, but Jerrod demanded his wife's and daughter's return. Francesca pleaded with her parents to let her and her daughter stay, but neither could afford the debts Jerrod now held."

Henry paused, allowing the silence to draw out the suspense. "Francesca took matters into her own hands and found a local Gullah woman and asked for a protection charm. She paid the woman in gold and received a magic charm designed to sink *Liberty T. Mitchell* if the captain insisted on delivering her to her husband. She didn't tell anyone about her visit to the Gullah woman, but Charleston was a small town in 1870, and word got around."

"The sea captain knew?" Talley asked Henry.

He nodded, narrowing his one eye. "He sure did. But if he told his crewmen, they would quit, and there would be hell to pay if he didn't deliver Francesca to her husband. He was caught between the devil and the deep blue sea."

"How could a charm sink a ship?" Bonnie asked.

Henry paced the deck. Behind him, the mellowing sun burned bright orange. He looked over his shoulder at the water and then back at the crowd. "The charm summoned sea monsters," he said.

Several of the dads chuckled, Mr. Manchester looked annoyed, and the mothers, including Mrs. Manchester, were watching Henry closely, many clearly admiring his physique. The children, including Bonnie, Dora, and Jessie, huddled closer.

"The voyage started out just fine," Henry continued. "No troubles. Smooth waters. And then about fifteen miles from these shores, after the captain refused to divert the ship, a storm came out of the south. Poseidon had unleashed his dragons, and their swiping tails churned up the ocean."

"What happened to Francesca?" Carlotta asked.

Henry's gaze lingered on Carlotta a beat, and then it wandered over the crowd. "She and her baby were huddled in their cabin as the ship ran aground and the waves began crashing into the vessel and flooding the deck. It was a terrible night. Rain. Lightning. High waves. The ship began to list. The sailors panicked because many didn't know how to swim." Henry shook his head. "Francesca was terrified as she realized her bargain with the Gullah woman had come to life. As the water filled her cabin, she opened a chest filled with blankets and nestled her baby inside. She placed a small cross with the child, praying the sea demons would take her instead of her child."

The crowd was quiet, everyone paying attention to Henry. He jumped down off the wreck. Like Carlotta, he liked his place on the stage.

"When the locals here came across the grounded vessel on shore, they immediately plundered her riches. As they were stripping the *Liberty T. Mitchell* clean, there was no sign of anyone. And then one of the men heard a baby crying. When they went to investigate, they found a baby girl in the chest, wrapped in a blanket and wailing as if her life depended on it."

Ruth watched Carlotta carefully, searching for signs that this story had struck a chord in her. Was she remembering the night she'd left Ruth?

"You found me in a pink blanket, right, Mama?" Ruth whispered.

Her mother laid her hand on Ruth's shoulder. Emotion tightened her voice. "All I remember is your sweet face," she whispered.

Ruth leaned closer. She wanted to ask Mama about Carlotta, but the words got trapped in her throat.

"What about Francesca and the sailors?" Bonnie asked.

Henry paused, letting his crowd stew just a little. "The sailors' bodies all washed up on shore, but there was never any sign of Francesca. And many locals reported seeing an Irish wolfhound running along the dunes, but no one ever caught the beast. Some said he'd arrived on the wrecked vessel. The only survivor was the baby."

"What happened to her?" Ruth asked.

"Taken in by one of the villagers, I hear. Beyond that, I don't know." He swiped his pointed finger across the crowd. "Are you wondering where the ghosts are in my story?"

Nervous chuckles swept the crowd.

"The ghosts of those sailors and poor Francesca are here now, walking these shores. And they will until the sea takes this vessel back into the dark waters. If you hear a wolfhound howling or a woman wailing for her lost baby, you'll know they're from the *Liberty T. Mitchell.*"

"What does Francesca's ghost look like?" Talley asked.

"I've never seen her with my own two eyes, but it's said she is as pale as the moon, and her long blonde hair is tangled with seaweed and seashells. Her eyes, I'm told, glow in the dark."

Mrs. Manchester downed the last of her drink and laughed. "A tall tale that'll ensure none of our kids sleep tonight."

Henry eyed the woman, but there was no hint of apology in his expression.

"Perhaps another song from Miss Carlotta?" Edna asked.

Carlotta had grown solemn during the story, but years of entertaining kicked into gear, and her lips widened. "I'd say that's just what the doctor ordered."

As Carlotta sang, the mood of the crowd lightened, and by the time she had finished, the smiles were less nervous.

Talley leaned close to Ruth. "I'm going to sleep with one eye open all night."

"Don't be silly. We were out here this morning, and we saw no ghosts. We'll be fine."

"But what if we see a ghost?" Talley asked.

"Then we'll ask her how she's doing and offer her a towel and a cold soda," Ruth said.

"You can't do anything for a ghost," Talley said.

"Why not? I bet they got wants and needs just like we do. If they didn't, they wouldn't be wandering in the dark with glow eyes."

"Don't say that!" Talley gasped.

Ruth's eyes widened, and she held up her hands and clawed at the air. "Gloooow eyes!"

Mama cleared her throat as she came up behind them, her arms filled with sandy blankets. "Ruth, looks like you're scaring Talley."

Ruth lowered her arms, pouting only a little. "Just talking about Francesca and everyone that died on that ship."

Mama handed a corner of the blanket to Ruth and took the other end, and together they shook off the sand. "Don't let Henry's stories get into your heads, girls."

"Do you think Francesca was real, Aunt Edna?" Talley asked.

"Henry loves a good yarn, and tonight he was showing off more than normal," Mama said, folding the blanket.

For Carlotta, Ruth reasoned. He'd looked at the singer like a starving man stared at pork barbecue cooked on the spit all day.

"Don't put any stock in his tall tales," Mama added. "There's no ghosts."

"But the ship is here, and whoever was on it likely died, right?" Talley asked.

Mama shrugged. "Unless the surfmen on duty were able to save them."

"Do you think they were saved?" Talley was determined to get her happy ending.

"Of course," Mama said.

Ruth winked at Talley. "Definitely."

"My mama always said spirits walk the earth because they're trying to fix a mistake or they've lost something," Talley reasoned.

"What kind of mistake did Francesca make?" Ruth asked.

"She went to that witch woman," Talley said. "And she left her baby behind."

"Sometimes a mother makes a hard choice out of love." Mama handed the edges of another blanket to Talley and Ruth.

"Don't matter why she left her," Talley said as she shook the blanket. "The truth is she did, and it bothers her to this day."

Pensive, Mama took the blanket and folded it. "You might be right about that."

Ruth's face burned as she stared at Carlotta. Had she come back to the Seaside Resort looking for her? Did she see traces of familiarity in Ruth's eyes, recognize the shape of her ears or the slant of her nose?

While she gathered up the folded blankets, Ruth searched Carlotta's smiling face as she chatted with a guest. She still saw no traces of herself, no matter how hard she searched. Carlotta liked taking her pictures, and Ruth enjoyed drawing. That could be a connection, but it was flimsier than eyes, noses, or even hands that looked the same.

Mama laid a hand on Ruth's shoulder. "It's time to get back to what matters and not fool around with these stories."

Ever since Ruth could talk, she had never been afraid of asking any question. Until now.

CHAPTER NINETEEN
RUTH

Thursday, June 22, 1950, 11:00 a.m.

The next few days ambled along as summer heat took hold of the days. Carlotta rarely appeared before noon, and when she did, she had her camera with her. She was never shy about asking for a picture and yesterday had grouped Talley and Ruth with Dora, Jessie, and Bonnie. The mainland girls had been charmed by Carlotta's easy manner and dutifully lined up, not a sneer between them. Next she'd turned her camera to the mothers sitting by the pool, and they, too, were delighted, each of them sitting up taller and thrusting out their chests slightly as they smiled. The evening shows doubled with each performance, and to accommodate the crowds, Mama placed all the restaurant chairs by the pool.

Ruth hadn't found the courage to speak to Carlotta. She delivered her lunch each day, and they talked about Whiskey, her sketches, and Carlotta's life on the showboat. But there'd been no mention of babies in pink blankets.

Now as Ruth stood in the towel hut, she watched Ann Manchester marching across the pool deck toward her mother and knew it was trouble. No one rushed toward Mama with such purpose with a compliment or a kind word. Ruth continued to fold towels but slowed her motions as she listened.

"Edna, I'm missing several pieces of jewelry," Mrs. Manchester said. "I left them on my dresser last night, and they aren't there now."

Mama's shoulders straightened as they did when facing a challenge. "When did you notice the pieces were missing?"

"When I woke up this morning."

Mrs. Manchester had staggered away from last night's performance early. It was becoming her nightly routine now that Mr. Manchester had arrived. He hadn't followed her back to their room but continued to drink and watch Carlotta. "Are you sure you haven't mislaid them?"

"I did not lose them. I put them in the same spot every night," she said tightly.

This type of drama played out in different versions every summer. Missing watches, shoes, earrings, necklaces—people on vacation were out of their normal routines and made more mistakes than normal.

"Would you like me to help you search your room?" Mama asked. "I'm very good at finding lost things."

"I've been through the room twice, Edna." Mrs. Manchester's tone tightened with each word.

"But I know the rooms very well," Mama insisted. "I've touched every nook and cranny in the bungalows over the years. I can tell you where the floors creak, windows stick, and the door hinges squeak."

Mrs. Manchester's face wrinkled as frustration flared in her eyes. "You won't find them in my room. In fact, I suggest you search your maid's room or the rooms of that singer. Showboat people aren't the most reliable, and cleaning staff often have sticky fingers. I could swear that Talley was wearing an old blouse of mine."

Mama's lips settled into a stark line. "I don't have a thief in my employ. I'm very careful about who I hire."

Blame traced across Mrs. Manchester's face. "We never know people as well as we think."

216

"Talley and I will go to your room now," Mama insisted.

"My husband is sleeping," she added quickly. "Once he's up, then you can clean and search to your heart's content."

"Very well." Mama stood still as stone as she watched Mrs. Manchester walk away. The fingers of her left hand flexed, but she said nothing.

Ruth hurried to her mother. "Talley and Carlotta didn't steal anything. They're good people, Mama."

Mama tucked a stray strand behind her ear. "I know that."

"Why's Mrs. Manchester saying things like this?"

"She's not been happy for a long time."

"Why?"

Mama shoved out a sigh. "Between you and me, Mr. Manchester is making life difficult for her. He's drinking heavily, like his father did when their family vacationed here before the war."

"He vacationed at the Seaside Resort?"

"His family were regulars for many summers. That's how he met his wife. She was working here as a waitress."

"Mrs. Manchester worked here?"

"It's good, honest work." Mama went silent for a moment.

"She acts like she was born rich."

"She married it."

"I don't like Mr. Manchester."

"Neither do I."

Hearing her mother's unvarnished honesty was a first for Ruth. "Maybe they shouldn't come back next year," Ruth said.

Mama pulled off her apron. "I'll be right back."

"Where are you going?" Ruth asked.

"To talk to Carlotta."

"Why?"

"Better we have a conversation now, in case Mrs. Manchester decides to make more trouble and call the sheriff."

"Can I come?"

"No, you stay here. I'll be back shortly."

Mama handed her apron to Ruth and then headed across the hot sand, oblivious to the heat and sun.

Ruth should have let Mama take care of the matter. Her mother managed every detail of the hotel, from guest registration to book-keeping to figuring ways to make more money. She helped Ruth with her math homework, kept Daddy on an even keel, and always had a job for Henry if he needed extra money. And she would see that Mrs. Manchester didn't cause trouble.

Still, Ruth had a vested interest in Carlotta, who could have been family. She followed in her mother's footsteps, careful to hold back so she wouldn't be seen. As the front screened door to Carlotta's cottage closed, she crept up the back stairs in time to hear her mother say, "Ann Manchester is making trouble."

"She's always enjoyed the drama," Carlotta said with some disinter-est. "*Mrs.* Manchester could stand to drink a little less. It would make life easier."

"Agreed," Mama said. "I'm worried her nerves are getting the bet-ter of her. She's always been a nervous one. She suggested Talley might also be a problem."

Carlotta shook her head. "Talley is sweet. She wouldn't know how to lie, even if you paid her."

Mama sighed. "She reminds me of her mother. Honest and naive."

"When is the last time you were back home?" Carlotta asked.

It had never occurred to Ruth that Carlotta would know anything about Mama's life before the resort.

"I haven't been back," Mama said.

"Why not?" Carlotta asked.

"Have you ever visited?" Mama challenged.

"No, but I write to my mother regularly."

Mama cleared her throat. "Patsy loves you very much."

A silence settled between them before Carlotta said, "Does Ruth know about the family?"

"The bare details."

Ruth didn't understand the unspoken meanings and crept closer to the door.

"None of us needs or wants trouble, especially now," Mama said.

"I'll be on my best behavior," Carlotta said.

"Thank you." As Mama exited the front door, Ruth crouched low, waiting for her to clear the dune before she headed out.

Footsteps creaked in the house, and the sleeping porch door opened. Carlotta looked at Ruth, her brow arched. "Does this cottage have a rat problem?"

Ruth rose and was relieved to see the amusement dancing in Carlotta's eyes. "I was worried."

"About what?"

"All the trouble," Ruth said.

"It's nothing your mother and I can't handle. We've crossed paths with trouble before."

"How do you know about Talley and Mama's family?" Ruth asked.

"You should ask your mother."

"Then she would know I've been snooping."

Carlotta cocked a brow. "It's okay for me to find you spying but not her?"

"She wouldn't appreciate it." Mama rarely raised her voice, but her disappointed looks were positively withering.

"What makes you think I do?" Carlotta asked.

"You're cooler than Mama."

"Am I?"

"Well, yeah. You travel around and see all kinds of things."

"Your mother has lived a full life, Ruth. She's more open minded than you think."

Carlotta's defense of her mother surprised Ruth. "You still haven't told me how you know Talley's family."

A crooked smile tipped the edges of her lips. "In that part of the state the world is small. Everyone knows everyone."

"And you knew Mama's family?"

"Some, yes."

"What are they like?"

"Nice enough, I suppose. Good, hardworking people who go to church every Sunday and read their Bible daily."

Ruth's mind shifted between Carlotta's, Talley's, and Mama's faces. Each was so different, and yet strands of familiarity threaded between them. Was it the eyes, noses, or tilt of their heads?

Carlotta walked down the porch steps. "If you want to know more about your mother's family, ask her."

"She never wants to talk about before." An old frustration twisted inside Ruth. "She always changes the subject."

"Then you should respect that. Not everyone wants to revisit the past."

"But I want to know more." That persistent hunger in her growled and grumbled. "Did you know I'm adopted?" She whispered the unspoken truth no one ever discussed.

Carlotta's lowering gaze hid something. Surprise? A realization? "Are you?"

"Mama said she found me in one of the bungalows, wrapped in a blanket. She said I was wailing my head off."

Her eyes softened. "You were a talkative baby? Imagine that."

Hints of brittle humor relieved some of the nervous energy buzzing in Ruth's ears. "Mama never found any traces of the woman who left me in that room."

"I can't imagine anyone sneaking in and out of this resort without your mother knowing."

Ruth studied her face closely, searching for any clue that she was that woman. "Are you saying Mama lied to me?"

"You're overthinking this," Carlotta said quickly. "You have a mother who loves you. I've met too many people on the road who would give anything to live the life you've had."

"But I have another mother out there, somewhere. And she doesn't love me." The worry spilled out of her like a crashing wave.

Carlotta's eyes held Ruth's. "Why do you say that?"

Tears welled in her eyes. "She left me alone in a hotel room in the middle of winter. Who does that to a baby?"

"You were wrapped in a blanket, in a warm room, and I would guess it wasn't long before Edna found you. Like I said, no one sneaks on this property without your mother knowing it."

"Mama said the woman must have arrived during the storm, delivered me, and then left."

"I've known of women who were alone with a baby on the way. Say what you want about this woman, but she cared for you in the only way she could."

"Are you *her*?" Ruth whispered.

Silence cut between them as Carlotta's expression grew tender. "No, Ruth, I am not."

Ruth studied the eyes that looked nothing like her own. Would Carlotta lie to her?

As if reading her mind, Carlotta said, "I promise you, I did not give birth to you."

Ruth swiped away a tear, seeing the truth in her gaze. All the anticipation that had built up in her the last few days burst like an overinflated balloon. "I thought you were."

"I'm not, honey."

She suddenly felt foolish standing here now. So stupid, to let her imagination mingle with her need to know. "Sorry."

"There is nothing to apologize for. When was the last time you spoke with your mother about this?"

"It's been a while."

"Talk to her again, Ruth. You're older now, and she might give you more information."

"Maybe."

"Talk to her, Ruth."

❦

CARLOTTA

Most nights Carlotta slept well enough, but tonight, she lay awake staring at the ceiling. Old feelings she had pushed aside a long time ago had found her when she'd looked into Ruth's eyes today. She wasn't sure what she'd hoped to accomplish by this sojourn by the shore and now wondered if it had been a mistake. There certainly were livelier places where she could have gone and made more money.

She had never handled loss well, and when faced with it, she ran. "Better not to dwell. Keep looking forward."

In the kitchen, she poured herself a whiskey and grabbed a packet of cigarettes and a lighter before heading to the sleeping porch. She sipped her whiskey and then, holding a cigarette between her lips, flicked the lighter until the flame flared. She held it to the tip and inhaled.

Carlotta stared out over the calm waters and blew the smoke out slowly. She didn't smoke often, because too much irritated her voice, but there were some nights that warranted a whiskey and a smoke.

Her mind turned back to Edna's and then Ruth's visits today. For all the words, so much remained unspoken.

She could not really ease Ruth's concerns, but she would handle Ann Manchester. She had learned to read couples, and though some were happy, most drifted into a no-man's-land of obligation, children, debt, and work. The Manchesters were tied not by love but by spite and stubbornness. Easier for Ann to accuse hotel staff of stealing than

222

admit to her husband she was too drunk to remember what she'd done with her jewelry.

As she stared through the smoke coiling around her head, she saw a man walking barefoot along the beach, his pants rolled up to his calves. A cigarette glowed from his right hand.

She thought for a moment it might be Mr. Manchester. His attention was never far from her when he was near. But as this man grew closer, she recognized his unhurried but purposeful pace and squared shoulders. Henry.

Allowing smoke to spill over her lips, she stabbed the butt into an ashtray. She and Henry had been flirting the last couple of days, each always finding a reason to tease or compliment the other. Moistening her lips, she clicked on a porch light, knowing he would notice.

He paused, the tip of his cigarette glowing red, and she felt his stare. In the ring of light, she rose and adjusted the tie of her robe.

Henry walked down the beach another fifty yards past her cottage, triggering disappointment. Was she losing her touch, or had she misread his lingering stares?

He stopped, turned around. His return trip was a bit faster, and when he shifted toward the dunes near her cottage, she smiled. Her touch was just fine.

Henry climbed the dunes and moved toward the stairs leading to the porch. He rested one foot on the bottom step as the moonlight caught the flash of even white teeth. "You're up late."

"It was your ghost story," she teased. "I still keep waiting for Francesca or the wolfhound to come floating down the beach. The guests will talk about it for years."

He climbed the stairs, opened the screened door, but didn't enter. "I always say, if you do something, do it well."

"Would you like a drink?" she asked.

"I have sand on my feet."

She looked down at his naked feet and ankles caked in damp, moist sand. "I'm sure you can figure out what to do."

While he sat on the stairs and dusted off his feet, Carlotta retrieved a second glass. The steady squeak of the porch door closing sent a slow thrill down her spine.

This close, he looked taller as he stared at her camera. "You a photographer?"

She handed him his glass. "I dabble. Strictly for fun. I travel so much the places blur, and the photos help me remember where I've been."

He took a sip. "Nice."

"Don't be boring, and don't drink bad whiskey."

"A woman after my own heart."

She topped off her glass. "Where did you come up with that story?"

"Pieces of the truth woven into a few embellishments."

"And what part was true?"

"The ship was likely called the *Liberty T. Mitchell*, which was headed from South Carolina to New York."

"And the baby?"

He gently swirled the amber liquid in his glass. "There were some legends surrounding a baby who was found in the shipwreck. Word is she was raised by locals."

"Why wasn't the child returned to her father?" Carlotta asked.

"As the tale goes, there was a note tucked in her blanket that stated she was safer in God's hands than her father's."

A gnawing curiosity left her a little breathless. "Who told you this story?"

"My grandmother," he said. "She knows most of the secrets on the Outer Banks."

"Maybe she's simply a gifted storyteller like you?"

Eyes glistened. "She very well may be. But my grandmother retold this story all her life, right up until her last days, when she was blind and bedridden. She insisted a shipwrecked orphan lived among us."

It was the kind of story a girl told herself when her mother left her. Ruth most likely had told herself similar stories. "Did she ever say if this girl was happy?"

"She lived a good life, with loving parents, according to my grandmother."

Carlotta eyed him, trying to determine if there was truth in this storyteller's happy ending. "And the orphan never had a desire to find this wealthy father?"

"She was happy. Said there was never a reason to go looking for trouble." From around his neck, he removed a silver ball chain with dog tags and a loop of wire holding a delicate cross. "When I joined the navy, my grandmother gave it to me."

"In your story, Francesca left a cross with her baby."

"Some whispered that my grandmother was that baby," he said.

Her heart beat faster for the mother and child separated by circumstance. "But she never said for sure?"

Windswept hair brushed over his forehead and eye patch, giving him the look of a sweet devil. "The Andersons never let truth get in the way of a good story."

She was charmed. "My goodness. That's quite a tale." She ran her thumb over the imprint of his name. "Atlantic or Pacific?"

"Atlantic."

She'd sung to enough soldiers struggling to leave the war behind. Many could during the daylight hours, but at night, near the witching hour, the ghosts returned to haunt. She handed him back the tags and cross. "Looks like your grandmother was your good luck charm."

"I kept her with me every step of the way." He strung the chain around his neck again but left it hanging roguishly outside his shirt.

"What has you out walking on the beach this late at night?" she asked softly.

"Why are you up?" he countered.

"I suppose we all have ghosts," Carlotta said.

Moonlight illuminated the amber depths of his whiskey swirling slowly in his glass. "Why would a lovely woman like you be haunted by ghosts?"

She had always known she was attractive. The boys had come sniffing around the house when she was thirteen. She'd run away at fifteen, and by sixteen, she'd fallen for a young man with a gentle heart and a powerful need to wander. "Who doesn't have ghosts?"

He regarded her over the glass lingering at his lips. "A husband? Boyfriend?"

"A restless soul who joined the navy in '37. He died of a fever that same year. For all his yearning for glory, it was sickness that got him." It had been a long time since she'd talked about Danny, who she'd met in Norfolk after one of her first shows on the *Maisy Adams*. After the ship had left harbor, he'd followed her to the next port of Cape Charles and after that West Point. She'd loved him, would have married him. And then he was dead. Even now, she couldn't bring herself to retell their story in great detail.

"He was willing to fight if it came to it. He gets high marks for that."

"Thank you."

"There anyone else in your life?"

"No," she said. "I travel too much to find anything permanent."

He sipped his drink. "What about on the showboat?"

"Most of the men on the ship are married. They've created an act with their wives. And I have a strict rule about married men."

"Well, in case you're wondering, I'm not married."

"You seem like a good catch for any girl around here. I've noticed the way the female guests look at you."

"They're trouble." A slight humorless smile tugged the corner of his mouth. "I learned that lesson long ago."

She finished her whiskey and set her glass down. "I'm not fond of extended engagements. A few nights in port hits the sweet spot."

He stared at her a long moment and then stepped forward. Inches separated them, but the energy crackling from their bodies reached out, collided, and coiled. Her body tingled.

He cupped the side of her face and slowly caressed her jawline with his thumb.

There'd been men since Danny, but not as many as most assumed. She was discerning. Careful. Because men, as fun as they were, could be trouble.

Carlotta leaned into a kiss and slid her hand down his flat belly. When her fingers brushed the hardness, desire melted through her. Sometimes a little trouble was worth the risk.

CHAPTER TWENTY

IVY

Monday, January 24, 2022, 8:00 a.m.

Ivy had cleaned and cleared out some of the last pockets of clutter. Finally, she had fallen into a restless sleep around one. Her unconscious mind must have known she'd forgotten to set her alarm because her sleep was filled with quirky dreams about shipwrecks, ghosts, and finally the howl of a large dog.

Suddenly fully awake, she sat up immediately. She swung her legs over the side of the bed, looked out the window over the dunes, and saw a large dog bounding toward the ocean. The wolfhound. She'd have dashed after the dog if not for the time. Eight a.m. Forty-five minutes until she was supposed to pick up Dani. Shit.

Within a half hour, she'd taken Libby out, fed her, showered, and dressed in dark leggings and that classic black V-neck sweater and boots. With less than twenty minutes to go, she drove from Nags Head into the town of Duck.

She missed Dani's house on the first pass, made a U-turn at the Wee Winks convenience store, and retraced to the house with a bright-yellow mailbox marked 272. She pulled down the wooded drive toward the small New England–style cottage located on a hill overlooking the

Currituck Sound. The house had been in the Manchester family since the early 1990s, when the main road had been paved only as far north as Duck. In those days, Pete Manchester had started buying up shore property when it was cheap. When selling started in the early 2000s, his values rose tenfold, and he made a fortune.

Ivy had been here more times than she could count. In the last dozen years, the house had gone through several renovations and was now covered in gray Shaker-style siding and black shutters. A sunporch addition faced the sound, primed to catch the blazing sunsets. A perfect artist's retreat.

She parked behind Dani's SUV and walked along the brick sidewalk to the front door adorned with a brass oval-ringed knocker.

Ivy knocked and listened inside to firm heeled steps approaching the door. She smoothed back her hair, suddenly wishing she had washed it and applied makeup because she would bet her net worth Dani had.

The door opened to Dani's tall, sleek frame. Hair in a ponytail, she wore a pink cowl-neck sweater, skinny jeans, and heeled black boots. Earrings dangled and sparkled.

"Are you sure we're going to a doctor's appointment?" Ivy asked. "You're dressed up."

Dani cocked a brow. "I'm always dressed up."

"True."

"Come inside while I grab my purse and phone."

Ivy stepped inside, closing the door behind her. Brightly colored works of art, carefully curated, filled all the walls. Impressed, she followed Dani into the kitchen and was met by an explosion of white marble countertops, custom kitchen stainless appliances, and wide-plank caramel wooden floors. On the large center island sat a hand-carved wooden bowl filled with lemons and apples.

"Place sure has changed since I was here last."

"Helps to be a decorator and work in a family construction business."

"Where does your dad live now?"

"He moved in with Dalton after I divorced Matthew. He said Bella and I needed our own place. I wanted him to stay, but he wouldn't hear of it."

"He's been batching it with Dalton for the last decade?"

"Dalton built a good-size garage for his truck and tools, and above it is Dad's apartment. It works out well for them both."

"I'm surprised Dalton doesn't have someone. He's been a catch since high school."

A grin tugged at Dani's lips. "He came close a couple of times but never sealed the deal with a ring. He admits he works too much to be a husband to anyone."

"I feel that pain," Ivy said. "I don't think I've made it past the third date in five years."

"You two are a lot alike." She dropped her cell phone in her purse. "Work, work, work."

"What's wrong with that?"

Dani snatched up her keys. "You tell me, *Ruth*."

"That so?"

"Take it as a compliment. If I had her drive, I'd have moved to New York and started a new life."

They stepped outside, and as Dani locked her front door, Ivy moved to her van. She turned on the engine, knowing the older car took longer to heat up.

Dani opened the front passenger door and glanced at the duct tape holding the tan leather of her seat together. "We can take my car?"

"Nah, I'm starting to bond with Mabel."

"Mabel?"

"My van. She has so much character; I think that she deserves a name."

Dani fingered the radio's broken volume button before she hooked her seat belt. "It would be comforting to know that we'll make it."

"We'll make it." Ivy wiggled the radio button and found the one channel it broadcast.

"No Bluetooth?"

"Built before it was invented."

Dani sighed. "Why did I bother to ask?"

Ivy wove along the highway through Southern Shores and took a right toward the Wright Memorial Bridge. "This is an eye appointment?"

Dani pulled large dark Jackie O–style glasses from her purse and slid them on. "That's right."

"You have to drive to Norfolk to see an eye doctor?"

"He's a specialist." She plucked an imaginary hair strand from her jeans and looked out the windshield toward the water.

"I've known you a long time, Dani. I'd say it's none of my business, but you know me. I've never shied away from the tough questions."

"No tough questions necessary. I just have an eye thing, and after the doc puts the drops in my eyes, I'll have to wait too long before I can drive home. I'm always at the house when Bella gets home from school."

Ivy had become the master of the dodge, and she could smell one a mile off. She also knew Dani well enough to know her old friend would dig her fancy heels in if Ivy pressed. She would find out what was going on, but all things came to those who were moderately patient.

Sunlight glistened on the water, and a crosswind from the north blew against the van as they neared the center of the bridge, forcing her to keep both hands on the wheel.

When she'd left the Outer Banks twelve years ago in her yellow Pacer, euphoria, fear, and nerves had tangled in her belly. But as she'd crossed the North Carolina line into Virginia, her resolve for a different life had frayed around the edges. Stubbornness had kept her going all the way through Virginia and Maryland and into Delaware. It wasn't until she saw the New Jersey state line that she had her first panic attack. She pulled into a rest stop, ordered a burger and fries, and sat in her car, staring at her cell phone. Once the burger's fat and carbohydrates had hit her brain, a little bravado returned. "If it sucks, I'll call tomorrow." She'd called the next day, told Ruth she had arrived safely and not to worry. If Ruth had heard the hesitation (which she always had), she'd said nothing.

And so it had gone for the next two months: panic attack, carbohydrates, and a call to Ruth to report good news only, no matter how dire. She'd never called Dani, fearing if she heard her friend's voice, the guilt over leaving would break her.

"I was surprised you didn't stay in town after Ruth's funeral," Dani said.

"I wanted to. But I had loose ends to tie up with my apartment and the restaurant. We get snarled in our lives, and it takes time to get free."

"It must have been hard to quit the job."

"In the end, leaving was easier than I imagined." It still stung that Mama Leoni had cut her loose so easily. A dozen years, and the woman hadn't batted an eye when she'd refused her request for leave. But again, she'd left her friends and family twelve years ago, leaving her own moral high ground shaky.

"New York has a vibe that's nothing like here. And I know that restaurant is missing your cooking."

"I've tried very hard not to check their social media page or any online comments about them."

"But . . ."

Ivy shrugged. "Recent Yelp reviews haven't been as great. I think they're struggling."

"Doesn't that give you a little satisfaction?"

"Not really. Maybe a little. But I remind myself that Vincenzo's hired me when I needed a job. I was at my wits' end when they took me on a trial basis."

"Don't feel too sorry for them. They had their chance to help you out, and they blew it."

"I had my chance to help you, and I blew it," Ivy said.

Dani shook her head. "Your leaving hurt, but it made me stronger."

They drove in silence for another forty-five minutes, with only the one country radio station to listen to. Ninety minutes after they'd left Dani's house, Ivy pulled into the medical complex. Dani directed her around the extensive parking lot and to a spot near a sleek building made of glass and chrome.

"Must be some kind of specialist," Ivy said.

"They're the best in the region." Dani got out of the car and closed the door, signaling she had no more to say.

Ivy followed her inside and up a bank of elevators to the third floor. Dani removed her dark glasses and easily located the practice's door, and they entered the plush waiting room. The walls were painted a pulsating blue, and the chairs were upholstered in vibrant reds. "It's a cheerful place."

"They believe in the power of color," Dani said.

"We eat with our eyes first."

"Something like that."

Ivy noted the nice coffee maker, the stack of magazines, and the television broadcasting the weather station's prediction of sunny skies.

Dani walked up to the receptionist. "I'm Dani Manchester, and I'm here for my appointment with Dr. Zacharias."

The receptionist smiled. "Yes, we have you here. Have a seat, and the nurse will be out for you in a moment."

"Thanks."

Ivy made herself a cup of coffee and offered it to Dani, who declined. She added two sugars and a cream and picked up a copy of the latest *Bon Appétit*. "Nice setup."

"Sometimes the appointments can take a couple of hours, so they like family to be comfortable."

"Will this take a couple of hours?" She'd banked on being gone five hours, which she hoped would not exceed Libby's maximum bladder time.

"This shouldn't take more than a half hour."

"No rush. If we run long, I can text Dalton and ask him to let Libby out."

"It won't take that long," Dani said with determined certainty.

Ivy sipped her coffee and was turning to the magazine's title page when the nurse called Dani's name. Without fanfare, Dani vanished down the hallway.

She shifted her attention to a brochure detailing the practice's mission statement, the list of their services, and the practitioners. She keyed in on Dr. Zacharias. Tall, with olive skin and a bright-white smile, he looked to be midforties. No wedding band. Dr. Hottie treated all forms of eye disease that extended beyond the average ophthalmologist's reach. "Stigma, my ass."

Ivy returned to the stylized platter of pasta with a red sauce, sprinkled with basil and flanked by a loaf of crusty bread. It looked nice, but she'd have done better.

She moved through the pages, pausing when she got to a restaurant profile of a former competitor. Luigi's was located down the block from Vincenzo's, and the two crews knew each other well and enjoyed a friendly rivalry.

Luigi had inherited the business from his father and grandfather and was now the primary chef. He was thirty-five but looked fifty. He'd once competed with Ivy in a local firehouse cooking competition. She'd beaten him. He was pissed.

"Look who's winning now," she grumbled as she turned the page.

She grazed through more glossy pictures of food and exotic locations. There'd been a time when this magazine and others like it would have fueled her dreams of a culinary future. Now she found herself wanting to tweak Ruth's fried-chicken and seafood-chowder recipes and maybe change the seasoning in her grandmother's coleslaw. There was also the barbecue recipe to update and the tempura-batter experiment she'd been mulling over.

The door opened, and Dani reappeared. "Ready?"

Ivy checked her watch and realized it had been forty minutes. She downed the last of her coffee, tossed the cup in the trash, and replaced the magazine. Glancing up, she caught a glimpse of Dani's watery, bloodshot eyes. "Everything all right?"

"Just the drops. They can be irritating."

That didn't ring true, but Ivy wasn't going to argue in the doctor's office. As soon as the elevator doors opened, Ivy hurried toward them and held the door open. Dani slid on her glasses and moved more slowly across the tiled floor. When she approached the doors, she slowed as if she wasn't quite sure where to stop.

"One step forward," Ivy said.

"I know that." And then, less sharply, "Thanks."

Ivy regarded her more closely now, not so sure she was seeing all that well. "Those must be some powerful drops."

"They are."

Ivy stayed close and opened the passenger-side door. Dani didn't complain as she slid into the seat, fumbled for her seat belt, and then hooked it.

Behind the wheel, Ivy started the engine and backed out of the spot. Neither spoke while Ivy navigated them out of Norfolk traffic and back onto the interstate. "I read the brochure. Dr. Zacharias is cute," Ivy said.

"He is," Dani said.

"He married?"

"You interested?"

"No, just thinking what a cute couple you two would make," Ivy said.

Dani brushed a piece of lint from her sleeve. "He's always very professional."

"All the more reason to want him," Ivy said.

"I've got bigger fish to fry than chasing my eye doctor."

"According to his brochure, he doesn't treat run-of-the-mill cases, Dani." Ivy let the comment stand, hoping Dani would spill.

"He does specialty cases as well as routine."

The nonanswer failed to deflect. "Tell me what's going on. This is the kind of errand your brother or father should have done. Not a questionable friend from the past."

"They're busy. And you're not questionable."

Was there a compliment buried in there? "That doesn't smell like the entire truth."

Dani rubbed her manicured fingers over the back of her neck. "The entire truth?"

"The last time you avoided the entire truth, we ended up not speaking for over a decade."

Dani sighed. "I'm losing my vision."

The words dangled between them as Ivy processed. "Like, you need better glasses?"

"Like, the glasses buy me some time, but by my midforties, I'll lose most of my sight. It's called retinitis pigmentosa. It's genetic."

"Who in your family had it?"

"I'm still not sure. I traced Mom's family back, and there's no blindness, but on Dad's side, I hit a brick wall with my grandmother, Ann. No one seems to know where she's from."

Ivy drew in a breath, held it before she slowly let it trickle over her lips. "Shit."

"My thoughts exactly." She adjusted her glasses. "I don't suppose there's a bottle of scotch rattling around in this van somewhere?"

She ignored the comment. "But you still drive."

"Only during the day when it's bright. I stopped driving at night last year after a fender bender. If I'm lucky, I'll be able to drive another decade. The hope is to make it beyond Bella's sixteenth birthday, and then she can get her driver's license and help out."

"What about Bella? Does she have any signs of the disease?"

"None. I've had her to Dr. Zacharias once, and he thinks she's in the clear. But we'll keep monitoring."

"Does she know?"

"About me? No. I'm not ready for that discussion. I want her to enjoy school and her friends without worrying about me. And she'll worry if I tell her."

Though Dalton had not said anything to Ivy about Dani, she was sure she'd have picked up on a worried glance or two, especially when the discussion of a puppy had come up. "You haven't told Dalton or your father, have you?"

"I haven't told them. Until now, I've not needed them. I've been able to make my appointments and modify enough to get by. But the days when I can function alone will come to an end."

"Did they really put drops in your eyes today?"

"They did. I've known for a couple of months I'd have to get a driver today. And my friend really did bail."

"I'm also assuming Matthew doesn't know."

"He does not. He'll be the last to find out. I don't need him micromanaging my life."

"He does have a tendency."

"Yes, he does."

"He wouldn't challenge you on your custody arrangement, would he?"

"I don't think he would, but I'm not putting anything related to Bella to chance."

"Why pull me into the loop?" Ivy asked.

"You're leaving soon, and you were also never the kind of person to get all worked up or make a fuss in the face of trouble. You put one foot in front of the other, just like Ruth did."

It made her sound a little robotic. "I've made a fuss before."

"When?"

"When I was in New York, I got worked up all the time."

"When your restaurant cut your salary, what did you say?"

"There wasn't much I could have said."

"Exactly. I would have been throwing plates. I threw a few after you left."

"I'm sorry."

"Don't be. Like I keep saying, you did us all a favor. And all your hard work put that place on the map."

"How do you know what I did for them?"

"I was already following your career when Ruth told me you were winning awards."

"Why?"

"You were my friend. And believe it or not, I was rooting for you. What happened between Matthew and me wasn't meant to hurt you."

A dozen years and success in her own right had allowed her to appreciate how her anger had propelled her during New York's early dark days. When the anger had faded, work had filled the void. She hadn't realized until now how alone she'd been.

Ivy tightened her hand on the steering wheel. "Is your vision the reason why you didn't move out of North Carolina?"

"Not at first. A baby and then a divorce within eighteen months were reasons enough. And then Matthew and I signed a custody agreement. We both agreed to live in North Carolina. Then I negotiated a deal on the gallery, and that took all my spare time to get it up and running. And then Dad hired me as the decorator for the company, which I really liked. I built a great life despite my dreams."

"When did you start to notice a change in your vision?"

"On Bella's eighth birthday party. We held it at night in the backyard, and as the sun set, the shadows were almost too deep and dark to navigate. Then it improved a little, and I convinced myself it was a onetime thing. When it came back, Ruth was the first person I told."

Her grandmother, in customary fashion, had not said a word. "What was her advice?"

"Live your life. Don't let the past or the future ruin right now."

"She gave me the same advice several times."

"And that's what I've done. But it's getting trickier to hide it."

Ivy heard Dani's fear and steered around it to the practical. "You won't be able to do it forever. And you have to tell Dalton and your dad."

"I will."

"When?"

"Soon. I'm still processing this latest vision shift for the worse. Every little bit I lose always catches me by surprise. It could improve again for a little while, but I'm not counting on it."

"Will you lose all your sight?"

"I have no way of knowing."

"Tell your family."

Worry carved creases at the corners of her eyes. "I will, but promise me you won't tell anyone."

"As long as I know you and Bella are safe, I'll keep my mouth shut. But if I think you're in trouble, I can't promise what I'll say."

"I'm asking you to keep this secret. You'll be gone soon, but I'll have to find a way to live this new life with these people."

"And I'm telling you, I will unless you or Bella are in danger."

"You don't get to dictate terms to me. You either keep the secret or you don't." Dani folded her arms over her chest and stared out her window. "I'd thought you'd be on my side."

"I am."

"Doesn't sound like it."

"If I didn't care, we wouldn't be having this discussion."

"Thank you for driving me today, but we're just old high school friends now. Neither of us owes the other anything."

CHAPTER
TWENTY-ONE
IVY

Monday, January 24, 2022, 1:00 p.m.

When Ivy pulled into Dani's driveway, a moody silence filled the car. They sat, neither moving until Ivy asked, "What can I do?"

"Nothing," Dani said. "It's not a fixable problem. But I'll figure it out."

"If you need anything . . ."

Dani reached for the door's handle. "Just keep my secret. I'll take care of the rest."

"I mean it. I will help you."

"Got it."

Ivy's grand exit twelve years ago had earned Dani's reticence. She might never fix the damage she'd done, but she could try. "Come see the pups anytime."

"Will do." Dani closed the door and walked toward her house.

For the first time, Ivy really paid attention to the way Dani moved and noticed the slight hesitancy in her steps, as if she were feeling her way along the ground, using touch to supplement her fading sight. When Dani opened the door, she didn't wave or smile before vanishing inside. Ivy backed out onto the street, wondering how she'd deal if her world were slowly going dark.

Twenty minutes later she pulled into her driveway and rushed up the stairs. Libby barked, and Ivy dashed to the kitchen island and dropped her keys and purse. "Miss Libby, I'm sorry."

Libby thumped her tail at the sound of Ivy's voice. The puppies jostled awake when their mother stood and moved toward Ivy. She picked Libby up and carried her out back toward the dunes. Libby ran around taking care of business as a cold January wind blew over beach grass. The sands had gathered around the shipwreck, and a portion of the interior beams had vanished. It wouldn't be long before the wreck was gone completely.

She stared up at the sky's vibrant blues and the stark whites of the buoyant clouds. A flock of gulls flew overhead, their long wings scoring the air. Closing her eyes, she tried to reimagine what she had just seen. How long could she keep this memory? How soon would the colors fade?

Even fully sighted, she could barely remember what her mother had looked like, and Ruth's face was already fading into the mist. People came and went from her life, and as painful as it could be, to have the entire world vanish from view was too much to consider.

Libby barked and trotted back toward Ivy, who picked her up. "Let's get you fed and change out your bedding." The dog licked her face.

Inside, she quickly swapped the blankets, carefully moving the puppies from old to new. Libby, as much as she seemed to like Ivy, kept a watchful eye on her as she handled her puppies.

Ivy held up the largest male and noted his eyes were barely beginning to open. His world was coming into view. She set the dog back down by his siblings and mother and left Libby to fuss and preen over her offspring until she was satisfied they were all still okay.

In the kitchen, Ivy made herself a pot of coffee, and after filling her mug, she sat at the dining room table and thumbed through the address book again, hoping she might have missed Carlotta's name. There was no address for Carlotta in the *C*s or *D*s, but Talley's name, initially listed under *J*, had been crossed out with a scrawled note to check *N*. In the *N*s the only entry was for a Mrs. Edward Newsome. Mrs. Newsome's address and phone number had changed several times.

Ivy shuffled through the black-and-white photos and found the picture of the young girls grouped together by the pool. She keyed in on the one with the light-colored ponytail. She glanced again at the name in the address book as she sipped her coffee. The fact that Talley was still in this book suggested she still mattered to Ruth.

She dialed the last number for Mrs. Newsome and listened as it rang six or seven times before it went to a mechanical voice mail recording. "This is Mrs. Newsome. Leave me a message." There was a long pause before she added, "After the beep."

Ivy waited for the beep and then said, "Mrs. Newsome, my name is Ivy Neale. I'm Ruth Wheeler's granddaughter. I'm reaching out to her friends listed in her address book. If you can, call me." She left her number and ended the call.

Restless, she considered calling the other names, but beyond the Manchesters, she knew no one, and dialing random strangers didn't interest her.

She moved into the kitchen toward the cast-iron skillet on the stove top. The fried chicken she'd made the other day had been good, but she wondered what it would taste like with slightly more modern flavors and lighter textures.

She removed the remaining pieces of chicken from the refrigerator and filled the pan with oil. As it heated, she collected the flour, salt, and spices from the cabinet and blended them in a shallow pan with panko bread crumbs. Her mouth watered at the thought of crispy, slightly sinful skin and tender meat. She preheated the oven and dredged her worries into the flour mixture. When the oil crackled and popped, she carefully lowered each piece into the hot liquid. The chicken skin sizzled.

Soon, she had cooked all six portions and placed them on a pan in the oven to finish cooking. She set the timer on her phone for ten minutes. Savory scents infused the house as she grabbed the coleslaw she'd made two days ago.

A knock at her front door had her turning to see Dalton standing there. Her thoughts jumped to Dani and promises made to keep her secret.

"Dalton?"

"I was at the jobsite next door and wanted to give you a heads-up. There's a Molly Gardner with the historical society who's going to be paying you a visit. Everyone on the beach knows about the wreck. We all know the ocean's going to take it back soon."

"Oh, right. Sure. She's welcome to stop by. I'm here just about all the time."

"I came by this morning, but you weren't here."

"I had errands to run. Paperwork. That kind of thing." Lies never rested easy on her tongue, and now they tasted especially bitter. "Hey, I'm making a batch of fried chicken. Don't suppose you're hungry."

"Is it Ruth's?"

"With my own twist or two. I can't eat it all, and it's always best hot."

"I wouldn't mind at all."

He wiped his feet on the mat and then followed her into the house, and as she moved to the kitchen counter, he regarded the cabinets that hung above it.

"And what does your contractor's eye tell you?" she asked.

"That these cabinets are solid and good, but they don't work in this space. Take them out, and the entire room opens up."

"I always hated peeking around them. Like a too-tall vase in the center of a dining table," she said.

"Drop the cabinets and then bump out the island a few feet, and you've got more room to move around the stove."

"Galley styles are efficient for one person."

"And if this place is going to be a summer rental, it'll need a kitchen that accommodates more."

She glanced around the space, imagining strangers in her house. Renters for the most part took care of properties like this, but they were rarely as careful as owners. "It used to be a rental when Ruth was younger. Took the overflow from the bungalows. Then Ruth and her mother sold the family cottage to raise money for resort repairs, and they moved in here with my mother, who wasn't more than one."

"How did Ruth meet your grandfather?"

"The story never filtered to me. I asked Mom a few times, but by the time I was really curious, she was gone. And Ruth never gave me a straight answer. All I know is that he died when my mother was an infant. Maybe he was vacationing here. Wouldn't be the first summer-romance baby."

"I don't think so," Dalton said. "I was quizzing Dad about Ruth the other night and asked about her husband. Seems she met him in the years she didn't live on the Outer Banks."

Ivy reached for a dish towel and opened the oven. Rich, full aromas rushed on a wave of heat. She shut the oven door with a kick of her foot. "Wait. Ruth moved away from the Outer Banks?"

"She did. When she was in her late teens. I'm not sure how long she was gone."

"She never told me." She touched the chicken skin, testing it for crispiness. Perfect. She positioned a leg and thigh on a white stoneware plate, dolloped a scoop of coleslaw, and then wiped the edges of the plate with her dish towel until it was pristine. She set a paper napkin and fork beside it.

"Mind if I wash my hands?" he asked.

"Go ahead," she said, nodding toward the sink.

He moved behind her, coming within inches of her as he flipped on the water faucet and reached for the soap dispenser. As he scrubbed, she was aware of his body and the heat and energy radiating from him.

She drew in a breath, trying to remember the last time she'd been with a man. So very long.

He dried his hands with a paper towel as he came around and pulled the two stools to the end of the bar.

She sat, and they both ate in silence for several minutes. Pleasure gave way to critiques as she considered the blend of spices. Not bad. But could be better.

"Fantastic," Dalton said. "Brings back a lot of good memories eating at the Seaside Resort." He took another bite as if chasing the past. "Our high school football team came by the resort every Sunday afternoon when practice was over. All the guys loved the fried chicken."

She remembered the boys rolling into the dining room, laughing, smelling of Dial soap hurriedly run over sweaty bodies, as well as clean cotton. She was fourteen with raging hormones and craving a boy's attention. Dalton was always polite, said "please" and "thank you," but he never looked at her like he did the cheerleaders.

"Ruth and I cooked double batches during practice season." Senses invoked the past better than facts and figures. Smell might be the strongest memory trigger, but taste was right behind it.

"I remember you," he said. "You always looked so serious."

"Not that serious."

"Serious." He grimaced. "Never smiled."

"How would you know? Beyond seeing me occasionally with Dani, we barely spoke. Your eyes were only for Casey Bailey." The tall blonde with the lightly tanned skin always looked good on his arm.

He grinned. "True. But that was a long time ago."

"Where is Casey these days?"

"Married with three kids. Lives in Raleigh."

"Rumor was you two were going to get married."

He pulled off a crisp piece of chicken skin. "We talked about it. I even looked at rings."

"But . . ."

"Like you, I just wasn't ready to pull the trigger on the life everyone thought I should have."

"I remember Dani saying you and your dad fought when you refused to go to college."

"More school wasn't for me. I wanted to travel, so I joined the navy and saw my share of bases."

"You weren't back when I left."

"We missed each other by three or four months." He set his chicken down and wiped his fingers on the paper towels. "I appreciate how you've handled yourself since you returned. Dani was worried about seeing you again."

"She seemed pretty relaxed."

"When she looks like nothing is bothering her, it is."

"A duck paddling on water."

"Exactly." He casually leaned back. "How was your dinner with Matthew?"

"Not bad. He's looking for a chef to run the kitchen of his new restaurant."

"You considering it?"

She chuckled. "Working for Matthew? He's sending over a proposal. It's supposed to arrive today."

"Ever considered opening your own place?" His smooth, easy tone mirrored Dani's.

She wasn't quite ready to say no out loud. "I know how hard it is. All the creative energy needed for the food gets zapped by the business side."

"When have you ever been afraid of hard work?"

She let out a breath. "Never. But whatever I make from the sale of this house will constitute my net worth. Gambling it all on a restaurant is a hell of a risk."

"This from the woman who packed up her Pacer and drove to New York City with no job or a place to stay."

"I didn't know any better. And I didn't have anything to lose then."

"You're smarter now. And you're young. Time is your best asset." He took another bite of chicken and carefully wiped the shimmer of grease from his lips. "What kind of restaurant would you open?"

"I've cooked every version of Italian for over a decade, so that would be the easy choice. But it doesn't speak to me anymore."

"Make fried chicken," he said. "I can think of a lot of folks who'd line up for this."

"In this day and age? I thought everyone was into vegan and low fat."

"Not if they're honest with themselves. Besides, folks always reach for the sinful food on vacation."

She chuckled. "Everything in moderation."

"Something like that." He took another bite. "This kind of cooking is your calling."

Cooking today had been natural and easy, but there'd also been no pressure to fill one hundred dinner orders. "I'll keep it in mind."

"Dani was out of town today." He pushed his plate of chicken bones slightly toward her.

"Oh."

"And you were gone today."

"Okay." She could have lied about a shopping trip, but she wasn't going to do that. "What's your point?"

"Dani's an adult. Her life is technically none of my business. But I'm her big brother, so I don't care about technicalities."

"You should be having this conversation with your sister."

"I've tried. I know something is off with her, but she keeps brushing me off. She insists she's fine."

"Why do you think she's not?"

"She's not painted in the last few months. I've invited her out to dinner more times than I can count, and she always has a reason why she can't make it. She's also keeping the gallery closed through February this year. She's never done that before."

247

"I don't know what to say." She set her chicken down, wiped her fingers with a paper towel. "Keep talking to her. She'll speak up when she's ready."

Gray eyes sharpened. "So there is something she has to tell me."

"I didn't say that."

"You did." He sighed and rolled his head from side to side. "Is she sick? Is it cancer? Mom died in her forties from breast cancer."

"Don't borrow trouble, Dalton. Talk to your sister."

"I will." A curse rumbled under the words. "Again."

"Good."

He was silent for a moment and then, "How are the puppies?"

"The biggest one's eyes are starting to open. Bella is in love with the littlest girl and named her Star."

"And Dani really said yes to a puppy?"

"She did."

"That's saying something."

"She surprised me too." She imagined him mulling over this new piece of information. Sooner or later, he would put it together.

"Have you hired a real estate agent yet?" he asked.

"No. I'll start making calls next week. I should have this place in good enough shape to show soon."

"I'm still bidding on the house."

"Seriously? Don't you have enough going on next door?"

"I've always liked this house. It's a great location, and the old-school vibe suits me."

"Would you like to see the upstairs? I've cleaned it out well enough to move around."

"Sure."

She rose and climbed the stairs to the top floor, outfitted with two bedrooms. She moved to the front bedroom, where she was now staying. She grimaced at her unmade bed and her suitcase overflowing with the clothes she'd hurriedly dug through this morning as he moved to the window. "Fantastic."

"I love waking up to that sight and the sound of the ocean. Don't miss the honking horns and all the city sounds."

"I can't imagine. I keep telling myself this place would be a profitable rental, but I'm also considering buying it for myself."

"Dani said your dad is living with you."

"He is. But the house is small, and it's set back in a wooded neighborhood. We both miss the ocean. There's enough space for the two of us here."

He looked in the other bedroom, frowned, and then headed back down the stairs. She followed, not sure if she should offer any color on the house or just let him process.

He opened the door to the spare room with all of Ruth's paintings. "Have you decided what to do with these?"

"No. But I'm not selling them."

"Good. She left them here for a reason."

"What makes you say that?"

"She didn't show these paintings to anyone. Once one was finished, she wrapped it up and started on the next. If she didn't want you to have them, she would have disposed of them."

"She had a heart attack. How could she know?"

"She'd become very nostalgic in her last few weeks. Connected with Dad and her cousin in Elizabeth City."

"Who was that?"

"Mrs. Newsome, I think."

"I called her and left a message."

"She couldn't make it to the funeral, because she's confined to a wheelchair now. Her generation doesn't check the cell phone messages as quickly. When she does, she'll get back."

"She's of sharp mind?" Ivy tried to visualize the young Talley in the photo after seven decades.

"According to Ruth, she's as sharp as a tack."

"How old is she?" Ivy asked.

"Mideighties. She was a couple of years older than Ruth. Their mothers were sisters, I think."

"There's so much I don't know about my family."

He regarded her with a pointed gaze. "Tell me about it."

CHAPTER TWENTY-TWO

IVY

Monday, January 24, 2022, 3:00 p.m.

Mrs. Molly Gardner called shortly after Dalton left, and they agreed she'd pop by in an hour. By the time she pulled up forty-five minutes later, Ivy had cleaned up the kitchen and taken Libby outside for a bathroom break.

Ivy stepped out onto the front deck and watched the midsize woman rise out of a gray SUV. She was late fifties, with gray-streaked brown hair, and wore faded jeans, a tan cable sweater under her peacoat, and rubber boots.

"Mrs. Gardner?" Ivy asked.

"Call me Molly. Ivy Neale?"

"Yes." Ivy stepped aside as Molly moved into the house. Libby barked as she peered out from behind her wall of boxes. "That's Libby. She's a new mom and nervous. I've wanted to remove the boxes for days, but she's calmer with them up."

"Can I see the puppies?" Molly asked, green eyes brightening.

"Sure. We have three, and the little female has been taken, but the boy and the other girl are looking for homes, in case you're interested."

Molly held her hand out to Libby and waited patiently as she sniffed and then licked her hand. "Oh my. They're so cute."

"Let me know if you want one. They're free to a good home." She let the words trail as if dangling a juicy carrot and not a wiggling puppy that required a fifteen-year commitment.

Molly nibbled her bottom lip. "My old dog just passed last month, and I promised myself I wouldn't get a dog for another year."

Ivy smiled, knowing that the softest sell could be the most effective. Plus, she didn't want anyone who wasn't really sure of the commitment taking a puppy. That thought led her to Dani, who might well lose her vision. "You can visit anytime, if you want to see them again."

Molly rose, holding up her hands as she drew in a breath. "You're tempting me, Ivy Neale."

"Yes, I am." When she'd waited tables at the Seaside Resort and even in her first days at Vincenzo's, even the staunchest dieters could be convinced to order the apple pie or the tiramisu when she was on the floor.

Molly stepped away from the puppies. "I came earlier today and explored the wreck. It's definitely the *Liberty T. Mitchell*."

"What do you know about the ship?" Ivy asked.

"There's quite a legend around it. My dad was a fisherman, and he was good friends with Henry Anderson. I grew up hearing Henry's stories. He told me his grandmother had been on board the vessel."

"Uncle Henry? He worked in Ruth's kitchen when I was little. She adored him."

"Henry was always close to the Wheelers."

"I'm surprised we never crossed paths."

"I was living in Raleigh from the late nineties to 2015."

About the time she'd been living here. "Henry never talked about the wreck."

"As I understand it, his grandmother was a little baby tucked in a steamer trunk found with the *Liberty T. Mitchell*'s wreckage."

"Really?"

"He swears he wore her crucifix with his dog tags when he served off the coast of Italy during World War Two."

Henry had always worn his dog tags, and she'd bet anything Ruth had buried him with them. "Do you think it's true?"

"I don't know. But you might very well have known a man linked to the wreck."

"It would be news to me."

Ivy moved to the dining table and collected the black-and-white pictures. "I found a camera that still had film in it. These are the pictures that came from that roll."

Molly carefully laid out each photograph on the table, her eyes lighting up with each new one. For a historian, it was Christmas Day and maybe a birthday all rolled up in one. "This is a fascinating piece of history."

Ivy lifted the picture of the Lana Turner look-alike. "Pete Manchester tells me this is Carlotta DiSalvo."

"He is correct. She was quite famous in the area during the years her showboat traveled up and down the coast. She joined the traveling troupe in 1941 and stayed with them until the midsixties. I've got some eight-millimeter film of her performing somewhere at the office. I'll see if I can find it."

"That would be terrific." Ivy was drawn in by Carlotta's light-colored eyes, which sparkled. "Why did she spend time at the Seaside Resort during her peak earning time? Even if the ship had been dry-docked, she could have performed in a bigger city and made more money."

"Edna Wheeler was her aunt. While the showboat was in for repairs, Carlotta took the opportunity to visit with family."

"My great-grandmother was Carlotta DiSalvo's aunt?"

"Carlotta was born Carol Jenkins in 1920 in a small town near Asheville, North Carolina."

Ivy studied Carlotta's arched, penciled eyebrows, her full, painted lips, and her bright smile. "She's a long way from the mountains."

"Edna did essentially the same thing in 1920. Picked up and came to the Outer Banks with a suitcase of clothes and five dollars in her pocket. According to Henry, Edna came to the barrier islands because she believed ghosts didn't cross water."

"What about the ghosts trapped here?"

"They weren't her ghosts, so I suppose she didn't care about them." Molly reached for her phone, scrolled through dozens of vintage photos, and settled on one of Henry taken in the 1950s. He was a very attractive man and conjured images of William Holden circa that time. "It was rumored Henry and Carlotta were lovers that summer."

"Wow, that's Henry? I can see Carlotta's attraction."

"He was a war hero. Earned a bronze star for service off the coast of Italy. That's where he lost his eye. And later he received several civilian awards for saving lives during storms. Estimates are he saved over fifty people."

"Do you think Henry's grandmother was really on the *Liberty T. Mitchell*?"

"In this part of the world, separating fact from a good yarn can be hard."

"Can you text me Henry's picture?"

"Sure." She handed the phone to Ivy, who typed in her number and hit send.

Molly's gaze dropped to the picture of young Ruth. "And you know this is your grandmother."

"Yes."

"She was quite the spitfire. Lived an interesting life. Did you know she joined Carlotta on the *Maisy Adams* a few years after this picture was taken? She worked as a cook on the ship and later as a stage assistant. She traveled with the ship for several years."

"Pete mentioned Ruth moved away for a time, but he didn't know where she went. He said she never talked about her years away, which apparently was where she met my grandfather."

"Her husband and father died about the same time, so she returned to the Outer Banks to help Edna run the Seaside Resort. Carol, your mother, was barely a baby."

"Did you ask Ruth about her travels?" Ivy asked.

"I did. She laughed, said ancient history didn't matter to her."

Ivy studied Carlotta's features and Ruth's. There was a resemblance in the eyes. "They look related."

"You know Ruth was adopted, right?"

Ivy shook her head. "I didn't."

Molly shrugged. "Henry let it slip. He was older, had had a few drinks after one of his Halloween performances that I'd attended. We got to talking about the Seaside Resort's history, and he mentioned Ruth's adoption. He realized his mistake and asked me to not tell."

"More ancient history Ruth didn't think mattered?"

Molly was silent for a moment. "I don't know."

"What happened to Carlotta?" Ivy asked.

"After she retired from the showboat in 1966, she returned to western North Carolina and settled in the Asheville area. She passed when she was in her midsixties. There was a short illness mentioned in her obituary, but details were never given."

Ivy chose to hold on to the image of the young, vibrant woman forever.

Molly skimmed her fingers over the old hotel register. "This is from the Seaside Resort?"

"Yes. It's the only one I could find. It covers the 1930s."

"Interesting choice of years." Molly carefully turned the yellowed pages. "Ruth was a pack rat."

"Don't I know it. I've spent the last week cleaning, donating, and tossing."

"The Seaside Resort was Ruth's life. It's hard to let go, especially as we get older. Our possessions anchor us to our best memories."

"Talley, Mrs. Edward Newsome, Ruth's cousin, is in assisted living. Do you have the address?"

Molly pulled up a contact on her phone and texted it to Ivy. "I do, as a matter of fact. Ruth asked me to call Talley after the hurricane and let her know she was fine. There you go."

Ivy's phone dinged with Talley's contact information. It chimed again with the historical society's information, including the website. "Thank you. Any information on the *Maisy Adams*?"

"Let me do a little digging on that one. I doubt there's any crew left alive, but there has to be some kind of trail out there. I'm very good at squeezing information from old sources." She turned toward the sleeping porch. "Mind if I have a look at the wreck?"

"Best view is from the back porch." Ivy crossed the main room and opened the door. A cold breeze whistled through the screens, brushing her skin in chilly strokes. She folded her arms over her chest.

"Henry told stories about the wreck and the souls that were lost," Molly said. "He became quite an attraction around Halloween, when local places were looking for tall yarns."

"I remember. His eye patch made him look like a pirate."

"He was a perennial favorite." Molly tilted her head as she stared at the old wooden ship's bones. "Have you seen any spirits?"

"All I've seen is an Irish wolfhound," she said, more to herself. "Last week I saw the hound and followed it over the dunes and under a house. I found Libby on the verge of giving birth. I also saw it this morning."

"Henry used to say the ship's captain had an Irish wolfhound."

Ivy hugged her arms around her chest. "I heard his name was Boris."

"That's right." Molly climbed down the stairs and crossed the sand to the wreck. "This really is fantastic."

Ivy followed. "Has the *Liberty T. Mitchell* appeared any other time than 1950?"

"Records indicate sightings in 1920, 1950, and 1980. This will mark its fourth showing. Each time it rose above the sands, the season was tumultuous."

The wind swept more sand over the vessel's remains as an unsettled feeling weighted the air. "You mean weather-wise?"

"No, for the locals. The *Liberty T. Mitchell* doesn't bring good luck or prosperity."

"I'd like to think it's going to be different this year."

"I hope you're right, dear."

CHAPTER
TWENTY-THREE
IVY

Monday, January 24, 2022, 6:00 p.m.

By the end of the day, Ivy had hauled the last of the clutter to the curb and dumpster. As she stepped back inside the house, her gaze wandered up the A-frame ceiling and then down along the stone fireplace. If Dalton bought the property, she'd bet he wouldn't change it much, but another buyer brought no guarantees that the cabinets, countertops, and floors wouldn't be replaced by slick manufactured products.

Saying goodbye to this place wouldn't be easy, but she didn't have much of a choice. She couldn't afford any repairs, and she needed the money from the sale to move forward. A little over a week until her birthday, and she'd make her proper goodbyes this time. The longer she lingered, the harder it would be to move on.

She sat at the dining room table and picked up the manila folder that had arrived on her front porch earlier. Her name was written in Matthew's bold script on the outside. Carefully she removed the three sheets of paper and read through the restaurant proposal.

It was as he'd said, only this time she had numbers to go with the dream. He had done his research, and he was a far cry from the kid in high school who hadn't really understood business. His income projections weren't out of line, and if they came to fruition, he'd have a good moneymaking operation.

Rising, she climbed the stairs to her bedroom and crossed to the walnut dresser, which she'd been avoiding. In the bottom drawer, she found all the pictures and precious memorabilia she had shoved in there before she'd left for New York. It had been one of the ways she'd hedged her bets. If New York didn't work out, she'd come home, open her drawer, put all her items back out, and resume her life.

But during the few times she'd returned in the last decade, she had never once opened the drawer. This was her past, and like Ruth, she wasn't fond of ancient times.

She removed a framed picture of Matthew, Dani, and herself taken on graduation day. Matthew had his arms slung around them both, and they were all smiling. Dani's and Matthew's expressions telegraphed hope, whereas hers signaled she was not only hungover but frantic to tell them she was moving to New York. They'd all been so young. Desperate to build their lives, they'd all made mistakes.

Ivy set the picture aside and found a framed photo of herself and her mother. She was about four, and her mother must have been thirty-six. They were on the beach, the ocean and blue skies behind them. She was wearing a pink-and-white polka-dotted bikini and her mother a slim navy one-piece. She guessed this must have been taken the year they had moved back in with Ruth.

Her cell rang. It was Dani. "Hey."

"Thanks for driving me to the thing."

"The doctor's appointment?"

"Yeah."

"No sweat." She pressed fingertips to her temples. "Dalton noticed I was gone. And that you were gone."

"He stopped by." Fatigue seeped from the words. "Didn't quite give me the third degree, but he suspects something."

"This is not a secret you can keep, Dani."

"I'm not ready to have the world see me differently."

"They won't."

"They did after Mom died. They will again."

"When do you think the time will be right? Is there a perfect alignment of stars in the sky?"

"Dalton has a lot of pressure on him right now. He's building the ten houses and needs to get them roughed in so they can collect the next installment from the buyers."

"It's that tight?"

"It always is and always will be. Dad drained the coffers to buy the land."

"There's never a good time to drop bad news. I know. I did it wrong on graduation night. I should have handled it better with you and Matthew. Do a better job than I did."

"What made you think of that night?" Dani asked.

"Finally cleaning out my old drawers. I found the picture of Matthew, you, and me taken at graduation."

"I remember that night. Matthew wanted to come after you, talk to you until you saw things his way. I convinced him to wait. Let you cool off."

"And the next day I left."

"He rested all his dreams on you working with us. When you left, we tried to make a go of the business, but we couldn't agree on anything. We needed you to be our glue. We lost the work-to-own deal two months after starting. My dad hired me, but working in my father's office and living at home made me feel like a loser. Matthew was struggling to get work too. We both understood how much it sucked to be left by you."

"I'm sorry."

"I'm not blaming you. Just explaining."

The old bruises on her heart could still ache. "You have Bella. You and Matthew are friends."

"*Yes*. And yes." Wariness shadowed the silence. "Are you going to go into business with him?"

"I have his proposal. I read it. But it doesn't change my mind."

"You really are leaving?" Challenge crashed against the caution.

"I'm not pulling any punches this time. Everyone's had fair warning that I'm leaving, so I'm not messing up anyone else's lives."

CHAPTER
TWENTY-FOUR
RUTH

Friday, June 23, 1950, 7:45 p.m.

The sun dipped closer to the horizon as Carlotta stood on the small stage of the shipwreck. A soft ocean breeze brushed over calm waters and ruffled the edges of her crimson skirt as she sang "Blue Moon." There were no horns or pianos, just the gentle rumble of the waves, but Carlotta's voice was so smooth nobody missed the instruments. The hotel guests, along with a couple dozen locals, had gathered chairs from around the pool and home to create a semicircle around the wreck.

Ruth and Talley stood in the back, ready to deliver cocktails to the guests, who, as the evening went on, charged more drinks to their rooms. Drink sales had risen, and Mama had already told Daddy earlier that they might turn a profit this summer. He'd chuckled as he rapped his knuckles against the wooden prep counter.

Mr. Manchester rose from his seat and moved away from the group, wobbling a little as he walked. His wife tossed him a worried glance and seemed to debate if she should follow. She glanced around, swallowed her worry along with the dregs of her gin and tonic, rose, and trailed after him. The two vanished over the dune, but seconds later the wind caught Mr. Manchester's angry voice before it faded with distance.

The song ended, and the crowd clapped. If they noticed the Manchesters, they were either having too much fun to care or too accustomed to their squabbles to be troubled.

"Are they fighting again, Mama?" Ruth whispered.

She frowned. "Yes."

"I haven't been giving him any more drinks," Talley said. "Just like you said."

Even for Edna there was a limit to profits. "He's been drinking from his flask."

"I didn't see it," Ruth said.

"He's clever," Mama said. "Let me go check on them."

"I can go with you," Ruth offered.

"No, you stay here." Her fleeting smile didn't spark much joy.

Ruth and Talley watched Mama walk across the sand and up over the dunes, her flat shoes digging into the earth like she was squashing a bug with each twist of her heel.

"Do you think your mama is going to give him a piece of her mind?" Talley asked.

Ruth flushed. "Yes."

"He's a scary guy," Talley said.

"That's never stopped Mama." Ruth didn't like Mama going toe to toe with men like Mr. Manchester.

"My mama said Edna was always a fighter. She never took guff off of anyone, even when she was a little girl."

"Who did she have to fight back home?"

"She fought with everyone. It's hard being the poorest in town. She never would let anyone talk down to her because of it."

These days Mama saved her fighting for men like Mr. Manchester, guests who refused to pay, or vendors trying to overcharge for a delivery.

A couple of times when the arguments grew too heated, Daddy stepped in. He never raised his voice, but men who were six feet four, even with wooden legs, didn't have to say much.

"I'm following her," Ruth said. And before Talley could object, she turned on her heel and hurried after her mother. She'd barely taken ten steps when Talley caught up to her.

"Are you getting your father?" Talley asked.

"He had to ride to the mainland to get more supplies for tomorrow. He won't be back until late."

"I'll come too," Talley said.

When they topped the dune, they saw Mama speaking to the Manchesters. She had screwed on her keep-the-peace smile, but it was stiffer than usual. Mrs. Manchester's face was beet red, while her husband's was tight with anger.

"If you won't serve me"—he stood with his feet braced, one fist clenched—"then we'll move to another hotel that will."

"We can help you move your belongings," Mama said.

"Peter," Mrs. Manchester said, pleading. "Let's go back to our room. We can rest for a bit and then rethink moving. It's too late tonight to do anything."

"Ann, shut up." Manchester ground out the words, along with a few unspoken ones that only the two of them heard.

Mrs. Manchester's smile faltered. "Peter, please. You're making a scene." In her world fights happened behind closed doors, and disagreements, like dust, were swept under the rug.

"Don't tell me what to do." He grabbed his wife by the arm. She tried to twist free, but his fingers tightened.

"Peter, please let's go back to the room. Please."

Ruth moved toward her mother, her fingers clenched, until a steady hand halted her.

"Is there a problem here?" Henry's voice was low, hardly loud enough to rise above the wind, but there was no missing the growl.

Mr. Manchester looked past the women to Henry, standing behind Ruth. His body was relaxed, as if he didn't have a care, but he looked that way when he took his boat out into the worst storms to rescue sailors. Trouble, he'd once said, was an old friend.

Mama's shoulders braced, but she didn't even toss Henry a glance. Mr. Manchester's jaw tightened. "No problem."

"You sure?" Henry's smile reminded her of a rabid dog her daddy had once shot. "Sounded mighty tense to me."

"It wasn't." Mrs. Manchester's gaze rose to Henry's.

In answer, Manchester took his wife by the arm and dragged her away. She hurried to catch up, stumbling several times as she tried to match his long strides.

Henry stood his ground, watching Peter Manchester.

Ruth, with Talley following, came up beside her mother, standing closer than normal as if she could siphon some of her strength. "He's mad."

"He's drunk," Mama said. "His wife knows he needs to sleep it off."

When Henry and her daddy broke open a bottle of gin, they'd laugh and talk most of the night, and then Henry would fall asleep on the couch and Daddy would find his way to bed. When they woke up, both were grouchy and slow moving but were back to their old selves.

"He'll really be all right in the morning?" Talley asked. "That might take some magic."

Mama's tense lips spread into a smile. "Maybe not perfect, but he'll be sober and too hungover to make much trouble." Her mother looked at Talley and her. "You girls be careful around him."

"What about Bonnie?" Ruth asked.

"She knows what her daddy's about. She knows to stay clear."

"And Mrs. Manchester?" Ruth pressed.

Drawing in a breath, Mama rolled her shoulders. "There's no talking to her anymore. She thinks she needs him."

"Why?" Ruth asked.

"I don't know. Now go on back to the show. The trouble is over."

"Are you coming back?" Ruth asked.

"No, I've lost my taste for entertainment."

"Go on now," Henry said. "The show on the beach is better."

"Okay."

The girls turned toward the sound of Carlotta's voice riding the wind, but Ruth dragged her feet, hoping to hear something of what Mama and Henry were saying.

"He's worse this year," Henry said.

"Not worse. Just willing now to show his true self."

"It's like he knows," Henry said.

Talley leaned toward Ruth. "Do you think the fighting is over?"

A few more steps, and they were out of hearing range and Mama's and Henry's voices. "For tonight."

"I've seen the look in Mr. Manchester's eyes. I've seen that look in Daddy's eyes. It never ends well. It's the reason Mama sent me here."

Ruth had heard stories of men who weren't good to their wives and children, but her father had never raised his voice, let alone his hand, to her mother. Gentle Giant was what she called him when they sometimes danced by the pool after the season ended.

"You won't have to worry about that here," Ruth said.

"Not until I have to go back home," Talley said.

"Do you have to go home?" Ruth asked. "You can stay in my room."

"The deal between Mama and Aunt Edna was for the summer."

Ruth shrugged. "If you decide you want to stay, just say the word. Mama and Daddy never say no to me on the big things."

Talley studied Ruth, her grim expression softening. "That's real nice."

"It's nothing. Be nice to have someone close to my age around the house."

CARLOTTA

Carlotta sat on her back porch staring out at the ocean, a whiskey in one hand, her other empty but aching for a cigarette she couldn't have because she'd exceeded her daily limit of four. She sipped, enjoying the subtle burn and the way it relaxed her muscles as a favorite song about stars and dreams rumbled in her head.

Her index finger rapped against her whiskey glass as her bare foot tapped the sleeping porch's sandy floor. Crosby's song "Swinging on a Star" was one of her favorites, and she'd sung it to countless audiences in the years right after the war, when broken soldiers and long-suffering wives and girlfriends wanted to rediscover their own destinies.

Yes, individual decisions counted in matters of fate, a lesson she'd figured out at a young age. But even the most careful and vigilant always faced the unexpected.

She had hoped Henry might return tonight. They'd shared a lovely evening, and he certainly liked her company. One more bite of the apple would be nice. She gulped the last of the whiskey.

Her last show had ended over two hours ago, and it was well past midnight. She guessed he wasn't coming. Too bad.

As she rose, a figure moved through the shadows along the shore. The small, feminine frame stumbled along the waterline in large, staggering steps that faltered as a wave brushed over bare feet and splashed the folds of a white skirt. Drunk, no doubt. Here to have a good time, drank beyond her limits, and now in trouble.

As Carlotta turned toward her door, the woman fell. Her head bowed, and the moonlight reflected on blonde hair tumbling forward. A wave smacked her, knocking her sideways.

Carlotta waited for the woman to rise. Another wave collided into her, and instead of standing, she coiled her body toward the water.

Annoyance snapped. Easy to drown in the waves if she was passed out. Carlotta walked across the porch and out the side door and moved over the dune. Tall grass brushed her calves and arms as cool sand worked between her sandals and bare skin. Down the dune, she stumbled, caught herself with a few quick strides. Annoyance growing, she kept walking until her sandals crunched seashells rimming the land's end.

Closer, the woman's white dress, covered in small red cherries, was plastered against her skin.

Carlotta nudged the woman with her foot as a wave crashed and splashed cold, salty water. "You need to get up."

The woman didn't speak, didn't look at her.

Unruly drunks and showboating went hand in hand, and she'd dealt with her share. Another wave crashed into the woman and swirled briefly around Carlotta's ankles, soaking her leather sandals.

"Get up!" This time Carlotta grabbed her arm and yanked with her full strength.

The woman pulled away, glaring up through the web of her hair. "Leave me alone."

Carlotta recognized Ann Manchester's voice immediately. She and her husband had left her show early tonight, and it took no guesses to know they'd been drunk.

Tugging again, she hauled Ann Manchester up. "You'll drown if you pass out in the surf."

"It's not that deep."

"A teacup of water is all it takes." Anyone who lived on the water had a story to tell about someone who'd drowned in little or no water.

Ann planted her palms on the sand, fisted them, and then pushed up until she stood. She wobbled, shoved back her hair, and licked the salt water from her lips. "I'm fine."

"You are not."

She swayed. "Why do *you* care?"

That was a good question with no answer. "Come with me."

"Where are we going?"

"Back to my cottage. You can sit on the sleeping porch until your head clears."

Chest heaving, she shook her head. "I don't need your charity."

"Edna would not be happy if I let you get injured."

Mention of Edna triggered grumbling complaints followed by staggering steps. Once Ann tripped and fell to her knees. Carlotta cursed, questioned her sanity, and raised the woman to her feet.

Ann's body suddenly convulsed; she jerked away, and this time when she doubled over, she vomited. The scent of sour gin drifted upward as Carlotta stepped back, giving her room. Finally, breathless, Ann sat back on her heels and dragged the back of her hand over her lips.

"Can you walk?" Carlotta asked.

"I think so."

She took her arm and again pulled upward. "We're almost there."

"Why are you helping me?" Ann asked, her voice ragged.

"That's a good question." Hearing the bitterness sharpening her words, she added more quietly, "We have all been in bad places."

"I'm not in a bad place." In the next step she turned, dropped, and vomited again. When the retching finally stopped, Ann's face was ghastly pale, but her bloodshot eyes were sharper.

Silent now, Ann rose and followed without any more complaints. When they reached the sleeping porch, Carlotta retrieved a robe and ordered Ann to undress. When she unfastened the buttons of her dress and peeled the fabric away, she exposed several bruises on her back and upper arms. The fabric fell into a pool around her ankles as Carlotta wrapped her in a dry robe, lowered her into a chair, and handed her a glass of water.

"Sip it slowly," Carlotta warned. "Edna would not appreciate you getting sick inside her house."

Ann took a small sip and then pressed the cool glass to her temple. "No, Edna would not like that."

A reddish-blue bruise darkened over a fading yellow smudge on Ann's thigh. Carlotta wasn't surprised to see evidence of old injuries. Peter Manchester wasn't a kind man, and his temper wasn't limited to drunken nights.

"I fell," Ann whispered as she covered her thigh with her robe.

"I'm not judging you."

"Of course you are." She swallowed, pushed sandy, wet bangs off her forehead. "Everyone judges."

Maybe she was looking down on Ann just a little bit because the woman held herself above everyone. She'd seen the type before—women who'd married money and cut themselves off from their pasts.

But she took no joy from the insight. Life had humbled Carlotta too many times for her to cast stones. "Where's your husband?"

"He passed out," she said.

"And the children?"

"Sleeping in the adjoining room."

"And you left?"

"I took his bottle of gin. I planned to pour it all out in the sand, but I may have had too much along the way."

"You were upset when you left earlier."

Ann looked up with bloodshot eyes. "You saw us?"

"I see everything from the stage."

"It's not his fault." The words tumbled out as if she'd rehearsed them in her mind a thousand times before.

"Of course it is. He raised his hand to you, didn't he?"

She shook her head. "He didn't use to be like this. The war changed him."

"It changed many men, but they don't beat their wives." Carlotta stared into the blue-green eyes, recognizing so much of herself.

Ann closed her eyes. "He saw so many terrible things. He has nightmares. He drinks to forget."

"That is not an excuse, Beth Ann."

Beth Ann looked up, shocked to hear a name she'd likely not heard since she left western North Carolina. "Don't call me that."

Carlotta raised her glass to her lips. "We've both done a good job of reinventing ourselves, haven't we?"

Her shoulders slumped slightly. "It was the only way to get out. You understand that, *Carol.*"

"We both found a way out. So did Edna. And now here we are. The three of us pretending that we never met each other."

Beth Ann's hand trembled slightly as she raised the misty water glass to her lips. She drank carefully, testing her stomach, and then set the glass down on a small side table. "We've all done well. Found better than what we would have gotten back home."

Home was poverty, a family deeply ingrained in the community and wedded to a way of life that should have ended in the last century. Both women had grown up hearing that they were too prone to trouble. *Spare the rod. Apples don't fall far from the tree.* Finally, one day Carol and Beth Ann had proved everyone right and run away.

"Why do you vacation here?" Carlotta said.

"Why are you singing here?" Beth Ann challenged.

"To see *her.*"

Carol and Beth Ann, two girls who'd discovered the truth behind their birth on their fifteenth birthday, had plotted together to leave Asheville and erase their pasts. Carol, blessed with a beautiful soprano voice, signed up to sing on the *Maisy Adams.* Beth Ann, the prettiest of the clan by far, wanted to see Edna, the woman who'd given birth to them and then given one daughter to a sister and her twin to their grandmother before she'd run away. The twins, who looked as different as night and day, had left the mountains together but gone their separate ways in Elizabeth City fifteen years ago.

"Why do you come back here, year after year?" Carlotta asked.

Beth Ann rolled her shoulders. "Peter shipped out right after we married in '38, and then I had Bonnie nine months later. He was gone for so long; then the war broke out. I guess I needed *her*. I floated the idea of a vacation here to the other wives, and they all readily agreed. We've been coming back ever since."

"And now he's back. And not the same man."

"No."

"Have you considered leaving him?"

Beth Ann shook her head. "I can't do that. His family is wealthy and powerful, and they would see to it that I never saw my children again, and that would kill me."

"Does he know about Edna?" Carlotta asked.

"I never thought so. Edna and I exchanged letters over the years, and when Peter and I moved a month ago, my box of letters went missing. I think he found them."

"Has he said anything?"

Beth Ann stared into her glass, swirling the water. "No. But he's changed. He's worse."

"What did you tell him about your past?"

A smile tipped the edges of her lips. "An orphan. No family. Father was a preacher."

"At least the last part is true."

"Easier to remember lies rooted in truth."

So here they both were, sisters raised as cousins, searching for something neither one could put into words.

"It's very late. I should go," Beth Ann said.

"Don't. Lay down on the couch and sleep for a few hours. You'll feel more like yourself and better able to handle what waits for you. You said yourself your husband and children are asleep. And I promise not to talk about family anymore."

In the morning, Beth Ann would sober up, and then Ann would be embarrassed by this moment. She would return to her husband and her life. Maybe one day she would decide enough was enough with Peter Manchester. But Carlotta had lived enough to know that that time was not now. Ann was not ready.

"Edna chooses very comfortable furniture." Carlotta fluffed a pillow for Beth Ann. "Lie down."

Beth Ann suddenly seemed too weary to argue. She lowered to the pillow, curled up her knees to her chest, and relaxed into the softness.

Carlotta covered Beth Ann with a blanket, gathered up the wet cherry dress, bra, and panties, and rinsed them out in the kitchen sink. Out on the deck, she pinned the dress and undergarments to the line.

Maybe Peter Manchester had banished his demons for a time, and they would be happy for a while. Flowers, chocolates, sweet words. That was the usual pattern with these couples.

Perhaps Beth Ann would see this moment as a chance to change her life again. Perhaps not.

When Carlotta woke, the sun was peering over the horizon, and Ann was gone. The only sign she'd been here was the half-drunk glass of water beside the folded robe and blanket on the couch.

Carlotta hung up the robe and looked out at the ocean. Normally, she slept until late morning, but Beth Ann's arrival had churned up long-buried memories.

She wanted to believe that, like Beth Ann, she never looked back to their days growing up in the mountains, but of course, in the difficult times she did. She dreamed of the adoptive mother who'd done her best to love her and Beth Ann, the sister-cousin she'd always seemed to find at family gatherings.

She took her camera and walked out onto the beach to see the wreck. She ran her fingers over the wood drying in the sunlight and hollowed by the sea creatures that had burrowed into it. She climbed up onto the deck and closed her eyes, thinking of young Francesca, sailing back to a cruel husband.

"Poor Francesca."

She turned, framed her image of the wooden hull, the ocean, and the rising sun, and snapped a picture.

"Miss Carlotta."

Hearing Ruth's voice reminded her of the girl's question yesterday that had struck such a familiar cord in Carlotta. "Ruth. You're up early."

"I like the morning light the best." She had pulled her dark, curly hair up into a ponytail. Freckles dotted the bridge of her nose under olive skin. She wore a yellow top and a white skirt that skimmed below her knees.

"Where's your cousin Talley?"

"She's running late because she's reading a book from the lost and found."

Talley and Carlotta's shared kin didn't come from a family of readers. The men went into the fields or the mines, and the women had children and kept home. Time was used to put food on the table and roofs over heads. Talley would have been an outlier in a world that distrusted readings beyond the Good Book. It wasn't lost on Carlotta that all the family's outcasts had found each other by this restless shore.

Carlotta walked down the side of the wreckage and jumped off the end. "Can I take your picture?"

"Why? I'm not that special."

"You are special," Carlotta said.

"But I'm not your daughter."

"No, but you are very special to me." They were sisters of sorts, with a shared mother, of sorts, who kept secrets from them both.

A slow grin curled Ruth's lips as she tucked a rebellious strand behind her ear. "Okay."

Carlotta framed her lens on the girl's face, taking time to catch the sun haloing her curls. "Now give me a big smile."

Ruth grinned.

Carlotta focused, refocused, and then snapped. "You're a pretty young girl, Ruth."

She rolled her eyes. "I guess."

"No guessing. You're pretty."

"I would rather look like you. I want to have more . . ." She glanced down at her flat chest.

"They'll grow in time."

"That's what Mama says, but it's taking forever. I look like a little kid. How old were you when you, well, yours grew?"

"Too young. Which isn't the blessing you think it might be. There's no rush to grow up."

"That's what Mama said."

"Edna knows best." The comment carried enough animosity that even a quick smile didn't quite hide. Logically, she understood there hadn't been a path forward for the young Edna and her fatherless infant twins. She'd done her best, leaving them in the care of family and sending home letters with worn dollar bills when she could.

Only on rare times now did the little girl who'd grown up believing she was less than resent Edna. And here that little girl was now, stepping from the shadows.

Ruth didn't seem to notice Carlotta's shift in mood as she hopped up on the wreck and walked toe to toe along the edge. "Do you think Henry's story was true?"

Carlotta cleared her throat. "About the ghosts?"

"The ghost and the lady. She left her baby in a chest wrapped in a blanket. Sad."

"He swears it's true."

"Mama and Daddy say they've never heard about Francesca's baby."

"Perhaps a family took in the child and decided to keep her story a secret. Sometimes the truth is too much trouble."

Ruth raised her hand over her eyes, peering out as a captain might. "Would you do that?"

"Hide a baby? If it meant protecting the child, I might. Why the questions?"

"Because Henry's story makes me remember the lady who left me here wrapped in a pink blanket. I want to believe she was like Francesca."

"I have no doubt she was," Carlotta said softly.

"I guess that lady has kept me secret all her life," Ruth said.

"Maybe."

"I don't have any good secrets," Ruth said. "Mama says that's just as well. She says they can get mighty heavy."

Few woke up in the morning deciding today would be the day to hide the truth. Beth Ann would wake up this morning, see her darkening bruises, dab makeup on them, and cover her arms with a beach jacket. She would do it, she'd say to herself, because she didn't want to upset her children, shame her husband, or shatter the illusion of her happy life. Her secret wouldn't hurt anyone but herself.

Edna would slip on her apron and begin her chores as if she could work her way clear of the past. And Carlotta would push away the insecure little girl who'd grown up on the outside, don her makeup, and take control of an audience surrounding her stage.

"Edna's right. Secrets are a burden."

CHAPTER TWENTY-FIVE

RUTH

Saturday, June 24, 1950, 3:45 p.m.

Ruth was at the front registration desk when the dark Ford pickup truck pulled up under the main building's carport. She recognized the driver, a fisherman who delivered goods to the Seaside Resort sometimes.

But she'd never seen the two young people climbing out of the vehicle. They were young, maybe early twenties, and she supposed they must be honeymooners. The Seaside Resort got its share of the newly married, fresh from church nuptials. If they'd arrived hoping for a room, they'd be disappointed. Even though it was Saturday, none of the families had checked out. Did they not see the lit-up **NO** next to the **VACANCY** sign?

The man was tall and lean and wore a crisp white shirt with a wide pointed collar that dipped into a V and polished two-tone loafers peeking out from dark striped pants. His hair, the color of wet sand, was slicked back with a thick layer of grease.

The woman's coffee-colored hair was cut short and curled around her pearl-clustered earrings. Her sunglasses were trimmed in red and angled upward like a cat's eyes. A bright-yellow blouse skimmed over small breasts and tapered into slim white pants.

Waving to the driver as the truck drove off, they picked up their suitcases and entered the front doors, each taking time to study the lobby.

"Can I help you?" Ruth asked.

"You can, young lady," the man said. "We're looking for Carlotta DiSalvo. She's the headliner here."

"She sings here, but I don't know if the Seaside Resort is big enough to have a headliner."

"She's the star wherever she goes," the man said.

Ruth didn't argue. "Who are you?"

"I'm Max Collier, and this is April Rivers. We perform with Carlotta on the *Maisy Adams*."

"Is the boat fixed, Mr. Collier?" Ruth hoped it wasn't.

"Call me Max. And no, our vessel is not repaired yet. Can you take us to Carlotta?"

"Well, this time of day, she's down by the wreck making sure it'll still work for the evening performance. What do you do on the *Maisy Adams*?"

"I'm a magician," Max said. "April is an acrobat."

"Do you do real magic?" Ruth asked.

Max grinned. "As real as you'll ever see."

"Can you take us to Carlotta?" April asked.

"Sure. Follow me."

As they cut through the lobby, her mother intercepted them. "Ruth, are these guests?"

"No, Mama. They're friends of Carlotta's. Meet Max Collier, the magician, and April Rivers, the acrobat. This is my mama, Edna Wheeler. She runs the place."

Max extended his hand to Mama, pausing a beat to study her face. "It's a pleasure to meet you, madame. Your daughter was just showing us to Carlotta."

"She's on the beach. I saw her a few minutes ago." Edna checked her watch. "I'll come along. I've a few minutes before I start setting up for the dinner service."

They followed Edna's quick pace out the back door and around the pool toward the beach. This was the quiet time of day, and the summer heat had driven everyone into their air-conditioned rooms to nap or read a book.

The exception was Mr. Manchester, who sat at a table by the pool, a refreshed drink in front of him, a full ashtray on his table, and a *Time* magazine in his hand. It was impossible to see his eyes under the dark sunglasses, but Ruth felt his gaze. Seemed he was always watching her.

Mr. Manchester had kept to himself since storming off from the show last night, and Mrs. Manchester had spent the day in her room.

Gulls squawked as they crossed the sand and walked toward the wreck.

"It's a real wreck," April said.

"It's pretty old," Ruth said. "It only shows up after bad storms."

April shivered. "Bad luck to spend too much time near a wreck."

"And this one is haunted," Ruth added.

"We don't know that for certain," Mama said. "Lots of stories but few facts."

"Who are the ghosts?" Max asked.

"Sailors and a dead woman looking for her baby," Ruth offered.

April laid her hand on Max's arm. "I don't like wrecks."

Max grinned. "We live on a ship, so we're naturally suspicious about vessels that meet a bad end."

They arrived at the remnants of the ship as Carlotta walked around the ocean-damp timbers. She hesitated when she saw the new arrivals.

"Max and April." She hugged them both. "What are you doing here?"

"The job in Norfolk didn't work out," he said. "The restaurant owner refused to pay us, and until the *Maisy Adams* reopens, we have nowhere to stay."

"We have no extra rooms." Mama's expression was pleasant, but Ruth knew it was her annoyed smile.

"There are extra rooms in my cottage," Carlotta said. "Perhaps they could stay with me, and they could perform in the evenings for room and board."

"What does a magician and acrobat have to add?" Edna asked.

Max reached behind Ruth's ear and out of nowhere produced a gold coin. April took a step back, set down her suitcase, and cartwheeled several times.

"They're quite popular on the *Maisy Adams*," Carlotta said. "They'll not be any trouble."

Ruth expected her mother to say no. She wasn't fond of surprises and didn't trust outsiders easily. Edna eyed Carlotta as if she were trying to peer behind the pleasant expression. "As long as they stay with you. And I'll expect two shows a night, just like you."

"That would be most acceptable," Max said as he glanced toward a nodding April.

"Then we have a deal," Edna said. "Carlotta can show you the cabin."

Max nodded. "Thank you, Mrs. Wheeler."

"Call me Edna; everyone does."

Carlotta eyed April, who seemed a shade paler since her acrobatic display. "Edna, would you mind if these two had a meal in the kitchen?"

Edna looked at the couple, and something in her expression softened. "Sure. There's plenty to eat. Get yourself fed and rested up before the six o'clock show."

"We appreciate that," April said.

"I'll take them to the kitchen," Ruth said.

"I'll do it," Carlotta said.

Her tone didn't invite questions or comments, so Ruth and her mother watched the trio walk back to the main building.

"I've never seen a magician before," Ruth said.

"Neither have I."

"Wonder why they came here?" Ruth asked.

"Something tells me Carlotta looks after them."

"Why do you say that?"

"Some folks are better at it than others."

"Like you," Ruth said.

"I suppose so. Let's hope they're as they seem to be."

"Who else would they be?"

"You would be surprised."

CARLOTTA

"Why are you really here?" Carlotta asked Max as they entered the cottage. They'd eaten sandwiches and fruit in the kitchen, and April's coloring was much improved.

April pulled off her scarf and relaxed her shoulders for the first time since she'd arrived. "Max got into a spot of trouble in Norfolk."

"What did you do this time?" Carlotta asked.

"April makes it sound very dramatic," Max said. "It wasn't."

"Out with it," Carlotta said.

"I was in a friendly card game," he said.

Carlotta shook her head. "The games are never friendly when you play with strangers."

"That's what I said," April whispered.

"The other players thought I was cheating." Max sounded offended.

Carlotta lifted a brow. "Were you?"

Max shrugged. "Technically, no."

"I won't ask what that means," she said.

"He had friends in the local law enforcement, and I was arrested. He lost fair and square and didn't like it. But I was able to talk myself out of trouble."

"He did magic tricks for the sheriff," April said. "The sheriff laughed and said he'd turn a blind eye if Max left town immediately."

"We hitched a ride and made it as far as the state line. Then we caught another ride and then another. It took us nearly a full day to get here." The drive should have taken two hours.

"So no fights?" Carlotta asked.

"Maybe a small one," Max said. "But I didn't hit any law enforcement."

Carlotta raised her hands in surrender. "I don't want any trouble here, Max."

Max's smile was easy and quick. "Of course not."

"You always say that, and yet . . ." On the *Maisy Adams* he usually limited his gambling to their last night in a port. If the games went badly—as they often did—then he was out of town before sunrise. More than once she'd seen him race down the docks as if the devil were on his heels and reach the gangplank seconds before it lifted.

"There'll be no troubles here," he said.

Of course he meant it. He never made a promise he did not intend to keep. But Max had a way of getting caught up in the moment, and his heartfelt promises vanished as easily as the cards did during his act.

Carlotta finished her second set shortly after eleven. As she had predicted, Max and April were quite popular with the guests. They both had a charm that was hard to resist, and she could tell by Edna's expression that she was pleased with her choice.

She'd seen no sign of Beth Ann at either of the evening shows, but Peter was there. Well on his way to drunk, he lit up when April appeared in her costume. She knew from experience to keep distance between Peter and April so there would be no trouble. As much as she wished Henry were here to keep the peace, she accepted that the job always fell to her.

When the last set wrapped, Max, April, and she lingered around to speak to guests who wanted to express their thoughts about the performances. Some loved Max's magic, and others wanted to know how the tricks were done. April dazzled with an impromptu balancing act on the wreck, as well as backflips and cartwheels. Several women, growing bolder with Carlotta, had suggestions about song choices, and one or two noted she had hit a few flat notes—which she had not.

Max and April, exhausted from their long day, made their way back to her cottage as soon as the crowds cleared. She considered remaining behind to thank Edna, but the woman was speaking to Ruth and Talley, who soon left for their cottage. As Edna gathered the folding chairs, her face was drawn with fatigue, and Carlotta wondered if Edna ever stopped moving. Maybe she, too, feared the demons lurking in stillness.

Carlotta left Edna to her task and walked back to her cottage. It was past midnight, and the lack of sleep last night was weighing on her now. She was more than ready to have a drink and go to bed.

High heels dangling from her fingers, she moved out of the light toward the shadows running between the bungalows and her cottage. As she walked, she sensed someone was following her, and twice she stopped, looked back, but didn't see anyone.

As she reached the cottage stairs, a man stepped out of the shadows. It was Peter Manchester. He planted his feet in the sand, swayed as a captain on a rocking ship might. He was drunk.

"Carlotta," he said. "Sounds like a made-up name to me."

"Go back to the hotel, Mr. Manchester," she ordered. "It's not safe to be out at night."

He glared up toward the darkened sunporch of her cottage, evidently searching for Max and April. Seeing no one, he said, "I know my way around. Not my first rodeo."

She thought about Max and April sleeping in the cottage. If she cried out for help, Max wouldn't hesitate to fight Manchester, and, based on experience, Max would end up in jail.

He moved closer, his fingers curling into fists.

She gripped the porch railing. "Go back to your room. Your *wife*."

He took a step closer. "I don't appreciate what you told my wife."

"I don't know what you're talking about." Lying, presenting a bold facade, and pretending were skills she'd long ago mastered.

"You told her to leave me." He sounded reasonable, dangerous. "She's *my* wife, and what happens in *my* marriage is none of your business."

"Your troubles fell at my feet. I didn't go looking for them."

An appearance from Henry would have been nice, but knights only inhabited fairy tales. A girl needed to make her own way. That explained the pair of brass knuckles in her purse, but her bag was on the cottage's dining table, the weapon swimming on the bottom with lipsticks, tissues, and coins. She gripped a high heel in each hand.

He stepped closer. "Stay away from her."

"I'm tired, Mr. Manchester, and I don't have time for this. Leave."

"This isn't your house. You're little better than a squatter. A pretender. Like my wife."

Reasoning with him amounted to wasted breath. But if she could dribble a little honey on her tone, he might calm, back off, and give her a chance to get inside and lock the door.

"You're right. I'm little more than a wanderer. I'll be gone soon, and in a few months you and your wife won't even remember my name. Go back to your wife, Mr. Manchester."

"My wife? I don't even know who she really is. I thought I did, but I don't."

Had he found the letters Beth Ann had mentioned? "Talk to your wife." The Beth Ann she'd once known would already be figuring a way to fix this problem.

"You both are witches." Dimming anger in his eyes gave way to a more ominous glint. "Both of you are chameleons who know how to charm and entrap men."

His gaze slid over her body, down the silk dress cinched at her waist, over her bare legs, to the red tips of her toes.

"Let me get you a drink," she said.

"Sure."

She was turning her back, ready to dash up the stairs, when he grabbed her by her hair and yanked her toward him. Surrendering to the pain, she stumbled, and when he shoved her hard sideways, she fell to the sandy beach.

"I found the letter from her mother. The woman she swore to me had died when she was a girl."

Beth Ann, for all her talk of never going home, couldn't completely walk away. "I don't know what you are talking about!"

"You're her sister. Her twin. What the hell else is she hiding?"

The truth, which hadn't been spoken out loud ever, stunned her. "I don't know."

Peter kicked her hard in the gut, knocking all the wind from her body. Pain radiated along her ribs and up her spine. She tried to scramble back, dropped one heel, but as she tried to stand, another blow sent her flying onto her back. She looked up in time to see Peter looming over her. His face was grim, angry, and determined. He wanted to hurt her, and she feared he would kill her.

He dropped down, pinning her body with his. His hand ran up her leg, under the hem of her dress, to her panties. He groped at the silk, pulling and ripping.

Carlotta gripped the remaining high heel in her right hand and hit him squarely on the back of the head.

He howled, recoiled, and then slapped her hard. "Bitch!"

In her left hand, she scooped up a handful of sand and then hurled it in his face. She hit him squarely in the eyes, and immediately he recoiled.

"Get off me, you pig."

She shoved him off her and was scrambling away when he grabbed her ankle. His fingernails bit into her skin.

She kicked hard, this time the heel of her foot connecting with his nose. He released his hold as blood erupted from his nose.

She made it to her feet and stumbled forward toward the stairs. She hurried up to the screened door, locked it and then the french doors leading to the sleeping porch. From her purse she fished out her brass knuckles and slid them on her hand, like a rich woman's diamond rings. Her heart pounded in her chest, but as tempted as she was to flee, she hurried to the window and peered out.

Peter Manchester lay on his back at the bottom of the stairs, clutching his nose. The blood looked black in the moonlight. He pushed up on his elbow, swept the blue-black hair off his forehead as he swayed.

A light upstairs clicked on. April's thin frame descended the stairs, a billy club—that showgirl's choice of a weapon—clutched in her hands. "Carlotta, what's going on?"

"Mr. Manchester was just heading back to the hotel."

April stood beside Carlotta, her gaze dropping to the man on the beach as he staggered a step and touched the trickle of blood dripping down his temple. He stared up at the two women. He might have made a run at one, but a second could inflict damage or escape to get help. Eyes narrowed, and without a word, he turned and walked along the beach toward the lights of the Seaside Resort.

"What was that all about?" April asked.

"It's nothing," Carlotta said. "Go back to sleep."

April regarded her. "Your face is bruising!"

Carlotta dabbed her cheek. Manchester wasn't the first patron to assume more than he should. "I'll put ice on it. It'll be gone by morning."

April reached for her arm.

Carlotta flinched in pain. "Go back to bed."

"I won't," she said. "Come into the kitchen. Least I can do is make an ice pack for you."

"No . . ."

"You're not in charge all the time. Come with me."

The force behind April's normally meek voice was charming. She lingered another moment at the window, and when she saw no sign of Peter Manchester, she followed.

April turned on the light, and Carlotta winced against the rush of brightness. April opened the freezer, grabbed the metal ice tray, and raised the lever until the ice cubes cracked free. Carefully she spread out a blue-and-white checkered dish towel, dumped the ice into the center, and then twisted the bundle until it was secure. She carefully pressed the ice to Carlotta's cheek.

"I saw him at the show tonight," April said. "He was on his way to drunk."

"His favorite pastime." Carlotta looked toward the window and caught her faint reflection in the glass. "How much did you hear?"

"Enough."

"Don't tell anyone."

"We all have pasts," April said.

Carlotta looked up the stairs. "Where is Max?"

"Sleeping. He took one of his pills. You know nothing will wake him up."

The pills came from a doctor in Baltimore, to help him with too many sleepless nights. "Better he not know."

April wiped away a smear of fresh blood from Carlotta's cheek. "Are you going to avoid Manchester for the next week?"

"If I have to. I don't want any trouble with Edna."

"I didn't understand why you were even bothering with this short-term gig. Now it makes sense."

Carlotta took the ice bag from April and glanced at the blood smearing the cloth before pressing it back to her face. "I thought it would be a nice change of pace. I've missed dry land."

"Since when?" April filled a glass with water and handed it to Carlotta.

She sipped, tasted a little blood before it washed away. "She's been nice to me. I don't want to bring any trouble to her door."

"You didn't. Peter Manchester did. The sheriff really should be told."

"I'll deal with Mr. Manchester." She smiled, grimacing when the battered muscles on her face shifted. "He won't bother me again."

"What are you going to do?"

"I'll take care of him."

CHAPTER TWENTY-SIX
CARLOTTA

Sunday, June 25, 1950, 6:00 a.m.

Carlotta had a restless night. She slept maybe three hours, and when she awoke, her body was stiff, and her head pounded.

She rose slowly and flinched as she swung her legs over the side of the bed, moved into the bathroom, and stared at her bruised reflection in the mirror. Her right cheek was slightly swollen but would have been worse without the ice. Makeup would take care of the discoloration. She pulled up her nightgown and glared at the swath of purple marks on her ribs. Bastard.

She let the gown drop to below her knees and moved into the kitchen to find Edna standing there. She had brewed a fresh pot of coffee and was pouring two cups.

Carlotta considered retreating into her bedroom and her makeup box, but a jab of anger kept her standing her ground. "Good morning."

Edna turned, coffee cups in hand. She hesitated slightly when she saw Carlotta's face before handing her a cup. She sipped from her own, and for a moment neither spoke as they stood in the silence.

"How did you find out?" Carlotta said.

"April came by the restaurant an hour ago looking for more ice. I told her to take as much as she needed."

"And you came to see why she wanted it." Carlotta opened the freezer to a large metal bowl filled with chipped ice.

"I like to know what's going on in my hotel."

"Nothing more to see here," she said. "There won't be any more trouble."

"I'm assuming it was Mr. Manchester. He's been more trouble every year, but this seems to be the worst."

"He found a letter from you to Beth Ann."

Her face paled a fraction. "Did he?"

"He knows the truth."

Edna stared at her. "What truth?"

"That Beth Ann and I are your daughters."

"Did he say anything else?"

Carlotta's eyes narrowed. "Like what?"

"Never mind."

"How did he meet Beth Ann?"

"Here at the resort. You know she worked here a summer. He was vacationing here and fell for her or maybe her beauty. They were married the next summer."

"She was selling her orphan story then."

"Yes. And I let her."

"Does Jake know?"

"Yes. He knows it all." She regarded Carlotta's bruised cheek. "I can call the sheriff. He owes me and will listen to any complaints I file."

"You would stand up for me?" Carlotta asked.

"Of course." Edna's tone warmed the words. "I ran from my girls once," she said, softly. "I'll never do it again."

Carlotta willed her eyes to remain dry. For once, the weight on her shoulders eased. "Beth Ann likes being a Manchester and won't give it up."

"That is her choice."

"I would like to finish the week."

"I know the guests and especially Ruth like having you here."

The idea of disappointing Ruth meant more than she expected. "I won't be run off by him."

"No, I wouldn't expect that you would." Edna set her cup on the counter and fished a bottle of aspirin from her pocket. "These will help with the pain and swelling."

Carlotta took the bottle. "Thank you."

"If you find you need to see a doctor, tell me. I'll make a call. He owes me."

"Who doesn't owe you on this island?"

"No one." As Edna moved toward the door, she paused. "Henry is leaving this evening. He's gotten work on a fishing boat, and the pay is too good to pass up. He's a sweet, gentle man, but he has a temper. He wouldn't like knowing Peter Manchester hit you."

Carlotta felt color warming her cheeks. She had nothing to be embarrassed about, but she was slightly with Edna. "Henry and I are friends."

"That is the sense I got. I saw him coming from this cottage a few nights ago, and the next day the man couldn't stop grinning."

Knowing she'd put a smile on his face pleased her. "I try to be discreet."

Edna crossed to the door and paused with her hand on the knob. "You were. Because I don't sleep much, not much gets past me here."

She would miss Henry when she left. And for a split second she imagined what it would be like if she remained on the Outer Banks and made a life here. She all but ran the *Maisy Adams*, so it wouldn't be much of a stretch to manage a hotel like the Seaside Resort. But as she painted herself into this version of her life, she saw herself growing restless and yearning to move to the next town.

"Thanks, Edna."

Edna turned partway, revealing a profile struggling with an unnamed emotion. "Of course."

Henry arrived at Carlotta's cottage as she was applying makeup for the evening performances. To her relief, the extra coat of makeup hid most of the bruising, and a scarf around her neck covered the marks. Not perfect but presentable.

A knock on the door had her turning, and she saw Henry standing by her back door. Her hand went to the scarf as she adjusted the knot. "Henry."

"Can I come in?"

She hesitated only a moment. Seeing him made her happy. "Of course."

"I wanted to see you before I left. Edna found work for me on a fishing vessel for the next week. The pay's too good to pass up."

Disappointment nudged her. "I'll miss you."

As he moved toward her, his gaze dropped from hers to her forearm. "You have a bruise."

"It's nothing," she said.

Frowning, he gently ran his finger over the purples and blues. "What happened?"

"I'm fine."

His gaze roamed over her, searching for more marks. He zeroed in on her scarf. Very carefully, he untied the soft silk and pulled it away from her skin. "Who did this to you?"

She captured his calloused hand in hers and kissed his fingertips. The anger ringing under the words was oddly touching. "It doesn't matter."

"It does, Carlotta. I need a name."

"I don't want trouble."

"It was Manchester, wasn't it? I've seen the way he's been watching you. And he doesn't treat his wife well."

"He was drunk."

"I don't care. Did he hurt you in other ways?"

She understood the meaning. "No."

Henry shook his head. "I wish I'd been here. I should have been here."

"It's not your job to take care of me," she said. "Normally, I can see trouble coming, but he caught me off guard." She kissed him on the lips. "I have an hour before my show. And I can think of something I'd much rather do than talk about Manchester."

When she kissed him, she could feel the anger holding him rigid. She ran her hand down his chest, already familiar enough with his body to know what he liked.

He groaned. "That's not fair."

"I know."

"You drive me crazy."

"Good."

CHAPTER TWENTY-SEVEN

IVY

Tuesday, January 25, 2022, 8:00 a.m.

Ivy couldn't sleep. She had spent most of the night again reviewing Matthew's proposal. It was as good an idea as it was risky. "Go big or go home," as he used to say in high school.

She rubbed her eyes and poured a fresh cup of coffee. A business failure would hurt, but it wasn't like losing her vision. She tried to imagine the world of darkness and shadows facing Dani.

Her phone rang. It was Dani. "Hey. Everything all right?"

"Yes. When are you going to examine the rest of Ruth's paintings? I was thinking now would be a good time. It's a nice, bright, shiny day."

Ivy sipped her coffee. "Sure, come on by."

"Good, I'm in your driveway."

She moved to the window. "You drove?"

"Just like I did the day before. See you soon."

Dani ended the call, and Ivy watched her walk up the cottage stairs. She was wearing black jeans, an oversize white cable sweater, and a leather jacket. Her boots were a bright red, and her hair was pulled into a high ponytail.

Ivy opened the door. "How do you do it all the time?"

"Priorities." Dani regarded Ivy's faded gray sweatpants and oversize NYC sweatshirt splattered with old grease stains. "You should try to make an effort sometime."

"I can pull it together once in a while."

"More often is better."

Ivy closed the door as Dani crossed the room to Libby and the puppies. She pulled a rawhide chew stick from her purse and offered it to Libby. "Mama deserves a treat."

Libby accepted the chew and began working on it immediately. Dani picked up the littlest puppy, the one that Bella had picked out, and took a picture of her. "I promised Bella another picture. She was ready to skip school today and puppy sit."

"They are moving around more. Won't be long before their eyes open," Ivy said.

Dani nuzzled her nose close to the puppy's. "They have a whole new world waiting to see."

That same world grew darker by the day for Dani. "You're pretty calm about all this."

Dani carefully replaced the pup and petted the others. "I'm freaking out. Good makeup and flashy boots are designed to distract."

"When are you going to tell Dalton?"

"Soon. I'm still not ready for him to freak out. Only one crazy Manchester allowed."

"And Matthew?"

She inhaled the scent of the pup and nuzzled her cheek close before she set her next to Libby. "Yeah, not looking forward to that one either. Have you looked at the numbers he proposed?"

"I have. He's a lot smarter than the eighteen-year-old Matthew with his grand idea of the three of us working together. He does want a financial stake from me. I suppose trust only goes so far now."

"We're all more cautious." Dani rose and surveyed the living room, now free of clutter. "You've made serious progress."

"My birthday is next week. Once I hit the big three-oh, I can sell it. I want to be ready."

"Has Dalton made an offer yet?"

"Not yet."

"He's always loved this place. Not to talk up my brother, but if you sold to him, he would never raze this place, even though the land is worth more."

"He said he really wanted the land."

"He's always had a soft spot for the older homes. By the way, he sold the last of the houses he's developing next door."

"That's great for him. Less stress for him. A good time to tell him."

"Not quite yet. Dalton won't take a deep breath until he's finished building the houses and closed on the sales."

"Ruth was sad to see the Seaside Resort go, but if anyone understood the value of a dollar, it was her."

"Speaking of Ruth. Show me her pictures. I'm going blind, and I don't have forever."

Dark humor was very Dani, but it still caught Ivy off guard. "It could be decades before you lose your sight."

"Or it could be a year."

"Really?"

Dani shrugged off her jacket and rested it on the back of a dining room chair. "No guarantees in life, Ivy."

"Point taken."

Ivy opened the door to the spare room. She'd been avoiding looking in here ever since she'd unwrapped the paintings. All the other parts of the house oddly didn't feel as personal as the art. This was a part of Ruth she'd kept to herself and rarely shared.

Dani flipped on the light. "It's too dark in here."

"Let me open the shades. The room gets great light this time of day."

She moved around the paintings wrapped in brown paper and the easel with the half-finished picture of the wreck, which, when Ruth had painted it, would not reappear for another month. She opened the blinds, allowing bright sunshine to pour into the room.

Dani blinked, and her shoulders relaxed as she crossed to the easel. She ran her fingers over cleaned paintbrushes sticking up from a mason jar. "The first time Ruth held Bella, she pronounced her the prettiest baby she had ever seen outside of you and your mother. My life was not going to be easy, she said, but it would be amazing. I thought she was going to be so mad, but she was so sweet."

"And you have been."

"And somehow will continue to be." She replaced the picture on the easel. "Enough about me. Paintings, please."

It took them nearly a half hour to clear the paintings out of the room and line them up along the walls in the living room, where they had more space to spread out the pictures. The sizes were fairly standard at twenty by twenty-four, though there were a few eight-by-tens and a large one that was thirty-six by forty.

"I also found sketch pads in the wooden chest under the window." Ivy had opened the chest and found dozens of sketch pads with pages full of drawings. "All I ever saw was her scribbling pictures on scrap paper. I had no idea she had so much talent."

"She didn't start painting until after you moved to New York. A lifetime of unpainted works couldn't be contained anymore. No more sketches. All her spare moments were spent bringing color to her art. Dorothy left Kansas and moved to Oz permanently."

"I wish she'd told me."

"She wasn't ready to share it with you."

"But she showed you."

"It was our common ground. Painting with Ruth kept me sane. Much like cooking with her kept you grounded."

"She recognized what we each needed." Ivy reached for a small painting of a fair blonde wearing a blue dress, facing the ocean. The vibrant colors oddly conveyed a sense of loneliness. "She said her mother always wore a blue dress. It was her trademark."

"What do you know about Edna?"

"Not much. She was born in the western part of the state in 1902 and moved here when she was eighteen. She found work at a small hotel and soon after met the man she would marry."

"When did they pass?"

"Jake died in 1960 and Edna in 1975. After Jake died, Ruth and Edna ran the Seaside Resort together. My mom grew up here before she moved to Richmond, and she and I were back five years later."

"You never talked about your mother when we were growing up," Dani said.

"I don't remember her really. Seems it's always been Ruth and me."

Dani drew in a quick breath. "It must have been awful for your mother to know she was sick. Just the idea of leaving Bella behind breaks my heart."

"You won't."

Outside, the ocean's rhythmic roar continued as it had and would forever. Ivy studied the picture of Edna. From all Ruth had said, Edna had lived a full life. She had never thought of her as lonely.

Dani selected a painting, tore off the paper, and was rewarded with a vividly colored portrait of a young Ivy and her mother. A riot of curls highlighted by the sun framed Ivy's grinning, round face. She was clutching fistfuls of sand as her mother laughed. "You must have just arrived here."

"I have faint memories of my mother driving us here. There was a song on the radio, but she wasn't paying any attention to it or me."

"She was sick then, wasn't she?" Dani asked.

"Yes. She lived another year. Ruth took care of her, me, and the hotel. I don't know how she did it."

"You've never mentioned your father," Dani said.

"I don't think he was ever in the picture. By the time I had questions about him, Mom was dead."

Ivy selected another picture. As soon as she removed the paper, she recognized the face instantly. It was Carlotta DiSalvo.

"The singer from the showboat," Dani said. "She must have made quite an impression on Ruth."

Ivy placed the image of Carlotta next to the paintings of Edna and the showboat. "Ruth worked on the *Maisy Adams* for several years, according to Molly Gardner."

"Really?"

"It was a surprise to me. Ruth never once mentioned Carlotta to me." She realized now how little she knew about Ruth beyond her narrow little world.

"Children don't always see their parents as people. Bella's guilty of it. I'm guilty of it. We seem to think their world didn't really begin until we arrived."

They continued to unwrap the paintings, and once they were finished, they discovered an array of bright colors and the faces of people— some recognizable and some not.

"I think this girl is my aunt Bonnie," Dani said. "She and my dad vacationed here often, right up until their father died."

"Peter Manchester, right?"

"He drowned. He was a drinker," she said. "The story was that he passed out in the surf and drowned."

"That must have been awful for them."

"If you ask Dad, he'll tell you his father was pretty abusive, but my grandmother Ann turned him into a saint after he died."

"Easier to be a widow of a saint, I suppose. She wouldn't be the first person to rewrite history."

CHAPTER
TWENTY-EIGHT
IVY

Tuesday, January 25, 2022, 4:00 p.m.

When Ivy's phone rang, she didn't recognize the number, but the 252 area code told her the call was local. "Hello?"

"I'm looking for Ivy." The woman on the other end sounded older, and though her voice was ragged, it was clear.

"I'm Ivy Neale."

"I'm Mrs. Newsome. Talley. Ruth's cousin."

"Talley." She tried to reconcile the young girl with the old voice. "Thank you so much for calling me back."

"Sorry it took so long. I'm not a fan of the cell phones."

"That's okay."

"So sorry to hear about Ruth. I always figured that I'd go first."

"No one expected it." She walked to the dining table and stared down at the image of the two young girls smiling. "There is so much I'd like to ask you about Ruth. Could I visit you?"

"You sure can."

"What about tomorrow?"

"I'm here all the time."

"How about ten?"

"Perfect."

Unanswered questions scratched in her throat. "The address I have for you is the assisted-living facility in Elizabeth City."

"Still there."

"Perfect. See you tomorrow."

"Can't wait."

The front doorbell rang just as she ended the call. When she opened it, she found Dalton standing on her doorstep. With wind-tousled dark hair, hands shoved in his pockets, and feet braced, he had the look of a nineteenth-century lightkeeper.

She pushed back her bangs, wondered quickly if this had to do with Dani. "Hey, what's up?"

"I saw your car. Can we talk about the cottage?"

Instinctively, she assumed he'd run the numbers and decided the costs of new bathrooms, a kitchen, and plumbing were too high. She couldn't blame him. The total amount had to be staggering. "Come on inside."

His gaze swept the main room. "Wow."

"Cleaned out and Ruth's pictures hung." She'd been staging the place just in case.

"I can see that." He moved to a painting of the ocean and the wreck. "If you decide to sell any of these, let me know. I'll buy any of them."

"I'll keep that in mind."

He reached in his pocket and pulled out a slip of paper. "This is my offer on the house."

She unfolded the paper and glanced at the bold handwriting. She'd searched comps and knew instantly his was more than a fair offer. "You still want to buy it?"

"Of course."

"I thought . . . never mind. Great. Okay."

"What does that mean?"

"Technically, I can't accept anything on the house until February second, when I officially age up."

"Am I in the ballpark?"

He'd knocked it out of the park. "Yes."

"If you think you could get more money by going on the market, then do it."

"I don't want to see the cottage dismantled, sold for parts, and wiped off the land."

"I've told you, I won't."

"I know." She could feel Ruth standing close, nudging her arm. *I gave you this place free and clear, but if you could save it . . .*

She extended her hand. "Consider this my official unsanctioned acceptance of your offer. When I'm thirty next week, I'll sign the papers."

He wrapped calloused fingers around hers. "I'll have the papers drawn up for your birthday."

"Terrific."

"How about I also take you out to dinner on your birthday? It'll be a celebration, and we'll make the sale official."

"That sounds fun."

"Great."

"Oh, and I'm headed into Elizabeth City tomorrow to meet with Talley. She worked at the hotel for several summers and was a friend of Ruth's."

"I'll be in Elizabeth City tomorrow to check on a load of supplies. You can tag along, and then we can see Talley."

"That could tie you up for hours. That's not necessary."

"I'd like to meet her. And it would give me a break from the job."

"If you don't mind?"

"Not at all. Looking forward to it. What time do you want to leave?"

"About eight. I have to be at her living facility at ten." She calculated the time. "I don't know if I can leave Libby and the kids alone that long."

"I can have my foreman check on them. He's been asking about Libby and the puppies. Turns out he was feeding her before you found her."

"I wondered why she didn't look underfed."

"He just lost his dog last year, and my guess is he'll fall in love with at least one or two of the puppies."

"Why didn't he come by before?"

He held up his hands. "I keep telling him to come by. But I can only lead a horse to water."

She laughed. "See you in the morning."

"Count on it."

She watched him hurry down the steps and cross to the work site. Ever since she'd arrived, he'd been helping her all along the way. As she closed the door, she lingered, watching him. He had the stride of a man in his element. Her cheeks warmed.

Her phone rang, jolting her thoughts away from Dalton. The display read: *Matthew*. She groaned. She had been avoiding him.

Rolling back her shoulders, she raised the phone. "Matthew."

"I hear you've been working hard on the house," he said easily.

"There's a light at the end of the tunnel."

"You're a superwoman to get it done so fast."

"No superpowers."

He cleared his throat. "Given any more thought to my offer?"

She might not clearly see her future, but backtracking wasn't the answer. "I don't think so, Matthew."

"Why not?" Annoyance mingled with surprise. In his mind, this was a no-fail idea.

"I don't know what my next step is, Matthew. But I don't want to work for anyone again." As she said the words, she realized how true they were. "It's not personal. I want my own thing, whatever that is."

"Is it the money? I can forfeit any investment."

"It's not all about money."

"You're opening your own place."

"I don't know what I'm going to do."

"Trust me when I tell you you're going to open your own restaurant. I know you better than you do yourself."

Maybe that had been true once. "You do not."

"You're not so different than when you left twelve years ago. Smarter, savvier, a better chef, but still independent Ivy."

"You make that sound like it's a bad thing."

"I thought it was once. No more. Especially now that I have a daughter."

"Progress."

"Not as much as you think. I'm going to take this as a maybe. We'll talk again."

"I'm not changing my mind."

"Think about what it takes to run the kitchen as well as the front of the house. It's a hell of a job for any one person. You run the kitchen one hundred percent, and I take care of the rest."

He was right. Running a café or restaurant alone was herculean. Over a hundred hours a week, easy. She'd have her freedom if she worked alone, but would she really be free to live a life if she was strapped to work all the time? Ruth had proved that was a long, hard road. "I'll be fine."

He was chuckling when he hung up.

CHAPTER
TWENTY-NINE
IVY

Wednesday, January 26, 2022, 6:00 a.m.

Restless, Ivy rose at six the next morning. In the windy blackness, she took Libby outside, fed her, and changed the puppies' bedspread. As her coffeepot gurgled, she jumped in the shower and, remembering Dani's comment about dressing nicely, took time to dry her hair and apply makeup. Jeans and a black V-neck were still her go-to, but they looked decent.

With still time to spare before Dalton arrived, she slipped on a coat, grabbed her coffee, and walked out to the wreck. The air was cold and the gusts brisk as the sun now smoldered below the horizon's edge.

More sands were gathering around the blackened timbers, and she suspected soon the beach would reclaim the *Liberty T. Mitchell.* She closed her eyes, listening to the gulls squawking and the waves crashing. No sign of the wolfhound or, thank God, the whisper of spirits.

Ivy skimmed her fingers along the wood. She was sorry to see it go. "Why appear now for me and for Ruth over a half century ago?"

The wind whipped the edges of her jacket and ruffled her hair around her face but offered no answers. The wreck's reappearance was coincidence, right? With no answers, she finally returned to the cottage, combed her hair, and finished another cup of coffee.

At 7:55, her doorbell rang, and in three quick strides she reached it and opened it a tad too quickly.

Dalton had showered, shaved, and combed back his dark, slightly silvered hair. The faint scent of aftershave floated in on a breeze, and the sight of him had her heart rushing to her throat.

"Ready?" he asked.

"Looking forward to it."

"Bert, my foreman, is coming by every two hours."

Ivy pulled her key off her ring and put it under the doormat. "Not highly secure but effective."

"The guys will keep an eye on the place."

She slid on her coat and did one last check of Libby before grabbing the register and tucking the black-and-white photos inside. After locking the front door, she followed him down the stairs and slid into the passenger seat of his truck, noting it had been freshly vacuumed. Her mouth curved. It said something when a man vacuumed for a lady.

Behind the wheel, he started the engine. "My stop should only take a half hour at most," he said. "Just confirming the order."

She smoothed her hand over the register resting on her lap. "Terrific. Where's Sailor?"

"Spending the day with Bert. He's getting old and not as fond of the day trips anymore."

He backed out of the driveway and made his way along the coastal road, and soon they'd cut over to the main highway and were crossing the bridge to the mainland. She gazed out the window, watching the waters of the Currituck Sound roll under the Wright Memorial Bridge.

"I hear you sold out," she said.

"Record time."

"Impressive."

"I never argue with good timing in the market."

Gulls flew overhead. "Agreed."

He drove onto the mainland past the restaurants, furniture stores, and gas stations. "Have you even gotten back to the mainland since you returned?"

"No reason to." The lie slipped off her tongue too easily. She didn't like hiding anything from him, but Dani had sworn she wanted to tell her brother in her own way. "Do you only build on the Outer Banks?"

"Yes. I'm lucky. Dad had the business up and running by the time I got out of the service. We've had a couple of tough dips, but for the most part, business is good."

"And you never wanted to live anywhere else?"

"I lived lots of other places in the service. And traveling was fun for a while. But this place is in my blood. What about you? How does it all look since you got back?"

"Slower than New York. Busier than it used to be. It's growing on me."

He grinned. "Be careful; you sound like someone who might stay."

When he hinted that she would move back, she didn't feel as riled as when Dani and Matthew pressed the issue. "I told Matthew I wouldn't work with him. His numbers looked good, but I just don't see it."

The corners of his mouth twitched. "There's plenty of opportunities down here if you want one."

"Very true."

"Any idea what you'll do next?"

"A few."

He didn't press, and they fell into an easy silence as he made his way along Highway 158. When the signs for Elizabeth City appeared, he veered to the left. Twenty minutes later, he parked at the lumber-supply company's lot. "Might as well come inside. They always have good coffee."

"I'll never say no to that."

She followed him to the front door, paused awkwardly when he opened it for her. "Thanks."

Inside they were greeted by the scent of freshly milled wood, a ringing phone, and the rumble of male voices. "Coffee's over there. Be right back."

"Sure."

Dalton crossed the room, and the man behind the counter extended his hand. They shook, and there seemed to be a mutual respect between them. She poured herself a cup of coffee, discovered it was indeed good, and walked around the showroom, studying the pictures featuring their lumber on a variety of projects.

She hadn't been alone for more than twenty minutes when Dalton reappeared with a stack of brochures and folders under his arm. "Never knew there was so much lumber, did you?"

"About as many as there are types of salt. Right product for the right job."

"You should be a builder," he teased.

"We both take raw ingredients and make something. Your products just last a lot longer than mine."

He opened the door. "I hope so."

Laughter bubbled in her as they both made their way to his truck. She could have seen Talley alone, but having him with her would make it easier. Hunting the past was always a risk.

He found the assisted-living facility on a wooded side street. The parking lot was half-full, allowing him to find a spot close to the front.

Her stomach churning a little, she climbed out of the car, the hotel-registration book tucked under her arm, and came around to the front, where Dalton met her. They walked inside, she introduced herself to the receptionist, and they were escorted to a large sitting room filled with lounge chairs and tables, where several of the residents were already playing cards or reading the paper.

Ivy tried to imagine Ruth here and could not.

An attendant rolled out a wheelchair carrying the small frame of a silver-haired woman. She was wearing a pink blouse and lipstick that brightened her face.

Ivy walked up to her. "I'm Ivy."

The smile mirrored the young girl's in the image captured so long ago. "I know who you are. Ruth has told me all about you."

Ivy turned toward Dalton. "This is Dalton Manchester. Pete's son."

Talley regarded him. "You don't look like a Manchester."

"Pete Manchester isn't my biological father. He adopted me when he married my mom."

Talley nodded. "You carry yourself like him. Pete always had a direct way of looking at a person even when he was little."

"That so?" Dalton said.

"That's a good thing," she said.

Ivy and Dalton pulled up chairs and sat at the table with Talley. The old woman fussed with the folds of her blouse and then rested her deeply veined hands on the table.

"It's good you don't look like your grandfather. His eyes always scared me," she said.

"My father was only six when he died, and he doesn't remember much."

"That's for the best. The older Manchester wasn't always kind."

"You were here the summer he died, right?" Ivy asked.

"It was my first summer on the beach. I'd just turned fourteen, and Aunt Edna had agreed to hire me."

"Aunt Edna?" Ivy asked.

"Ruth's mother and my mother, Jolene, were sisters. Edna was the oldest; then there was her twin, Aunt Patsy; then my ma; and Aunt Beth Ann. Edna moved away when she was seventeen, long before I was born."

"You said Aunt Edna agreed to hire you?" Ivy asked.

"Mama wrote to her and asked if she had a spot for me. The family had hit hard times, and she decided I'd be better off at the shore. To this day, I'm grateful for that decision. Changed my life."

Ivy removed Carlotta's photos from the registration book. "I found these in a camera that Ruth had tucked under a bed at the house. I was surprised to see the pictures turned out so well."

Talley removed pink glasses from a pocket and slid them on before she dropped her gaze to the photos. Immediately, a smile played across her lips as her mind seemed to drift back. "That was quite the summer. Ruth was only about twelve, but she was older than her years in so many ways." She picked up the picture of Ruth. "There were times I thought she was older than me."

"You must have known Carlotta." Ivy marveled at the youthful light that flickered in the old woman's eyes.

"Oh, I sure did," she said. "A few years later she invited us to work on the *Maisy Adams*, and we went together."

"You and Ruth worked on the *Maisy Adams*?"

"For three seasons. Ruth left in 1960 when her dad and then her husband died, but I stayed on two more years. I met my Bernie while working on the ship."

"I'm surprised Edna let you two go."

"The *Maisy Adams* wasn't a wild place. Carlotta ran a tight ship. She kept strict rules about keeping the young girls away from the male customers and crew members. It was a great time for us both. We saw all up and down the East Coast. I ate my first grapefruit in Florida."

"What did you two do on the *Maisy Adams*?"

"Ruth ran the kitchen. She worked hard, just like she did at the Seaside Resort. Takes a lot to keep a crew fed. And I worked the ticket booth."

Ivy leaned back in her chair, trying to imagine her grandmother anywhere else other than the Seaside Resort. "Who was my grandfather?"

"A young boy in Baltimore. Carlotta always warned us against any dockside romance. But Ruth was swayed by his smile." Talley's stooped shoulders bent forward a little more. "They married, but he was killed in a fishing accident right after Carol was born. It was Carlotta who told her to move back home. Edna would take care of her and the baby, and Ruth would take care of Edna."

"Edna must have really trusted Carlotta," Dalton said. "I'm not sure I'd let my niece go off with just anyone when she was so young."

"Well, Edna and Carlotta were kin. Trust comes more naturally in family, I guess," Talley said.

"Edna was Carlotta's aunt, right?" Ivy asked.

"Well, that's what everyone thought." Talley grew silent, as if weighing what she was about to say. "Truth was Edna was Carlotta's real mama."

"Edna had another daughter?" Ivy asked.

"She had two other daughters. Carol and Beth Ann. Edna had her twin girls in 1920. She gave one of the girls to Aunt Patsy to raise and the other to Grandma Jenkins." Talley was quiet for a moment as she traced the faces of the young girls in the photograph. "When Carol and Beth Ann were fifteen, they left town together. The aunts and cousins sometimes whispered about their leaving during my growing-up years. Carol—we didn't know her as Carlotta then—would send money home to her parents to help out. But no one heard from Beth Ann."

"Carol and Beth Ann would have been about thirty in 1950," Ivy said.

"Thereabouts, yes."

Dalton tapped the picture of Carlotta and the group picture of the women gathered around the poolside table. "Carol became Carlotta. And Beth Ann became . . ."

"Ann Manchester," Talley said.

"My father's mother," Dalton said.

"That's right."

This explained why Dani had not been able to track her grandmother's lineage. The woman had created a new identity out of thin air.

The trio was silent for a moment before Ivy asked, "Was this the first time Edna had both Carlotta and Ann at the Seaside Resort together?"

"It was. But no one talked about it," Talley said. "Mrs. Manchester was nervous and jittery around her husband. I'm sure she was terrified he'd find out about her past."

"She was afraid he'd find out she wasn't an orphan?" Dalton asked.

"Yes," Talley said.

"What about her family made her so ashamed?" Dalton asked.

"They were poor mountain folks. But good people for the most part," Talley said.

Ivy sensed there had to be more. Was poverty such a sin that Ann felt she had to wipe out her past?

Dalton didn't appear satisfied by the narrative, either, but instead of pressing shifted tactics. "My grandfather died in the summer of 1950."

Talley adjusted her glasses. "That's right. He drowned. He was a drinker, and everyone believed that he'd stumbled and fallen into the surf."

"That's what everyone says," Dalton said carefully. "Was it true?"

Talley looked up at Dalton but didn't answer.

"My father, Pete, is a good man," he said. "And if I could find out what happened to his father, I would."

"He drowned in the surf," Talley repeated softly.

"That's never rung true with me," Dalton said.

"Mr. Manchester's death was for the best," Talley said. "He wasn't a kind man."

"What did he do?" Ivy asked. "Did he hurt Ann?"

Talley fussed with the folds of her blouse. "I was always up early or late reading that summer. I saw more than I should."

"What did you see?" Ivy asked.

Talley knit her hands together and settled them in her lap. "It was the night before Peter Manchester died. He and his wife had not been getting along. They'd both had too much to drink at Carlotta's show."

Ivy imagined Talley rewinding an old tape, tensing as she readied to hit play again on a movie that she had no desire to see. "Where were you reading? I always liked being by the pool late at night. It was very peaceful."

"I liked the pool as well," Talley said. "The waters were so calm and quiet at night, and I could stretch out in the lawn chair and read under the floodlight."

"What did you see?" Ivy said softly.

"I've bottled this up for so long," Talley said. "I never even told Ruth all this, and for so many years we told each other everything."

Dalton sat back, and Ivy could see he was struggling to be patient. He was a decisive man, and he didn't mince words, but for Talley's sake he allowed her story to find its own meandering path.

"These pictures came from Carlotta's camera, which Ruth left for me to find in the cottage. I think they wanted all the stories to be told," Ivy said.

"I heard the wreck is back," Talley said.

"Yes," Ivy said. "How did you hear?"

"I've friends who have family in the area. Word gets around."

"So you've heard it stirs up spirits," Ivy said. "Say what you need to say so they can have peace."

Talley drew in a breath. "Mrs. Manchester came running out of her room and toward the pool deck. I was sitting in one of the deck chairs reading. I curled up in a small ball and did my best to look invisible. Mr. Manchester grabbed his wife by the arm and got right in her face. Said he'd found the letters when he was moving boxes at their new home. He knew her secret."

Ivy glanced to Dalton's curious expression. "What secret?"

"I guarded this secret for a long time," Talley asked. "I should have told Ruth, but I didn't."

"There's no one to hide it for anymore," Ivy said.

Talley shook her head. "I should have told Ruth, but Aunt Edna begged me not to."

Peeling back the layers wasn't as easy as it seemed. Some stuck, others tore, and instead of ending up with neat, even layers, all that was left was shredded pieces.

"Edna had learned to be a midwife from her mother. She didn't get a chance to learn it all, but she had a good understanding even at seventeen how to deliver a baby."

"Ruth was born on the Seaside Resort property." All her life Ivy had thought Edna had given birth to Ruth, but now she knew her grandmother had been adopted.

"Yes."

"Are you saying that Edna delivered Ruth?" Ivy asked.

"She did."

Ivy ran her finger down the names in the old registration book.

"The Outer Banks in January 1938 might as well have been on the moon," Dalton said. "Good place for a woman to give birth in secret."

"I would learn later that most of the women who came to Edna in the winter months heavy with child didn't have a husband. And in those days, many folks were struggling to eat. Edna must have found homes for a dozen babies in those years."

"These weren't legal adoptions, were they?" Ivy asked.

"Maybe some were, and some weren't. She never did anything behind a mother's back. But like I said, times were hard, and tough choices had to be made. Edna's name was whispered in a lot of circles."

"What does this have to do with Ann and her husband fighting?" Dalton asked.

"The letter Mr. Manchester found was from Edna to Ann. The letter warned Ann not to tell Ruth about their relationship."

"Wait a minute," Dalton said. "Are you saying Ann was Ruth's biological mother?"

"That's what Mr. Manchester said that night; however, Ann was crying, denying it. But her husband didn't listen. He hit her hard, she pushed him, and she was able to get away. She ran toward the beach. I was worried, so I followed her. She spent the night at Miss Carlotta's."

Ivy scanned the list of names in January 1938. She stopped at the name B. A. Jenkins. Beth Ann Jenkins. "You said Beth Ann never kept up with the people back home. But she kept up with Edna because of Ruth."

"That's right," Talley said.

"She vacationed at the Seaside Resort during and after the war," Dalton said. "To see Ruth."

"I suppose she just needed to know how Ruth was doing."

Ivy sat back. "I thought Carlotta was Ruth's birth mother."

"That's what I thought at first. Ruth thought it too. Made sense to think that Carlotta got in the family way, considering the life of a singer on a showboat. But it was Ann."

"Peter Manchester discovered all this?" Dalton said.

"And he was mad. I think he wanted to kill Ann, Carlotta, even Ruth."

"But he drowned in the surf," Ivy said carefully.

"Not exactly," Talley said.

CHAPTER THIRTY
EDNA

Monday, June 26, 1950, 1:00 a.m.

Edna had barely slept more than three hours a night since Beth Ann and Carol had arrived at the Seaside Resort. It had never been her intention that the two would ever be here at the same time. In fact, she'd never thought she'd see Carol again. But when Carol had written and asked for a summer job, she couldn't keep herself from saying yes, even though she'd be here during Beth Ann's two weeks.

Since Carol had arrived, they hadn't hugged or really said much to each other beyond what was necessary, but just having her close, even for a short time, confirmed in Edna's mind that she had done right by the girl.

Beth Ann, on the other hand, was a worry. She'd been the prettier of the two girls from the day they were born. But she was small boned and delicate, and for the first three days of her life when they'd been together, she'd cried constantly.

When Beth Ann had shown up on her doorstep thirteen years ago, looking for summer work, Edna had been nervous and excited all in one instant. She'd told Jake who the girl was, and he'd suggested she hire her for the summer. "You deserve to know her," he'd whispered in her ear while they'd lain in bed. "Have you talked to her about who you are?"

"I don't have the words to do it," she said softly.

Her Beth Ann had become Ann by then, and she seemed happy to be working as a waitress. She loved the sun, the beach, and the steady stream of new faces coming in and out of the hotel.

Henry, on leave from the navy, drove down from Norfolk and flirted with Ann, who answered all his compliments with a smile. The two talked a lot, but Edna never saw anything to cause her worry.

Then Peter Manchester and his family arrived in early June of 1937. He was vacationing with his family, and Edna heard Ann tell Peter she was an orphan and then watched with growing worry how the two grew close. As he and his family were leaving, they promised to write and keep in touch.

And then the summer ended, and her girl left for a typist job in Elizabeth City. They wrote once or twice, but neither spoke about their own relationship or the baby. She learned about it the day Ann showed up at the Seaside Resort near New Year's, shrugged off her jacket, peeled back her girdle, and revealed her rounded belly.

Edna and Jake had been married fifteen years at that point. They'd not been blessed with children, but they had each other, and the resort had become their baby of sorts. Still, she felt the pang of envy as she always did when she saw a woman with child. At this point, she'd delivered a half dozen babies to women who couldn't care for them, but there'd always been a family ready to take the infant. Besides, the way she saw it, she'd turned her back on the two babies God had given her, so she didn't feel she had the right to another.

Ann's delivery was easy. For such a thin, delicate woman, she pushed that squalling little girl into the world as if it were nothing. All Edna had to do was catch the baby and wrap her in a pink blanket.

God, but she loved that little baby girl. All the wounds to her heart healed, and for the first time she felt whole. Jake was crazy about the baby. They cooed and fussed, marveled at her dark, curly hair, and laughed at how she fisted her hands when she took the bottle.

Beth Ann wouldn't hold the baby or even look at her, and when she'd told Edna she was returning to Elizabeth City without the child, Edna didn't try to stop her. To this day she wondered if Ann's life might have been different if she'd encouraged her to raise her baby out here at the end of the earth.

But she'd let Ann go, named that squawking, high-spirited infant Ruth after Jake's mother, and never looked back.

Now as she sat on the deck of her house sipping a whiskey, she watched Peter Manchester stagger toward the beach. A lifetime of maternal worries and regrets roiled inside her as she thought about Beth Ann, who had taken to her room today. After the words the couple had had the other night, it didn't take much to know Beth Ann was hiding bruises.

When Edna stood and followed Peter Manchester, she didn't have a plan. Maybe they would talk. Maybe she'd beg him for his silence. Maybe she'd threaten him with the sheriff.

Peter staggered toward the surf and fell to his knees. A wave rushed over the moist sand and struck him broadside. He toppled over but pushed himself up to a kneeling position. His white shirt clung to his bare chest, and his combed hair now twisted around his head.

"Damn it," he shouted.

Edna slipped off her shoes and set them in the sand. She was wearing her favorite blue dress, and the idea of salt water drenching it didn't sit well. But one did what one must.

Cold water brushed her toes, sending a shiver as she moved closer to Peter. He tried to stand, but he lost his balance again and tumbled face forward into the sand. He coughed and sputtered.

"Peter." She wanted him to hear her voice, see her face.

He craned his neck, looked at her with narrowing bloodshot eyes. "Edna."

"Is there a problem?"

"Other than my fucking wife is a whore, and you're raising her bastard."

Rage churned through Edna, and for a moment she couldn't speak. It had been foolish to write Ann each year, but she'd wanted her girl to know Ruth was doing well.

Edna stared at Peter, watching him fight to stand.

"That's why you hit Beth Ann?"

"Who?"

"Beth Ann, *my* girl."

"Your girl? What are you talking about?"

She'd buried the truth so deep, and she wasn't sure she could speak it out loud. But when she did find her voice, the words tumbled out, and the pressure fisting in her chest eased. "Ann is my child."

He laughed. "You? That's ridiculous."

"She's my flesh and blood."

He pressed the heel of his hand to his forehead. "Why am I surprised she also lied about her past. That's all she's done, is deceive." He sneered. "You must be proud of yourself. Your bastard had a bastard."

Edna took a step back, watched as another, larger wave rolled up the shore and struck him hard. He fell forward, his face again hitting the sand.

"Help me stand!" His words slurred, and she wondered how much he was processing.

"Of course, Peter." Another surge of water struck, splashing his face and her skirt.

She approached as he lumbered up onto an elbow. More water hurled in from the ocean, forcing her to stagger her stance to maintain balance. Cold water sizzled on her hot skin as Peter spit out a mouthful of water.

She raised her hands and, instead of grabbing his arm, cupped the back of his head and pushed. He resisted, tried to twist free, but she leaned into him, pressing his face into the sand. More water struck them, but she didn't notice now as tension rippled through her muscles. Peter tried to raise his head, but she gripped his hair and kept pushing. As the seconds ticked, his strength waned.

Edna didn't know how long she kept his mouth and nose against the sand. When she looked up and saw Talley staring at her with wide eyes, she released his head, feeling his muscles still. His body lay motionless now, and his chest did not rise and fall.

Edna took a step back and faced Talley. What could she say to the girl? How would she explain this?

Talley held her ground. "I won't say a word."

"Talley . . ."

"He's a bad man, Aunt Edna. I won't ever say a word. Family sticks together."

She had no way of knowing if the girl could keep a promise that carried such weight. If Talley went to the sheriff, her world would change. Jake's and Ruth's lives would change.

"Are you sure you can?" Edna asked.

"I'm sure," Talley said. "I'll do it for Ruth."

And without another word, the two walked back to the cottage.

CHAPTER
THIRTY-ONE
IVY

Wednesday, January 26, 2022, 1:00 p.m.

Ivy and Dalton stopped for lunch at the small restaurant where the beach and bypass roads met. The sun was still high and warm enough to tempt them to take one of the outside picnic tables. The waitress brought them menus. Dalton already knew what he wanted to order, and Ivy, feeling overtaxed, told the young woman to make it two of the same.

Soon they had sodas and a basket of nacho chips. "Do you think Ruth understood the value of the hotel-registration book?" Dalton asked.

"She must have. It's the only one she saved."

"Did she ever talk to you about it?"

"No. Never."

"But she didn't hide it from you, either," he said. "She left the registration book out for you to find."

As they waited, her phone rang, and she glanced at the number. "New York area code. If it's important, they'll leave a message."

"Another job offer?" he asked.

"Likely a Vincenzo's vendor looking to get paid."

The waitress returned with their sodas, napkins, and silverware.

"Maybe Ruth needed me to know a truth she could not articulate. Ruth was a woman of few words." She sipped on her soda. "She was also never good with feelings. She let her actions do the talking."

"Like Edna?"

She shook her head. "How do you feel about Edna? If what Talley said is true, Edna killed your grandfather."

He traced his finger down the condensation on the glass. "I have no attachment to the man. And my father still doesn't like to talk about him."

Their burgers arrived, and she bit into hers. It was decent, good really, but she would have added more salt and pepper.

"You'd cook it differently," he said.

"I would." ,

"You can still take Matthew up on his offer."

"Are you trying to talk me into a partnership with him?"

"No. Definitely not." His chuckle was deep and throaty. Sexy. The air crackled. Both ate in companionable silence for several minutes.

"If what Talley said is true, it means you and I are related," she said.

"Dad is not my biological father," he said, as if he needed to make the point. ,

"But our families are linked."

"You and Dani both share Ann," he said.

That made them all second cousins, or a version of. Dalton by marriage, Dani by blood.

"Have you considered going into business with Dani?" he asked. "She's a hell of a businesswoman."

"I know. But she has a lot on her plate." She wondered how Dani would negotiate parenthood, the gallery, and her decorating business as her vision diminished. "Dani will find this new wealth of ancestry interesting. She mentioned that she can trace your mother's family way back but that your dad's line ended with Ann."

He balled up his napkin and pushed away his plate. "Why would Dani care about genetics?"

A flush of color warmed her face. "Doesn't everybody care about it?"

"No. Why does Dani care?"

"I don't know."

"You do. You've got that look on your face."

"What look?"

"The caught-with-the-hand-in-the-cookie-jar face."

Ivy touched her cheek. "Too much time in the sun."

"Nice try." He sighed. "Haven't we learned anything about secrets today?"

She felt overwhelmed by him, Dani, her family. "Look, if there's something you want to ask your sister, then ask her."

"I've tried the direct and honest approach with Dani. She's as cagey as she was as a five-year-old."

"I can't get between the two of you, but I do encourage you to talk to her."

His expression sobered, grew serious. "I'll drop you off and go see her right now. Unless you want to come with me. Keep the peace between the two of us?"

Dani wanted Ivy's silence, and she'd given it. But if she showed up with Dalton, Dani would feel outnumbered, maybe even betrayed. "She can handle you just fine."

"She needs to be honest with me."

"I agree. But this is your family business."

"Technically, Cousin Ivy, you are part of the family now," he said. "Come with me. No matter how this goes down, she's going to be pissed at you and me. Might as well take it on the chin together."

Ivy and Dalton arrived at Dani's house twenty minutes later. The bus had just arrived, and Bella and Dani were walking up the front sidewalk. Bella was chatting a mile a minute while Dani shouldered her daughter's book bag.

When Dalton pulled up, Bella's face broke into a wide grin. Dani's tightened with suspicion as Bella ran toward Dalton. "Dalton! What are you doing here?"

"Why aren't you in school, squirt?"

"Half day!"

He picked her up and hugged her close. "Ivy and I had lunch, and we thought we'd stop by."

"Did you bring me anything?" Bella asked.

Dalton chuckled. "I did not. But I hear you have a puppy coming soon?"

"I do! Her name is going to be Lulu!"

"Not Star?" Ivy asked.

"That was yesterday," Bella said.

"I have more puppy pictures," Ivy said. "Want to see Lulu?"

"Yes!" Bella leaned in as Ivy pulled out her phone and played the video of the puppies yipping and wobbling around.

"Their eyes aren't open yet," Bella said.

"Not yet. But they're trying to stand," Ivy said. "And bark. Lulu is a little bossy."

Dani looked at the video, none of the wariness on her face softening. "She'll have to be bossy to keep up with us."

"When can we take her home?" Bella asked.

"About six weeks," Ivy said.

"What about the other puppies?" Bella asked.

"I'll find homes for them," Ivy said. "Don't worry."

"Maybe they'll live close, and they can have playdates with Lulu," Bella said.

"That might happen," Dani said. "Why don't you go inside and eat your afternoon snack? I made you a sandwich."

Bella hit replay on the short video, watched the puppies play one more time, and then ran inside.

When the door closed, Dani said, "Not that I don't love puppy updates, but what's really up?"

"I went into Elizabeth City to see Talley. Dalton had a stop at the lumberyard, and he came along."

"Wasn't that convenient," Dani said as she eyed her brother.

"Talley knows more than we realized." Layers of meaning lingered under Dalton's words.

"Did she?" Dani asked.

Ivy relayed what they'd learned from Talley about Ann, Peter, and Ruth.

Dani listened, took it all in, shaking her head. "Ruth always said we were family. I thought she meant it metaphorically."

"Literally," Ivy said, sensing Dalton's growing impatience.

He finally cleared his throat. "What's going on with you, Dani?"

Ivy ducked her eyes as she shook her head. Subtle as a bull in a room full of glass.

"I don't know, Dalton," Dani said. "What is going on?"

Ivy could feel Dani's gaze but didn't say a word.

"Don't give Ivy the look," Dalton said. "She's said nothing. You, however, are speaking volumes."

"What's that mean?" Dani folded her arms over her chest.

Ivy wished she had her car now. These two did not need an audience, especially a newly discovered cousin, for this conversation.

"What's wrong, Dani?" Dalton asked in a softer tone. "I want to help."

"What if I don't need help?" Dani challenged.

He grumbled an oath. "We're too old for guessing games."

Dani sighed, tapped a ringed finger on her bicep. "Ivy."

Ivy held up her hands, no longer willing to nurse a secret in light of all that she'd learned today. "You need to talk to your brother. He needs to know."

"Shit," Dani muttered. "You finally got your chance at payback."

"What?" Ivy asked.

"For Matthew, for taking what wasn't ever mine," Dani said.

Ivy shook her head as she took a step back. "I'm going for a walk," she said. "There's a coffee shop down the road. I'll be there."

"Take my truck home," Dalton said, frowning. "Dani and I'll have a nice long chat, and then I'll get the truck later."

"How will you get back?" Ivy asked.

"Plenty of people I can call."

"Sure," Ivy said.

He dropped his ring of keys in her hand. "Thanks."

"You really should stick around," Dani said. "You started this, *cousin*."

"I didn't start it," Ivy said through gritted teeth. "But you need to finish it."

Dalton walked Ivy to the truck. "The second gear sticks a little, but it runs fine."

"I used to drive the Seaside Resort's truck all the time. If I can manage that piece of junk, this will be easy."

"I'm sorry to put you in the middle."

"No, you're not. But that's okay. Better you talk to her now. In six weeks, I'll be gone, and she'll need you."

He opened the door, she slid behind the wheel, and as she clicked the seat belt, he closed the door.

She shifted into reverse and backed out onto the road. The car slid easily into first, and second was a little tricky, but before she'd gone a mile, she'd figured out the truck.

When she pulled into her driveway, it was after three, and she tried not to picture what mess Libby might have created. When she reached the front door, there was a note. *I'll take the little brown pup if he's not taken. My sister may want the other one. Will talk to you about it tomorrow. Bert (Dalton's foreman).*

She tugged the note free and opened the front door. She owed it to Libby to make sure the puppies were taken care of. And then she would sell the house to Dalton. And then she and Libby would find a new life. It was all falling into place.

As she crossed to the kitchen table and set the registration book down, Libby ran to her, her tail wagging. "Hey, girl."

The dog licked her hand and then, teats wagging under her belly, walked to her food and water bowls, which looked freshly filled. Bert. A good sign.

She skimmed her fingers over the frayed fabric cover of the registration book. She thought about Ruth. Had Edna told Ruth the truth about her birth? Or maybe Carlotta had told her during her years on the *Maisy Adams*? Had Ruth known what Edna had done to protect Ruth, Ann, and Carlotta?

"So who was the daddy, Ann?" Ivy asked. "I know you know." The room crackled with silence. "You don't have to tell me. I'll find out. I've never met a question I was afraid to ask."

CHAPTER
THIRTY-TWO
IVY

Wednesday, January 26, 2022, 5:00 p.m.

"Luigi," Ivy said. "Sorry I missed your call."

"Ivy Neale," he said. She could hear the buzz and clatter of his restaurant's kitchen, which would be throttling up toward full speed for tonight's dinner service.

"I saw your recent magazine piece. Very nice."

"It was very flattering." No missing the pride.

"What can I do for you?" She walked to the sleeping porch and stared out over the dimming sun and toward the wreck, which was vanishing into the sand.

"I heard you left Vincenzo's. That Gino was a fool to let you go."

She let the comment pass. "You didn't call me to hear restaurant gossip this close to the dinner rush."

The background clatter eased, and she pictured him slipping into a side office. "Come work for me," he said.

"You?"

"You would be my sous chef, and if all goes as I'm hoping, you'll be chef in this kitchen in a year."

"Where are you going?"

"Opening a second location."

"Congratulations."

"Say yes," he said.

The breeze caressed her face. "Email me details," she said.

"I'll do it right now."

"I'm not making any promises."

"But you're listening to me. That's all I need for now."

She ended the call, trying to reimagine her life back in New York. With the sale from the cottage, she could get a better place, closer to work, and she wouldn't be worried about always making her monthly bills. It would be a different, better experience.

The doorbell rang, and she closed the doors to the porch and moved toward the front. Dalton was standing on her front porch; the lines in his face were etched deep in a way she'd not seen before. "Want to come inside?"

"Yeah."

He passed by her, petted Libby on the head when she came up to greet him, and then sat at the kitchen counter. "I'm sorry about what Dani said."

"I'd be lying if I said it didn't hurt."

"I know. Dani is stubborn as hell, and when she's backed into a corner, she comes out swinging."

Ivy folded her arms over her chest. "Did she tell you?"

"About losing her sight. She did. And thanks for driving her to Norfolk. I should have been the one to do it."

"I didn't mind." She set up the coffeepot to brew. "Where does she go from here?"

"She's not going anywhere. She's staying in her house. Living her life, and when her vision dims to the point of not being able to drive, she'll figure something else out."

"She's got to be freaking out."

"She is. The steadier and more determined she is, the more afraid she is. She was like that when she was pregnant with Bella. Dressed up every day, always had a smile on her face, and never faltered. I can't tell you how many times she bit my head off."

"What's next?" Ivy asked.

"One foot in front of the other, just like when Mom died and Dani got pregnant. Life goes on."

"Have you told your dad?"

"She wanted to do it. She promised me she'll talk to him in the morning. She doesn't like to drive at night anymore."

"That's a good thing."

"Explains why she insisted on hosting Christmas dinner last year and why she's turned down all my dinner invitations."

She poured him a cup of coffee and set it in front of him. "If anyone can do this, it's Dani."

He reached for the cup. "Do me a favor—don't let what she said get in the way of being her friend. She reached out to you first, and that's saying something."

"I'll call her before I leave town."

He traced the rim of his cup. "I keep forgetting you're leaving. I just assume you'll see reason and stay here."

"See reason?"

A half grin tugged at his lips. "I was hoping you'd remember all the good times you had here."

"How would you know about the good times?"

"Dani spent more time at your place than at home. How many times did I pick you two up and drop you at the movies or the mall?"

"Millions." A memory flashed of a young Dalton standing by the pool at the Seaside Resort, his hair a wild mop and his sun-soaked skin a deep brown. She was thirteen, maybe, and Dalton was sixteen. Even then, being close to him had made her stomach flutter.

"I have this vivid memory of you two running a bingo game by the Seaside Resort pool," he said. "You must have been about thirteen."

She remembered. "That was fun."

"Everything I heard from Dani suggested you loved it here."

"The Seaside Resort and Ruth are gone. They were my anchors." She sighed. "That call from New York was from a restaurant associate. He's offered me a great job."

"Do you want to take it?"

It would have been a no-brainer six months ago. "I'm not sure."

His coffee untouched, he came around the counter. "You have more here than just the Seaside Resort and Ruth. You have Dani."

"Do I?"

"Talk to her." He stood close, and his quiet energy made her aware that she'd been alone for a long time.

Energy snapped between them. If she left never having kissed him, she'd wonder. And if she kissed him, she wondered if she could leave. "Can I kiss you?"

Tension and relief collided. "Yes."

As she rose up, he bent his head, cupped her face in his hands, and pressed his lips to hers. Testing. Tasting.

Her breath halted in her chest. She could sleep with him and move on. Matthew hadn't kept her from leaving. She was stronger than any ties she had to this place.

When the kiss ended, she tipped her forehead into his. "Can you stay for a while?"

"I sure can."

CHAPTER
THIRTY-THREE
RUTH

Monday, June 26, 1950, 6:45 a.m.

Ruth was up early. Sometimes her body was so full of energy it was all she could do to sit still until she worked out the wiggles. Walking was one of her best ways to move her muscles and calm her mind and body.

Talley was still sleeping, but no wonder. She'd been up late reading, and when she'd finally fallen asleep, she had tossed and turned and several times moaned in her sleep.

Ruth rose out of bed, picked up her clothes, and slipped out of the room to the bathroom, and when she returned, she was dressed and ready to leave. She reached for her shoes.

"Where are you going?" Talley asked, her voice thick with sleep.

"For a walk on the beach."

"I'll come." She rolled on her back and rubbed the sleep from her eyes.

"You don't have to," Ruth said.

"I want to. Give me a second." Talley tossed back the covers and slid her feet into worn slippers. She hurried down the hallway and, as promised, was back in minutes.

"You were reading late last night," Ruth said.

Talley's face was pale, and dark smudges hung under her eyes. "That Nancy Drew."

They climbed down the steps and over the dunes, and the buttery-yellow sun peered toward the horizon. Ruth inhaled. Mornings were the best time.

As they walked along the beach, she looked up toward Carlotta's house and saw that the lights were on. "She's not usually up this early."

Talley's gaze trailed hers. "I imagine she keeps all kinds of hours. Days and nights always mixed up."

As they moved down the beach, she noticed that the ocean was reclaiming the wreck. It was nearly covered in sand. She was sorry to see it go but glad the spirits would be put back to rest.

Beyond the wreck, Ruth spotted what looked like a creature lying in the surf. She'd seen her share of dead animals on the beach. Crabs, fish, birds, even an old sea turtle once. But as she hurried toward it, she realized it was a man and stopped short. His face was buried in the sand, but she recognized the trousers and shirt from yesterday. It was Mr. Manchester.

Talley screamed and jumped back.

As her surprise wore off, Ruth's curiosity grew. She walked up to him and nudged him with her foot, thinking maybe he had passed out or was playing some kind of bad joke. He would be the type, and she could almost imagine him sitting up and yelling, *Gotcha.*

"Get away from him," Talley said.

Ruth kicked the scuffed bottom of his wing tip shoe. His leg wobbled back and forth, but there was no resistance in the muscles. Still, he could be clever.

She nudged his midsection, where the damp shirt clung to his skin. "Time to get up, Mr. Manchester. You can't lay in the surf."

"He ain't getting up," Talley said.

"How do you know?"

"Because he's dead!"

Ruth searched for signs of blood or trauma, but his body looked as it had yesterday, only it was so still. And he wasn't breathing.

When the wave rolled out to sea, she rolled him over and looked closely at his face. His lids weren't open or closed but hung suspended between both. There was just enough of a gap for her to see his eyes, which were cloudy and distant.

The next wave rolled in, catching her by surprise and splashing her skin and shorts with cold salt water. She stood up and stepped back quickly.

Ruth gripped Talley's hand.

"We need to get help," Talley said. "Your mama will know what to do."

As they ran toward the hotel, she looked back at Carlotta's house. She thought for an instant Carlotta stood on the screened porch, but whatever she saw was gone as quick as it came.

She remembered Henry's story about ships and ghosts trapped on these shores. Was Mr. Manchester now among the spirits that haunted the beach? She hoped not because she had little hope death would improve his character or disposition.

Running faster, she pumped her arms harder. Breath burned in her lungs, and the morning sun, turning hotter by the moment, sent beads of sweat rolling down her back. Panic welled up in her, and all the fear and worry delayed by the shock came into focus. There was a dead man on the beach, and she had looked in his eyes.

She raced into the kitchen's back door with such force it slammed open and hit the wall. Talley was steps behind her.

Her parents turned from the stove. Instantly her father put down his spatula, stepped away from the sizzling bacon, and went to her. He dried his hands on his apron and placed them on her shoulders.

"What is it, Ruth?" Daddy asked.

The words rattled in her head, but she couldn't make them come out of her mouth. She was breathing hard, and her head was spinning.

"Take a deep breath," Daddy said in a steady voice.

Mama, eyes filled with concern, walked toward her. "Tell Daddy, honey."

"Th-there's a man on the beach," Ruth said.

Talley nodded, opened her mouth, but no words materialized as she looked toward Mama.

"What man?" Her father's voice sharpened with an edge.

Ruth breathed in once and then twice. "Mr. Manchester is on the beach."

"What's he doing on the beach?" her father asked.

"Nothing," Ruth said. "He's dead."

"She's right, Uncle Jake," Talley said. "He's dead."

The lines furrowing Daddy's face deepened. "Stay here with Ruth. Let me go see."

"Maybe we should call the sheriff first," Mama said. "We don't know what kind of trouble is out on the beach."

"Stay here," he said.

Daddy grabbed a bat that he kept by the back door and marched out.

"Are you girls all right?" Mama asked.

Ruth looked at Talley and then at her mother. She wanted to be brave and pretend that what she'd seen didn't matter. But her bravado crumbled, and she hugged her mother tightly.

Her mother wrapped her arms around Ruth and Talley, holding both girls close. "It's all right, baby girls. It's all right."

Ruth savored the scents of cinnamon and sugar that clung to her mother's dress. "You haven't called me 'baby' in a long time."

Her mother smoothed her hand over the wisps of hair that had escaped her barrettes. "Because you don't like it when I do. And I suspect Talley thinks she's all grown up too."

Talley shook her head. "No, ma'am."

Ruth hugged her mother again. "Do you think Mr. Manchester's spirit will come and get me?"

"Why would you say such a thing?" Mama asked.

"Henry said ghosts live on the beach near the water."

"Henry makes up stories," Mama said. "Most of everything he says isn't real. That's what makes his stories so much fun."

She drew back and looked up at her mother's face.

"Henry looked serious, like he meant every word."

Mama smiled. "Sometimes I think he believes all his stories. As long as you don't take him too seriously, he's harmless."

"I've never seen a dead body," Talley said.

Mama drew in a steady breath. How many behind-the-scenes problems had she handled like this? "Let Daddy have a look. Mr. Manchester might be passed out."

"He didn't move," Ruth said. "His chest didn't rise and fall even a little bit."

The back door squeaked open. And when Ruth twisted around and looked at her daddy's face, she saw the grim resolve. "I need to call the sheriff."

"Is it Mr. Manchester?" Mama asked.

"Yes." He looked at the two girls, his face etched with worry. "And he's dead."

Mama held the girls close. "How?"

"It looks like he drowned. But the sheriff and the doctor will have to make that decision."

EDNA

When the sheriff came, Edna let Jake do the talking. Jake and Sheriff Hank had grown up within a few miles of each other; they'd hunted and fished together, and both had served in World War I.

Sheriff Hank lifted the blanket covering Peter Manchester's body as it lay in the sand, dragged out of the tide's reach. He stared at him a long time, studied his neck, checked his hands and his pockets. He found the bracelet that Ann had reported missing to Edna days before. Ann accepted the bracelet but didn't offer an apology.

Next, the sheriff spoke to Ann, who reported Mr. Manchester had drunk heavily. "He's been trouble since the war." As if that explained it all.

In the end, the sheriff declared the death an accident and called the funeral director on the mainland, who came and toted the body away. When the sheriff and body were clear of the island, Jake called a local man to drive Mrs. Manchester and her children home.

It was close to three in the afternoon when the sheriff was gone and the body was cleared away. Jake told Edna he was going to take Ruth and Talley into Kitty Hawk for a soda and maybe an ice cream. She readily agreed and was relieved to see the three drive off.

Edna walked across the hot sand to Carlotta's cottage and found her sitting on the sleeping porch having a smoke and a whiskey. She'd used makeup to cover the bruise on her face, but it would darken before it faded.

"The sheriff is gone," Edna said.

"Is that so?" She stamped out her cigarette.

"No need to worry about Manchester anymore."

"I was never worried about him," Carlotta said, rising. "I've crossed paths with many Manchesters before."

"I think it's best you leave," Edna said. "The sheriff isn't looking too close, but your bruises will bring up questions."

"I'm already packed. So are Max and April. He's pulling the car around. I was just waiting for you and Ruth."

Edna stared at the young woman whose presence reminded her too much of the boy she'd foolishly loved in a time that was nearly forgotten. "Jake took Ruth and Talley into Kitty Hawk. I thought it best she not be here when you left."

Carlotta frowned. "I would have liked to see her. Does she know the truth?"

"What truth?" Edna willed tears away.

"About Ann."

"What about her?" To the end, Edna would protect her children whether they wanted it or not.

"Ruth looks like Grandfather Jenkins," Carlotta said. "I know you didn't pass those looks on to the girl, and neither did I."

Edna felt her skin flush. "Ruth knows I found her in a pink blanket. She knows Jake and I love her. That's all that matters."

"She asked me if I was that lady, the woman who left her. I told her no, but I'm not sure she believes me."

"If she asks, I'll assure her you are not."

"And she'll believe you?"

"Of course."

"She's young, Edna," Carlotta said. "One day she's going to press for answers."

"Answers don't fix everything. Sometimes things are the way they are, and all you can do is get on with your life."

"Is that how you felt after Ann and I were born?"

Sadness fisted in Edna's chest when she thought back to the small infants lying in dresser drawers by her mother's fireplace. Both had been crying, and her breasts, so full of milk, had ached. That moment was rarely far from her thoughts. "It was the only way I knew how to protect you."

"For what it's worth, we were happy. But I guess there was enough of you in us that made following the rules hard." Carlotta reached down and picked up the little dog, rubbing her gently between the ears. She handed a card to Edna with a PO box address on it. "I've left my camera for Ruth."

"That's very extravagant."

"Not really. You'll see that she gets it?"

"Yes."

"Tell Ruth to write me. I'd like to hear from her."

Edna flicked the edge of the card. Carlotta was right. Edna and her children weren't afraid of breaking the rules to have a better life. And Ruth was going to be no different. "I'll give her the card."

"What about Beth Ann? Is she going to be all right?"

"She's got her children, a good home, and money."

"I feel like I'm abandoning her," Carlotta said.

Edna's spine stiffened. "You can't help someone who does not want it. If she needs help, she knows where to find us."

"It's for the best?"

Edna heard the bitterness as she took a long look at her daughter's face. "Yes, it is."

CHAPTER
THIRTY-FOUR
IVY

Thursday, January 27, 2022, 9:00 a.m.

When Ivy walked out on the sleeping porch, she discovered the wreck was gone. The waves and winds had layered it with sand, swallowing up the timbers as if it had never been there. She was sorry to see it go, though it gave her some satisfaction to know the spirits once again rested. Maybe now the living could find peace as well.

Ivy drove to Dani's house but didn't find her car in the driveway and took a chance she was at her gallery down the road. She had promised Dalton when he'd kissed her this morning that she'd go see Dani. She hadn't made any big promises but had decided a small one was easy enough.

The only car in the gallery parking lot was Dani's SUV. Ivy parked beside it and walked up to the glass front door. She stared past the CLOSED sign to inside the shop but didn't see Dani. She knocked.

Seconds later Dani peered out from a back room and approached the door slowly.

"I think we need to talk," Ivy said.

"So that you can explain again why you let me down."

"That's a low blow," Ivy said. "I never said anything to Dalton."

"But he figured it out."

"Because he's not stupid!" Ivy shouted.

Dani unlocked the front door and opened it, and Ivy walked inside. She was instantly taken by the light-gray space, the vaulted ceiling, the whitewashed timbers, and the windows that let in so much natural light. "This is really pretty."

"I know."

"I mean, I wouldn't expect you to do anything other than top of the line, but this is great." She walked to a seascape done in oils. "It's nice."

"He's very talented. Lives on the mainland but spends a lot of time here."

She glanced at the price tag and winced. "Ouch."

"That's a lifetime of work and study on the canvas. Experienced talent does not come cheap."

Ivy considered the endless hours refining her skills in the kitchen. "Point taken."

"Why are you here?" Some of the bite had left her tone.

"I've been offered a job in New York. Luigi's. In fact, I was reading an article about them while I was waiting for you in the doctor's office. It would be a huge step up for me."

"So this is goodbye?" she snapped.

"Why are you getting upset with me?" Ivy challenged. "I didn't tell Dalton about you! And I'm trying to be more mature about leaving this time than I was the last!"

Tears welled in Dani's eyes. "I'm not upset. This is a happy moment, right? You're going to take your money, move back to your old life, and find your bliss. I'll remain here and get on with my life, just like I always have."

"I haven't said yes to the offer yet," Ivy said.

"Why not?"

"I don't know. Maybe I feel like I'm abandoning you and I want to help."

"How? No one can help. And I will not be responsible for you sticking around here and being miserable for the rest of your life."

"Why are you so sure I'd be miserable here?"

Dani shook her head. "There's nothing you can do. Nothing anyone can do. It's a problem with no fix."

"I know. I know."

Dani closed her eyes and rubbed her temple as a tear ran down her cheek. "Don't stay for me."

"What if I stayed for me? This area has a lot of new challenges for me, and I can cook Italian food in my sleep."

Dani looked at her. "I'm sorry. I was shitty to you yesterday."

"Yes, you were."

"I didn't mean it."

"Maybe you did a little."

That prompted a half smile. "Either way, I'm sorry. Low blow."

"Apology accepted."

Dani shoved out a sigh. "I told you that I did a little genetic research on my family. I was trying to figure out where the vision issues came from."

"And?"

"It didn't make sense to me at the time. Patsy Jenkins Rogers was distantly related. She had vision issues. I had no idea how the Jenkinses/Rogerses were connected to me."

"Ann's biological aunt. Edna's sister."

"I know now, thanks to you."

Ivy was silent for a moment, thinking about the wreck that had now vanished. Even if the world between the living and dead wasn't as transparent as it had been, she hoped Ruth could hear them now. "Do you think Ruth knew about Ann?"

"She had to have known."

Ivy pictured Ruth wiping the edges of their plates as she served Dani and Ivy a late-afternoon snack at the hotel restaurant.

"It would have been nice to hear it all from her," Ivy said.

"Random clues was about the best Ruth could muster."

Ivy smiled. "I don't suppose we could put my DNA into the system and figure out who was Ruth's biological father."

"It wasn't Peter Manchester," she said. "Ann and Peter were O-positive blood types, according to the genetic site. Ruth was AB negative. But I'll throw your DNA into the mix and see if there are any hits. I might be able to figure it out."

"What would Ruth say if she heard us talking about her birth parents so openly?" Ivy imagined Ruth turning away to stir a pot of fish stew or scrub a pan.

"She'd say it doesn't matter."

Ivy walked deeper into the gallery space, staring at the blank walls. "What do you think about displaying Ruth's work here?"

"You want to sell?"

"No. But her work deserves to be seen."

The tension in Dani's shoulders eased slightly. "Have you ever considered having limited-edition prints made of her work?"

"Never really thought about it."

"I think they could do very well. And there wouldn't be the sticker shock of original art."

"It would be worth the investment."

"What about your next life? Your New York promotion?"

"What if I commit to stay for a while? See how it goes. What if we sold prints of Ruth's work?"

"We?"

"Dalton said you're one hell of a businesswoman. I'll even put up a financial stake if that helps."

Dani regarded her with narrowing eyes. "Is this a pity venture?"

"Not at all." Nothing had felt righter. And it wasn't because of Dani or Dalton. "Besides, Libby might like to see Lulu from time to time."

"Diamond."

"What?"

Dani shrugged. "The puppy's name is Diamond now."

"Right."

"Don't question the mind of an eleven-year-old. Just run with it."

"Will do. What about my idea?" Ivy asked.

"I could be persuaded to consider it. But no promises. One step at a time."

"No promises," Ivy said, smiling.

"And while we're talking about this venture, can you tell me why my brother sounded so relaxed and happy this morning when he called?"

Ivy moistened her lips. "Good to see I haven't lost my touch."

Dani's laugh was hearty and full. "I knew it."

"I like him."

"Are you staying for him?" Dani asked.

"You know me better than that," Ivy said. "I'm staying because all this feels right for me."

"If you break Dalton's heart, I will hunt you down and turn you into barbecue," Dani said.

"You can't cook."

"I'll figure it out."

Ivy met Dani's gaze. "I'm not running again."

"Okay, then." Dani reached for her phone. "This just might be good."

EPILOGUE

IVY

Ruth's art exhibit opened a week before the summer season kicked off. Dani argued that the traffic would be less congested, and so her regular customers, decorators, and the press would be more likely to attend. Sales might not be as high, but that would come. The exhibit was scheduled to remain up until Labor Day. But the streets were already busy with early vacationers, and there'd been a good bit of buzz in local media about Ruth's work.

For the opening buffet, Ivy's menu was an homage to Ruth with her own twists. She'd made panko-fried chicken nuggets, mini buttermilk biscuits, and small cups of fish chowder. For dessert, she'd made bite-size apple-and-fig pies. The drinks were colas in glass bottles (a nod to Ruth and Talley) and martinis (a shout-out to Ann and Carlotta.)

Fifteen minutes before opening, Ivy stood in the space staring at all the paintings, all tangible expressions of the deep feelings Ruth had held so tightly all her life. Spread among them were the framed black-and-white photos Carlotta had taken over seventy years ago.

"Drink it all in." Dani's heels clicked against the wooden floor as she moved toward Ivy, the full skirt of her blue dress swirling around her as she moved. She'd pinned her blonde hair up into a twist and wore sparkling earrings, along with red lipstick and fingernail polish. It was her nod to Carlotta.

"It's incredible," Ivy said.

"It is," Dani said. "It wouldn't have happened if not for you."

"Me?"

"Because you left here twelve years ago to chase a dream, the rest of us had to get our act together and find our own path. Ruth began painting. I made a baby and a career. It all happened because you left."

"I never thought about it that way."

Dani picked up two martinis and handed one to Ivy and kept one for herself. "I'm toasting you, Ivy Neale."

Ivy raised her glass. "Right back at you."

Dani sipped, glancing toward the parking lot. "Where's my brother and child?"

"Dalton should be here soon. He said there was traffic from Elizabeth City."

Dalton had offered to drive to the assisted-living facility in Elizabeth City and pick up Talley, who was thrilled to be invited to the event. Bella had asked to go, and the two had left here two hours ago.

After Ivy had sold the beach cottage to Dalton, she'd gotten a small apartment on the shore. There was enough money to tide her over, and she'd not been in a rush to commit to anything. But of course, when you weren't looking for something, it had a way of finding you. She'd been hired to cater a couple of small parties, which had led to catering a store opening and a fundraiser. Word was spreading quickly that she was a top-notch chef, and several opportunities had presented themselves to her.

She'd decided to pass on the New York job and the restaurant space that had once been the tackle shop. But she and Dalton had been dating steadily the last five months. The more time she spent with him, the deeper her feelings grew.

A knock on the door had them both turning to see Bella grinning at them. Dani crossed, unlocked the door, and kissed Bella on the cheek.

"Mom, I have to go check on Rosie," she said.

Bella and the puppy, a.k.a. Rosie, were nearly inseparable now, according to Dani. "She's fine, Bella. She's with Libby and Sailor, and they're hanging out at our house."

"But she misses me."

Dani tucked a stray curl behind Bella's ear. "I'll have Uncle Dalton run you back to the house in a little while. It's important you be here now."

"For Ruth."

"She was our best pal."

Bella nodded. "Can I have a soda?"

"You can have two."

Ivy moved out to the parking lot and walked to Dalton's truck as he removed Talley's wheelchair from the bed. She tossed him a smile, and he winked as she opened the driver's side door and kissed Talley on the cheek. She wore a navy dress with a matching jacket, pearls around her neck, and hints of rouge brightening her cheeks. Her freshly styled hair curled gently around her face, accentuating bright eyes.

"Ivy," Talley said. "I thought we'd never make it. Traffic is crazy this time of year."

"But you made it, and now we can celebrate."

Dalton pushed the wheelchair around the car, and Ivy helped Talley into it. "Ready to go."

Ivy leaned toward him and kissed him on the lips. "Thank you."

"I was glad to do it," he said. They pushed Talley inside the gallery.

Pete pulled up, parking beside Dalton's truck. He shook Dalton's hand, hugged Ivy, and kissed Talley and then Dani on the cheek. Pete had visited Talley several times, and the two had spent a good deal of time talking about the summer of 1950. The truth wasn't always easy, but airing it had helped them both.

"You've outdone yourself, kiddo," Pete said.

Dani grinned. "I know." She leaned over and kissed Talley. "Let me give you both the grand tour."

"I would like that," Talley said.

Dani smiled, spun the wheelchair around, and pushed Talley with Pete in tow toward the first set of black-and-white photos.

"Dani looks good," Dalton said. "More relaxed than I've seen her in a while."

"She's the one that made this night happen. She arranged the art and photos, and thanks to her, the limited-edition prints arrived two days ago."

He wrapped his arm around her shoulders. "How did the eye appointment in Norfolk go yesterday?"

"Not great. She's lost a little ground. It could reverse, but no guarantees."

Dalton's expression remained stoic even as tension radiated through him. "I feel helpless."

"She doesn't," Ivy said. "And so we'll have to take that and run with it."

He leaned closer, his lips near her ear. "Have I told you I love you lately?"

"It's been ages. At least since this morning."

"I love you."

She kissed his lips. "Back at you."

Dani moved to the front window and studied the collection of cars filling her lot. "It's almost showtime, people."

Matthew walked up to the door with a tall brunette in her late twenties. They were holding hands.

"This is going to be a hit, Ivy," Dalton said.

Dani opened the doors, and Matthew and the others entered. Bella came to her dad and showed him the misty bottle of soda. He cringed only a little, knowing today was the kind of day rules got a little bent.

"Ivy," Matthew said. "Looks terrific."

"It's all Dani."

"More like a team effort," he said as his gaze wandered to the food table. "I'd like you to meet Jennifer."

Ivy shook the woman's hand. "Welcome."

"This is something," Jennifer said.

"It's all Dani."

"I've been hearing about the menu from Bella," Matthew interjected. "She says it's fantastic."

"She's my taste tester."

"It's really good, Dad," Bella said. "Come try it."

"I will."

As Matthew, Bella, and Jennifer moved toward the food table, Dalton took Ivy's hand in his. "I think I can safely say the renovation of the cottage is done."

"The countertops came in?"

"As of yesterday."

She'd not seen the cottage in a couple of weeks and was excited to see all the pieces finally together. "Can't wait."

"The refinished furniture arrived yesterday. We now have a bed that faces the ocean."

"We?"

"I'd like you to move in."

"Really?"

"And if it doesn't make you feel too pressured, I'd like us to get married and have six or seven kids." His smile didn't quite soften the worry behind his eyes.

"Okay."

"Okay to?"

"Moving in. Marriage down the road. Six or seven kids might be a stretch, but I'm willing to negotiate."

He kissed her. "I'm always open to discussion."

Family Tree

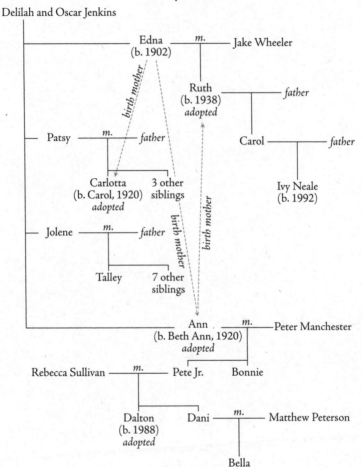

ABOUT THE AUTHOR

Photo © 2017 Studio FBJ

A southerner by birth, Mary Ellen Taylor has a love for her home state of Virginia that is evident in her contemporary women's fiction. When she's not writing, she spends time baking, hiking, and spoiling her miniature dachshunds, Buddy, Bella, and Tiki.